halfhead

Stuart MacBride, without the 'B', is the bestselling author of a series of crime novels featuring DS Logan McRae and set in Aberdeen. He won the International Thriller Writers best debut novel award, and has been shortlisted for the Barry Award, and twice for the Theakston's Old Peculier Crime Novel of the Year award. In 2007 he won the Dagger in the Library, awarded for a body of work, and in 2008 he won the ITV3 Crime Thriller Award for Breakthrough Author. *Halfhead*, published under the name Stuart B. MacBride, is his first foray into Science Fiction.

Stuart lives in north-east Scotland with his wife Fiona, cat Grendel, and a vegetable plot full of weeds.

By Stuart MacBride

STUART B.
MACBRIDE
halfhead

HARPER
Voyager

HarperVoyager
An imprint of HarperCollins*Publishers*
77–85 Fulham Palace Road,
Hammersmith, London W6 8JB

www.harpercollins.co.uk

This paperback edition 2010
2

First published in Great Britain by
HarperCollins*Publishers* 2009

A catalogue record for this book is
available from the British Library

ISBN: 978 0 00 734926 5

Set in Meridien by Palimpsest Book Production Ltd,
Grangemouth, Stirlingshire

Printed and bound in Great Britain by
Clays Ltd, St Ives plc

Mixed Sources
Product group from well-managed
forests and other controlled sources
www.fsc.org   Cert no. SW-COC-001806
© 1996 Forest Stewardship Council

FSC

For Grendel
(my own fuzzy little serial killer)

Without Whom . . .

This book has taken a hell of a long time to go from a first draft to the finished thing, and a lot of people have helped along the way. So I'd like to thank Phil Patterson, Luke Speed, Sarah Hodgson, Jane Johnson, Amanda Ridout, Allan Guthrie, James Oswald, and Christopher MacBride, for all their time and trouble. And believe me, I've caused a lot of trouble.

But most of all, thanks go to Fiona and Grendel, who've been putting up with this nonsense for years.

1

There's blood everywhere.

It sparkles in the artificial light like diamonds scattered onto dark-red velvet. It fills the air with the scent of burning copper and hot rust, tugging at her belly. It soaks through her jumpsuit, making the cheap fabric cling to her gaunt body like a second skin.

It's wonderful.

She falls to her knees in the filthy toilet cubicle; shuddering in ecstasy. With a trembling hand she reaches forward and touches something that looks like boiled beetroot, but isn't.

Memories burst across her tattered brain: succulent, delicious memories. The hunt. The kill. The sweet, sweet release. She wants to moan, but no sound comes out. . .

For a long time she just sits there, surrounded by the fruits of her labour. And then, bit by bit, her mind begins to return. A mind she hasn't used for over six years. All sharp edges and buzzing noise.

Bees and broken glass.

For the first time since the trial, she understands where she is: this is a toilet. Cheap, municipal tiles encrusted with human filth and coated in a film of blood. Pine disinfectant fighting against the acrid stench of old urine. Slowly she stands, the sticky handful falling from her numb fingers, splattering against the floor.

As she steps out into the low room a cloud of flies startle into flight and dance drunkenly through the boiling air, intoxicated on haemoglobin.

Not bees. Bluebottles. They're pretty.

She holds out a hand and one lands on a sticky red fingertip. Hairy little legs. Fragile glass wings. Her thumb jabs forwards, trapping the wriggling shiny body. Holding it there. It buzzes and wriggles. A tiny life.

And then, slowly, she squeezes till it pops. A little explosion of yellow. A tiny death.

Broken bluebottles and glass.

There's a mirror mounted on the wall above the sinks. It's cracked, layered with graffiti. Mimicking the room's shabby contents: the dirty walls; the streaks of arterial red; the flies; and the thing in the bloodstained orange and black jumpsuit, staring right back. . .

Broken.

Suddenly everything is still. Even the bluebottles settle, not daring to spoil the moment.

Tears blur her eyes as she finally understands what she has become. The face in the mirror is not the face of a human being, it's the face of an animal. A killer. A halfhead. No hair, no mind and no lower jaw.

She can't even scream.

2

'Control, this is Delta One Four, do you copy?'

'*Affirmative Delta One Four. You are cleared to proceed.*'

'Jacobs, you're on sweep. Phillips: back door. I'll take point. On three, two, one. . .' The heavy plastic door slammed back against the toilet wall and suddenly the low, stinking room was full of flies. 'Move! Move! Move!'

Jacobs charged in, his Field Zapper pointing everywhere at once. Out in the corridor Phillips was facing back the way they'd come, covering the entrance. Detective Sergeant Cameron ran into the toilets . . . then slithered to a halt on the blood-smeared tiles. Seven years with the Bluecoats and she'd never seen anything like this. There was something dark and sticky smeared all over one of the toilet cubicles. It used to be a man.

DS Cameron reached one hand up and keyed the little switch buried beneath the skin of her throat.

'Control. . .' She turned her back on the butchered remains. 'We've got a problem.'

'Now, can anyone tell me what this is? Anyone? Yes, Sophie?'

A small girl in a neon-blue tabard dropped her hand and grinned a gap-toothed grin. 'It's a bad person.'

'That's right Sophie!' The teacher smiled. They were good kids. 'Now, can anyone tell me *why* they cut bad people's heads in half?'

There wasn't even a moment's pause: all twelve of them leaped up and down screaming, 'Because they've been naughty!'

To be honest, the halfhead they were staring at didn't look all that naughty, just another poor soul who wasn't going to cause any more trouble. A man with half a face, a fried brain, and a barcode tattooed on his forehead. He was slowly mopping his way across the entrance lobby, cleaning the marble-tiled floor until it sparkled. The small group followed him, ignoring the priceless works of art lining the walls. They'd found something much more interesting. Some of the children pulled faces, sticking out their top teeth, pulling in their chins and rolling their eyes. One or two of them pretended to clean the floor with special, invisible mops. It was amazing just how much imagination they had.

'Now, then,' the teacher said as they rounded the corner, 'what do you think the bad person did? Nigel, what do you think? What did he do?'

Nigel examined his boots for a minute. 'Wath he mean to thomebody'th cat?'

'Ooh, that *would* be naughty wouldn't it?'

'Yes!' they screeched.

'Excuse me.' The voice came from a well-dressed man waiting for the lift.

'Just a moment. Young persons, what do we say to the nice man?'

'We don't talk to strangers!'

'That's right!' The teacher turned and beamed at the gentleman in the dark-blue suit. 'Aren't they clever!'

There was a slight pause, then the man said, 'Delightful.'

'We like to come here and look at all the pretty paintings, don't we?'

'Yes!'

For the first time the stranger smiled. Obviously the children had worn down his initial reserve. They'd taken someone they'd never met before and, in a matter of seconds, turned him into a friend. They were wonderful that way.

'I couldn't help overhearing your question, "What did he do?"'

Nigel jumped up and down, waving his hand in the air, desperate to be the centre of attention again. 'He wath mean to thomebodie'th cat!'

The stranger reached forward and ruffled Nigel's hair, bringing an even bigger grin to the lad's face.

'He was indeed. A lot of them are to begin with. Before they escalate.' The man dropped down and winked at the circle of children. 'Moths, frogs, cats, dogs. . . Then this one turned his attentions to little boys. He liked to cut their fingers off, one by one, and stick them somewhere dark and private.'

'Ooh!' A little girl tugged at the stranger's sleeve. 'Did he stick them up their noses? Did he? Nigel's *always* sticking his fingers up his nose.'

'No I don't! Don't lithen to her, she'th a poo-head.'

'Am not!'

'Are too!'

'Er, look, I don't think this is entirely appropriate.' For the first time the teacher noticed that the stranger's smile didn't go as far as his eyes. In fact, now that he *really* looked, there was something decidedly sinister about the man. 'Come on, children, we . . . er . . . have to be going.' He gathered them together, trying to get them to safety, but the nasty man kept on talking.

'Then, when they didn't have any fingers left, he would cut off their toes. If they were lucky they died from shock. If not, they were still alive while he opened up their tummies. With a kitchen knife.'

'That's disgusting! How dare you!'

The lift doors pinged open and the man stepped backwards through them.

'When we caught him there were fifteen little boys buried under his floorboards and three more in the freezer.' His expression hardened as he stared straight into the teacher's eyes. 'Try and remember that next time you feel like taking the piss.'

A soft chime sounded and the doors began to slide shut. 'What's your name? I'll report you to your superiors!'

Clunk. With a dry whirr the lift departed taking the horrible man and his unpleasant stories with it.

Safely cocooned within the glass-walled car the nasty man in the dark-blue suit reached up and keyed his throat-mike.

'Control, this is Hunter, *please* tell me the staff lifts are going to be back online soon!'

A voice crackled in his earpiece: *'Sorry, sir, Maintenance are still working on it. Won't give us a completion time.'*

'There's a surprise.' Outside the lift's glass walls Glasgow baked, waiting for the rains to come. They were late this year, the unbearably hot summer dragging on and on, outstaying its welcome by months. Everything looked on the verge of death. Himself included.

He watched his reflection slide across the glass, not liking what he saw. Dark-purple bags slumped under his eyes; his proud, squint nose sitting on a face that needed at least another eight hours sleep and a better shave than the one he'd given it. Somewhere along the way, genetics had sneaked up on him, startling his unruly mop of dark brown hair into a slow retreat. Every year a little more forehead went on display. Have to get a clonegraft organized. Not for a couple of years, but soon enough.

He dragged his eyes away, letting them drift across the Network's shadowed forecourt. Here and there, small pockets of wilted vegetation waited for the blistering morning sun. Another party of school children was being shepherded towards the main entrance, to be lectured on the importance of maintaining law and order. Look at the pretty paintings. Or just make fun of the halfheads.

Bloody teachers.

A delicate ping heralded his arrival on the thirteenth floor and William Hunter stepped out into the corridor. Someone was waiting for him.

'Sir.' Private Dickson snapped off a salute. She'd swapped her usual grey jumpsuit for a dress uniform in black and chrome, a huge Bull Thrummer slung causally over her shoulder. The siege rifle was almost as big as she was, its massive tremblers sticking up past her head, the tines dangling down by her ankles.

'Lieutenant Brand said to tell you the team's assembled and ready to go, sir.' She stood to attention and Will couldn't help but smile.

'Are you sure that's what she said?'

'Yes, sir.'

'Those were her exact words?'

Private Dickson wouldn't look at him. 'Em . . . more or less, sir.'

'I can check, you know.'

She sighed. 'Sir. The Lieutenant said: "Tell him to get his arse in gear before I kick it half way to Edinburgh for him." Sir.' Dickson's face had turned a delicate shade of pink.

'Well, we'd better not keep her waiting then.'

At the end of the corridor a pair of double doors hissed opened onto the staging zone. Will followed Dickson out onto the roof and into the open air. The sudden change from climate-controlled comfort to baking heat was like being punched in the chest. Every breath was an effort as they marched past the hopperpads towards a waiting Dragonfly.

The gunship sat on four squat, hydraulic legs, a huge

asymmetrical salmon sculpted from blackened steel. All of its weapons' bays were closed; they wouldn't need heavy artillery where they were going.

As Will and Dickson cleared the barrier rail the Dragonfly's engines growled into life, the concrete landing pad shimmering in the downdraught.

They clambered up the rear ramp and into the relative cool of the gunship's darkened interior. A familiar voice sounded in Will's ear, '*Mr Hunter, how nice of you to join us. . .*'

'Morning, Lieutenant.' Will made his way down the ship's drop bay, nodding at the troops as he passed, looking for a vacant compartment. They'd kept one for him at the far end, next to the passageway that led through to the cockpit, directly opposite the six-and-a-half-foot-tall cylinder no one wanted to look at.

He clipped himself in.

Immediately the sound of the ship's engines changed, roaring up through the octaves to a high-pitched whine. The ground beneath his feet surged and Will went with it, riding the wave of steel as the Dragonfly leapt into the sky and accelerated away.

It was a quiet journey: none of the usual banter that went on in the belly of a Network gunship. They stood, quiet in their bays, thinking about where they were going and how close they'd been to joining Private Worrall.

Will tried not to blame himself for what had happened. Why should he? It wasn't his fault: Worrall had been careless. Worrall wouldn't follow procedure. Worrall *had* to be the big hero.

Silly bastard. . .

But it didn't stop Will feeling responsible.

Someone tapped him on the shoulder.

'Are you going to speak, or do you want me to?' Lieutenant Emily Brand sounded a lot more subdued than she had when he'd clambered aboard. She leant on the rail surrounding his compartment, shifting her weight effortlessly as the Dragonfly roared through the sky.

Emily was built for this type of work: lean, muscled, auburn hair cropped so short it was almost shaved. Like the rest of her troops she was in dress uniform: black, tailored, four chrome bars on her shoulder to show her rank. They'd be sending Private Worrall off in style.

Will glanced across at the metal cylinder. 'Don't worry about it. I'll talk if you're not. . .' He was going to say 'up to it', but to Emily that would sound like a challenge. 'I'll do it. God knows I've done enough of these things; got the speech off by heart.'

'Yes.' She looked away. 'That'd probably be for the best.'

The Dragonfly tilted and Lieutenant Brand headed back to her command station next to the pilot, leaving Will with an almost inaudible, 'Thank you.'

He watched her go then reached forward to switch on the monitor mounted above his booth. The screen crackled and fizzed with static from the engines, but the view from the ship's front gun ports was still recognizable beneath all that white noise: Glasgow.

The river Clyde sparkled like a barbed-wire fence, winding its way slowly to the sea, hemmed in by the massive barrier walls that cut the city in two and wrapped all the way around the outside. Keeping the Atlantic Ocean and the North Sea from swallowing it whole. On the south side of the river the city changed; there were none of the great 'revivalist architectural projects' or trendy sandstone communities. Over there it was all foamcrete and industrial plastic, a grey landscape of compressed urban habitation units sweltering in the sun.

Will watched as sunlight caught the windows of a massive connurb block, shining like a warning beacon against the depressing, angular landscape. 'Stay away' it said. Something cold marched down his spine. He didn't need to be told twice.

'Landing zone acquired: touchdown in three.'

He lurched against the harness as the Dragonfly's engines howled into reverse, bringing the gunship to a juddering halt in midair. Didn't matter what they were doing, they always flew these damn things as if they were going into battle.

The word *'Arse'* sounded in Will's earpiece, and then the signal cut out.

Up in the cockpit Lieutenant Emily Brand was arguing with someone on the comlink – Will couldn't make out the words, but the tone was clear. It didn't sound as if she was winning.

Finally her voice crackled over the tannoy. *'Sorry people: change of plan. Bluecoats need backup and an SOC team. That means us. None of the other units can attend. I know it's shitty and I know it stinks, but it's orders. Start your engines people, Private Worrall's funeral will just have to wait.'*

The ship swung in the air and the engines roared again. Will watched as the nice side of the city disappeared from his monitor, replaced by the foamcrete jungle. They were heading straight for the towering connurb blocks.

'Oh no. . .'

'Listen up, people: we're going into a known hot zone and there are Bluecoats onsite, so no itchy trigger fingers and no heroics! I don't want to be carting anyone else back in a body-bag.'

Almost everyone stole a glance at the canister opposite Will's booth.

'Target is: male toilets, main entrance lobby, Sherman House.'

Oh no. No, no, no, no, no. . . Will tightened his grip on the handrail, palms suddenly cold and damp. Curses flew around the drop bay as the troopers moaned about the target. But there was worse to come.

'ASD Hunter will be in charge of the pickup team. Anyone who doesn't do exactly what he tells them, when he tells them, will suddenly find themselves having a very bad day. Understood?'

Will barely heard the half-hearted chorus of, 'Yes, ma'am.' He was too busy trying not to throw up.

'I can't hear you!'

The steel walls reverberated with the deafening shouts of, 'Ma'am, yes, ma'am!'

'Better. We have an ETA of two minutes thirty. I suggest you make sure all weapons are locked and fully charged. Chitin will be worn! I see you out there without it and I'll shoot you myself.'

All around him Whompers and Thrummers were buzzing into life, their targeting beams illuminating the dim interior with a sickly green glow.

Will reached for his throat-mike and asked as calmly as he could what the bloody hell Lieutenant Brand thought she was doing putting him in charge of the pickup team. Sending him out there.

'It'll be good for you.'

Will closed his eyes and gritted his teeth. Some very well-paid people with expensive leather couches and degrees in psychology had told him the same thing. If you don't confront your fear it will always haunt you. He hadn't believed them either.

'ETA one minute, people. Smooth and clean. In and out. No drama. No problems.'

It was too late for Will to back out now and he knew it. It would make Lieutenant Brand look bad in front of her troops and it would make *him* look even worse.

Shit. Shitty . . . fucking . . . shit.

Thanks, Emily, thanks a heap.

He pulled his Zapper out from its shoulder holster and checked it was still fully charged. The small, pebbled disk sat in the palm of his hand, the dial on the top turned to a conservative 'Heavy Stun'.

Just because he was going back to Sherman House it didn't mean history would repeat itself. And besides, *this time* he had a heavily armed assault team for backup. There was nothing to worry about. No one in their right mind would pick a fight with half a dozen of the Network's finest. It would be suicide. Madness.

He shifted uncomfortably against his harness; the residents of Sherman House weren't exactly known for their good mental health.

Sod it. Will grabbed a Whomper from the recharging rack. The assault rifle's plastic casing was cool beneath his fingers as he ran a thumb over the power indicator. Telltales sparkled into life, indicating a full battery and the weapon's readiness to blow a dirty big hole in anything it was pointed at. At least this way he could take a few of the bastards with him.

'Heads up, people, we have visual.'

Monstrosity Square filled the small screen in front of him. Four massive connurb blocks with more than sixty thousand people shoehorned into each. And if that wasn't bad enough, there were another eleven identical squares on this side of the river: half of them rebuilt in the aftermath of the riots.

God help Glasgow if their residents decided to go on the warpath.

Again.

Static crackled across the picture as the Dragonfly pitched into its final approach, dropping like a cannonball.

Lieutenant Brand stalked back into the drop bay, bracing herself as the gunship started twisting and turning – making itself a difficult target. She walked the length of the bay, checking everyone was chitined up before barking orders at them. 'Nairn, Dickson, Wright, you're on point. Floyd: rear-guard. Beaton, you and Stein are on SOC. The rest of you form a defensive perimeter around the ship.' There was a pause as Will's escorts unbuckled themselves. 'Stay *focused*, people, we're not in Kansas any more.'

The engines slammed into full reverse. This was it: Sherman House, they'd arrived.

Oh God. . .

Before the landing legs had even touched the tarmac the rear ramp was open, letting in the harsh morning sun.

Emily nodded: game time.

'Move it, people!'

The four-man defensive perimeter sprinted into place, body-wires spooling out behind them like armoured spiders. Sunlight glistened off their chitin as they scanned the crowded square, heavy weapons searching for possible targets. The blocks' residents froze in place like waxworks: silent, staring. Hostile.

Then the advance team charged down the ramp; running for the nearest monolith, the crowds parting like a Red Sea of the unwashed and unwanted.

Will tightened his grip on the Whomper as the three Network troopers disappeared into Sherman House. The entrance had been grand and imposing once: a wall of plexi-glass and chrome the size of a football pitch, moulded marble plinths and the most fashionable sculpture public money could buy. But the glass had lost its sparkle long ago.

There was no sign of the dancing figures in bronze, or the mottled-steel animals, or even the full-sized granite sperm whale. They'd all gone during the riots: blown apart by Shrikes, or Thrummed out of existence. Only ash-black shadows remained.

When the all-clear crackled in his earpiece, Will realized he'd been holding his breath.

This was a *very* bad idea.

'Come on,' he said, keeping his voice low so no one else could hear, 'this is for your own good.' He took the first step onto the ramp and stopped. His pulse thudded in his ears, chest tightening, stomach churning, mouth suddenly dry, the Whomper shaking in his hands.

Beaton and Stein stood behind him, wrestling with the ungainly scanning gear: a canister that looked disturbingly like Private Worrall's coffin. They were expecting Will to take the lead.

Lieutenant Emily Brand's voice sounded in his ear. *'You waiting for an engraved invitation?'*

He crossed the threshold into the harsh sunlight. It was like walking into an oven with a two-ton weight tied to his bowels. Sherman House. . .

Sweat pricked across his forehead.

The forecourt was crowded with angry, silent faces, staring at the armoured troopers. Most of the locals were dressed in the colourful eclectic rags that were all the rage the year before last; some wore the tight, formal clothes that had been in vogue the year before that. On this side of the river they only followed fashion from a distance.

There'd be more of them, glowering down from the floors above. Watching. Waiting for the blood and the darkness to start all over again.

Will tightened his grip on the Whomper and marched across the sun-bleached tarmac, eyes fixed dead ahead. The building getting bigger with every step, until it blocked out everything.

The crowd just stood there, gaily-coloured tatters fluttering in the downdraft from the Dragonfly's engines.

Only ten feet to go. Eight. Six. Four. . . Will pushed through the cracked and grimy doors into the shrouded atrium.

The huge, glass front wall was now almost opaque, a jigsaw of splintered panes and cloudy plasticboard. Green mould coated the glazed panels, throwing the huge room into shadow.

It should have been cooler in here out of the sun, but it wasn't.

All around him, hundreds of people stood in silence, just like the crowd outside. Staring.

Beaton and Stein burst through the door behind him, dragging their Scene of Crime equipment, Private Floyd bringing up the rear. Will keyed his throat-mike.

'We're in.'

'*Roger that. Perimeter defence: prepare for dust-off in five, four, three. . .*' Outside, the ship's engines built to a muffled roar as the Dragonfly leapt free of the ground, fading as it accelerated away to safety.

Now they were on their own.

Will nodded at the six heavily armed men and women surrounding him.

'Let's do it.'

Sergeant Nairn led them deeper into the building, heading for the toilets. As the pickup team moved the crowd moved around them. No one came within six feet, as if beyond that distance they would be safe from the Whompers and Thrummers.

By the time they reached the stairs to the mezzanine level sweat was trickling down Will's back. He wasn't sure if it was the heat or being back in Sherman House that did it, but he felt terrible. He'd been right to stay away.

At the top of the steps the main lobby stretched away on both sides, circling the building's central well. The space it surrounded was supposed to be a 'landscaped oasis in the urban jungle'. From what little Will could see it looked more like an open landfill site.

They found the toilets next to the elevators.

'Sergeant Nairn,' Will pointed at the cracked blue door, 'I want you, Floyd and Wright to guard the entrance. No one in or out without my say so.'

'Understood.' Nairn and his troopers took up their positions, weapons pointing at the crowd. The nearest inhabitants shifted uncomfortably, but the six foot bubble stayed exactly the same.

'Dickson, you're with us.' Will eased the door open and stepped inside, blinking at the sharp, eye-nipping reek of ammonia. Bloody hell – it stunk in here: rancid piss, laced with bile and sweat. Will stopped short and gasped. God, you could even *taste* it. . .

Behind him Dickson swore.

Three separate toilets – male, female and differently-abled –

15

took up a wall each. Beaton and Stein humped the SOC kit into the corridor. 'Jesus, Dickson, smells worse than your house.'

'Fuck you Stein.' She shifted her grip on the massive Bull Thrummer, its spinners crackling, the tines trembling in the reeking air.

The door to the male toilets was slightly ajar. Covering his mouth and nose, Will pushed it all the way.

'What th' hell?' A large woman wearing the distinctive navy jacket and brass buttons of a beat cop went for the Field Zapper strapped to her hip. Will had just enough time to duck before a sheath of blue lightning arced over his head and into Private Dickson.

There was a muffled squeal as all the muscles in Dickson's body contracted at once, sending her flying. As she hit the far wall her Bull Thrummer bellowed, tearing the concrete floor into a thick mist of crackling dust.

The outside door battered against the wall as what looked like Sergeant Nairn burst in, the lightsight on his Thrummer making a solid bar of green in the cloud of concrete particles. 'ON THE FLOOR NOW!'

'DON'T SHOOT!' Will stepped forward, then froze, arms pinwheeling, one foot hovering over the edge of a huge hole, straight through to some sort of maintenance room on the floor below. 'Shit. . .' He staggered backwards. 'We're on the same side!'

The woman with the oversized Zapper stayed where she was, the snub barrel pointing straight at Will's face.

'Prove it.'

'OK. I—' He coughed up a lungful of concrete dust. 'I'm reaching into my inside pocket to get my ID card. Are we all happy with that?'

She didn't object, so Will slipped the small plastic rectangle out of his wallet and showed it to her. The hologram on the front looked like someone had startled a chimpanzee, but it seemed to do the trick.

'Well, well, well: an Assistant Section Director as I live and breathe. What's th' matter, Network?' she asked, 'You think us poor wee Bluecoats would screw it up without you here to hold our little handies?'

'You asked for SOC support, OK? Urgh. . .' He grimaced and spat: gritty saliva. 'And for the record, I think it's bloody ridiculous they cut your budget, *again*. How are you supposed to—'

'Save it for someone that cares, Mr Assistant Section Director, cos I've had my share o'patronizin' bullshit this month.' She stepped aside and jerked her thumb over her shoulder. 'In there.'

Will bit his tongue – fighting with her wasn't going to get them anywhere.

On the floor behind him Private Dickson was groaning her way back to consciousness. He made sure she knew what day it was and how many fingers he was holding up before ushering the SOC team into the gents' toilet.

It was a filthy room, the metallic smell of fresh blood adding to the oppressive urine reek. The tiles had been white once, now they were stained a dark cherry red. Bloated flies filled the air, drifting in fat, lazy circles. A couple of younger Bluecoats stood in the corner, keeping as far out of the way as possible. One of them was pale grey, shivering, and as Beaton and Stein started assembling the scanning booms, Will found out why. The smell was bad, but the sight was worse.

'Was the body like this when you found it?'

A voice sounded behind him: 'No, it was all in one piece. We hacked it up for a bit of a laugh.'

You know what? Screw this: if the Bluecoats wanted a fight, they could have one.

'Right,' he said, slowly turning around. 'I have had enough of your lousy attitude. We're here because we have to be, *not* because we want to be. You. . .' Will drifted to a halt.

He'd been prepared for another blue uniform carrying a

grudge the size of Peebles, but instead he was confronted with the most violently green suit he'd ever seen in his life. Its occupant was female, slightly taller than average, with skin the colour of milky coffee. Her hair was gathered up on top of her head in an asymmetrical bun – very fashionable. The frown she was wearing was almost as unpleasant as the suit.

'Oh, I see.' She crossed her arms. 'What a *shame* you've been dragged all the way down here to play with the lower classes. What's the matter, Network? Termite lives don't count? This not white collar enough for you?' Somehow she'd managed to clench her entire face.

Will's voice never rose above a low growl. 'We don't want to be here because one of our team got blown apart yesterday. We don't want to be here because right now we're supposed to be·placing him in the long walk, and I'm supposed to be telling his wife and his daughter what a great man he was.' Will stepped forward, staring Ms Green Suit straight in the eye. 'We don't want to be here because this is not a Network job. But some bean-counting mincehead decided to slash your budget and give all the extra work to us, so here we are. And I do not have the time, or the inclination, to fight with you about it: I have a funeral to go to.'

She tilted her head to one side and studied him for a moment. The scowl slid from her face. 'I see.' She pointed at the cubicle done out like an abattoir. 'Victim's an I-C-one male. Roughly five foot eight, hundred and ninety pounds.'

Will opened the cubicle door all the way. The remains were slumped back on the toilet, chunks of meat and innards lying in sticky clumps on the blood-soaked floor, smears of scarlet and black all up the walls. The head was almost unrecognizable. 'Wow. . .'

'Chest cavity was split with a knife, at least eight inches long, probably serrated. No sign of the murder weapon on scene. Internal organs have been removed and slashed. The same chevron pattern is evident on both thighs.'

Will squatted down in front of the tattered body, peering into the emptied chest cavity. 'Anything else?'

'Teeth and jawbones were shattered by some sort of blunt instrument. There's something in his mouth: think it's his genitals, but I can't tell for sure till your Scene of Crime bods are finished with the scanning. No idea what happened to his eyes.'

Hard light flickered through the low, stinking room as Stein and Beaton finally got the scanning booms set up. Any minute now it was going to get very noisy in here.

Will levered himself back to his feet.

'You'll agree,' Ms Green Suit said, as he stepped gingerly over the cables snaking across the sticky floor tiles, 'that the attack pattern looks frenzied, disorganized. Furious. I'd say our killer was white, male, aged between twenty-four and thirty-two. Slovenly appearance. Lives alone or with his mother. She's got no idea what he's up to.' She didn't need to say unemployed, on this side of the river that was a given.

Will smiled – it was the classic serial killer profile, straight out of the field manual. 'I know this isn't my case, but are you *sure* your killer's disorganized?'

'Course he is. Attack's too messy for him to be anything else.'

Will pointed at the remains. 'Look at the hands.'

She frowned. 'What about them?'

'The fingertips are pulped, so we can't take any prints. The jaws have been demolished, so we can't use the dental database. The eyes have gone so we can't take a retinal scan. The only way we're going to get an ID is if our victim's got a record and his DNA's still on file. If not: chances are we'll never know who he was.'

Her lips moved soundlessly for a moment. Then, 'So the killer must be organized enough to cover his tracks.'

'At the very least.'

The scanning array gave a low rumble and a clank, then

fell silent. Stein treated it to a brief bout of swearing and a good hard kick. The machinery started up again, the sonics grumbling and buzzing like a catarrh-filled geriatric full of wasps.

'OK, people,' Beaton flipped a switch on the side of the casing, 'time to vacate the premises if you don't want to be immortalized in glorious, invasive scanovision.'

They all shuffled out into the corridor, avoiding the hole in the floor, and waited for the scanners to do their thing. The low phlegmy rumble turned into a deafening whine – the closed door cut the noise a little, but not much.

The concrete particles were settling, coating everything and everyone in a thin layer of gritty grey dust. Private Dickson stood at the far end of the group, cradling her Bull Thrummer and nursing what looked like a pretty big grudge; glowering at the Bluecoat who'd treated her to that bout of electro-convulsive therapy.

Ms Green Suit leant over and said something Will couldn't really hear.

'What?'

'WHY DIDN'T YOU CALL?' She had to shout directly into his ear before Will could hear her over the scanners.

'WHAT? CALL WHEN?'

'WHEN YOU CAME BARGING INTO THE TOILETS. WHY DIDN'T YOU CALL AND LET US KNOW YOU WERE OUT HERE? IF YOU HAD, YOUR LASS WOULDN'T HAVE GOT HERSELF ZAPPED.'

Will swore under his breath. 'I. . .' He couldn't come up with a good excuse, so he kept his mouth shut and waited in silence like the rest of them.

The floor beneath their feet trembled as the subsonics kicked in and Will shut his eyes, leaning back against the wall. That way he didn't have to look at the large hole in the floor, or Dickson's angry face. Good job Bluecoats weren't allowed to carry anything stronger than a Zapper, or Will would have another funeral to speak at. And this one really would have been his fault. Stupid, stupid, stupid. . .

At last the scanners gurgled and pinged to a halt.

'Right, that's your lot.' Stein stuck a finger in his ear and wriggled it. 'Give us two minutes to pack up and we can all go home.'

They filed back into the blood-smeared toilet, doing their best to stay out of the way as Beaton and Stein battered and cursed the equipment into its casing, then chucked it out into the corridor for Private Dickson to look after. Beaton produced a body-bag, squatting to pick up chunks of red and purple meat from the sticky tiles.

Now that the scanning gear was out of the way there was nothing obscuring Will's view of the dirty room. Broken sinks. Walls covered with graffiti. Cracked mirror. The floor was peppered with dead flies, their little shiny bodies not robust enough to stand up to the scanners. Blood everywhere. Will didn't envy the poor sod who'd have to sanitize the scene when they'd gone. . .

He frowned. A set of cleaning equipment sat abandoned in the corner: mop, wheely-bucket, scrubbing brushes, big container of industrial disinfectant.

'What happened to the halfhead?'

The Bluecoat in the green suit frowned. 'Halfhead?'

Will pointed at the mop and bucket. 'Know anyone else who's going to be scrubbing urinals in this part of town?'

'Damn.' Her mouth became a thin line. 'I'll get someone to look in to it.'

That was two points he'd picked her up on. Have to watch that if he didn't want the old hostility back.

'Of course,' she said, while Will did one last tour of the crime scene, 'down here halfheads go missing all the time. We're pretty sure it's the local militia: they grab them, torture them for a couple of days, then kill them. Never any proof, but we know they do it.' She gave a short laugh. 'Believe it

21

or not, there's a rumour going round that they *eat* them. Kind of a ritual cannibal orgy thing. Can you believe that?'

Something cold slithered down Will's spine. All he needed now was the sound of homemade drums in the darkness. Corridors. Death. Blood. His heart hammering rusty nails into his chest.

He wiped a hand across his damp forehead, then turned to see if Beaton and Stein had finished, so they could get the hell out of here . . . but something made him stop.

The SOC team were wrestling the victim's torso into the body-bag. Beaton's dress uniform was covered in a thin film of dust, the chrome buttons smeared with dark red. Will reached out and stopped her from closing the tags over the body.

There was something tugging at his memory, something dark and familiar.

'What's wrong?'

Something he'd seen before.

'Hello?' – Ms Green Suit was staring at him.

'What? Oh . . . nothing.'

He stood back and let Beaton seal the bag. The last tag snapped shut, hiding the victim's ruined face from view.

There *was* something here. Something he half recognized, but couldn't quite grasp.

Something that had killed before.

3

The bluebottles have flown away, looking for something dead
to feast upon, letting the buzzing in her head settle down to
a dull ache. Everything hurts: the colours, the sounds, the
smells. Sharp and sparking. Like electricity dragged across her
brain. . .

She does not think about that. She shuts it out and keeps
on walking.

Sparks, and the smell of burning meat.

SHE DOES NOT THINK ABOUT IT.

She stops, one hand resting against a wall of hot brick, the
surface rough beneath her fingers. Warmed by the sun and
the beat of the darkened heart.

This is what happens when she does not take her medication. Things . . . break.

A bird lies in the gutter, on its back, a ragged hole in its
side, wings crawling with mites. Beak open. Praying to the
beating sun in the voice of dead things.

It's a lovely sound.

She wants to sing. Like the dead bird. But she can't, because
of the sparks and the burning meat.

Because of Him.

She struggles on the operating table, fighting against the

restraining straps. It won't make the slightest bit of difference, but this is no place for rational thought. She's authorized enough halfheadings to know that. These sharp, broken, terrified thoughts will be the last ones she'll ever have.

The surgeon tries to say something, but she screams him down. Her mouth is operating on automatic: hurling abuse, obscenities, threats. Then the pleading starts: wild bargains and promises to change. The small part of her that is still lucid watches all this with detached interest: a professional behaviourist, categorizing the mental stages of the condemned mind. She wets herself.

An orderly presses a hypo against her shoulder and pulls the trigger – pins and needles swim through her body as the sedative rides her bloodstream.

She opens her mouth for one last scream, but nothing works anymore. All broken. Her body sags against the chilly metal.

The man is talking again, describing the procedure to the viewing gallery. She closes her eyes and does something she's not done since she was a little child. She prays. She doesn't pray for salvation, or forgiveness, or world peace, she prays that the surgeon will fuck this up and kill her on the operating table. That she won't have to spend the rest of her life like the other lobotomized slaves. That she won't. . .

And then the sound starts.

The surgeon pulls the ultrasonic blade from its holster. The sound jumps to a screech as he runs it across the test block – just a few practice incisions – getting a feel for the wand's hair-trigger with his long, thin fingers.

'We begin,' he says, 'by splitting the lower jaw.'

Gloved hands pull at her lower lip and the wand screeches. Ionized blood and bone fills her mouth. It's the last thing she'll ever taste.

She tries to tear her head away, but the only things she can move are her eyes, sweeping the operating theatre, the viewing gallery, looking for something, *anything* to stop this from happening. This is not how it's supposed to end. She was careful. She was so very careful.

There is a cracking noise. Her whole head shifts, as the surgeon works one half of her jaw free of its socket.

Then her eyes find *Him*.

He's sitting in the front row, His face close to the glass, Network-issue, dark-blue suit almost invisible in the dim light of the viewing gallery. Here to watch her suffer. The ragged scar she gave Him is just a faint purple line now, snaking its way down His face like a tear of drying blood. Soon there will be no trace of it left, scrubbed away through the miracle of modern medicine. But the scar she's given His soul will be there forever.

Will stood underneath the cooling unit, enjoying the breeze on the back of his neck. Outside, the sun was at its zenith, broiling the air until it shimmered. But in here it was nice and cold.

It was always cold in the mortuary.

'Any luck yet, George?'

The man in the green plastic overalls looked up and shook his head. A human jigsaw was spread out on the slab before him and, as Will watched, the pathologist dropped something unsettling onto a tray then smeared his hands down the front of his chest.

George waddled over to a little sink and rinsed his gloves off. 'How was Worrall's funeral?'

'Hour and a half late. The family weren't particularly impressed.'

'No pleasing some people. . .' George sniffed, pulled out a handkerchief, and made horrible sticky snorting noises into it. 'Machine's still trolling through the database, but while we wait for an ID, want to see what I pulled out of your dead friend here?'

'Not really, no.'

George smiled, stretching his podgy face as far as it would go. 'Thought you weren't squeamish.'

'I'm off for lunch in twenty minutes. Cafeteria do a good enough job of putting people off their food, they don't need any help from you.'

'Ah, funny you should mention lunch. . .' He grabbed a clear plastic bag from the bench behind him. 'Tada! Stomach contents!'

'Wonderful.' Will took one look at what was sloshing around in the pouch and changed his mind about having the ratatouille.

'Knew you'd like it.' George gave a huge, gurgly sniff. 'Want to know what's in it?'

'Surprise me.'

'Oh, I can do that all right: human flesh.'

Will's face froze. The drumming started again; the long dark corridors sticky with blood; the mutilated faces. . . *Please* tell me it was his own.'

The pathologist shook his head. 'Nope. It's someone else's. Consumed at least eight hours before he popped his clogs.' George grinned, obviously happy to have ruined someone's day. Rotten little gnome that he was. 'Now you go off and enjoy your lunch. I'll give you a shout if the machine comes up with anything.'

Will's new office was a lot larger than the last one, but there was the same lack of personal detail. No paintings, no knick-knacks, no holos, not even a framed plaque. If it weren't for the words 'ASSISTANT SECTION DIRECTOR WILLIAM HUNTER' on the door, there would be no sign that anyone worked here at all.

He reached out for the mug, sitting on a bland grey coaster, and took a mouthful. Gagged. Then spat it back into the cup. It used to be tea; now it was a cold, beige, watery liquid with a film of artificial milk scumming the surface.

He carried the offending beverage out into the corridor and poured it into the nearest pot plant.

'Mr Hunter?'

Will froze. Oh . . . bugger.

He turned to see the woman voted 'most likely to inspire murder' at last year's Christmas party. In her stocking feet she would have been an unremarkable five foot four, in her power heels she was an unpleasant five foot seven. Her hair hung round her head in a no-nonsense pageboy cut, framing features that could be generously referred to as 'lumpy'.

'Ah, Director Smith-Hamilton. How nice to see you.'

His boss beetled her neatly trimmed eyebrows. 'What *exactly* are you doing, Mr Hunter?'

'I. . . The . . . plants were looking a little dry. Probably the weather. Thought I'd give them a drink?'

'Ah: that's what I like to see! People thinking of their working environment as more than just a series of walls and windows. Very good.' She placed a hand on his arm. 'Studies have shown that plants have a positive effect on morale. And anything that improves morale, improves productivity.' Director Smith-Hamilton gave his arm a squeeze. 'But then, I don't have to tell *you* that!'

'Yes, well, if you'll excuse me, I have to—'

'Anyway, that's not why I came to see you, William.' She leaned in close, eyes sweeping up and down the corridor, voice dropping to a loud whisper. 'I had a meeting with the Justice and Defence Ministry: they're cutting the Bluecoat budget *again*. How those poor souls are supposed to maintain law and order with what they've got left is beyond me. So as part of a damage limitation exercise I have decided to launch an initiative!' She beamed at him.

Oh God, not another initiative – they still hadn't finished clearing up after the last one.

'Really?' He did his best to sound positive.

'The last thing we need is the rank and file resenting the

Network because we get more funding than they do. We need their cooperation when we're out in the field. Especially as we're all going to have to work a lot more closely now. So my initiative,' she said, 'will be to get the Bluecoats onboard. Bring in a couple of the middle ranks to liaise and work cases with us. That way they stay in the picture, we make them feel valued, and they'll be more inclined to cooperate.'

Will was surprised: he tended to think of Smith-Hamilton as an unnecessary evil, but every now and again she proved that you didn't get to be a Network Director by being a *total* mincehead. It really was a good idea, and he said so.

'Knew you'd be onboard!' She punched his shoulder again. 'I've asked control to assign each of them an office on the premises: you know, share with an experienced Special Agent, get to know the ropes, that sort of thing.' She stole a glance at the glowing numerals set into the skin of her wrist and tutted.

'Oops, must dash. Got the First Minister waiting, and you know what a prima donna he is. . .' She favoured Will with one last smile before marching off down the corridor.

He shook the last drips of cold tea from his mug. Well, that could have gone a lot worse. It wasn't as if—

'Oh, Will.' Director Smith-Hamilton popped her head back round the corner. 'Before I forget: I've moved the ASD meeting up to three instead of four, scheduled you in for a case evaluation at two thirty and I believe the first of our Bluecoat liaison officers is already here: bright young woman, definitely going places. So if you could just nip down and sling her through induction that'd be super.'

And then she was gone.

He took it all back – she *was* a total mincehead after all.

Will stomped back into his office, keying his throat-mike. 'Control: the Director's new Bluecoat liaison officer, where have you put her?' The sooner he got the induction out of the way, the sooner he could get some real work done.

There was a pause, then, *'In with Special Agent Alexander, sir. Do you want me to put you through?'*

'No, thanks anyway.' He killed the link and rode the lift down to the fourth floor.

Agent Alexander's tiny office had two grey desks shoehorned in, facing opposite walls. One was a mess of battered dataclips, the trays overflowing with unfinished files and open cases. Old-fashioned, two-dimensional photographs covered the wall above the desk; a lot of them pictures of Will and the office's owner. Restaurants, birthday parties, pubs, standing about like stuffed penguins and grinning like idiots at some ceremony or other. Back when they both had a lot more hair.

An explosion of foul language pulled Will's eyes towards a pair of lurid green trousers sticking out from under the other desk, and as he watched, the desktop terminal hummed into life, beeped twice and then flickered off again. This time the frustrated cursing bore all the hallmarks of impending violence and Will was almost afraid to ask,

'Anything I can do to help?'

Ms Green Suit, the Bluecoat from the Sherman House toilets, stuck her head out and pointed at a pile of cabling. 'Pass us over the red one. . . . No, not that one: the one with the big square bit on the end.'

She flashed him a smile, but it turned into a scowl when she saw the space the red thing was supposed to fit through.

Will kept his mouth shut as she did her best to shove the 'big square bit' through a small round hole in the plasticboard. There was a thump. Then: 'Fucking cock-monkeys!' She crawled out from under the desk, sucking a set of raw knuckles.

'You want some ice to put on that?'

'Only if it's keeping half a pint of gin company.' She sat back on the office floor and scowled at the tiny drops of blood beginning to form.

Will dropped into a crouch and peered under the desk at the offending 'big square bit'. The hole it was supposed to go through was less than half its size. 'What's on the other side of the wall?'

'No idea. You want me to go look?'

He nodded and she marched out of the door and into the other room.

'See anything?'

Her voice echoed down the corridor, 'Just a manky pot plant. Junction box is further down.'

'Good. Move the plant.' Brian always kept a spare Palm Thrummer in his desk. Will spent a whole fifteen seconds bypassing the securilock, then went rummaging through the junk-filled drawers. Brian was a good enough Agent, but he had a nasty habit of turning every place he worked into a pigsty.

Will found the Thrummer – looking like a stainless steel vibrator – beneath a pile of discarded plastic things and dragged it out into the open. If he was lucky it would still have some charge left. He twisted the two halves of the cylindrical casing till something went 'click' and the tines slid out.

'Stand back from the wall.' He pointed the weapon at the offending small, round hole and thumbed the trigger. The Palm Thrummer growled and a fist-sized section of wall disappeared in a cloud of dust. There was a shriek from the other room.

A stunned face gawked at him through the hole. 'Do you not think that was a bit over the top?'

'Call it lateral thinking.' He grabbed the 'big square thing' and tossed it through.

She grabbed the connector before it hit the carpet and laughed. 'You're not right in the head, you know that?'

'Look, we got off on the wrong foot this morning, how about we start again?' He stuck his hand through the hole for shaking. 'William Hunter.'

'Detective Sergeant Jo Cameron.' Her handshake was firm,

but warm. Made a nice change to find a professional female who didn't feel she had to prove something by crushing all the bones in his hand. 'You going to be my new room-mate then?'

'Not really, no.' He stood, waiting for her to come back round to the cramped office.

'Ah . . . I get it.' She pointed at the nameplate on the door 'SPECIAL AGENT BRIAN ALEXANDER'. 'This isn't your office, but your picture's all over the wall. What are you two, lovers or something?'

'No, I'm his boss. Assistant Section Director.'

'Ah. . .' She raised an eyebrow.

'Brian and I came up through the ranks together.' That wasn't strictly true, *he'd* come up through the ranks, Brian's career had stalled at Special Agent.

'You two aren't an item?'

'Don't think Brian's husband would approve.' Will settled back against the cluttered desk. 'So, how come you got lumbered with the liaison job?'

'They stuck the posters up a fortnight ago, thought it sounded like a good idea. Put my name down.'

'You've known about this for *two weeks*?'

'Yeah. Why?'

Will closed his eyes and had a swift mental fantasy involving Director Smith-Hamilton, a seven-foot skewer, an open fire, and some barbecue sauce.

'No reason.' He forced a smile. 'So, shall we start your induction DS Cameron?'

'Sir, if you're the ASD you have to call me Jo.'

'Sir?' Not what he'd been expecting after this morning's run in.

'Just because I'm a Bluecoat, doesn't mean I can't follow the chain of command. And anyway,' she shrugged, 'I might want to join the big N some day.'

*   *   *

They went through the building from the top down: toured the rooftop landing zones, walked the corridors of power on the seventh floor; pointed at the other Assistant Section Directors on the sixth; glided past the Special Agents on five, four and three; poked their noses in on the juniors and trainees on two and one; stuck their heads round the control room door on the ground floor; did more pointing at the famous paintings in the public areas; sauntered through the legal department, briefing rooms and operation zones on the first sub level; ignored the canteen and VR reconstruction suites; and ended up deep in the building's bowels. Outside the mortuary.

Will didn't take long to warm to his task as tour guide. DS Cameron was likeable, bright, and she'd joined in when he'd poked fun at the tourists gawping their way around the ground floor.

'Quite some place,' she said. 'Beats the crap out of the clapped-out Victorian pile I work in.'

'City Central?'

'Yeah, for my sins. Than and the occasional jaunt out to Monstrosity Square: keeping an eye on the termites.'

'Termites?' He stopped with one hand on the mortuary door. 'They're not insects, they're people.'

Her chin came up. 'You've never been in a fire-fight down there, OK? So don't tell me—'

'Virtual Riots. Sherman House. We were three days out of the Academy.'

'Oh. . .' She blushed.

'Dehumanizing them doesn't help, Jo. Trust me.' He pushed through the tinted double glass doors into the mortuary's reception area. A pretty blond in tight-fitting patent leatherette looked up from a datapad and smiled as they stepped onto the immaculate marbled floor.

'Assistant Director Hunter!' The receptionist bustled out from behind his desk, arms out as if he was expecting a hug. 'How *nice* to see you again.'

'Afternoon, Duncan.' Will turned to introduce DS Cameron and stopped when he saw the expression on her face: cheeks twitching, eyes all sparkly. Making little snorting noises. 'Is George in?'

The shiny young man nodded. 'Popped out earlier, but he's back now. If you like I can give him a shout? Ask him to come out and meet you?'

'It's OK, we can manage.' There was no way Will was going to hang around here with DS Cameron for any longer than was strictly necessary. Not when she was on the verge of the giggles.

'God, did you *see* his suit?' she said as the mortuary door hissed shut behind them. 'I've not seen anything that shiny since I worked vice!'

Given the neon-green monstrosity she was wearing, she was in no position to criticize.

Will led the way along the long, antiseptic corridor to a door marked 'Storage & Examination'. Someone had stuck a cartoon up beneath the sign: a hunchback and a mad scientist on the beach, playing volleyball with a brain. Frankenstein's monster sat by the net, the top of his head open like a pedal bin. It was captioned: 'Igor's Day Off'. And just in case that was too subtle, the word 'Igor' had been crossed off and 'George' written in its place. It was a surprisingly good likeness.

The man in question was sitting on one of the slabs, drinking a mug of something that sent sweet-lemony-menthol steam into the cold, circular room. His lunch was spread out on the stainless steel beside him, and as they crossed the floor he popped a slice of CheatMeat in his mouth and made blocked up chewing noises.

'Supposed to be teriyaki swan,' he said, voice echoing off the metal walls, 'but it tastes more like old socks.' He polished off another slice. 'Who's this you've brought with you?'

'George: Detective Sergeant Jo Cameron. She's going to be

with us for a while, helping coordinate Network–Bluecoat investigations and resources.'

'A veritable vision in green. . .' A smile pulled at George's podgy face, making his cheeks swell and his eyes disappear into little wrinkly slits. Like a short-arsed Buddha on an off day. He reached out and took the hand Jo had stuck out for shaking, turning it at the last minute to kiss the back. 'What's a lovely creature like you doing hanging around with Mr Misery Guts here?' He beamed up at her, apparently having no intention of giving her hand back.

Indecision flitted across DS Cameron's face and Will got the nasty feeling she was about to punch the pathologist's teeth down his throat. But she didn't. Instead she performed a graceful little curtsey and batted her eyelashes.

'Well now. . .' she treated George to the full strength of her smile. 'How else would I get to meet a man as handsome as yourself?'

George just giggled and blushed.

'If you two have quite finished.' Will marched over to the centre console and brought up the file on the mangled remains they'd retrieved from Sherman House that morning. The lights dimmed and an old holo projector flickered into life: 3D shots of the victim's remains crackling in the air as the carousel started to turn – its long mechanical arms selecting the appropriate bodypod from the pigeon-holes lining the walls.

An examination slab creaked up out of the floor and the carousel clicked the metallic canister into it, retreating back to the roof as George waddled over and unclipped the tabs. With a faint poom of trapped air, the tube fell open, revealing a collection of pale-yellow body parts, all neatly labelled and categorized.

George had forgotten to put the top of the skull on, exposing a nasty interior view of their victim's head. 'Oops.' He popped the hairy lid back in place and secured it with a squirt of skinglue. 'Ladies and gentlemen, may I present Mr Allan Brown.'

'You got an ID?' Will was impressed. 'How the hell did you manage that?'

'Ah.' George tapped the side of his nose, scrunched up his face, and sneezed explosively. Then snorked into a scabrous hanky. 'Mr Brown was part of the PsychTech programme. They kept full records: dental, retina, DNA . . . you name it they kept it.'

PsychTech. Jesus, even the word was enough to make Will's stomach churn. He swallowed hard, wondering why it suddenly felt hot in here.

The little pathologist waved a hand at the holo image. Nothing happened, so he did it twice more, cursed, then stomped back to the console, kicked it, and stabbed a couple of buttons. A naked child appeared next to the cutting slab, fizzling in and out of existence. A little blue tag, floating next to his head, said 'ALLAN BROWN – 5 YEARS OLD'. The image lurched as the child grew, the counter increasing with every holographic scan. The last one in the series showed Brown at eighteen, six years before someone decorated a stinking toilet cubicle with his innards. An unremarkable young man with nothing but pain and death in his future.

George hauled a transparent plastic bag from the canister. There was a large, unmistakeable, gelatinous-grey lump sitting in a puddle of yellowy liquid.

'You're not going to like what I got out of his brain.'

Will forced a smile. 'Can't be any worse than the stomach contents.'

'You'd be surprised.' He waved at the display again, and this time it worked: a large schematic of the victim's brain appeared, bright green, yellow and red bands glowing in the dim mortuary light. 'See it?'

Will frowned, trying to work out what the different colours meant in terms of neural chemistry. He'd only ever learned to recognize two patterns: one was the distinctive mark of the confirmed serial killer, the other was far more dangerous. Right now he was looking at a combination of the two.

'You're right. I don't like it.'

'There's more.' The little man pulled a datapad from his pocket and typed in a rapid stream of numbers. Another naked figure flickered into life beside Allan Brown, only this one looked like a jigsaw puzzle where half the pieces were missing. 'Mr Kevin McEwan, he came in day before yesterday. They found bits of his family all over the apartment. Wife and two children.'

A second brain appeared, turning slowly in cross section. Large chunks of it were missing – most of the back where the brainstem should have been was gone – the edges all torn and frayed.

'Doesn't have the same level of prefrontal lobe activity, but everything else is the same.'

DS Cameron stared up at the floating brains. 'I don't get it. . . What are we looking at?'

Will pointed at the one on the right. 'This is the guy we scraped off the toilet floor at Sherman House this morning. You see the yellow banding? That's caused by a lack of serotonin and glucose; it means a loss of activity in the prefrontal lobes. When that happens, you get someone who has a great deal of difficulty controlling their base urges. More often than not they don't even try. It's a classic indicator of a disorganized serial killer.'

She nodded. 'So this could be a revenge thing: our victim—'

'It's also indicative of something else.'

'What?'

The pathologist pulled out his hanky again. 'Remember the VRs?'

'You're kidding!'

George blew his nose, then sighed. 'I wish. The brain

patterns are almost identical. I started looking for a connection as soon as I got an ID on the stiff you brought in. They're both from Sherman House. Lived two apartments away from each other.'

Oh shit. . . This was *not* good. This was not good at all.

Will stared at the ceiling for a moment. Took a deep breath. Swore. 'We're going to have to go back there, aren't we?'

DS Cameron turned on him. 'What do you mean, "*we*"? This is *my* investigation, you were only there for SOC backup. All that bollocks you spouted about cooperation, and first chance you get you steal my case!'

'I don't have any choice, OK?' Will ran a hand across his eyes. 'If this really is an outbreak of VR syndrome it's a Network matter. Fuck. . .' He kicked the nearest chunk of machinery. Didn't make him feel any better: his stomach was still full of snakes. 'Better grab your coat DS Cameron: we're going on a little field trip.'

4

High above the streets lazy, golden clouds drifted slowly westward. A pair of Scrubbers floated in the stale air: huge rusty metal shapes, dripping condensation from their swimming-pool-sized filtration units onto the buildings below, where it evaporated as soon as it hit the hot concrete. The advertising hoardings bolted to the Scrubbers' sides juddered, the pictures out of sync; misaligned and fuzzy. What was the point of fixing them? No one looked up any more.

If anyone had, they'd have seen a Network Dragonfly jinking past the out-of-focus displays, heading for the south side of the city. Half a mile out it dropped to street level and banked right, roaring between the huge connurb blocks.

And there was Monstrosity Square: dead ahead.

Will watched it growing on his monitor. Calm. Stay calm. Breathe in through the nose, out through the mouth, in through the nose, out through the mouth. Nothing to worry about. Everything was going to be fine. They were OK this morning, weren't they? In through the nose, out through the mouth.

Fuck, fuck, fuck, fuck, fuck.

In the next bay, Detective Sergeant Jo Cameron lolled against her harness, fiddling with the Thrummer she'd borrowed from the armoury. She was whistling to herself, something cheery and upbeat that Will could almost recognize over the Dragonfly's engines. She didn't look worried about going back to Sherman House, but then she hadn't been there eleven years ago. She'd been too young. She'd been lucky.

Will unclipped his Whomper from the recharging rack and checked the battery for about the twentieth time: still fully charged.

In through the nose, out through the mouth.

'*Right, listen up, campers.*' Lieutenant Brand's voice was curt and businesslike. '*They've already had two visits from the Network this week; chances are they'll be getting restless. So keep it tight! I do not want this turning into another episode of "Everyone Gets Their Arse Shot Off". Understood?*'

The trooper in the bay opposite crossed himself as he and his colleagues barked, 'Ma'am, yes, ma'am!'

'*Good. ETA: forty-five seconds. Buckle up, people, it's going to be sudden.*'

At the last moment the Dragonfly leapt, twisting almost vertically to climb the side of Sherman House. Jo shrieked and laughed; Will closed his eyes and tried not to throw up. As the gunship fishtailed to a halt on the building's roof, he released his death grip on the supports and unsnapped his safety harness, watching as the bays around him erupted into life.

'*First team: GO!*'

The rear ramp swung open, exposing the rooftop in all its tatty glory. When the connurb blocks were new this was all lush, vibrant gardens, arranged around the building's central well. Twisting paths for romantic walks, picnic areas, and sports facilities. Now it was an unkempt jungle, punctuated by the blackened circles of forgotten bonfires. Drifts of rubbish slouched in every corner like dirty, lumpy snow, and here and there, the tumbledown ruins of community buildings were visible through tangled rhododendrons and brittle brown ivy, their walls crumbling and vandalized.

The first team sprinted out into the undergrowth, searching for an entrance to the lower floors.

Huddled in the safety of the drop bay Will looked out on the blocks that made up the other three corners of Monstrosity Square. Two hundred and forty thousand people were crammed into these four huge, ugly buildings. No jobs, no hope and no future.

No wonder they'd all gone crazy.

From here, sixty storeys above the roasting streets, Glasgow was laid out like a vast, concrete cancer. It stretched in every direction, further than the eye could see, grey and dirt brown, sweltering in the evening light. Home sweet home.

A voice sounded in his ear, making Will jump: *'Entryway is secure.'*

The second team burst out of the Dragonfly, taking up positions. And then Beaton and Stein lumbered after them, dragging the bulky scanning equipment through the scrub. The bashed and dented canister trundled along on tiny wheels that quickly became ensnared in the yellow grass. They swore and cursed all the way. Amazingly their grasp of the profane was nowhere near as comprehensive or inventive as DS Jo Cameron's.

Will checked his Whomper's battery one last time, then stepped into the sweltering afternoon. In through the nose and out through the mouth. . . Everything smelled of dust and dry earth.

He scanned the landing zone, finally spotting DS Cameron meandering along the edge of the roof. She had her Thrummer slung casually over her shoulder – like a long, deadly handbag – her hands in her pockets and a smile on her face.

Will shook his head and joined the advance team.

They'd found one of the minor access escalators: a small plexiglass bunker squatting on the building's roof. The transparent panes were all scratched, covered with fading graffiti tags, the plexiglass swollen and blackened in one corner, where someone had tried to burn the place down. The moving steps were gone, exposing a ramped tunnel that disappeared into the depths of the building.

Will looked down into the hole. 'This the only option we have, Sergeant?'

Nairn nodded. 'Aye, sir. If we want to steer clear of the main access points it's this or we go down the outside on wires.'

Will tried not to shudder – there was no way he was going out over the edge of Sherman House on the end of a body-wire ever again.

Nairn gave the orders, sending Privates Dickson and Wright scurrying down the ramp into the darkness. He gave it a count of ten, then waved at the SOC team. 'Beaton, Stein: you're next. And keep the noise down this time! I don't want every psychotic wee lowlife in the place using your bloody scanning equipment as a homing beacon.'

'What do you mean "our scanning equipment"?' Stein slapped the battered canister. 'Just cos we've been lumbered with this shite four times in a row don't mean we're makin' a career out of it!'

'Shut your cakehole! You will hump that bloody scanning stuff about and you will like it. Or I will connect your rectum to your bloody ears with my boot!' There was no smart reply from Private Stein, he just picked up his end of the SOC canister and clambered into the tunnel. Nairn nodded. 'Better. Rhodes, Floyd: you're on rearguard.'

Will picked his way carefully down the slippery ramp. Six feet in, the track twisted back on itself, doglegging around a support pillar, and as he turned the corner Will's innards clenched. The toilets downstairs had been bad enough. But this was. . . This was. . . Jesus.

The breathing exercises weren't working any more.

41

Stupid. It was just a building. Nothing to worry about.

So how come his legs wouldn't move?

Inside, Sherman House hadn't changed much in the last eleven years: dingy corridors, lined with silent, shuttered apartments. All the horrors locked away and secret. At least this time the carpets wouldn't be sticky with blood.

Grubby plastic spheres lined the passageway, giving off a pale, insipid glow that did more to exaggerate the shadows than illuminate things. More graffiti lurked in the gloom, covering the beige walls like cheap tattoos. People trying to leave their mark on a world that had already forgotten about them.

Someone tapped him on the shoulder and Will flinched. 'No offence, sir,' said Sergeant Nairn, 'but think we could get a move on? I'd kinda like to get out of here before the natives go apeshit.'

'Right. Sorry. . .' Will cleared his throat. 'Good point.'

He forced his feet to move again, following DS Jo Cameron down the broken escalator into the depths of the building.

'You know,' she said as they passed the fifty-first floor, 'you seem a bit tense.'

'Really.' Will frowned in the darkness. It stank of mildew in here, stale air, and something sickly sweet and floral – not quite covering up the sour background smell of damp carpet.

'Yeah, ever since George showed you those brain scans you look like you're holding a hand grenade between the cheeks of your bum. I've visited Sherman House dozens of times, it's not as bad as you think any more. Honestly.'

Will turned the next corner – looking out at another identical corridor. 'Think we could just focus on the job in hand?'

'If you don't want to talk about it, just say so.'

'I don't want to talk about it.'

She shrugged. 'Suit yourself.'

It seemed to take forever to work their way down to the forty-seventh floor.

Will hadn't seen a single living soul since they'd arrived on the roof; nearly sixty thousand people lived in Sherman House and there was no sign of any of them. Like the place wasn't creepy enough.

DS Cameron stepped off the escalator ramp, took one look at the shabby hallway, and summed up all that human misery and squalor in five words:

'Can you smell cat pee?'

Stein and Beaton were hauling their scanning equipment along the threadbare carpet, swearing their way towards the late Allan Brown's last known address. Past them Will could just make out the faint glimmer of a Whomper's telltales: that would be Private Wright, standing guard. The sinister shape of Private Dickson and her Bull Thrummer lurked down the other end, cordoning off the whole area. Anyone wanting to cause trouble would end up missing a large part of their anatomy.

From the outside, flat 47-126 didn't look like much: just another shabby brown door in a long line of shabby brown doors. Nairn motioned Floyd and Rhodes into position on the opposite side of the passageway, their weapons trained on the flat's door at chest height. The sergeant reached into his mouth and pulled out a wad of chewing gum, rolled it into a sticky ball, then pressed it over the spyhole. He flattened himself against the wall next to the door, nodded at everyone, then reached out and knocked. . .

No reply.

Nairn pointed. Rhodes?'

The trooper clicked a button on the chunky oblong strapped to the barrel of his Thrummer, peered into the weapon's sight. Pulled his head back. Frowned. Slapped the oblong twice. Then went back to the sight again, sweeping the Thrummer back and forth. 'No sign of movement.'

Nairn turned to Will. 'You want us to force it?'

He was about to say yes when DS Cameron walked over

and crouched down in front of the keypad lock set into the wall beside the door. She popped the cover off with a pocket knife, pulled a thin piece of bent wire from her asymmetrical hairdo and stuck it into the circuitry. As she fiddled about, the display panel flashed warning red. Then ten seconds later a small bleep sounded and the lights went as green as her suit.

'Open Sesame.' She pushed the door open on silent, plastic hinges, revealing a small, dark hallway.

Will stared at her. 'I don't believe you just did that. A hair-grip?'

'Yeah, well.' She stood and worked the impromptu lock pick back into place above her left ear. 'That's technology for you.'

'Unbelievable. . .' He stepped into the tiny hallway, opened the door on the other side, and walked into a nightmare.

A fug of hot air washed over them, bringing with it the stench of rotting garbage. Like a bin bag left in the sun. The windows were covered with broad straps of black plastic. Slivers of light found their way through the gaps, falling across the cramped space in horizontal bars. One wall was given over to a collage made up of little bits of paper scrawled with dense handwriting, all glued together to form the life-size silhouette of an angel. Only this angel didn't have a harp, it had a sword. A big red sword that dripped blood. But that was nothing compared to what sat in the middle of the room.

The paper angel stood guard over a pile of severed heads. Severed halfheads to be precise.

'Oh – my – God.' Jo Cameron stared at the mound. 'So *that's* where they all went to!' There were at least fifteen of them, possibly more, all neatly arranged in a heap.

Will dug a reader out of his suit pocket and pressed it into her hand.

'Get the barcodes.'

Biting her bottom lip, she reached forward and slid the

electronic eye over the nearest disembodied head. The reader gave a disapproving clunk. She scowled at the display. 'Non sample error. Must be all the wrinkles: thing looks almost mummified. . .' Jo snapped on a pair of thin, blue plastic gloves and tried smoothing out the skin on the forehead. Then had another go with the reader. Clunk. 'Come on you little sod. . .'

Will left her to it, picking his way through the rest of the squalid flat. Rubbish spread out from huge piles in the corners of every room, hiding the floor from view. The kitchen was awash with green, hairy mould. He opened the fridge door, gagged, then slammed it shut again, bathed in the un-mistakeable sickly sour smell of rotting meat. Holding his breath, Will tried again, one hand clamped over his nose. In with the bloated plastics of milk and black slimy vegetables were thick cuts of pale meat, with a fatty, goose-pimpled rind. The flesh a nasty greenish-grey colour, speckled with black mould.

The light didn't come on. Power was probably dead, which explained the smell.

Will closed the fridge door, then hurried through to the bedroom before he had to breathe in again.

It was a dark, cramped little room, stuffed with rubbish. Another six-foot angel collage dominated the wall above the bed, just visible in the gloom. Mr Brown had done a much better job of taping over the bedroom's tiny window. Will punched the lightsight on his Whomper up to maximum, bathing the room in its eerie green glow. It leached away all the colours, turning the whole scene into a monochrome landscape of half-seen garbage.

He stepped forward and felt something crunch underfoot. He froze. Please don't let it be what he thought it was. . . Gingerly, he lowered the Whomper's barrel, spotlighting the refuse beneath his feet.

Emerald light glittered back at him from dozens of cracked

plastic cylinders. It was just discarded HotNoodle tubes, their biodegradable plastic littering the nest like gaily patterned animal bones.

He waded through the filth to peer at the angel and its blood-soaked sword.

Each bit of paper in the collage bore the same handwritten quotation:

> 'And the third angel followed them, saying with a loud voice, If any man worship the beast and his image, and receive his mark in his forehead, or in his hand,
>
> The same shall drink of the wine of the wrath of God, which is poured out without mixture into the cup of his indignation: and he shall be tormented with fire and brimstone in the presence of the holy angels, and in the presence of the Lamb:
>
> And the smoke of their torment ascendeth up for ever and ever: and they have no rest day nor night, who worship the beast and his image, and whosoever receiveth the mark of his name.'

That explained a lot.

Back in the lounge, DS Cameron was still cursing her way through the pile of severed heads, scowling at the reader. 'Come on, you little—'

'I know why he did it.' Will said as she banged the hand-held device against the floor. 'No, scratch that. I don't know *why* he did it, but I know why he *thought* he was doing it.'

She hurled the reader at the heads, settled back on her haunches, then looked up at him, her face all pinched and lined. 'Why does nothing ever sodding work?'

'The angels: there's another one in the bedroom. They're made up of little bits of the Book of Revelation. Chapter fourteen.'

She frowned for a moment, then started to recite in an almost singsong voice, '"If any man worship the beast and his image"—'

46

'"And whosoever receiveth the mark of his name."' Will pointed at the heap on the carpet. 'It's the tattoo.'

He turned the lightsight on his Whomper down to a more reasonable operating level. 'Tell the SOC team to start scanning the place. When they're done, have them bag and tag anything that looks like a body part. Start with the fridge. But tell them to get a shift on. Sooner we're out of here the better.'

'OK.' She stood, then stooped to pick up the discarded reader. 'What are you going to do?'

'The other body George showed us, he lived two doors down. I'm going to take a look.' He turned and made for the door. 'Oh, and see if you can dig a VR set out of this midden. If our halfhead-hunting friend really did have VR syndrome, there'll be one in here somewhere.'

The door to flat 47-122 swung open after a small amount of fiddling with the lock. It wasn't as quick as DS Cameron's hairgrip method, but it didn't leave any physical evidence of tampering. The tiny hallway was as nondescript as its neighbour, but the rooms beyond it were completely different. Allan Brown's flat had been a lair. This had been a home. Right up to the moment when Mr Kevin McEwen came home and shot his wife Barbara in the face. Then he'd gone into the second bedroom and done the same thing to his two children, before turning the gun on himself.

The council clean-up crew had stripped the place back to the fixtures and fittings, leaving it bereft and lifeless. Will stood in the middle of the empty living room and tried to imagine it before Kevin McEwen wiped out his entire family.

Like all connurb block flats it was surprisingly small, even with all the furniture removed: a lounge with a screened off kitchen, one master bedroom, a toilet-shower, and a secondary sleeping cubicle. The rooms were decorated in ancient wallpaper: the pattern a mixture of dirty yellow and green, faded with age. Picture frames had left shadows on the walls, keeping rectangles of wallpaper rich and vibrant. A faint dark line marking the top edges. The McEwens must have been a house-proud pair, because other than that, the whole place was scrupulously clean.

A faint rumble sounded from down the hall. The SOC team had started scanning.

Will wandered from tiny room to tiny room; amazed that anyone could live somewhere this small, let alone raise two kids here. Every apartment in Monstrosity Square was the same: a testament to the ingenuity and inhumanity of the planning department.

Compressed Urban Habitation they called it. Cram as many people into as small a space as possible, then sit back and wonder why they start killing themselves. And each other.

He checked his watch, gave the meagre flat one last look, then headed back out into the hallway, locking the door behind him.

As Will hurried up the corridor the floor started to tremble. By the time he'd reached Allan Brown's flat the sonics were in full swing. He had to shout to be heard over the din in the kitchen.

'HOW MUCH LONGER?'

Stein puffed out his cheeks. 'DONE THE LOUNGE AND BEDROOM, BUT YOU KNOW HOW IT IS: SOMETIMES THE MACHINERY WORKS FIRST TIME, SOMETIMES WE HAVE TO KICK THE HELL OUT OF IT.' He aimed a boot at the scanner's dented canister. 'AND IT'S ALWAYS US! I MEAN IT WOULD BE FAIR ENOUGH IF IT WAS SOMEONE ELSE'S TURN NOW AND AGAIN, BUT FOR GOD'S SAKE: EVERY SODDIN' TIME?'

Thankfully the howling scanning booms meant that Will could only catch snatches of the rant. He nodded in sympathy and when the subsonics kicked in mimed his concern and buggered off through to the main bedroom.

It was slightly quieter in here, but not by much, even with the door shut. DS Cameron and Sergeant Nairn were picking through the mounds of rubbish. A transparent evidence sack sat in the middle of the cluttered bed – there wasn't much in it.

'ANY LUCK?'

DS Cameron squinted at him. Then cupped a hand over her ear. 'WHAT?'

'HAVE YOU HAD ANY LUCK?'

'A BIT. WHAT ABOUT YOU?'

'WASTE OF TIME. THE MCEWENS' PLACE IS CLEAN AS A WHISTLE, READY FOR THE NEXT POOR SODS TO MOVE IN. NOTHING LEFT.'

'SORRY, CAN'T HEAR A THING OVER THAT BLOODY—' The scanners fell silent and DS Cameron paused for a moment, then sighed. 'God, that's better. . . What were you saying?'

But Will was heading back to the kitchen: the scanners still had another cycle to go. If they were quiet *now* it meant they weren't working. He burst into the room to see Stein and Beaton on their knees, poking at the equipment.

'What's wrong with it?'

Beaton jiggled one of the leads. 'It's buggered: that's what's wrong with it.'

Will checked his watch again. They'd been here almost fifteen minutes. Give it another six or seven to get back to the roof. Twenty-two minutes. Even then that was probably going to be tight. Running at full tilt the scanners would have interfered with all electronic activity within six hundred feet: that included the public virtual reality channels. Robbed of the only real escape they had, the locals would start looking for something else to fill the gap. Religion might have been the opium of the masses, but VR was their crack cocaine.

And no one liked going cold turkey.

'How long to fix it?'

49

'Don't know.' Beaton looked up at her colleague who gave a shrug. 'Five, maybe ten minutes?'

That made it over half an hour. Will shook his head – there was a difference between reasonable risk and reckless stupidity. 'You've got two.'

'No chance. We've got to recalibrate the whole array or it'll just fall over again.'

'Then pack it up. We're leaving.'

Stein shook his head and smiled as if he was talking to a small child. 'You don't understand—'

'If you two aren't ready to go by the time I count to ten, we're leaving you behind. You can take your chances with the natives.'

'But we—'

'One. Two. Three—'

'But,' Stein pointed at the machinery's dented casing. 'The subsonics—'

'Five. Six—'

'We've got to recalibrate, or—'

'Eight. Nine—'

'But—' He was beginning to go red in the face.

'Ten. Time's up.' Will turned and shouted into the bedroom, 'Sergeant Nairn, get your team together. We're pulling out.'

'Yes, sir!' Nairn emerged from the bedroom with an evidence bag slung over his shoulder. DS Cameron was carrying one too, lurching after the sergeant into the lounge. With fifteen severed heads stuffed into the transparent sack, she looked like a macabre Santa Clause.

'Did we get a VR set?'

'Nairn's got it,' she said, as the man in question marched out the front door. 'All twisted up into a pretty little shrine decorated with finger bones and jelly babies.'

Will closed his eyes. Blood and drums in the darkness. *Definitely* time to go.

'Come on then.' He ushered her out into the corridor.

A muffled, rapid conversation erupted in the apartment behind them: Beaton and Stein arguing over whether or not they'd really be left behind. Then there was the sound of mechanical scrabbling and professional swearing. The SOC team tumbled out of the flat, forcing their battered equipment back into its casing as they went.

'All right, all right! We're coming.'

Will reached up and keyed his throat-mike. 'Lieutenant Brand, this is Hunter: prepare for dust-off.'

'Roger that, Hunter. We are hot to trot.'

'You see,' said Detective Sergeant Cameron, hoisting her evidence bag, 'nothing to worry about. I told you this place isn't half as bad as you think.'

And that was when the shooting started.

5

It started out as a faint crack, like the sound an ice cube makes dropped into warm water. Then another. And another. Then the sound changed, grew deeper, got closer. Gunfire echoed down from the floors above, and Rhodes' voice crackled in Will's earpiece:

'. . . repeat, we have hostiles!'

No: this wasn't fair! He'd been careful. They were heading home!

Sergeant Nairn punched up the power on his Thrummer and shouted: 'Dickson, Wright, get your arses back here on the double!'

They all sprinted for the broken escalator. Nairn jumped onto the ramp, his Thrummer searching for targets. 'Talk to me Rhodes, what the hell's going on up there?'

'. . .Fifteen, maybe more. Automatic projectile weapons; I think I see a Zinger.' The harsh burr of a Thrummer tore through the air. 'Orders?'

Nairn looked at Will and waited.

'We. . . It. . .'

'Sir, I hate to hassle you, but now would be a good fucking time.'

'But we. . .' Deep breath. In through the nose, out through the mouth.

'Fine.' Nairn hit his throat mike again. 'Rhodes, you are cleared for deadly force. I want everything neutralized and—'

'No!' Will grabbed the sergeant's arm. 'We've had two cases of VR syndrome on this floor in one week, probably hundreds more we don't know about. You have to keep any contact to a minimum or this whole place will explode.'

'Oh Jesus. . .' Nairn swallowed, hard. 'Rhodes – disregard last order, *non*-lethal force only.'

'Sarge? Have you gone off your fuckin'—'

'Shut up and do what you're told. People: we need dust-off and we need it now!' He charged up the ramp, with privates Dickson and Wright hurrying after him, leaving Will, DS Cameron and the SOC team behind.

Angry noises filtered up from the floors below: it didn't matter that the scanners had been turned off and packed way, it would take time for the building's local network to reboot. Sherman House was suffering from VR withdrawal. And if the residents couldn't have computer-generated death and destruction, they could always have the real thing.

'Erm. . .' Beaton shifted from foot to foot. 'Not meaning to be funny or anything, sir, but shouldn't we be getting the hell out of here?'

Stein fiddled with the Field Zapper at his hip. The SOC team only carried small arms – anything bigger would have made manoeuvring the scanning equipment impossible. He was flicking the power switch on and off, on and off, never quite allowing it to get fully charged. Eyes darting up and down the corridor. Licking his top lip. The sound of gunfire was getting louder. 'It's going to be OK, right? No problem. . .'

Will pushed them towards the ramp. 'I'll take point; DS Cameron, you're back door.'

She nodded, a faint sheen of perspiration speckling her

brow. The bag of severed halfheads swung as she spun round to face back down the ramp, making her stagger. There was no way she could provide covering fire carrying a sack full of heads and Will told her so.

'We can't just leave them, they're evidence!'

'OK, fine . . . give them here. I'll take—'

A soft 'phfwoom' sounded from the floor above and suddenly the entire corridor was bathed in flickering orange light. Then a sheet of flame exploded down the ramp.

'GET DOWN!'

Will leapt, bouncing off the wall and twisting on the rebound to land behind the escalator, putting its bulk between himself and the fireball. Stein wasn't so lucky. He was still straining with the scanning equipment when the blaze caught him. Beaton cowered on the other side of the scanner as the fire rushed past; leaving her unscathed while her colleague burned.

Stein staggered off the ramp, his hair and clothes ablaze, screaming.

Will tore off his own jacket and dived on top of him, smothering the flames. Stein's thrashing body gradually fell still.

The bitter tang of smoke filled the air, and the corridor's sprinklers finally kicked in, bathing the hallway with luke-warm, stale water.

'Damn it!' Will flipped Stein over onto his back and felt for a pulse. The trooper's face was scarlet and swollen, blackened in places, the skin split open on his cheeks and forehead, wisps of steam drifting up into the ineffective drizzle. There was a faint tremor beneath Will's fingers, but Stein wasn't breathing.

'Is he dead?'

Will looked around to see DS Cameron struggling to her feet. The back of her bright-green suit was burnt, crackling and flaking as she moved. Her meticulous asymmetric bun was ruined: from the nape of her neck up, her hair was tattered and crisped, angry red skin showing through under-neath. She was shaking.

More gunshots. Closer now.

Go back to Sherman House, Will. It'll be good for you, Will. Will it bollocks.

He waved DS Cameron over. 'Get him into the apartment.'

She stood, looking down at Stein's roasted body, her face grey and smudged with soot. 'He's dead, isn't he.'

'He will be if you don't stop fucking about!' The corridor was getting darker as the flames on the floor above guttered out in the artificial rain. 'Move it!'

DS Cameron gritted her teeth, grabbed a handful of Stein's baked-on jumpsuit, and dragged him back towards flat 47-126, swearing all the way. Will scrambled up the escalator ramp, helping Beaton manhandle the SOC gear down onto the soaking carpet. They hauled the heavy metal canister along the corridor, following DS Cameron into Allan Brown's flat.

Will slammed the front door shut behind them, and keyed his throat-mike.

'Sergeant Nairn? What's going on up there?'

The signal was crackly, the older man's voice breathless and worried: *'Escalator's impassable. Some spragger's brought down the ramp.'* Will could hear gunshots, like small pops of static between the words. The jarring roar of Dickson's Bull Thrummer drowned out what was said next, but when the noise died down Nairn was saying, *'. . .concussion, and Floyd's been shot in the shoulder. We're laying down covering fire, trying to keep the wee bastards' heads down. Can you make the stairs?'*

Will watched Private Beaton clamber on top of Stein, rip open his chitin, and start chest compressions.

'Don't you dare die on me, Dick. You hear me?' Keeping a steady rhythm on top of his heart. 'Don't you fucking dare. . .'

DS Cameron had her lips clamped over Stein's mouth, forcing breath into his lungs. There was no way they could carry him up all the way up to the roof and keep him alive at the same time.

'Negative. We need another option.'

'We can't get down to you. Not without a lot of dead bodies.'

And then the violence would spread and spread until the whole bloody building went up. Will swore.

DS Cameron shouted across the room, 'We're losing him!'

'What do you want us to do?'

Outside in the corridor, the gunfire was getting louder. The locals were coming.

Plan. Need a plan.

Will scanned the room: he had two Network troopers – one on the verge of death – a traumatized Bluecoat, and a knackered set of scanning equipment. And none of the evidence they'd just risked their lives to collect.

'Where's the bag of halfheads?'

'Sir? What should we do?'

'Shut up and let me think!'

He stuck his head out into the corridor: the evidence bag lay against the wall by the escalator ramp. He was halfway down the hall before he realized what he was doing and by that time it was too late to turn back.

The wall lights were overflowing with stale water, casting wriggling snakes of dim light as Will splashed past. Now that the fire was out, the sprinklers were little more than an incontinent dribble. They'd probably done more damage to the building than the flames had.

He slithered to a halt by the escalator, grabbed the discarded evidence bag and hefted it over his shoulder – staggering under the weight. He peered up the ramp. Half way up, it came to an abrupt end, dirty orange rebar sticking out of the fractured foamcrete. Sergeant Nairn was right: there was no way anyone could jump that gap. Not without a body-wire. . .

'Fuck.' It was like a kick in the goolies, but it was the only option.

He reached up with trembling fingers and clicked on his

throat-mike, trying to keep his voice steady: 'Lieutenant Brand, I need you to get that Dragonfly airborne.'

'Forget it. We're not leaving you behind!'

'Just do what you're bloody well told, for once.' There was something rectangular and half-melted at Will's feet: Stein's Field Zapper – the one he'd kept fiddling with – its plastic casing blistered and cracked. As Will bent down to pick it up, the building went ominously silent.

Not good. *Definitely* not good.

Will splashed his way back down the corridor, lugging the heavy bag of severed heads. 'I want that gunship outside apartment one twenty-six, forty-seventh floor – drop out five bodywires and a cargo net. We're going for hard D.'

'From inside a building? Are you mad?'

'If you've got any better ideas, let's hear them, because I'm all out.' His earpiece went silent. And then,

'Nairn, get your team back to the ship. Pickup in forty-five seconds.' Static burst across the signal as the Dragonfly's engines went to full power. *'I hope you know what you're doing, Will.'*

Struggling along the gloomy, waterlogged corridor Will hoped so too.

He was almost at the flat's front door when a hard crack sounded behind him. A plume of water danced at his feet. Another shot and the bag on his back jumped, throwing him forward. Will just managed to stay on his feet as more bullets tore into the walls around him, sending out puffs of paint and shredded plasticboard.

He scrambled into the flat and slammed the door shut.

'We've got company!' He heaved the bag of heads into the middle of the room. 'Get Stein ready to move. Beaton, clip his bodyharness to yours, I don't want him bashing his brains out on the window frame. Cameron,' he pointed at the broad strips of black plastic blocking out the world, 'tear that crap down.'

She grabbed a corner and tugged. Light flooded into the room.

Will turned Stein's burnt Field Zapper over in his hands. The battery lights were still winking away merrily to themselves: with any luck it wouldn't short out and electrocute him.

'Where the hell's that damn Dragonfly?'

Right on cue the sunlight disappeared again. The flat's windows rattled in their frames as Lieutenant Brand's gunship twisted in the air, dipping its nose down to expose the double drop bay doors in its belly.

A single bullet thudded into the apartment door, ripping a hole straight through it and into the tiny hall. And then another one. And another.

'That's as close as you get!'

Will pulled up his Whomper and thumbed the trigger. The assault rifle kicked in his hands – its bark deafening in the confines of the filthy lounge – and the front door tore itself apart. One moment it was there, and the next it was a hail of sizzling plastic, pattering down on the threadbare carpet. He slung the Whomper over his shoulder and powered up Stein's Field Zapper. The weapon's lights flickered then died.

'Fuck.' He thumped it against the wall. Shook it. Tried again.

A tatty, ginger-haired figure leapt into the gap where the door used to be.

She was big-boned rather than fat, dressed in the same eclectic, colourful rags they'd seen this morning. Tribal scars twisted across her pale skin, pulling at the corners of her ice-green eyes. She was carrying an old F24, virtually an antique, and as she brought it up, a smile split her face. Teeth filed to points.

Will shot her.

The arc from Stein's Field Zapper caught her in the chest, throwing her back into the sodden corridor. Stepping forward, Will pointed the weapon at the waterlogged carpet and held the trigger down.

A chorus of shrieks and squeals erupted in the hall as the blue lightning danced down the corridor. Then there was the sound of bodies hitting the floor. And then silence. Will didn't risk sticking his head out to check the results: someone might have been wearing insulated boots.

DS Cameron forced the lounge window open. Debris leapt into the air, dancing and spinning in the hot backwash from the Dragonfly's engines, like angry, paper seagulls.

Sergeant Nairn dropped from the ship's belly, a cluster of body wires reeling out behind him. He grabbed at the open window with both hands and DS Cameron lunged forwards, dragging him into the room. Before his feet could even touch the carpet, gunfire was clanging off the ship's hull: a Network Dragonfly made a big and inviting target.

Something bellowed from the floor above and the whole craft lurched.

'Come on people, get a move on: we can't hang around here all bloody afternoon!'

Will helped Nairn clip on Stein and Beaton's bodywires while DS Cameron wrapped another set of wires through the handles on the scanning canister, finishing them off with a huge, inelegant knot. The bag of heads went into the cargo net.

That just left Will and the Detective Sergeant.

As they struggled into their harnesses a tubular canister bounced in through the door and landed on the grubby carpet – little red lights chasing each other round and round the ends.

'Oh shit. . .' Will punched his throat-mike and braced himself. 'Hard D. Now!'

The Dragonfly leapt away from the building, yanking them out of the living room window. The scanning canister caught the frame side on, glass and twisted aluminium spraying everywhere. Someone screamed, the sound whipped away as the gunship rolled into a tight turn, accelerating hard.

The explosion tore Allan Brown's apartment to shreds.

*   *   *

The sun hangs in the dirty blue sky like a jewelled furnace. It's blurred around the edge, a faint shimmer of chemical fog that grows thicker as she watches. The wind must have shifted, bringing with it the firestacks' industrial perfume.

She's been wandering the streets for hours, drifting through her own personal smog. Faces swim in and out of focus: colleagues, patients, victims. . .

Something flashes overhead and she turns to watch it roar across the sky. Small figures dangle beneath it, slowly being drawn up into its belly. The shape is familiar, haunting: like a bad dream only half remembered. But right now everything is like that.

She doesn't even know who she is.

Her stomach rumbles and she flinches, startled by the sound. It's been six years since she's felt anything as profound as hunger. She knows this because one of the city's big, floating Scrubbers carries a flickering advert with today's date.

Six years.

Six years since she's been able to feel anything at all.

Hunger. Love. Anger. Pleasure. Revenge. Lust. Pain. Seven perfect words, much hotter than a mere ball of burning gas ninety-three-million miles away. Pretty words: shiny like the blade of a knife.

She drifts on, ignoring everything but the growing hollow in her belly, unable to do anything about it; she can't feed herself, they saw to that on the operating table.

Six years of intravenous nourishment. Nil by mouth.

They took it all away. . .

But she's going to get it back. Oh yes. She's going to get it *all* back.

'One, one-thousand – two, one-thousand – three, one-thousand: breathe.' Private Dickson straddled Stein's scorched body in the darkened drop bay, pumping away at his heart. Every time she said 'breathe' Private Rhodes pinched Stein's nose and blew into his mouth. Then they would wait for his lungs to deflate and the whole pattern would repeat again.

'One, one-thousand – two, one-thousand – three, one-thousand: breathe.'

Sergeant Nairn was up to his armpits in the resuscitation unit mounted on the drop bay wall. Cables snaked out from it, lying in coils at his feet, little sparks fizzling away in the depths of the circuit boards, adding the smell of hot plastic to the harsh tang of burnt hair and burnt flesh.

'One, one-thousand – two, one-thousand – three, one-thousand: breathe.'

Beaton sat on the mesh floor of her cubicle, head back, face pale, clutching her left wrist where it had caught the flat's windowsill on the way out. She hadn't taken her eyes off Stein since they'd laid him out on the central walkway like a fish for filleting.

'One, one-thousand – two, one-thousand – three, one-thousand: breathe.'

Will lurched back along the walkway to where Private Floyd was slumped against the bulkhead. The drop bay was baking hot, but Floyd was shivering, his forehead glassy with cold sweat. The front of his battle dress glistened with blood, but at least his heart was still beating.

'One, one-thousand – two, one-thousand – three, one-thousand: breathe.'

Will knelt in front of him and peeled away the sticky fabric surrounding the wound. When Sergeant Nairn said the trooper had been shot, Will had expected some sort of flesh wound, not a gaping hole. It looked as if someone had welded a dozen nails onto the business end of a sledgehammer and then pounded merry hell out of Floyd's shoulder.

'What on earth did you stand in front of? A truck?'

Floyd hissed a couple of short breaths through clenched teeth, then tried for a smile. 'Think it was an old . . . old P-Seven-Fifty.'

'One, one-thousand – two, one-thousand – three, one-thousand: breathe.'

Will dug into the small first-aid locker at the side of the cubicle and pulled out a handful of blockers. He snapped three of the small, plastic ampoules into the injured man's neck, waiting for them to take effect before popping the cap off a tin of skinpaint.

'How's . . . how's Stein?'

'Something's wrong with the crash kit: no oxygen, no EKG, no defib. Nothing.' He gave the tin a shake, then sprayed thick, pink mist into the wound.

'One, one-thousand – two, one-thousand – three, one-thousand: fucking *breathe* damn you!'

The paint bubbled where it touched raw flesh, sealing the ruptured veins, bridging the gap between the tattered muscles. It didn't look very pretty, but at least it would hold Floyd's shoulder together till they reached Glasgow Royal Infirmary.

The trooper blinked. 'Woah. . .' Then a broad, lazy smile stretched his face wide. Three blockers had probably been a bit much, but Will didn't really care – and from the look of things, neither did Private Floyd.

'You going to be OK?'

Floyd just beamed – so Will left him to it, lurching back up the drop bay.

'One, one-thousand – two, one-thousand – three, one-thousand: breathe.'

'What's our ETA?' Detective Sergeant Cameron stood holding onto the edges of her booth, staring down at Stein's pale body. Trembling.

'Two, maybe three minutes.'

She nodded. Cleared her throat.

'How you doing?'

'Is he. . .' She took one hand off the railing and ran it across her soot-smeared cheek. 'I don't get it. I mean, one minute it was all fine and the next it was . . . everywhere. We didn't even *do* anything. They just. . .' She shuddered.

Will gave her shoulder a squeeze. 'You did OK back there.'

She wouldn't look at him. 'Is that what it's like in the Network? Everyone wants to kill you?'

'Look: why don't you give Nairn a hand with the crash kit? You cracked that securilock in ten seconds flat, maybe you can get it going too.'

DS Cameron nodded. Wiped a hand across her eyes. Took a deep breath. Marched over to the tangled mass of wires and levered Sergeant Nairn out of the way.

One minute later she'd got the machinery working.

Two minutes after that, Private Richard Stein was dead.

The hours all melt into one another, slipping by, carrying her along with them. Sunset paints the horizon with violent red. The sky is bleeding just for her. One by one the city's street-lights flicker on, a Mexican wave of sodium fireflies as the day slowly dies, their light giving the greasy city an unhealthy yellow pallor.

A garishly painted Roadhugger hisses to a halt beside her. She ignores it, just keeps trudging along the baked pavement. And then the voices start:

'Jeeeesus, would you look at the state of it! That blood?'

'Some bugger must've cut it. Disnae matter, just shove it in the back with the others.'

Rough hands grab her shoulders, but she's too tired to resist. They haul open the back doors and bundle her into an empty bay. Then paw at her flesh.

'Cannae see any wounds,' says a man who looks like a ruptured pig. His face is fleshy and bloated, a thin fringe of hair outlining the uppermost of his many chins. 'Think we should take it straight tae the hospital?'

'Bugger that. Only got another six to pick up and then I'm

aff home for the night. Let them worry about it back at the depot.'

Pig-Man frowns. 'There's an awful lot of blood here Harry, what if someone's chibbed it? What if it dies?'

'If it dies, it dies. It's just a fuckin' halfhead! Who cares?'

Pig-Man is quiet for a moment, then he sniffs. 'Yeah, suppose you're right.' He pulls the restraining bar down, clambers back out into the night, and slams the door. Then waves through the window at them, sharing a joke with his ugly friend as they walk back around to the cab.

The engine starts and she lurches against the bar, blinking. Light-headed. Hungry. Sharp and broken. Bees and broken glass.

She needs to take her medication. Or someone will – get – hurt.

Another lurch, and one of the halfheads stumbles. They're all around her: freakish faces devoid of thought or emotion. The rancid smell of their sweat is everywhere. Bluebottles and dead birds. The one in the next bay is staring off into the middle distance, the barcode tattooed over its left eye fresh and sharp. A new convert to the ranks of the living dead.

She reaches up and touches her own forehead, trying to feel the tattoo she knows will be inked into her own skin. The colours faded, the edges blurred after all these years.

It holds the key to everything she is and was. It holds her name.

The Roadhugger grumbles from stop to stop, and each time the back door opens, Pig-Man pushes another halfhead into an empty compartment. It doesn't seem to worry him that his cargo was human once. That they were shiny things with dreams and feelings. Because that doesn't matter any more: their brains have been burned away. They're just lumps of barely sentient meat to be used as slaves. Walking, mutilated, orange-boilersuited reminders that crime doesn't pay.

Or rather, that getting *caught* doesn't pay.

Caught by a man in a dark-blue suit, with a jagged scar on his face. The scar would be invisible after all these years, but the face would be the same. A little older. Maybe a little more grey in the hair. . . Would his screams still sound the same?

The Roadhugger stops outside a large, featureless, concrete building, then the vehicle slowly judders backward towards an open loading bay. Beeping.

She knows this place: she's seen it every morning and every night for the last six years. A sign on the wall, in cheerful orange and blue, reads: 'SERVICES, UNIT 47 EAST. H-HEADS: LOADING AND UNLOADING'.

They will clean her and feed her and give her a place to rest until morning. She is home.

There will be plenty of time for revenge later.

6

Drums pound in the darkness, like the heartbeat of something huge and hungry. Creeping down the pitch-black corridor, Sergeant William Hunter grits his teeth and keeps moving.

The carpet scritches and screltches beneath his feet, sticky with blood. He can't see it, but he can smell it: hot copper and burnished iron. Every single floor is like this, shrouded in darkness and drenched in blood. Like a nightmare he can't wake up from.

Cramp screams across his back again and he stops for a moment, gritting his teeth and swearing quietly. Private Alexander weighs a bloody ton and Will's been carrying him around for long enough to resent every last ounce. He unclips the trooper's harness and struggles the almost dead weight onto his other shoulder.

'Bloody hell. . .' his voice is barely a whisper, '. . .why did you have to be such a *fat bastard*?'

Private Alexander isn't the only weight he's carrying: the whole building's pressing down on top of him, grinding him into the blood-soaked carpet. Making every step a battle. Add to that one empty Whomper – the battery as dead as the rest of the Dragonfly's team – and Will has all the fun he can handle.

He fastens their harnesses together again, then pushes off the wall and staggers on in the dark: one hand held out in front of him, the other brushing the wall at his side.

Plastic doors bump beneath his fingertips, each one hiding its own horrible little story. A murdered family. A VR shrine to the building's new digital god. A tattered corpse, mutilated and half eaten. . .

It's been a day and a half since the Dragonfly crashed head-first into this freak show, thirty-nine floors up, and so far the only people he's seen have all been very, very dead. . .

He stops. Something has changed, but it takes him nearly a whole minute to figure out what: the drums are silent. The bloody things have been his constant companion for a day and a half, pounding away at him, and now they're gone.

Thank God.

He slumps against the nearest wall and closes his eyes, enjoying the blissful peace. Could go to sleep now. Kick in the door to one of the flats, chuck the dead bodies out into the hall, and barricade himself inside. He sighs. Never going to happen. If he doesn't get Private Alexander to a medic soon, he's going to die.

Slowly Will pulls himself upright and forces his legs to move, carrying the trooper's fat arse through the blackness.

The corridor seems to go on forever, stretching away into the dark. On and on and on.

Door, wall, door, wall, door, wall, door, wall, door, wall. . .

And then a rush of warm, foetid air brushes Will's face.

He freezes. Then reaches out a hand. There's a little metal lip, and then nothing. Lift shaft? There's no sign of the actual lift, just that column of dank air, laced with the smell of machinery and grease.

'Oh you wee *beauty*.' He can feel the grin spreading.

The stairwells are too dangerous – blocked with piles of furniture, lit by flickering torches – but the lift shaft is another matter. He double checks Fat Boy Alexander is securely strapped in place, then inches forwards until the floor comes to a sudden, terminal stop.

Holding on to the open elevator door with one hand, he reaches out into the void, searching along the lift shaft's rough foamcrete walls for the maintenance ladder he knows is in there.

Climb down to the ground floor, break out through the front doors, and run like hell for freedom. Easy. No problem at all. Leave this dark, scary shitehole behind and go back to the real world, where people don't mutilate themselves with kitchen knives.

The sound of drums explodes all around him and he flinches, stumbles, grabs at the wall, trying not to scream. . . He scrabbles back into the corridor, heart hammering faster than the deafening drums. He stands there, trembling for a moment, then wipes a hand across his eyes. Frowns. Blinks.

There's a light, flickering weakly at the far end of the passageway.

It's getting brighter.

Oh Jesus. . .

They're coming.

Will sat bolt-upright in the middle of the bed, surrounded by clammy sheets, sweat running down his chest, heart pounding. He dragged in a couple of ragged breaths and swore.

Hadn't had that nightmare for nearly four and a half years.

'Lights.' The controller bleeped, filling the apartment with dazzling brightness. 'Argh. . . Down, down!' They slowly faded to something less likely to burn his irises off.

Will slumped back on the bed and scowled at the ceiling. *Not* a good start to the day.

By the time he'd showered, dressed, and caught the shuttle into work, it was half past seven and the dream was gone.

Network Headquarters was enjoying the quiet lull before

the day shift kicked in. Services were delivering their daily consignment of halfheads, herding them through the squeaky corridors. Giving them their instructions in small, easy to understand words, then handing each a wheely-bucket full of cleaning supplies and leaving them to get on with it.

Sweep. Mop. Polish. Tidy. Dust.

One of the bigger halfheads bent to pick up a cloth and cleanblock from the bucket at its feet, then shambled over to polish the lift doors. What was left of its surgically truncated features was covered in spiral tattoos, a brand new patch of pink skin grafted onto its forehead with the barcode right in the middle. It looked vaguely ridiculous, but then that was the point. Will stood for a moment, waiting for the halfhead to finish, then decided that he'd really rather take the stairs.

Somehow the lift didn't appeal today.

An hour and a half later his desktop terminal bleeped at him. Incoming call. Will scowled at the little camera mounted into the unit. The bloody thing had resisted all attempts at sabotage. He'd even tried sticky tape over the lens, but the halfhead who did the offices cleaned it away every time it came in to empty the bins.

Will stabbed the 'receive' button and barked, 'Hunter,' into the microphone.

'Aye, very good.' A familiar, podgy face filled the screen, one eye a milky ball of grey with little flashes of light going off inside it. The image was slightly distorted, stretched by the tiny wide-angle camera attached to the end of the caller's fingerphone. *'Nice haircut byraway, circus in town?'*

Will ran a hand through his unruly locks, unable to stop the smile breaking out on his face.

'Morning, Brian. Had a dream about you last night.'

'Oh aye? Don't tell James, he gets affa jealous.'

'Don't flatter yourself.' He settled back in his chair. 'How's tricks?'

69

'Lousy. The Munchkin From Hell keeps givin' us cases Sherlock Holmes couldn't fuckin' solve.'

'That's because you're her special little soldier.'

'Aye, and my farts smell of rainbows.' A scowl turned his features ugly. 'Every time I see the old bag I get another impossible case.' He shook his head. 'She's gettin' her own back for what happened at the Christmas party. Did I tell you. . .'

Will listened to Brian rant for a while, nodding his head every now and then to pretend he was paying attention. Brian was wrong about Director Smith-Hamilton, yes she had it in for him, but her grudge went back a lot further than last Christmas.

'What can I do for you Brian?'

'Oh, right. . . It's your new girl, DS Cameron.' There was a squeaking noise and the background swooped past Brian's head – probably swivelling his chair around – settling on a patchwork of old, two-dimensional photographs as he dropped his voice to a whisper, 'She's dodderin' about this mornin', looking like somethin' the cat shat out. What the hell did you do to her yesterday?'

'George found traces of VR syndrome in two bodies from Sherman House. Natives got restless when we went back to search the victim's apartment.'

Brian blinked. 'What do you mean, "when we went back"? You're no tellin' me you went with her!'

'If it's an outbreak of VR it's out of Bluecoat jurisdiction. You know that.'

'Sherman House. . .' Brian's face shuddered. 'Jesus an' the wee man. I mean, I find it hard enough and I was away with the fairies the whole time. Last time I bagged and tagged a set of Termies there thought I was going to pee myself. . .' He trailed off. 'You sure you're OK?'

'I lost Stein.'

'Aw, Jesus.' Sigh. 'I'm sorry. Two in one week. . .'

Will changed the subject. 'Anyway: DS Cameron?'

Brian's round, pink face suddenly loomed on the screen, until Will was staring straight into one huge, magnified eye. *'She doesn't know I'm telling you this – and she'd probably throw a blue hairy if she found out – but she's no doin' as well as she's kiddin' on.'*

Will nodded. He'd seen the look on her face when the mortuary techs wheeled Stein's body away. The life of a Bluecoat wasn't easy, but it was nothing compared to what the Network went up against every day.

'Can you no' get her to take some time off?'

'Don't know, Brian: she only started yesterday. If I send her home it's going to look like I don't think she's up to the job.'

'What's more important? You lookin' like a shite in a suit, or her being able to cope?'

'Point taken.'

'Knew you'd see sense.' The image zoomed out again, showing off a big toothy grin. *'Oh, and while I'm on, James wants to know if you're free for dinner tonight?'*

'I don't know if I can—'

'Bollocks. My place: seven thirty. And bring a bottle of somethin' drinkable this time, you tight-fisted bastard.' There was a muffled sound from the room behind him and the picture jiggled around until Will was looking at DS Cameron. She was carrying two steaming mugs. Brian reached out and took one. *'Thanks, that's smashin'.'*

'Got you some biscuits too. . .'

Biscuits? First George, now Brian. Maybe she had a thing for strange little fat men?

Will shook his head. 'I'll let you know how I get on.' He killed the link and went back to the paperwork.

The crime reports should have been interesting – high-tech transgression, murder, fraud, espionage, disappearances, kidnappings, hostile interventions – but somehow his team of agents always managed to make everything read like stereo instructions. He waded through as many as he could before near-suicidal boredom set in.

He dumped the last two inches of cold tea from his mug in the nearest sickly pot plant and headed for the fourth floor.

There was no sign of Brian in the tiny office, but Detective Sergeant Jo Cameron was at her desk, grumbling away at something on her screen. Her hair was even more fashionable than before – the tightly-wound bun sitting at a bizarre angle to accommodate the new bald patch. The back of her neck was a swathe of fresh skinpaint, the shiny pink surface looking out of place against her caramel skin. But what *really* grabbed the attention was today's suit. It hadn't looked too bad on Brian's fingerphone, but in person it was . . . hard to ignore. Bright blue with a narrow, luminous orange pinstripe, orange buttons, and orange lapels.

Will stared at her. 'What would you have got if you'd won the bet?'

'What?' She swivelled her seat around. Her eyes were puffy and tight lines feathered out from the corners of her mouth, but other than that she looked as good as anyone could dressed as a plastic of Irn-Bru.

'Came past to see how you were getting on.'

She pulled her face into a smile. It didn't go anywhere near her eyes. 'I'm feeling fine, sir.'

'How's the neck?'

'Bit itchy . . . other than that. . .' She shrugged, one hand going to that patch of artificial pink. 'MO gave me some blockers.'

Will pushed the door closed, then perched on the edge of Brian's pigsty desk.

'You know,' he said, picking his words carefully, 'when we go into hot zones we put our lives on the line, and sometimes the stress . . . well, it can do a lot more damage than you'd think. If you don't give yourself *time*, it can creep up and really sink it's teeth in your arse. And if it does that in the field, chances are you're coming home in a plastic bag.'

DS Cameron's brittle smile disappeared. 'With all due respect, *sir*, I resent that. Just cos I'm a Bluecoat and a *woman*, doesn't mean I'm going to fall apart the first time things get shitty!'

'That's not what I meant.'

'Really?' Her mouth turned down at the edges. 'Well then, just what *did* you mean?'

'I've been there, OK? I've done the whole therapy and counselling thing. And I've seen people playing it macho: refusing help. I've spoken at their funerals.' He sighed. 'Look, Jo, I'm just trying to make sure you're not suffering in silence because you think the Network will think you're weak if you don't. I downloaded your file this morning: you've got the makings of a damn good agent, if you get the call. And if you don't get yourself killed first.'

She blushed. Rubbed at her neck again. Stared at the carpet. 'Thanks. . .'

Will nodded at the neat stack of printouts on her desk. 'What they got you working on?'

'Special Agent Alexander's asked me to assist on a couple of cases. Burglary at Teretcor Engineering, about a dozen cases of Unauthorized Data Access at PowerCore.'

Will put on his innocent face and said nothing.

'And,' she pointed at a holo pinned to the board above her desk – an elderly couple sitting on a floral couch, grinning at nothing, their eyes like glittering beads of glass, 'these very rich, very dead OAPs keep turning up. Big chunk of money missing from their bank accounts. Look like they've been stuffed. . . It's bizarre.'

'Yeah, that sounds like Brian's caseload.' Will checked his watch: half ten. 'You got anything urgent on?'

'Nothing that won't wait.'

'Come on then: if we're lucky George has done something

73

with those severed heads. If we're even luckier we'll be in and out of there before he digs out his holiday snaps.'

'Detective Sergeant Cameron! How nice to see you again!' The plump pathologist slapped something purple and slimy onto a cutting slab, then wiped his hands down the front of his green apron. 'What can I do for you this beautiful morning?'

DS Cameron smiled at him. 'Please, if we're going to be friends you'll have to call me Jo.'

'Jo. . .' George sighed. 'Lovely.' He stood there with a soppy look on his face for a moment. Then blinked and frowned, as if noticing Will for the first time. 'Suppose *you're* here for those halfheads?'

'Where are they?'

The pathologist sniffed. 'You see what I have to put up with, Jo? No "hello", no pleasantries, no nothing. Man's got no manners at all.' He dug a hanky out of his pocket and made splattery noises into it. 'Still, I bear it because I am a gentleman.'

He snapped his bloody gloves into a cleanbox, then wandered over to a large trolley, draped with a sheet.

'Tada!' George whipped off the cloth, revealing three rows of severed heads. Most of the skin was still wrinkled, the close-cropped hair making them look like mouldy prunes, but their foreheads were smooth and shiny. The barcodes perfectly clear.

Jo squatted in front of the partially mummified features, stroking one of the heads. 'Wow: how did you manage that?'

'Ah. . .' He winked at her. 'That would be telling!'

Will lent forward and sniffed. 'Hand cream?'

'Hand cream?' George stuck his nose in the air. 'Don't be *ridiculous*, why on Earth would I use hand cream on severed heads? Hand cream . . . pffff.' He cleared his throat. 'It's face cream. Been slapping it on since yesterday.'

'George, you're a star.' Will grabbed a reader from the

worktop behind them. There was something red and gluti-
nous on the handle, but he didn't notice until it was all over
his hands. 'Oh for God's sake. . .'

The pathologist shrugged. 'It's strawberry jam. I dropped
my sandwich.'

Will handed the sticky piece of equipment to DS 'call me
Jo' Cameron and went to wash his hands. By the time he'd
finished she was running the reader over the last head in the
row. It made a reassuringly positive beep.

She nodded at him. 'Got ID numbers on all of them.'

'Right,' he said, drying his hands on the back of George's
labcoat, 'now we need some names. Get onto Services: tell
them to run a match.'

'Hoy!' The little pathologist snatched his coat-tails away.
'You're very welcome, I'm sure!'

'George, you know I have nothing but the utmost respect
for your phenomenal professional acumen.'

'Bollocks. Jo, it's been a pleasure having you again, feel
free to pop in any time.' George bent and kissed her jam and
face cream flavoured hand before turning to Will. 'But you
can bugger off and never come back.'

7

Services ran their operation – and most of the city – from an imposing tower of foamcrete, pink marble, and green glass. An unattractive wart that had gone slightly mouldy.

The elevator pinged, then the doors slid open. Twenty-seventh floor: Offender Management Department – South. Will and Jo stepped off the escalator into plush, beige carpeting. A medium-sized trundle case followed them, squeaking along on juddering caterpillar tracks as they made their way to the long, low reception desk. Six people manned the desk, all of them talking into fingerphones, the low murmur of their conversations barely audible through the sonic dampening. When a mousy blonde finally deigned to look his way, Will pulled out his ID and smiled.

'Will Hunter: Network. I'd like to speak to someone in records please.'

'I'm sorry, sir, but all those lines are busy right now.' Her left eye faded from glossy grey to spider-veined pink, the iris shining, vivid and yellow as she took off her finger-phone.

'I called earlier: case of severed halfheads need identifying. I have a list of the ID numbers, so if you could just—'

'I'm sorry, sir, we can't give out any details without formal identification taking place. All remains have to be signed over for identification.'

Will nudged the trundle case with his foot. 'That's why we brought them with us.'

'One second.' The receptionist slipped the blue plastic sleeve back on her index finger, then pointed at her own face. Her owl's eye went grey again, lights flickering in the depths. 'Steve? It's Marjory, listen I've got some bloke from the Network here and he wants some halfheads ID'd. . . Yes. . . Yes, I told him that, says he's got them with him. . .' She swung her finger around, pointing at Will instead. '. . .Yeah, that's what I thought too. . .' And then she was pointing at herself again. 'OK, thanks Steve.'

She dragged out a datapad and made Will sign half a dozen different forms in triplicate, then summoned a tattooed youth to take the trundle case away. As it disappeared through a door marked 'Private' she nodded at a small waiting area over by the floor-to-ceiling window. 'If you'd like to take a seat someone will see you shortly.' And then her eye went grey again, and she was off.

Will settled into a chair that was a whole lot less comfortable than it looked, Jo easing herself down beside him. From here they had a perfect view of Glasgow's main transport hub – shuttles, Groundhuggers, Behemoths, all in the process of coming or going. Little one-person Bumbles vwipped through the air, following complicated holding patterns, twisting and turning like flocks of starlings as a huge blue Behemoth slipped its mooring and lumbered up into the sweltering morning.

Two minutes later it was just a distant silhouette against the dirty-yellow sky.

DS Cameron, stretching out in her seat. 'How long you think we'll have to wait?'

'Your guess is as good as mine.'

Fifteen minutes later they were still there.

Jo turned in her seat and scowled back at the reception

desk. 'All they've got to do is scan the codes into the computer. How hard can it be?' She fidgeted. 'Can't you just stick your ID back under that frumpy wee cow's nose and pull rank? You're the sodding Assistant Section Director!'

'Wouldn't make any difference: Services are a law unto themselves. Far as they're concerned they run the city. Everyone else is just window dressing.'

'Hmmmph,' Jo folded her arms and slumped back in her seat, 'and there was me thinking it was just us Bluecoats that never get any respect. Joined-up government my arse. Tell you: I had my way we'd slap the bloody lot of them in the Tin for obstruction. Bunch of tight-sphinctered, penny-pinching, halfwit—'

'Excuse me?' DS Cameron's favourite 'frumpy wee cow' was waving at them. 'Someone from records can speak to you now.' She pointed to a short corridor next to the lifts. 'Booth number three.'

The cramped cubicle contained two seats and a narrow shelf bolted beneath the large screen mounted on the wall. Will and Jo squeezed in and closed the door. Thirty seconds later the screen flickered into life and the someone from records they'd been promised appeared: a man with a huge head, wild cloned hair and a trendy pixel tattoo that made abstract patterns as he spoke. *This going to take long? Only I've got a conference call in five minutes.*

Will tried not to sound as pissed off as he felt. 'I just signed over seventeen severed halfheads for identification: I need names, postings and dates to go with them.'

'And you are?'

'William Hunter. Assistant Network Director William Hunter.'

'How nice for you.' He looked off the bottom of the screen for a moment, and the sound of a keyboard clicked out of the speakers. *'One moment.'* The screen went blank.

Jo muttered something under her breath that would have made the Marquis de Sade blush.

Three minutes later he was back. *'And are these the same halfheads that a. . .'* Pause. Frown. *'Detective Sergeant Campbell enquired about this morning?'*

'DS Cameron. That's right.'

The man on the screen sighed. *'As we explained to DS Campbell, we can't give out that kind of information over the phone.'*

Will gritted his teeth. 'We're not on the phone, you are.'

'Have you signed over the severed halfheads to a representative from resourcing?'

'I told you that at the start, remember?'

'Until they're signed over to a representative from resourcing we can't give out any details.'

'We signed them over!'

'I see. And have you received notification of identification?'

'No, that's why we're sitting here. I want *you* to tell *me* who the halfheads were!'

'I'm sorry I can't give out that information over the phone.'

Jo couldn't contain herself any longer.

'Listen up you scribbly-faced bag of shite, either you get your finger out and—' She was cut off by a beep from the speaker.

'I'm sorry, our time is up.' And with that the screen went blank.

'What the *fuck*?' She slammed her palm against the screen, making the whole thing shake. 'WE'VE BEEN HERE HALF A BLOODY HOUR!' Jo turned to Will. 'Can you believe this shite?'

'Watch the door.' He pulled a small, flat pack from a hidden pocket in his Network-issue jacket. It was full of wire tools, a tube of metaliglue, and a battered cracker. Will slid one of the thin metal slices into the joint between the screen's control panel and the wall, then twisted. The panel popped open, revealing a small chip rack and a rats' nest of wires.

'Are you sure that's a good idea?'

He pulled a pair of wires from the jumble and slapped a

connector onto each. 'Most security systems are designed to stop people hacking in from the outside. So if you want to break into them, do it from the inside. . .'

The cracker's keypad rattled beneath his fingertips as he inveigled himself into Services' local network. 'Makes the guardian AIs a lot less sceptical.'

Two minutes, thirty-seven seconds later the cracker bleeped. Will grinned. 'We're in. Who's first?'

Jo checked her notes. 'S R dash O dash nine six two dash nine five eight.'

Will punched the code into the cracker, and the room's main screen filled with personal details.

'Thomas Simpson, thirty-seven. Convicted of serial rape eight years ago, been missing for four. Working at Brewster Towers when he disappeared. Next?'

'M H dash D dash five three two seven dash eight eight seven.'

'Hold on . . . Alison Campbell, forty-five: multiple homicide. Halfheaded three years ago. Went missing from Sherman House.'

It didn't take long to see the pattern: Allan Brown liked to hunt close to home, only taking halfheads sent to clean the four connurb blocks that made up Monstrosity Square. Preying on a steady diet of murderers and rapists. There was even a serial killer in the collection of severed heads – a cannibal called Iain Foreshaw who'd butchered seven nursing students and two prostitutes. It was a fittingly ironic end to a predator's life: brought down and eaten by one of its own kind.

In his own twisted way, Allan Brown had put himself at the very top of the food chain.

Now all they had to do was find out who'd killed him.

The mop slops dirty water from one side of the toilet to the other, back and forth, back and forth. Greasy ribbons of filth making patterns on the grubby tiles. The smell doesn't really bother her any more. It did when they'd dropped her off here this morning, bundling her out of the Roadhugger with a mop and a pail, speaking to her like some sort of trained monkey: 'Go in. Clean. You come back when called. Understand? I said, do you understand?'

Patronizing bastard.

For a moment she thinks about taking her mop, snapping it in half, and using the splintered end to gouge the man's face into tattered, bloody ribbons. Pluck the eyes right out of his head. . .

She has always loved eyes. They look so pretty, lying in the palm of her hand.

It takes a lot of control to squash the desire. She hasn't had her medication and it's getting more and more difficult to keep it buried deep inside where it can burn bright and fierce. But somehow she manages. She nods and trudges into the connurb block like all the other good little halfheads. Trembling inside with bees and broken glass.

The morning passes in a reek of human waste and disinfectant, memories flickering in and out like a distant firework display. The sparks too far away to taste properly. On the tip of the tongue she doesn't have any more.

Some time around noon the front pocket of her jumpsuit starts buzzing and she stands staring at it. Buzzzzzzzzzzzzz. Busy little bees. Buzzing against her broken glass chest.

Hungry.

She drops the mop and walks out into the baking sun, following the other halfheads. The pig and his friend are there with their bright yellow Roadhugger. They plug a tube into her arm and fill her full of intravenous nutrients, but it doesn't ease the gnawing ache.

Then the ugly men are gone again, and she's left to clean and mop.

The afternoon is more lucid. Thoughts are starting to stay in her head where she can focus on them, follow them. *Plan*.

Food will be the biggest problem. If she disappears, the man who looks like a pig won't feed her any more.

She stops mopping, frowning at her reflection in the dirty water. Remembering soft-green walls, squeaky flooring, men and women in long white coats. Where every room smells like the stuff they put in the buckets. The smell of safety.

She'd have smiled then, if she had enough face to do it with.

'OK,' said Will as they pushed their way through the crowded lobby back at Network Headquarters. 'What do you want to do now?'

'String that Services shitebag up by his goolies.' A gaggle of children in garish school uniform stopped right in front of them, so they had to detour past a bus party of OAPs ogling a Cézanne.

'I meant about the investigation.'

She narrowed her eyes. 'Lot of murders in that bit of town go unsolved. Thousands of potential witnesses, but no one ever admits to seeing anything. From the state of the body, I'd say whoever did it, this wasn't their first time. Won't be their last either.'

'Pretty safe bet.'

'I dumped all the crime scene data into the system this morning, MO's pretty damn distinctive so we're bound to get a match.' She grinned, eyes sparkling. 'Nice to have the resources to really go after a case like this for a change, instead of just handing it over to the Future Boys. . . No offence.'

'None taken.'

They slipped into one of the staff lifts and punched the button for the fourth floor.

'You know,' said Jo as the doors closed, shutting out the noisy lobby, 'I was wondering. . . You've got a kind of reputation— Urrrgh. . .' She staggered, face screwed up in a grimace, teeth bared.

82

Will grabbed her, holding her upright.

'Damnit!'

'You all right?'

'No. . .' She stayed where she was – wrapped in his arms, eyes closed, breathing deeply. In and out.

Will looked down at the top of her head. 'What the hell was that?'

'Coffin dodger. Someone's gone missing.'

It might have been the confines of the lift that made Will feel suddenly uncomfortable, or it might have been the sensation of Jo's breasts rising and falling against his chest as she breathed. Whichever it was he could feel his temperature rising inch by embarrassing inch.

She opened her eyes and looked up at him. 'Thanks. They're supposed to put out a warning on the comlink before they do a broadcast. Give us a chance to prepare.'

Will let go. Stepped back. Cleared his throat. Stuck his hands in his pockets, hiding his embarrassment. 'No problem.'

'Jesus.' Jo shuddered. 'Nothing like a transmitter going off in the base of your skull to put a shiner on the day.' She rubbed a hand over the patch of shiny new skin at the back of her head. 'Why they can't just send the bloody signal out to the poor bastard they're looking for, I don't know.'

'Is it always that bad?'

'Caught me off guard that's all. They broadcast the "come in number six: your time's up" message to every Bluecoat in the city and the things in our heads jump about like it's Hogmanay. Doesn't matter if you're number six or not. System was meant to be selective, only trip the locator in whoever's gone missing, but the IT company fucked the installation up and we haven't got the budget to fix it.' She stopped and frowned at him. 'You don't have them do you?'

'Nope: security risk. It'd be too easy to spot an agent when they're undercover. Network doesn't care if it can't find our dead bodies.'

'Lucky bastards.'

The lift arrived on the fourth floor with a small, metallic 'ping'. Will slapped a professional smile on his face as the doors slid open, but left his hands in his pockets.

'Well . . . I have all that lovely paperwork to get back to. Let me know how you're getting on with the case, OK?'

'Yes, sir.' She snapped off a salute, turned on her heel and marched away.

As the lift doors slid slowly shut Will closed his eyes and sighed. 'Bloody hell.' He was definitely getting too old for this.

Six people sit around the dinner table: two men, three women and one little girl, all are dressed up in their Sunday best. Which is funny because it's not Sunday, it's Tuesday.

Their suits are all neat and clean, shirts ironed, ties tidily tied, shoes shined, party hats on their heads. Everyone is smiling. One big happy family. No arguments. No temper tantrums.

No one moves. No one says a word.

The silence is beautiful.

Full of love.

The sound of running water comes from a room off to the side, interspersed with snatches of VR jingles: Fruity Pops. Poppa Steve's Family Pizza. CheatMeat – the tasty cloned treat. The singing isn't loud: just someone entertaining himself, whistling along softly to the bits between the words. Whistling while he works.

Through in the bedroom there's a stain, exactly eight pints of O rhesus negative wide. There's another one on the hall carpet, next to the cupboard. The rest is slowly disappearing down the plug hole, in a froth of pink, soapy water.

And last, but not least, there's the birthday girl. She lies curled up in front of the VR terminal, hands and feet tied behind her back, a wire in the back of her sinful head. She stopped struggling half an hour ago; now she just lies there, shivering and sobbing while a wholesome, computer-generated fantasy flickers inside her retinas.

Eighteen years old.

Filthy, dirty, impure . . . lovely. . .

She's not as lucky as the ones sitting around the table.

For her death is still a long, long way away.

8

Outside, on the roof, the heat was overpowering. Three steps off the escalator and sweat was beading on Will's forehead. Over to the west, clouds were beginning to form: the rains were coming. About bloody time. After the oppressive, drawn-out summer, it would be nice to come up here and just stand in the downpour. Let everything wash away. But right now it was like standing in a frying pan.

He hurried along the rooftop walkway, heading for landing bay twelve: where Lieutenant Emily Brand and a nice cold beer were waiting.

She was standing with her back to the hangar door; dress uniform replaced by a plain, concrete-grey jumpsuit, the sleeves knotted round her middle, showing off neon-red sports webbing, muscled arms and broad shoulders. He watched her pull a Shrike from the Dragonfly's port weapons pod – shifting the heavy air-to-target rocket as if it were made of papier-mâché.

She was every trooper's fantasy: early thirties, five foot six, athletic, strong chin, freckles, button nose. . . Her team took great delight in winding up newcomers: fanning the fires of their ardour, knowing full well that Emily would only put up with so much before beating the crap out of the poor sod.

The last one ended up with a broken arm, three missing teeth, and concussion.

Emily might scrub up well, but she was *not* the sort of person you messed with.

Will stepped into the shade of the hangar. It wasn't *that* much cooler in here, but being out of the sun made him feel less like a slice of bacon. 'It's half five: where's that beer you promised?'

She hooked a thumb over her shoulder, towards the Dragonfly they'd taken to Sherman House yesterday. 'Help yourself.'

Will unlocked a hatch on the Dragonfly's hull marked 'WARNING: ENGINE COOLING SYSTEM'. A six-pack of brown plastic tubes nestled in a homemade hammock between the coils and the burner. It had taken Emily about two months to get it positioned *just* right. Too close to the coils and you got beer-cicles, too close to the burners and you got an engine compartment full of boiling foam and melted plastic.

He popped two loose from the mesh and threw one over.

Emily caught it and held the cool container against her forehead. Sighed. She ran the tube through her close cropped hair and down to the nape of her neck. 'Can't remember summer ever going on this damn long. . .'

'Cheers.' Will pulled the tab and swigged a mouthful of cold, dark-brown beer. 'Won't be much longer: Monsoon's on its way. They're saying Thursday, Friday at the latest.' He slumped down onto a box of pod rockets. Loosened his tie. 'God . . . that's better.'

'Serves you right for wearing that ridiculous suit the whole time.'

'Privilege of rank: you get to "set an example".'

'Get to sweat like a pig in a sauna too: sod that.' She leaned back against the Dragonfly's dented hull and stared at him for a bit. 'You know,' she said at last, 'you look like shite.'

'Good', I've been practising.'

'Trust me, you can stop practising. You've reached perfection in the "looking like shite" stakes. They ever decide to make "looking like shite" an Olympic sport, you can represent Scotland. You're gold medal material.'

Will took another swig and smiled. 'Thanks for the vote of confidence.'

'Don't mention it.' Emily crossed her arms and examined the scuffed toe of her grey boot. 'How's the new girl getting on?'

'Jo?' He suppressed a beer-fuelled burp. 'OK, I suppose. Get the feeling this liaison job is a bit more . . . *difficult* than she'd expected.'

'Yeah, everyone thinks it's all glamour, heroism, and medals . . .' Emily looked away. 'Want to see why the crash kit wouldn't work yesterday?'

She marched around to the far side of the ship. Will hauled himself to his feet and followed.

'Shite.' There was a tattered hole in the hull, about the size of a small child, just in front of the starboard air intakes. Pipes, wires, and cables blackened and torn.

'Outer casing slowed it down a bit, but there was still enough oomph left to roast the controller circuits. Whole thing's completely fucked; it's a miracle your new girl got it working again.' Emily's voice dropped. 'Two minutes earlier and we might have saved Stien. . .'

Will peered into the hole. 'What was it?'

'Best guess? One of the old P-Seven-Fifties. Probably the same one that took a chunk out of Floyd's shoulder. Damn thing must be an antique.'

They walked back to the hangar's entrance together, standing just out of the sun's reach.

'Funny the way it works out, isn't it?' Emily snapped a pair of shades over her eyes. 'Team before us were in and out, not even a whiff of trouble.' She smiled. 'Mind you, spent two days getting the blood out of their drop bay.'

'Tell me about it. I remember this one time. . .' He stopped as his brain caught up with what she'd just said. 'Wait a minute, why did they have to clean the drop bay?'

'Told you: all that blood. Gets gummed up in the mesh flooring and if you don't get rid of it sharpish, the whole ship smells like fusty black pudding and rotting—'

'No. I mean why was it covered in blood?'

She shrugged. 'They tramped it in from the scene. Lieutenant Slater said the flat looked like an abattoir – had to sponge the guy's wife and kids into their body-bags.'

'But. . .' He frowned. 'The Kevin McEwen murder? Flat forty-seven one-twenty-two? Two doors down from where we were yesterday?'

She nodded and took another swig of beer. 'Killed his wife and kids, then topped himself.'

'But I *saw* the place. It was clean.'

'So? Services probably sent in a sanitation team. Stripped the whole thing back to the plasticboard and repainted. Big deal.'

Something in Will's stomach lurched. 'Who was the investigating agent?'

'I think it was Brian. Why are you so—'

But Will had already clicked his throat-mike, 'Control, this is Hunter, where's Agent Brian Alexander?'

'One moment, sir. . .' There was a small pause, and then, *'He's overseeing SOC at the Martian Pavilion with DS Cameron. I'm not getting any response from his phone – must have the scanners running. You want me to give him a message?'*

'Tell him I want to see him in the reconstruction suites, soon as he gets back.' Will killed the link and dropped his half-drunk plastic in the nearest bin. 'Got to run. Thanks for the beer.'

'You're welcome. . .'

Blood. Everywhere. On the floor, up the walls, spattered across the ceiling. Will fumbled with the sizing band on the dusty VR headset one of the technicians had dug out of the stores for him. The old-fashioned gloves weren't helping, the wires kept getting tangled in the straps. . .

Flat 47-122 looked nothing like Will remembered it. There were holes in the recording: fuzzy blobs of no data caused by interference, but nearly everything else was stained red. An avatar stood next to him: a muscular, computer-generated man with hair hanging down to the middle of his back – which was either wishful thinking, or a serious case of self-delusion. A dark-blue label floated above its head with 'AGENT ALEXANDER' written on it.

Will walked forwards and touched the scarlet-stained wall, the glove giving a small tingle of feedback as he ran his finger-tips across the pixel-perfect wallpaper. 'Are you *sure* this is the right apartment?'

The avatar that didn't look anything like Brian nodded. 'Trust me, it's no' the sort of thing you forget. Bits of body all over the shop, blood everywhere. Aye, this is it alright.'

The carpet beneath their computer-generated feet was almost black with blood, the SOC team's footprints still clearly visible in the matted fabric. Over by the door, some-thing that had once been a father of two was sprawled against the wall.

'So where's the rest of him?'

Brian's avatar pointed downwards. 'You're standing in it.'

And that's when Will realized what the fist-sized lump lying beside his left foot was. 'Wonderful. . .'

Kevin McEwen's lower half coated the middle of the room, what was left of his torso acting as a doorstop. Mrs McEwen was smeared across the tiny kitchen, the two children all over the second bedroom. Will worked his way from room to room, just as he'd done when he'd visited the real apartment yesterday.

How on earth could this be the same place? The flat he'd seen was spotless; this was straight out of a cheap horror film.

The murder weapon was lying behind the sofa, power lights flickering in the reconstruction. Will gave it a cursory once over and then went looking for the VR unit. It was lying on the floor, the casing battered and cracked, as if someone had smashed the thing repeatedly against the wall until it was little more than a large, electronic maraca. Will bent down and picked the computer-generated replica off the carpet, his gloves tingling in a half-hearted attempt to simulate weight and texture. One of the headsets was bent into a perfect figure of eight, the lenses cracked, the cables ripped from their sockets, leaving small tufts of multicoloured spaghetti behind.

They still didn't know what caused VR syndrome, but they knew the symptoms well enough. Something goes very wrong with Kevin McEwen's brain chemistry. Then, one day, the only escape he has from his shitty life – the public virtual reality channels – goes on the blink. Maybe his VR unit blows a fuse, or maybe one of his kids tries to stick a slice of buttered toast in the drive, whatever, it doesn't matter: the results are the same. Kevin McEwen goes out, gets himself an old MZ-90 and kills every last member of his family.

Will took another look at the room. The bloodstains. The chunks of meat. The big holes of nothing in the corners of the room, where the walls joined the ceiling, jagged with interference. 'It's a bloody awful recording.'

'What do you expect? Every SOC team kicks seven shades of shite out the machinery. I'm no' surprised it's buggered.'

Will closed his eyes and pictured the place he'd visited: a cramped, scrupulously clean rabbit hutch without so much as a stain on the carpet.

'It didn't look anything like this yesterday.'

'We really need some new SOC kit. Any chance you could have a word with the Demon Dwarf? Buy somethin' that actually bloody works?'

'The place was spotless.'

91

'Aye, well, this is how it looked Sunday when we picked up the stiffs: freshly decorated in "internal organ red". James threw a hairy when he saw the state of ma suit.' Brian's Avatar shrugged. 'Maybe Services redecorated? You know, givin' it the once over for the next lot of poor bastards.'

'If they did, they used recycled wallpaper. There were shadows on the walls where pictures used to hang.'

'Nah, look at it: there's no way you'd *ever* get that crap off the walls. Them stains is there to stay. Must've been a different flat.'

Will took his headset off and the crime scene disappeared, replaced by a bland beige room. 'Not unless there's two flat one-twenty-twos on the forty-seventh floor.'

Brian was sitting in the corner, both eyes a milky shade of grey. 'Even if it was the same place – and I'm no sayin' it was mind. . .' He reached up and unplugged the jack from the socket in the base of his skull. 'But if it *was*, why the hell would anyone bother to make it look like it'd been lived in for years?'

'That's what I intend to find out.'

The décor in Director Smith-Hamilton's office was probably meant to be 'restrained executive chic', but to Will it just looked like a Martian theme pub. The walls were clad in burnished bronze, hand-crafted rivets picked out in delicate verdigris. Genetically engineered pot plants sat on the deep ochre carpet, their manmade fronds an oasis of green and red in the shining dessert. The director sat in leather splendour behind a sandstone desk big enough to sleep six, toying with a two-foot holo of Mars.

'I'm sorry, William, but it's out of the question,' she said, flipping the planet on its axis. 'We've had too many incursions into Sherman House already. Look what happened yesterday!'

He shifted in his chair, and tried to explain the situation for the third time. 'But—'

'Give it a couple of weeks to cool down. Let them get back to their little routines. Then we can look at a small expedition, one that doesn't involve anyone getting shot.'

'There's definitely something going on at Sherman House. We've got two confirmed cases of VR syndrome and a disappearing crime scene. Flat forty-seven one-twenty-two was a *bloodbath* when Agent Alexander's team collected the first set of bodies, but three days later—'

'It was clean. I know, you said.' She pinched the bridge of her nose for a moment. 'Look, William, whether you go back to Sherman House today or next week, the room will still be there. There's no point risking lives for the sake of a couple of days.'

'But—'

'I understand your need to get to the bottom of this, and I admire your determination, but my decision is final.' She pushed the holo away and stood, frowning down at him. 'Until the situation at Sherman House has stabilized, there will be no more Network intrusions. Is that understood?'

Will sighed. 'Yes, ma'am.'

'Good.' The frown vanished, replaced by a beaming smile. 'I'm glad we had this talk, William, it's so seldom we get to discuss ongoing cases. Tell me. . .' She teetered around the desk, took his elbow, and escorted him to the door. 'How is Detective Inspector Cameroon getting on?'

'Detective Sergeant Cameron is doing fine.'

'Excellent. Well, don't let me keep you.' And with that she closed the door.

Will counted all the way to ten before he started swearing.

'Bastarding shite-bags!' The pig-faced man glowers up at the sky, as if it's God himself who's just crapped down the back of his overalls. A one-sided Rorschach inkblot in stinky grey and white.

His partner grins. 'Don't know what yer whingin' about. On you it looks good.'

'Fuckin' birds. . .' Pig-Face shoves another halfhead into its bay in the back of the Roadhugger. The halfhead stumbles – falls like a bag of potatoes onto the dirty metal floor.

'Get up you stupid fuck!' Pig-Face kicks the prone figure. Putting the boot in. Venting his anger on something that can't even cry out in pain. Just because a seagull did what seagulls do. . .

And that's when she decides to kill him.

Medication be damned. She likes the sound of bees and breaking glass.

She steps quietly out of her little compartment and taps him on the shoulder.

Pig-Face turns, his flabby face swollen and flushed. Eyes glittering like beautiful black opals. 'The fuck you want? Eh? GET BACK IN YOUR FUCKIN' BAY!' He draws his fist back. It's big, and rough, and ugly. Just like he is.

Her first blow catches him between the legs: a strong knee that ruptures his left testicle. He folds in the middle, gasping for air, a streamer of spittle twisting free from his slack mouth. She grabs the back of his head and shoves *hard*, bouncing his face off the metal corner of an empty bay. He gurgles, bright red splashing from the remains of his nose like streamers from a party popper. Little jewels of torn skin stay behind on the metal surface. Three teeth lying on the floor.

Pretty.

She wraps her fingers into his hair and smashes his head forward again. And again. And again.

Now his whole body is limp, but she doesn't stop. Smash, smash, smash – until his features disappear into a bloody pulp. Nothing left.

Someone says, 'Oh Jesus God. . .' and she looks up.

It's Pig-Face's partner: the ugly bald one who drives the truck. He stands at the Roadhugger's tailgate, his stupid, wet mouth working up and down. 'But. . . What. . . Steve?' Then he does something very, very silly: he steps up into the truck.

She lets go of Pig-Face's hair and the body hits the deck with a wet splatching sound. A puddle of dark cherry red expands across the scuffed yellow floor.

The ugly man stops moving when his friend starts pooling around his feet. 'Oh God. . .' His face pales, eyes bugging like a startled goldfish, one hand clamped over his mouth. Then he lurches, once, twice, and vomits all over himself.

She waits for him to finish retching before she bashes his brains in.

Nothing fancy. Nothing personal. Just straightforward, mechanical death.

His body is still twitching as she selects a female halfhead of roughly the same size and build as herself from the collection in the back of the Roadhugger. Undressing it is easy enough – though the orange-and-black jumpsuit stinks of stale sweat – then she dresses it in her own clothes, taking care not to get too much blood on her new outfit.

She stares into its eyes, looking for some sign of life. For some spark to tell her there's still a human being in there somewhere. . . But all she sees is the familiar, indifferent gaze of someone who has gone away, never to return. So she is merciful.

She pats it on the cheek, then caves the left side of its face in with a heavy metal wrench. Turning the barcode into a ruined mess of torn flesh and fractured bone.

And then she works her way around the rest of the bays, checking on her fellow halfheads. Putting them out of their misery, one by one. They don't even blink.

Fifteen minutes later the Roadhugger crashes through the

retaining wall of the Connelly Memorial Flyover. It plummets fifty-two feet to the carriageway below, killing everyone onboard the municipal transport that breaks its fall. A beautiful fireball of amber and gold. The smell of crackling skin and greasy tallow. Bees and broken glass.

By the time the emergency crews arrive she is long gone.

9

Tuesday evening was muggy and unpleasant – the promised rains were tantalizingly close, but for now Glasgow sweltered. Sitting alone in his sixth-floor office, staring out of the window at the heat-hazed streets, Will brooded. The rest of the day shift had knocked off hours ago, but here he was, still obsessing about flat 47-122, Sherman House.

He'd checked the scanner logs a dozen times. Gone through the recording with Sergeant Slater. Twice. It was definitely the same place. Kevin McEwen had gone home on Sunday night and blown his wife and children into bite-sized chunks. Drenched the flat in blood.

So how come two days later it looked as if nothing had happened there? Services hadn't been near the forty-seventh floor of Sherman House for months – he'd checked.

But *someone* had. . .

There was a flash of light against the gathering clouds – one of the massive Scrubbers catching a ray of sunshine. Tons of rusting machinery, hanging above the streets and houses, glinting like a big, dirty balloon.

Will closed the blinds.

Director Smith-Hamilton was right: they couldn't send another team in there. The natives were volatile at the best of times, but three visits in as many days had left them ready to explode. And he *really* didn't want to be the one who lit the fuse.

But he wanted to know.

So he went back down to the reconstruction suite and ran the recording again. There had to be something he'd missed.

The first evening is rough: huddling in doorways, doing her best not to be seen. Avoiding the Bean-Heads and the Mincers. Just because they're little children, it doesn't make them any less dangerous – all wired and jittering with combat pharmaceuticals. Hunting in packs for fresh meat.

She finds somewhere safe to wait, near the service entrance, behind a pair of industrial wheely bins that smell dark and meaty. The 'WARNING – BIOHAZARD' label all scuffed and peeling. For once the bees are quiet, their wings still sticky with Pig-Face and his partner's blood. Fat and contented. She dozes, trying to ignore her own hunger and thirst. . .

By the time the bright-yellow council Roadhugger appears the sky has faded from pale blue to dark orange, the city's sodiums coating everything in sickly light.

The Roadhugger's warning lights flash as it reverses up to the main entrance, then a man gets out of the cab and goes around to the back. He struggles with the tailgate for a moment then leads his cargo out onto the grubby forecourt and lines them up, ready for work. The previous shift of halfheads wanders out through the hospital doors and the man loads them into the empty bays. Then drives away.

She steps out from behind the bins and joins the line-up. She doesn't look up at the sign that says 'GLASGOW ROYAL INFIRMARY' – that would be suspicious. Halfheads don't take any interest in their surroundings.

She's slightly dirtier than the others, and her jumpsuit smells, but the bored orderly in green and white doesn't seem to notice. He just steers them all in through the service doors and starts handing out the night's tasks.

It's been six years since she was last here. This was where they cut her face in half, removed her breasts, stitched up her orifices and burned away her brain, but before that she'd been in and out almost every day. That's how she knows she'll be safe.

She worked here, hunted here. She knows this building, knows where to get what she needs.

The intravenous nutrients they give to coma patients are almost the same as the ones they use for halfheads. It won't give her quite as much energy, but she can always take supplements. All she has to do is get to the central store.

When the orderly turns his back she disappears, taking a mop and wheely-bucket with her for camouflage. No one sees halfheads anyway: they're invisible.

She works her way into the bowels of the building, pushing the bucket ahead of her.

Little has changed down here: the walls are still two-tone institution green; everything still smells of stale sweat, rotting cauliflower, and cheap detergent. There are miles of these little corridors, winding their way through the earth. Laundry, Waste Disposal, Protein Recycling, Incinerators. . .

Her broken glass memory brings up a face: Gordon Waugh. Long hair, high forehead, piercings. He'd screamed and begged when she'd beaten him, mewled as she'd slid the knife into his belly, popped and crackled when she dumped him in the furnace. . .

Strange. She can see all that, sharp and clear and perfect, but she can't even remember her own name.

She stops outside a door marked, 'AUTOMATED STORE: NO UNAUTHORIZED ACCESS'. The securilock looks new. She reaches out and strokes the buttons lightly with her fingertips, feeling them bump beneath her touch like stiff grey nipples. The display says 'ENTER PASSCODE'.

Passcode.

She pauses for a moment. Listening.

A pair of thick Fife accents are arguing somewhere off in the subterranean corridors. The air management system rumbles. The plumbing gurgles and clanks. Other than that, she is alone.

Perhaps she should go looking for someone? Someone on their own. 'Persuade' them to give her the code. Slice them up nice and thin, peel back their skin like. . .

She closes her eyes, shudders. The bees are back, loud and insistent. Hungry.

There are drugs in the store that will help control them. Help her think more clearly.

But first she has to get that code.

A sound from down the corridor: the voices from Fife are getting closer. She jerks upright, looking for somewhere to hide. And then remembers what she is: nobody sees half-heads. As the two men turn the corner, all she has to do is pick up her mop and push it back and forth across the floor.

'No it *wasn't*.'

'Yes it *was*!'

'It *can't* have been. The peritoneal cavity just isn't *big* enough for a whole melon!'

'It *is*!' They walk right past her.

When their singsong voices fade into the distance, she lets the mop fall to the floor and squats down in front of the securilock again.

Frowns at the keypad. Fingers twitching.

She can feel half-remembered shapes – not numbers or letters, but a pattern of motion. A memory written in muscle and bone. Shutting her eyes she places her fingertips against the buttons and lets them find their own way through the combination.

There is a soft ping and she opens her eyes. The display

has changed from 'ENTER PASSCODE' to 'CODE ACCEPTED'. They haven't deleted her old access code. Sloppy.

She steps inside and closes the door behind her.

The room stretches out beneath the building, a vast forest of shelving and racks disappearing into the distance. Automated pickers glide between the aisles, fetching and carrying everything needed to run one of the world's biggest hospitals. The metal arms load their cargo into the many dumb waiters that pepper the cavernous room, a ballet of steel and medical supplies, played out to the soft click and hum of machinery. It is beautiful.

Human intervention is not required down here: machines stock the shelves from a subterranean shuttle station, machines check the stock levels, and machines carry the supplies up to the wards and the operating theatres and the mortuary and the canteen.

A beautiful mechanical world where she is the only living thing.

It takes almost an hour to find the coma ward nutrient pouches, perched in the far corner, between acres of toilet paper and racks of skinglue. She rips open a box, pulls out one of the flattened jellyfish shapes, and pops the seal, watching as the bag swells with all the things she needs to survive. It will take a minute or two for the mixture to settle and clear and she spends the time digging out an intravenous line to attach to the socket in her arm.

As the liquid trickles into her veins, the dull ache at the back of her head begins to lift, the tightness in her throat lessens, her stomach stops growling – even though she hasn't actually eaten anything. She closes her eyes and drifts for a moment. Happy.

Grabbing another pack from the pile, she clambers up a wall of toilet paper and makes a little nest for herself beneath the coolant fan. Surrounded by a protective wall of extra-soft quilted tissue she slips the new pack into place and settles down to sleep. For the first time in six years, she is comfortable. Safe.

There are many things that still need to be done, but for now she is content just to rest.

10

'So this is where you've been hiding.'

Will peered out from beneath his VR headset. Lieutenant Brand was lounging against the reconstruction suite wall, wearing another grey jumpsuit – urban concrete-coloured camouflage. Only this time she didn't have her bra on show.

'I'm not hiding.'

'Bollocks you're not. You've been down here all morning, looking like something off the History Channel. Headset and gloves: you're such a sodding luddite. Why can't you get a jackpoint like normal people?'

Will stuck two fingers up at her.

She shrugged, sighed, then pointed at the room's terminal. The chunky evidence cartridge with the scans from flat 47-122 was plugged into it, chugging and creaking as the computer interpreted the data into three dimensions. 'That your mystery room?'

'Want to take a look and tell me what you think?'

She unspooled a lead from the wall; breathed on the little gold connector; polished it against her sleeve; checked it was clean; then felt for the socket in the back of her head with her other hand, freezing just before she clicked the jack into place. 'You spring for lunch afterwards?'

Will nodded. 'Deal.'

He was as good as his word. Thirty minutes later they were sitting in the cafeteria, eating stovies. They'd been over the deep scan readings, the narrow band and the subsonics; they'd even run simulations to track the order of events. None of which explained why flat 47-122 looked so different before and after.

'So,' he speared a little chunk of cloned lamb from the mound of stodgy potato and onion on his plate, 'what do you think?'

'We have to go back. If that place was redecorated the way you said it was—'

'And it *was*.'

'Then something frinky's going on.'

He looked at her. '"Frinky"?'

'Not my fault you're stuck in a time warp.'

'Yes, well. . .' He loaded up another forkful. 'Sherman House is off limits: the Fairy Princess vetoed all Network intrusions for at least a fortnight. We go back in there with another pickup team we'll start a riot.'

'Then we don't take a pickup team.' Emily cast a quick glance around the crowded canteen, then dropped her voice to a whisper. 'She said no *Network* intrusion: didn't say anything about you and me visiting a sick friend who just happens to live there.'

'A sick friend?'

'Trust me, if we don't get caught we won't have to go into any details. We can hop a public shuttle from the Pavilion.' She waggled her knife at him, speaking with her mouth full. 'Better get a change of clothes: you'll stick out like a sore thumb in that monkey suit. We'll do it this evening, about half five?'

'It's a date.'

Emily raised an eyebrow, but didn't say a word.

A shadow fell across the table and Will turned to see DS Cameron in a canary yellow suit, Brian lumbering after her. 'Ah, here you are,' she said, eyes sparkling in the overhead light. 'Guess what: we've identified that halfhead who went missing from the Sherman House toilets!'

'You got Services to talk?' Will was impressed; he'd forgotten all about the abandoned mop and wheely-bucket. 'Who was it?'

'And,' a big smile spread across her face, 'we've got a match on the MO used on our murder victim. You're not going to believe—'

'Wheesht!' Brian cut her off. He sank down into the chair next to Will. 'The missin' halfhead was S H dash O slash D dash one zero two eight six. The dead body in the bog was killed the same way as twenty-seven of her victims—'

'Oh God. . .' The fork fell from Will's hand, skittering across the tabletop, spreading little droplets of pickled beetroot juice. Like a blood spatter pattern. 'She's still out there. . .'

Brian shook his head. 'She's no' anywhere Will: she's dead. The Roadhugger takin' her back to the depot went over the Connelly Memorial Flyover yesterday evenin'. Fell fifty foot onto the back of a bus. No survivors.' He paused. 'They've got what's left of her on a slab down the city mortuary, if you want to see her?'

Lieutenant Brand reached across the table and took hold of Will's hand. 'You OK?'

DS Cameron stuck a datapad on the table, crime scene photos from the Sherman House toilets fading in and out in a macabre slideshow. 'It's a classic copycat killing. Perp finds out who she is, then stalks her for a couple of weeks, working on the fantasy, waiting for an opportunity to perform. Probably made her watch as he butchered Allan Brown.'

It didn't seem to bother her that no one else was celebrating. 'Doing a background search on the Roadhugger's crew now. I'm betting one of them has a record of psychological problems. You know: got the job so he could work with killers and rapists, waiting for his chance to be just like them.'

Will lurched to his feet. The room was beginning to pulse. Hot. Hard to breathe. Mouth coated in grease and the taste of meat. Bile.

'Need to get some air. . .'

'Feeling any better?' Lieutenant Brand settled back against the handrail.

Will straightened up, wiped a hand across his mouth, shrugged. Mouth rank with the bitter taste of vomit. 'Not really.'

The landing bays were empty, no one about on the roof of Network Headquarters to see him spatter a half portion of stovies all over the walkway. Brian had stayed behind, keeping DS Cameron busy and out of the way.

It was stifling up here, the afternoon pressing down on him like a steam iron. The layer of clouds above the city was getting thicker, turning ominous and dark. Threatening what everyone so desperately wanted: an end to the terrible heat.

He clutched the rail and stared out into the distance, wondering if he was going to be sick again.

A gentle hand brushed his shoulders. 'You want to talk about it?'

'No.' He sighed. Looked out across the sweltering city. 'Haven't thought about her in years. . . Well, except for anniversaries, birthdays, Christmas, you know – things like that.' He ran a finger along the thin band of pale skin where his wedding ring used to be. 'Funny isn't it? How. . .' He stopped. Cleared his throat. 'When Brian said the MO matched. . . I know she's been cleaning toilets and sweeping the streets for the last six years, but she was a halfhead. You know what I mean? She wasn't really *alive* anymore. And then suddenly bang! Back to square one.'

They stood in silence for a while, leaning on the rail, not really looking at the view.

And then Will straightened up. 'I want to see her.'

'Good idea – stinks of puke up here anyway.' Emily linked arms with him and steered him towards the lifts. 'How about we knock off early? Get smashed at one of those stuck-up freezy joints. Embarrass a few of the idle rich with our rough, working-man's banter.'

'Thought we were going to see that sick friend of yours.'

'No chance.' Emily hit the button for the Network's shuttle station. 'You need to let off steam, and until you do, you're dangerous. Tonight we get plastered. Tomorrow we go visiting.'

The chief pathologist at Glasgow Royal Infirmary checked their IDs again, even though the security guards had done it three times already on their way down here. Tall, thin, with a hooked nose, and mane of fading ginger hair, he was straight out of a Brothers Grimm fairytale.

The hospital mortuary was huge, all four walls dominated by refrigerated corpse pigeon-holes. A dozen post-mortem tables dotted the floor, stainless steel islands in a sea of cracked grey tile. Most of them were occupied, the bodies being taken carefully apart by teams of anatomical pathology technicians.

When the chief pathologist was finally satisfied that Will, Brian, and Emily were who they claimed to be, he handed their IDs back, nodded, and punched the case number into the console with long, delicate fingers.

The carousel pulled a bodypod from the huge collection that surrounded them, clicking the metallic sarcophagus onto an empty table.

The pathologist wrinkled his nose. 'You may wish to hold your breath at this point.' He popped the toggles, exposing what looked like an over-cooked side of pork with fragments of melted plastic fused to it. With a small cough the pathologist pulled out a metal pointer and began his monologue.

'The skull has suffered severe structural damage, as have both arms and most of the upper torso.' He used the pointer to flip the switch that turned the body. 'As you can see most of the epidermis has been charred – extremely high temperatures – no doubt due to the fuel cell in the municipal transportation being ruptured upon impact. Primary cause of death was blunt trauma to the cranium, probably caused on impact. The other damage was almost certainly post mortem.'

Will looked down at the human barbecue and suppressed a shudder. It was unrecognizable.

'You sure it's her?'

The pathologist pointed at the charred head.

'As you can see, the barcode tattoo on the forehead has been rendered illegible by impact and fire damage, but. . .' He pulled a reader from beneath the table and slid it over the melted remains of the jumpsuit. It bleeped when he reached what was left of the breast pocket. 'The ID chip is still intact. It matches the manifest.'

He twisted the reader, showing Will the display panel.

'SAMPLE 4: ID: SH-O/D-10286'

Will's mouth went dry. 'DNA?'

The pathologist raised an eyebrow. 'There were sixty-two people in the bus that Roadhugger hit, Mr Hunter.' He waved his skeletal hand, indicating the vast collection of refrigerated bodypods. 'And that's in addition to all the other deaths we have to deal with on a daily basis. You'll appreciate that there may be a little bit of a backlog.'

Brian stepped forwards. 'Aye, and you'll appreciate that you'll be in a world of shite if you don't shift this one to the top of your fuckin' priority list.'

The pathologist blinked. 'I see. . . Well, I shall chase up the records department as soon as I get a chance and—'

'I'm sorry, did I no' make myself perfectly fuckin' clear?'

There was a pause, and then the thin man pulled a little blue cylinder from his top pocket, slipped it onto the end of his index finger, and pointed at his own face. 'Records.' His left eye clouded over. 'Yes, I sent a DNA sample up an hour and a half ago, reference: S H dash O slash D dash one zero two eight six. . . . Yes, I know, but I want you to expedite it. . . . I know there's a backlog.'

His one clear eye swept across Brian's angry face, then looked away quickly, voice lowered to a hiss. 'I don't care, just *do* it. . . . Yes, I'll hold.'

Two minutes of awkward silence later the pathologist slipped the fingerphone back into his pocket. 'It's a match. The DNA profile is the same as the one we have on file for this halfhead's medical records. Obviously we don't have a name, but when Services collect the remains for formal identification I can—'

'It's all right,' said Will. 'I know who she is.'

After all this time, she was finally dead. She could burn in Hell where she belonged.

'Come on.' Emily laid a hand on his arm. 'Let's go get pished.'

Eighteen floors beneath their feet a figure stirs in her sleep. The dream is lovely and warm, woven from other peoples' nightmares. The last, terrifying moments of their lives. A slow, intimate waltz of blood, that slowly turns into something altogether more sensual. More special.

In the dream she looks exactly the same as she did on the day that they caught her: flowing golden hair that spills out in soft waves to her shoulder blades; soft, claret lips; long slender neck; and crystal clear, baby-blue eyes. Thirty-six years old and not looking a day over twenty-seven. The perfect predator.

The air is heavy with the sound of busy bees, and she is bathing naked in a bath of fresh, warm blood. There are pale bodies all around the bathtub, holding their slit wrists above the surface, dripping their last drops in her honour. She throws back her head and moans in sheer rapture at the sticky, warm delight.

And then a shadow falls across the room: The Man In The Dark-Blue Suit.

She shivers in her sleep. He's here. He's come to steal her face! She thrashes awake, knocking rolls of toilet paper flying. He's here! He's. . .

Her eyes dart back and forth. The room is quiet, peaceful, safe. The ceiling fan rotates above her, the pickers glide along their rails, the store hums away to itself. Everything is normal. He's not here.

She sinks back into her nest and waits for her heart to stop pounding. She has *never* known fear like this before. Illogical. Irrational. Terrifying. . .

She examines the feeling, turning it back and forth in her mind, analysing her reaction and its cause.

The Man In The Dark-Blue Suit.

There's only one thing to do: she has to confront her fear or it will always have power over her. She's told hundreds of her patients the very same thing.

She slips from her nest to the storeroom floor.

The man who haunts her dreams isn't a God, or a monster, He's just a human being. But in order to confront her fear she must put a name to Him. And when she knows who He is, she can obtain closure.

Preferably with a very sharp knife.

11

Will and Emily stepped off the escalator and into the crowded lobby of Sherman House. Thursday morning, and the huge room was loud and sweaty, packed with sullen faces, all lit with the greasy green light that filtered in through the mould-covered plexiglass. A couple of halfheads pushed floor polishers across the atrium, redistributing the dirt. Someone nodded past, the sound of a cheap sub-dermal music player echoing out of his mouth. Bitter smells of stewed coffee, the dusty scent of mildew, the sweet tang of aerosol narcotics.

Will rubbed his palms dry on his trousers.

Nothing to worry about. He could do this. Deep breath. He could definitely do this. Nothing to worry about.

Why was it so damned hot in here?

He hauled at the collar of his eclectic rags – rescued from a seedy, second-hand shop on Nesbit Road – a patchwork of clashing colours and patterns, the trailing edges flapping as he moved. Emily wore hers like a native, but he looked like someone's dad in fancy dress. It had been years since he'd gone undercover and it showed.

'Relax,' she said, scanning the crowd. 'Everyone's going to think someone shoved a dead cat up your arse.'

'Feel like a bloody idiot.'

'Look like one too.' Emily frowned at him. 'You might as well be carrying a six-foot placard saying "Undercover agent, please shoot me!" *Relax* for God's sake.'

Will slouched, letting his arms dangle as they sauntered carefully across the crowded atrium.

'Better. But still crap.' She pulled the tabs on the two beers they'd bought at a little off-licence vending machine at the Martian Pavilion, and handed one over. 'Try to look more vague. If anyone says anything just mumble incoherently, I'll tell them you're on Tezzers.'

'Thanks a heap.' He took a gulp from the tube, grimacing as the fizzy liquid burnt on the way down. Too much to drink last night: toasting the dear departed bitch's memory with Emily and Brian in a variety of pubs, ending up in a pretentious little freezy joint on Sauchiehall Street. Where the drinks were every bit as ridiculously overblown as the music.

'OK,' he said, stifling an acidic belch, 'how do you want to play it?'

'You're my half-wit, good for nothing boyfriend. I am a strong, independent woman and you follow me about, like some sort of smelly Alsatian.'

'Woof.'

'Good boy.' She set off for the lifts, Will shambling along behind her, still trying to get into the part. Hunched up grunting obscenities under his breath.

About a dozen youths were gathered around the bank of lifts, dressed in the skin-tight formal wear that was so fashionable three years ago. Some were staggering about, giggling, others slumped back against the wall with big wet grins and eyes the colour of tarmac. The outskirts of the pack looked jumpy, as if they were waiting for their turn to go off to cloud-cuckoo land, but didn't have enough money for the bus.

Emily leant over and whispered at Will, 'Think they're on Tezzers?'

'More like H, or Mouse. They'll be turning over anyone who looks like they haven't already swallowed their daily allowance.'

He hooked an arm though hers and staggered slightly, blinking slowly, trying to look as if he'd just swallowed a whole week's ration of government-issued narcotics. 'You want to take the escalator instead?'

Emily shook her head. 'We're too close. If we turn round and go the other way it'll look like we've got something worth having.'

'And they'll try and take it.'

'Got it in one.'

They reached the outer edges of the group. One of the jumpy kids stepped in front of them. Sharp features, squint teeth, a monocle tattooed around his right eye. 'Gotta pay the taxman, yeah?'

Emily stared at him. 'Get to fuck, you wee radge.'

Monocle smiled. And that's when Will realized that the young man's teeth weren't squint – they were filed to points. All the better to eat you with. . .

'"Get to fuck," is it?' Monocle turned and held his hands out. 'You hear what the bitch says to me? Eh?' When he turned back there was a six-inch serrated knife in his hands. 'You know what? For an old bird you're pretty fit. . .' He ran the knife blade up and down the colourful tatters on Emily's sleeve. 'Bet you like it rough, eh? Bet you're just fuckin' gaspin' for me and my mates to take you round the back and bang the shit out you. Yeah?'

Will stepped forwards. 'Who do you think—'

'Shut it, Grandad.' Now the knife was an inch from Will's throat. 'We won't forget about you, you know? Malcolm here likes breakin' in auld mannie's arses for them. Don't you Malcolm?'

A fat youth with pimples and a shark's-tooth-grin nodded. 'Fuckin' gay you up *brilliant*, man.'

'Aye, so. . .' Monocle looked back at Emily. 'You got a dirty mouth, bet I got something that'll clean it for—ulk. . .'

The knife wavered, then dropped to the tatty floor. The kid's eyes bulged in his head, lips twitching, face turning pink. Emily had her hand buried in his crotch, twisting cloth and skin and testicles into a tight fist.

'Ahhh, Jesusfuckfuckfuck. . .'

She smiled. '"Bang the shit out of me"?' She screwed her hand around another quarter turn and Monocle's knees gave way. Emily wrapped her other hand around his throat, keeping him upright. 'I'm out of your league, Funshine.'

And then she let go.

Monocle collapsed, curled into a ball, and made a high-pitched keening noise. Like a deflating balloon.

Emily turned to the rest of the troupe. 'Anyone else?'

They all took a step back, leaving a clear path to the open lift doors.

'Didn't think so.'

Inside the graffiti-covered compartment, Emily stabbed the button marked '47' and settled back against the scarred metal wall. As the doors slid shut, the youths stood and stared at Emily with something close to hero worship.

The lift lurched to a halt on the second floor, and a handful of people got on. Then it was off again, the sound of squealing metal marking the time between floors. More figures in colourful tatters got on at the seventh. A couple left at the ninth.

Then the destinator pinged for the thirteenth floor and a large woman squeezed into the crowded lift.

Shit. Shit, shit, shit, shit!

Will grabbed Emily and pulled her against his chest, engulfing her in a deep, groping kiss. Her back went rock-hard beneath his fingers . . . and then she loosened up, weaving her hands into his hair and making happy little moaning sounds.

114

On the other side of the lift, the large woman scowled, her green eyes flicking like razorblades across the faces in the car. Big-boned rather than fat, with ginger hair and tribal scars, dressed in the same set of multicoloured rags she'd had on when Will shot her in the chest with Stein's Zapper.

Floors passed, and each time the lift juddered to a stop more people squeezed their way out of the car, doing their best not to brush against the big woman. Keeping out of trouble.

Twenty levels later the doors slid open and the redhead stomped off down the corridor. Now Emily and Will were alone in the lift, and as the car began to rise again, he pulled back from Emily's lips.

'Why Mr Hunter,' she said with a smile. 'How impetuous of you.'

Will grinned and let her go. 'Thought she was never going to leave!'

The expression on Lieutenant Brand's face didn't alter much, but it took her a heartbeat before she said, 'Who was it?'

'She was the first of the mob to reach Allan Brown's place. I had to zap her.' He slumped back against the handrail and scrubbed his face with his hands. Heart still thumping. 'Sorry about jumping on you like that. It was the only thing I could think of at the time.'

She kept the smile on her face and straightened out the tatty hem of her tunic. 'Don't worry about it. Just try to give me a bit more notice next time. Maybe dinner and a spot of dancing. Something like that.'

She stands there in the storeroom, with a brand-new reader in her hands, the packaging torn and discarded at her feet. The reader hums as she runs it across the barcode above her left eye. And then it bleeps. It knows who she is.

Holding her breath, she lowers the device and reads the words on the small screen: 'SAMPLE 1. ID: SH-O/D-10286'

Disappointment.

She tries again, but all it says is, 'SAMPLE 2. ID: SH-O/D-10286'

What good is that? How is that supposed to help?

She was expecting a name, something that would trigger her memory. Something that would tell her who she was.

'SAMPLE 3. ID: SH-O/D-10286'

The reader explodes when she hurls it to the floor. She stamps on the plastic fragments, kicking them away into the store. All she wants is a name, is that really so much to ask for? Is it?

IS IT?

She closes her eyes, taking deep shuddering breaths.

Calm down. Calm. Slow breaths.

Stay in control.

Bees and broken glass. . .

She stares off into space, tapping her fingetips gently against her exposed teeth. There will be records in the system somewhere. They halfheaded her in one of the theatres upstairs, they will have her records on file. What she needs is a doctors' terminal: one with direct access into the hospital's secure patient database.

Maybe she'll find someone to satisfy her *other* needs on the way? Someone to while away the hours with. Someone to spread across the floor like raspberry jam. . .

Just as long as she's careful. Just as long as she stays in control.

That's what went wrong before: she stopped taking her medicine, because she thought she didn't need it. She stopped taking her medicine, because she thought she could control herself without it. She was wrong. She needs her medicine . . . but she can't take her medicine – can't remember what it is.

But once she finds out who she is, everything will be all right.

She will take her medicine.

She will be good.

She will behave.

She promises herself that.

Carefully, she slots her mop into the bucket she stole yesterday and wheels it out through the storeroom door.

Cool. Calm. And in control. Dragging a cloud of bees behind her.

The elevator doors slid open on the forty-seventh floor of Sherman House. There was a faint, lingering smell of burned bacon as they walked up the scorched corridor. Fresh graffiti marked the wall in shiny red paint where Stein had caught fire: 'ONE – NIL!'

Allan Brown's stinking nest had been boarded up since they were last there; large plasticboard sheets welded over the entrance. Two doors down, flat one twenty-two was safely locked. Will punched in the entry code and scowled as the lock went 'clunk' at him.

'Problems?'

'Code's been changed. . . Hope they haven't assigned the place to new tenants.'

He knocked and they waited. Then knocked again.

No answer.

Will popped the cover off the lock and thirty seconds later they were standing in the empty flat. The place was exactly as he'd remembered it: tidy, but shabby.

Emily stared at the faded yellow-and-green wallpaper. 'This isn't the place on the recording. It can't be.'

'It is. I double, triple and quadruple checked. And then I got Brian to do the same. This is where Kevin McEwen slaughtered his family.' Will walked from room to room, retracing his steps. There was no sign of blood anywhere.

117

'If the place's been cleaned, how come it looks so tatty?'

'Exactly.' Will rubbed a hand across the wall nearest the kitchen. 'Scrub that much blood off the walls and you'll take half the wallpaper with it. I wonder if they've. . .' He took a step back. Frowned. That couldn't be right. There was no *way* that could be right.

'What? What have you found?'

He pointed at a shadow on the wall – ingrained dust showing where a picture had hung for years. The grime framing the rectangular silhouette was made up of tiny dots of cyan, magenta, yellow and black.

'The dirt's not real, it's been printed on. . .' He lurched to the other side of the room. There was a little stick-figure family scribbled on the wall in red crayon. The smiling figures were made up of the same magenta and yellow spots. Everywhere he looked, he found more and more counterfeit squalor.

Emily announced that the kitchen was full of the same fake grime, but Will wasn't really listening. He'd positioned himself in the middle of the room, just where the SOC team's scanning equipment would have sat. The computer reconstruction was full of holes, blobs of no data, and as he stood there he got the nasty feeling he knew why. The blobs hid the upper corners of the room, just where you'd put surveillance equipment if you wanted to keep an eye on the flat's occupants.

'This gets weirder,' said Emily emerging from the kitchen, 'there are damp patches under the sink and they've been printed on too. Inside a cupboard! Who in their right minds. . . What are you doing?'

'Give me a leg up.'

Emily braced herself into the corner, hoisting him up as if he was barely there.

Will peered at the join between the walls and the ceiling. It looked normal enough, but then it would, wouldn't it? Reaching into his pocket, he pulled out Brian's Palm

Thrummer, twisted the little canister open, and set it on minimum. It burred in his hand, numbing his fingertips as he carefully stripped the upper layers of wallpaper and plasticboard away, turning them into a cloud of grey dust that billowed out into the room.

There was something in there. . .

Will took a deep breath and blew, clearing the fog away. Two sonic probes and a small jammer were bolted into a little metal box, mounted behind the plasticboard. The whole array was lit up: the probes grumbling away to themselves as they recorded him and everything else in the room.

'Shit!' Will leapt to the ground. 'We've got to get out of here. Now!' He grabbed Emily and hauled her towards the door.

'What the hell's got into you?'

'How long have we been in here?' He pulled back his tatty rag sleeve and glanced at his watch. 'Five minutes. Shit, shit, *shit*!'

Will slammed the door of the apartment behind them, and hurried down the corridor, back towards the lifts, muttering all the way. 'Come on, come on. . .'

'Where are we going?'

They rounded the corner just as the lift doors pinged opening. The car was full, and standing right at the front was the big-boned woman with the red hair and tribal scars.

'Fuck!' Will snatched at Emily's sleeve, stopping her in her tracks. 'When I say, run for it.' Two steps back and the lifts were hidden from view. 'Run!'

They almost made it.

There's no sign of the man whose name adorns the diplomas on the office wall, but just in case he turns up she locks the door before powering up the terminal on his desk. The same code that worked on the storeroom door gets her through the system's security check.

She calls up the hospital's patient database and punches in the reference code the reader gave her: SH-O/D-10286.

The machine chugs away to itself for almost three minutes, searching through the millions of people held on the system. And then the result comes back. 'ACCESS RESTRICTED. FOR MORE DETAILS CONTACT SERVICES – OFFENDER MANAGEMENT DEPARTMENT'

She has an almost overwhelming urge to grab the monitor and smash it against the wall. And then she realizes that this is how the system is supposed to work. Halfheads are non-people. Nothing is allowed to connect the lobotomized slave to the crimes they committed. Nothing for anyone to idolize or respect.

She sits back in the doctor's mock-leather chair and scowls at the screen.

But it's her name.

HER FUCKING NAME.

If *anyone* has the right to know what it is, it's her.

Deep – calming – breaths.

They haven't deleted her user ID from the system, maybe there's another way to find out who she is. . .?

She calls up the email program and enters the same pass-code again.

'WELCOME DOCTOR FIONA WESTFIELD. YOU HAVE NO NEW MESSAGES.'

Doctor Fiona Westfield.

She frowns. She'd expected everything to come flooding back, but it doesn't.

She puts the name into the patient database and this time the screen fills with information. *Everything* is here. The details of her halfheading: the attendees, the surgeon – just reading his name makes her shudder – case notes on the bladder infection she'd contracted as a result of a poorly sterilized catheter.

And a photograph: her at a conference receiving an award. She reaches out and caresses the screen. Long blonde hair, little button nose, sparkly blue eyes. Her face. She wants her face back so badly it *hurts*.

The hospital system has been a busy little bee, automatically finding links to a potted biography, cross-references to her trial, post mortems on her victims. . .

Beautiful, beautiful pictures of torn abdomens and ragged flesh.

The images spark things inside her head: memories and thoughts from a time when she was a real person. Before they hacked her jaw away. Before she became a monster.

But as she reads she knows that's not true.

She has *always* been a monster.

12

His head falls back, eyes closed, shuddering, breathing hard. Sweat running down his naked back. With a final thrust everything goes bright and sharp. . . Oh God. . . Yes. . . And then he falls forward, panting, feeling wonderful. Feeling spent. Feeling happy.

Over on the bed – held nice and tight by all those chains and straps – the birthday girl stares at him. She's still wearing a little badge saying: 'I Am 18', even though it's not really her birthday any more. She stopped sobbing fifteen minutes ago, now she just trembles, whimpering something over and over behind the gag.

He doesn't say anything, because she wouldn't understand. No one *ever* understands.

Sometimes it makes him cry, but not today: today is a day for celebration. That's why he's let her watch.

He slips himself free, patting the other woman on the head as he does so. The lucky soul is almost gone – one eye swollen and bloodshot, a string of dribble hanging from her slack mouth. He's filled her up with as much life as he can, and soon the angels will come and take her to their bosoms. Another soul that he has saved.

He smiles and winks at the birthday girl, tucked up all nice and cosy on the bed. It'll be her turn soon enough. He's ᵦ more than enough life to go round.

Will groaned. He shifted his weight, trying to find a position that didn't hurt quite so much, but he could barely move. Cramp lurched up and down his body, pausing every now and then to kick him in the kidneys.

He prised one eye open. Bright light. Pain. It felt as if someone was ramming a red-hot poker into the socket. 'Fuck. . .' It was like the worst hangover he'd ever had. He closed his eye again.

Someone slapped him. Hard enough to fill his mouth with the taste of blood.

Will coughed, retched, spat a mouthful of hot copper down his own front.

Slowly the room lurched into focus. A wall of muscle was standing over him, dressed in a grey-black jumpsuit. The kind with sergeant's stripes on the sleeves.

'Aye.' The bruiser was rubbing his right hand, talking into a throat-mike. 'That's 'em baith conscious now. Ye'd better let Himself know.'

'So, you're not dead then.'

Will inched his head around, slow and careful, just in case it fell off. Emily was strapped into an interrogation chair next to him, still dressed in her eclectic-tatters outfit. A fresh bruise covered her left cheek, her lip was swollen, and her expression was murderous.

'Where are we?' It came out as a croak.

'No idea. By the time I woke up we were in here. The restraints weren't as good as these ones. . .' she flexed against the straps, going nowhere. 'But they learned fast.'

Will swore. Winced. Then looked around the room, trying to figure out what the hell they were going to do now.

It was a dimly lit, circular room, empty except for Will, Emily, the two interrogation chairs, and the man-mountain.

was one continuous mirror that wrapped all the
...nd, their distorted figures reflecting back at them.
...ould be cameras and scanners on the other side of
...ss, recording everything, right down to their blood
p...ure and pupil dilation.

So it was official – they were fucked.

But at least they weren't dead yet.

Will spat out another sliver of blood. 'How far did you get?'

'About a hundred yards.' Emily's scowl turned into a smile.
'There's at least three of them won't be walking home tonight.'

'Two of them,' said a cheery, educated, mid-Atlantic voice,
'may never walk again. Not without some serious surgical intervention anyway.' The newcomer stood in a doorway that hadn't
been there the last time Will looked. The man was backlit,
turning him into a silhouette against the painful glare. 'Gotta
admit: I *like* a woman who knows how to take care of herself.'

Emily's eyes narrowed. 'Blow it out your arse!'

'Ah, touché.' The silhouette folded its arms and leaned
against the doorframe. 'Well, now we've got the witty repartee
out the way, I wanna know who you are and exactly what
you're doing at Sherman House.'

Silence.

'OK . . . let's try again. We know you don't live here, so
what are you: Newsies? Hope-Heads? Malkies? Don't tell me
you're *Flatworlders*, that would be too disappointing. No? Neo-
Christian Jihad?'

More silence.

The man shrugged. 'You know, I don't have to do this. If
you like, we can just pump you full of chemical co-operation.
Save everyone a load of time: I get what I need to know and
you get moderate-to-severe brain damage. No skin off mine,
is it?'

Will cleared his throat. 'I don't know who you are, but I
can promise you we're not journalists, religious freaks,
enforcers, or Terra-rists.'

'Glad to hear it. Your girlfriend's too spunky for all "space is for the Martians" bullshit.' The silhouette cocked its head. 'So what *are* you then?'

Will threw the question back: 'What are you?'

'Nope, sorry, that's not the way it works. You answer my questions, or you end up taking your meals through a tube. So one last, and *final*, time: Who are you?'

Will shut his eyes. Tell the truth or lie?

Given the setup here, they'd be monitoring everything right down to his pupil dilation and skin temperature. If he tried to lie they'd know about it before he'd finished the sentence. And then the interrogation drugs would come out. Moderate-to-severe brain damage – there was no way he could do that to Emily.

He brought his chin up. 'William Hunter: Assistant Network Director for Greater Glasgow and Central Section. This is Lieutenant Emily Brand, Rapid Deployment Squad Team Lead.' He tried to put a bit of steel into his croaky voice. 'Now *exactly* who and what are you?'

But the man in the doorway wasn't playing.

'If you're a Network ASD, what you doing poking round Monstrosity Square without armed backup? Mind you, considering the mess your girlfriend made of Davis, McLean and Simpson, maybe you didn't need it.' There was a pause. 'Why Sherman House, Mr Assistant Section Director?'

In for a penny: 'Last week an SOC team was called out to flat one-twenty-two, forty-seventh floor. Their scene-of-crime scans show the place covered in blood, but when I went back there on Monday it was stripped clean. No bloodstains; just an old, tatty flat with faded wallpaper.'

'You came all the way down here because someone tidied up?'

'Two of the bodies we collected from Sherman House this week tested positive for VR syndrome. We need to know if there's another outbreak brewing.' It wasn't the whole wasn't a lie either. The machines wouldn't get

'that

...he figure took a step back and the doorway faded, ...thing behind but mirrored glass. That fake Amer-... echoed around the room, *'Don't go anywhere, will you?'*

And then Emily hissed at Will, 'Why the hell did you tell him who we are?'

'You *want* your brain fried with chemicals?'

'You have no idea who he is! Terra-rists, Neo-Christian Jihad, even Gaelic Nation Separatists for fuck's sake. They didn't know who we were, and you just handed them a Network ASD for a hostage!'

Will nodded at the mountain of muscle in the dark-grey jumpsuit. 'Look at him: he's not a fanatic, he's military. This whole place stinks of Black Ops.'

She looked at him. 'That doesn't exactly make me feel any better.'

Ten minutes later, the dim room blossomed into full light, sparkling back off the mirrored wall. A door popped open somewhere behind them, and that same transatlantic voice said, 'Angus, please unfasten our guests.'

'Yes, sir.' The man-mountain started on Will's restraints.

A figure wandered into view, hands in the pockets of his sharp, bottle-green suit. Late twenties. His hair was mousy brown and wavy, his eyes unremarkably blue. The kind of face you wouldn't remember clearly when you were questioned by the police. He walked with a pronounced 'clip clop', on a pair of dark brown Cuban heels that added an extra inch-and-a-half to his height, and even then he only just scraped five-foot-eight.

'Sorry for the inconvenience, Mr Hunter, but we gotta be real careful about who's wandering about down here. Someone kicks something off and "boom"; we got ourselves a full-blown riot.' He stuck out a hand. 'Ken Peitai, Senior Social Engineer, Ministry for Change.'

They shook, then Peitai handed over a plain business card.

Will pointed at the sergeant untying his feet. 'Since when does the Ministry for Change need military backup?'

'Since Sherman House.' The man in the bottle-green suit smiled, eyes twinkling. 'They keep a lid on things: neutralize flare-ups before things get out of hand, tidy up afterwards, make sure it doesn't explode like it did during the VRs. Couldn't do our job without them.'

Peitai helped Will to his feet. 'See, that's why the apartment you visited didn't look like the SOC recording. We erased the crime scene when you'd done with it, scrubbed the place from top to toe.'

Will winced, pins and needles making him hobble. 'The wallpaper had stains printed on it.'

'Yup.' Peitai watched the man-mountain trying to unstrap a glowering Lieutenant Brand without getting anywhere near her. 'Our psych boffins figure if we leave the place spotless and smelling of paint, the next load of occupants will know something horrible happened in the flat before they got it. Imaginations run riot, they start to obsess, and next thing you know they're out in the corridors blowing off steam by kicking someone's head in. So we print on a bit of grime; make the place look lived in. So far it seems to be working.'

Will nodded – it actually made sense. Which meant that all the sneaking around he'd done had been a stupid, and dangerous waste of time. Dragging Emily down here, getting them almost killed. . .

Moron.

He cleared his throat. 'Sounds like a good plan.'

'You know,' said Ken, 'there's so much Spontaneous Violent Aggression down here we're pretty sure the original Virtual Riots weren't actually caused by them shutting down the VR channels after all. That was just the trigger. And when you got so many people living on top of each other in connurb blocks like this, there's plenty other triggers to choose from.' He started to recite facts and figures, throwing hands about to emphasize various points.

The mountain of muscle in the grey jumpsuit finished untying Emily and retreated to a safe distance, watching as she stretched out her hamstrings and flexed her fists. Now she was a 'guest' instead of a prisoner, she outranked him, but Will got the feeling the big man just didn't want to end up being the fifth person she'd crippled that day.

Ken stood at the door to the mirrored room, holding it open. 'You guys want a tour?' He tipped a thumb at the corridor outside. 'We don't get a lot of visitors – you know, keeping the whole thing under wraps – but I'd love to show you round?'

Will nodded. Still feeling like an idiot. 'Thanks.'

The place was a rabbit warren, the walls painted a cheery shade of yellow and decorated with abstract works of art. Various coloured lines ran along the floor beneath their feet, occasionally branching off as they came to a junction.

'We reckon about half the guys living in Monstrosity Square got some degree of VR syndrome,' said Ken as they stepped through a set of double doors into a control room. One wall was given over to a bank of monitors, stretching from floor to ceiling, each screen showing a tiny flat like the one Kevin McEwen had killed his family in.

'Got monitors in about a third of the apartments. We're getting the rest wired up, but it takes time, you know?' He slid his hands over a control plinth, making the screens jump from flat to flat. Most of the residents were plugged into VR headsets, their gloved hands waving about in front of them, making things happen that only they could see. No one down here was rich enough for a cranial implant.

'That's about the only thing thirty percent of them ever

do: all day, every day. We had to make Comlab insert food and toilet breaks into their programming, because the poor sods would end up with malnutrition and bladder infections. The remaining seventy percent spend anything between four and twelve hours plugged in. Why live in the real world when you can live in a full-immersion fantasy instead?' Ken sighed. 'It's not the VR that's addictive, it's the escape it represents.'

Will watched the rooms and their inhabitants come and go on the screens. 'What happened to the McEwens?'

Ken grimaced and traced a figure of eight in the air – every monitor changed to show the same thing: Apartment 47-122. He reeled it back and figures flickered in reverse through the place.

Will saw himself and Emily in their tatty rags . . . then the flat was empty . . . then there he was again, poking around just before Stein died . . . then empty again . . . and then it was the clean-up squad, stripping off the wallpaper, painting the walls with blood. Then Brian Alexander and his Network team dropped the chunks of dead body back where they'd found them. And finally the victims came back to life, made whole by the assault rifle in Kevin McEwen's hands.

Ken twisted the control back to 'PLAY'.

Kevin raised the gun and blew his wife and children apart.

Ken hit pause. 'By the time the response team got up there it was too late. We're still trying to find out how he got his hands on an MZ-90. I mean, Jesus: the damn thing's an antique.'

He waved his hand over the plinth again and the screens flickered back to real time views of the different flats. Then Ken ushered Will and Emily back out into the corridor.

'Primarily we're trying to find out what really triggered the VRs,' he said as they followed a green line in the floor. 'Eleven years on and we still can't pinpoint an *exact* cause. Compressed urban habitation is obviously a key factor, but if we can find out what's actually causing their brain chemistry to change, making them go off the rails, do terrible things. . . Well, we could make a huge difference to these people's lives.'

A pair of technicians came out of a door marked 'AUTHORIZED PERSONNEL ONLY!', nodding a greeting at Ken as they wheeled a trolley away down the corridor.

Will watched them go. 'Any success?'

Their guide gave Will a lopsided smile. 'Not as much as I'd like. But we'll get there.' He pushed through the door the technicians had come from, leading Will and Emily into a medium-sized laboratory, lined with expensive-looking bits of equipment. The walls in here were the same happy yellow as the corridor, but the paintings had all been replaced by digiboards and cell diagrams.

A handful of serious-looking men and women were dressed in light-blue lab coats, bent over scopes, scanners, gene sequencers, and test tubes.

Ken pointed at a woman manipulating a big computer-generated holo of a human brain, the familiar red and yellow bands clearly visible in the frontal lobes. 'We're also working on methods to reverse the changes VR syndrome causes. I figure that if we can make a cure airborne and combine it with a heavy-duty sedative, we can just flood an infected building through the ventilation system. Knock 'em out and fix 'em up at the same time, before they can hurt themselves or anybody else.'

Ken clapped one of the scientists on the shoulder. 'It's a tough job, but if anyone can do it, it's these guys.'

The man in the white lab coat grinned.

Will waited until they were back out in the corridor. 'Why didn't you inform us you were running trials down here?'

'Ah.' Ken shrugged. 'You'd have to ask my boss that one. Me? I think the fewer people know half of Glasgow's probably still got VR syndrome, the better. That gets out there's going to be panic, hoarding, mass hysteria, civil unrest. . .'

Will had to admit he had a point.

They followed a blue line in the floor, Ken going on and on about psychological empowerment and how it was still possible for the people crammed into Glasgow's connurb blocks to have a better quality of life.

But Will wasn't really paying attention. He had his mind firmly fixed on a long shower, a carry-out, a bottle of wine, and a change of clothes. His gaily-coloured tatters were beginning to smell. He'd had enough of feeling, and looking, like an idiot for one day.

They'd reached a pair of frosted-glass doors marked, 'SHUTTLE STATION'.

Ken ushered them through to an unassuming platform, the concrete tunnel stretching off into darkness on either side. 'Well, this is where I have to leave you folks. I gotta re-home about three dozen families before the end of the day. Fight broke out in the lobby this morning. Starts out as a tiny scuffle – some kid gets his testicles mashed – and next thing you know, boom: six dead, twenty seriously injured. If we hadn't got a team in there pronto God knows how many more would've been hurt.'

He called for a private car, then offered Will his hand.

'Nice to meet you Mr Hunter; sorry we had to zap you back there.' They shook. 'Give me a shout next time you're coming down: we'll have lunch and I'll introduce you to some of the guys.'

'I'd like that.'

Emily didn't offer to shake Ken's hand, but he didn't seem too put out, just waved goodbye and left them alone on the deserted platform.

She scowled at the closed doors. 'You buy all that horse-shit?'

'I've heard dafter things. And if they *can* come up with a cure for VR: can you imagine it?'

'That wee shite is up to something.'

Will shrugged. 'Everyone's up to something.'

131

He could hear muffled voices in the corridor behind them: a man and a woman. Gossiping, discussing their caseloads, telling dirty jokes. He couldn't really see them through the frosted glass, just two blobs of light and darkness going about their day.

Will turned his back on the doors. 'Have I told you the one about the two nuns in a hydroponics garden—' The growing roar and buffeting wind of an approaching shuttle drowned out the rest.

Emily stepped back from the platform's edge. 'SO THAT'S WHY THE CUCUMBER SANDWICHES ALWAYS TASTE FUNNY?'

'YOU'VE HEARD IT?'

The tunnel was growing lighter, the stanchion lights flickering on as the shuttle car decelerated out of the gloom. Green and shiny, like an exotic beetle. It came to a halt right in front of them.

'I told it to you in the first place.'

The shuttle's door popped open and slid back on its runners, exposing a clean, well-appointed interior. Not like the shabby ones the Network always used. They climbed onboard. 'NETWORK HEADQUARTERS' was already programmed into the destinator.

With a gentle hiss the door slipped back into place and the shuttle began to move, pulling away from the station.

Will settled back in his plush seat, taking one last look at the entrance to Ken Peitai's little subterranean kingdom. It was amazing the things that could go on right under your. . .

He froze.

Just coming through the frosted doors was someone he recognized. Her wild ginger hair was now tied back in a neat ponytail and she was laughing, her green eyes twinkling in the strip-lights. The tribal scars were gone, only a faint trace of puffiness remaining where she'd peeled them off. The woman from Sherman House – the one he'd zapped.

He didn't get much of a look at her companion, just a flash of a tall man in a long black cloat, its straps fluttering in the wake of the departing shuttle.

The car accelerated to cruising speed, leaving the platform far behind.

Oh shit.

If Ken's little social engineering project was so damn altruistic, how come his agents were running around stirring things up? When Stein died, the ginger-haired woman hadn't been trying to 'keep a lid on things', she'd been running at the front of the pack, with a projectile weapon in her hand and a crazy glint in her eye. She'd tried to kill his team for God's sake!

Then there was the rest of them – the ones who'd chased Will and Emily through the corridors. . . How the hell did Ken Peitai get away with running his private militia in a building full of VR syndrome? It was like sticking a firecracker in a wasps' byke.

Emily was right not to trust the little git.

Will scowled, watching the lights vwip past.

Out of the frying pan.

13

The rains arrived that evening, right on schedule. A flash. A single peal of thunder. The first drop spattered against the hot concrete, evaporating almost immediately. And then another drop. And another. Growing faster, thicker, heavier, until it was bouncing back from the pavement.

Gradually the streets filled with people, standing with their faces turned to the downpour. They danced and sang, celebrating the end of the oppressive heat, passing plastics of whisky and beer around. An impromptu carnival that rivalled any New Year's Eve.

And then the temperature began to drop – slowly at first, just a couple of degrees an hour – until everyone was soaked and shivering. So they left the streets to the rain.

Summer was over. Now it was the turn of the monsoon.

'That does *not* explain why you disobeyed my direct order to stay away from Sherman House!'

The shuttle had dropped Will and Emily off at Network Headquarters almost two hours ago, dressed in all their tattered finery. Fifteen minutes later the summons to the Director's office had arrived. She'd kept them waiting in the anteroom for ages before calling Emily in. Director

Smith-Hamilton was a professional, she did not believe in public bollockings. That meant Will had to sit outside while she tore a strip off of Lieutenant Brand. And then wait some more while she made a few phone calls. And then wait some more on top of that, just to make sure he knew he was in trouble.

He stood to attention while she paced back and forth in front of the panoramic glass wall, rubbing at her forehead. 'I mean, I could understand it if you were one of the junior agents, but you're an *Assistant Section Director*, William! I have to be able to trust you to follow the chain of command. If you don't, how can we expect anyone else to?'

Behind her, Will had a perfect view of the city. Grey skies, sheets of rain. Glasgow was drowning. He knew how it felt. 'I can only say—'

'I'm not finished yet. When I decided to promote you to Assistant Section Director, I faced a great deal of opposition. "He's too young," they said. "He lacks discipline," they said. I told them they were wrong: that despite your youth and *unsavoury* connections, you had a good, solid head on your shoulders. That you had what it took.' She stopped pacing. 'Was I wrong, William? Should I have listened to them and left you with the rank and file for another five years?'

'Well, you—'

'Don't interrupt. It was bad enough you went back to Sherman House against my direct orders, but did you really have to drag Lieutenant Brand along with you? Are you looking to ruin *her* career as well as your own?'

'I only told Lieutenant Brand where I was going once we were aboard the shuttle. She insisted on accompanying me to ensure my safety. She was not able to contact Control to inform them of my intentions because we were surrounded by residents who could have overheard, putting both of our lives in jeopardy.'

'I had Governor Clark on the phone for twenty minutes this afternoon, demanding your head on a stick!' Director Smith-Hamilton leant back against her huge sandstone desk. 'You can consider yourself lucky the people running Sherman House have decided not to make a formal complaint. A Mr Peitai called me an hour ago to speak on your behalf: you owe him. Were it not for his support your position here would have been untenable. Do you understand?'

'Yes, ma'am.'

'Obviously, I can't let this disgraceful breach go unpunished. I'm fining you one month's wages and cutting your holiday entitlement by four days.'

'Thank you, ma'am.'

She sighed. 'What are we going to do with you, William? I always had high hopes of you following in my footsteps. I thought that one day – when I move on to take a seat at the Ministry – I'd be able to leave the Network in your hands.'

Smith-Hamilton turned to face the downpour. Cleared her throat. Fidgeted with the cuffs of her jacket. 'I understand they found Dr Westfield's body yesterday. It must have come as a terrible shock.' She paused. 'Perhaps that's why you went against my exclusion order on Sherman House?'

He didn't answer, but she nodded anyway, then walked over and put a hand on his shoulder. Up close she smelled of lavender and bergamot. 'I think you should take the rest of the week as compassionate leave. We'll hold down the fort here and you can come to terms with. . . Well with whatever you have to come to terms with.' She guided him towards the door.

'Remember, William, we have a team of highly trained therapists who can help you through this. I want you to feel free to give them a call. Make them work for their money.'

Which was pretty much exactly the same speech he'd given DS Cameron.

Will murmured something noncommittal and thanked the Director for her time. Then marched off down the corridor, back straight, head up.

As soon as he heard her office door close, he slumped to a halt and swore. She could keep her highly-trained therapists – he'd had enough analysis to last a lifetime, thank you very much.

He got into the lift and hit the button for the lowest level. Brooding all the way down.

There was no sign of George's shiny receptionist, so Will went straight through.

The 'Frankenstein's Day Off' cartoon was gone, replaced by a large sign taped to the mortuary door: 'GEORGE'S HOUSE OF FUN'. The Network's chief pathologist was inside, up to his elbows in someone. As Will stomped in wearing his gaudy rags, the little fat man looked up, his mouth hanging open, cheeks twitching, eyes wide.

'What the bloody hell do you look like?' George sniggered, but that caused nasty things to come out of his nose. 'Is the circus in town?'

'I need a favour.'

He dragged out a scabby hanky and blew. 'OK, I'll do you a favour – if you do me some balloon animals.' He snapped off one of his gloves, pinched the wrist hole together and blew, inflating the thing into a bloated hand-shape. 'Look, it's a stegosaurus!' The fingertips were smeared with blood.

'Very funny.' Will grabbed it off him and dropped it in the bin. 'I need you to run a complete med-scan on me.'

George stopped laughing. 'Me?' He frowned. 'Why not get the MO to do it?'

'Because I don't want the MO knowing I dress up like Bobo the Bastarding Clown on my days off. You know what an old gossip he is, I'll get bookings for children's parties!'

'Point taken. So why a med-scan?'

'Emily and I got taken down at Sherman House. Might have been a Zapper, but I'm not sure. We lost about two hours; I want to make sure there's no nerve damage.'

'Well. . . But all my equipment is designed to work on dead people. It'd be really cold. *And* uncomfortable.'

'I'll live with it.'

'That'll be a novelty, none of my other clients ever do.' He took off his bloodstained cutting apron and pulled on a fresh pair of gloves. 'Strip off and jump up on a slab and we'll get started. Mr Arthur here is in no hurry for his cranial evacuation.'

Will got undressed, then settled down to an excruciating half hour of cold probes and bright blue lights.

Norman bit his lip and suppressed a giggle. Kris was the most exciting thing that had ever happened to him. Just five minutes ago they'd been running some old biddie through the imager, and now here they were 'Going Down Below' as Kris liked to call it. Going. Down. Below!

He was going to marry her. Hadn't asked her yet, but she had to know he was thinking about it. Hop a shuttle to Dundee, get hitched in one of the big casinos by someone dressed as Elvis.

The elevator slid to a halt and they tumbled out into the utilitarian-green corridor.

No one about – as usual – so Kris punched the passcode she'd stolen from Dr Brooms into the storeroom keypad.

'Come on, then.' She pulled him inside. 'I'm a *very* sick woman. You'll probably have to perform a full, in-depth, thorough, hands-on, no-holds-barred, medical examination.' She punctuated each word with a small, delicate bite on the tip of his nose.

Norman groaned, his 'special thermometer' rising to the occasion. Kris danced away down the aisle, waving to him as she disappeared behind the stacks of disinfectant.

'Now then, Miss Barrons,' he said in his most commanding and respectable voice. 'As your physician it is important that you do exactly as I tell you. Do you understand?'

A giggle from around the corner, followed by, 'Oh *yes*, Doctor.'

Norman straightened his tie and advanced towards his patient. 'In order to examine you properly I'm going to have to ask you to remove all of your clothing.'

'Oh, Doctor! Are you *sure* that's necessary?'

He loved saying this bit: 'Trust me. I'm a doctor.'

'Well, you know best. . .' The sound of buttons popping open made his pulse quicken. A white labcoat flipped over the top of a stack of Germaway, closely followed by a set of blue scrubs. There was a pause, as delicious as it was predictable.

'Can't I even keep my bra and panties on?'

Panties. . . Norman gulped. It didn't matter how many times she said it, it always turned him on.

'Don't worry,' he said, trembling slightly, 'it's for your own good.'

A gloriously lacy piece of underwear joined the pile on top of the disinfectant, quickly followed by its skimpy associate.

'Excellent. Now if you'll just step out here, I'll begin the examination.' Norman straightened his tie again. He wasn't allowed to get undressed. Not yet.

A long, silky leg appeared from behind the crates, teasingly slow. She stepped out into the aisle, naked as the day she was born. Her long auburn hair hung over her shoulders, the ends just dancing above the tips of her gorgeous, pointy breasts. The smile she wore was wide and inviting, painted in dark-red lipstick that glistened in the artificial lights.

'Oh, *Doctor*. . .' She pouted. 'I feel terribly hot!'

'Then we'd better start by checking your temperature.'

She slunk towards him, biting softly on her bottom lip, dropped to her knees and unzipped his trousers.

* * *

139

The grey-haired man behind the table steepled his thin surgeon's fingers and said, 'Tell me about him.'

Ken Peitai waved his hand over the control console, and a double-sized human head appeared above the boardroom table. The face looked as if it hadn't slept properly in weeks, thick blue bags hanging beneath the bloodshot eyes, hair sticking up in random directions, a bloody lip.

'Assistant Network Section Director William Scott Hunter: 32.' Ken waved his hand again and the head slowly rotated. 'Youngest ever to hold the position. Four years at the Academy: graduated with a degree in Unauthorized Data Access. Came third in his class. Bit of gossip for ya: the guy who came first is doing thirty to life in the Tin for blowing up that deep-space research lab in Dundee. Some friends, huh?'

The old man reached into a top pocket, bringing out a test tube half-filled with thick green liquid. The glass rod danced across his fingers like a sliver of light. 'Go on.'

Ken tried not to stare. His employer never missed a beat – if he did, they'd both be dead in minutes.

'Four months before graduation he gets called up: Virtual Riots. He's on a scholarship so he's got no say in the matter. Works his way up to sergeant before his Dragonfly crashes into our very own Sherman House, thirty-nine floors up. William here rescues his buddy Private Brian Alexander from the cannibals and carries him out to safety.' Ken smiled. 'There was talk of making a big budget movie out of it, but it all fell through. When the VRs finish, the Network decides not to release his commission. Since then he's been their golden boy.'

Ken paused for a moment, letting the disembodied head turn in silence.

'Best predictions have him taking over the Network Directorship within five years, senior position at the Ministry for Defence and Justice in nine.'

The old man nodded, holding the test tube up like a conductor's baton.

'And yet he claims he was here because a crime scene had been *cleaned*?'

Ken stroked the control pad again and schematics flashed up on the wall screens – pulse, pupil dilation, skin conductivity, thermal images. 'All the monitors say he was telling the truth. I checked the recordings from apartment forty-seven one-twenty-two: he spent the whole time staring at the wallpaper.'

The old man set the test tube dancing again. 'What about his employer?'

'I threw a bit of weight around and had Governor Clark call her this afternoon: read her the riot act. Let her know she'd never get a Ministry seat if she pissed us off. By the time he was finished she was fallin' over herself to cooperate: said she was going to have a "quiet word" with our Mr Hunter. I listened to it; she tore a strip off his ass a mile wide.'

The old man smiled. 'Good. It would be a shame if we had to have Mr Hunter killed.' He sat back in his chair and popped the test tube back in his top pocket. 'Keep an eye on him, Ken. Make sure that doesn't become necessary.'

She has no idea how long she's been asleep: down here, in the bowels of the hospital, it's hard to measure time. The rhythm that's been such a major part of her life for the last six years is gone. There's no early morning alarm, followed by feeding, followed by getting into the truck, followed by getting out of the truck, followed by scrubbing and mopping and picking up litter. . . She doesn't miss the work, but her body misses the routine.

She rolls over in her nest, sits up beneath the low ceiling fan, and frowns. The storeroom is supposed to be unmanned, but she can hear giggling. Somewhere in the aisle below, two people are playing doctors and nurses.

Quietly she slides forward, peering over the wall of toilet paper. And there they are: a woman with perky breasts lying back on a big box of surgical gloves, her companion kneeling in front of her. She's got her hands behind her head, moaning and squirming as he licks and slurps between her legs. And then it happens. The woman opens her eyes and realizes she's being watched. She's pretty. Not beautiful – her face is too pointed for that – but she's definitely pretty. It is a shame she'll have to die.

A frown flits across her face – does she tell her partner there's someone staring at them, or does she close her eyes again and sink back into the moment?

She makes the wrong choice. 'Norman?'

Dr Westfield would have let her come before killing her. After all, she's not a monster. Not *all* the time.

'Norman!' The woman slaps her partner on the head and points up towards the nest of toilet paper.

'Ow, Jesus, Kris! What was that for?'

'Up there!' she says, pointing again. 'Someone's watching us.'

'What?' Norman jumps to his feet and stands there, erection bobbing about like a cheeky pink sausage. 'Jesus! Oh Jesus!' He scrambles back into his trousers. 'I knew we shouldn't have come down here! Oh Jesus, we're for it now!'

They've been playing doctors and nurses. Now it's time to play killer and victims.

Dr Westfield slips out of her nest and down to the store-room floor, spilling toilet rolls everywhere.

The naked woman narrows her eyes. 'What's a halfhead doing in here?'

'Why did I let you talk me into this?'

'*I* talked you into this?'

'It'll go on our permanent records!'

'Oh really?' Kris places one hand on her hip and pokes

him in the chest with the other. 'I didn't hear you complaining five minutes ago when I was sucking your dick!'

'I can't afford to lose this job!' He drags his shirt over his head and bends to grab his labcoat from the pile of discarded clothes. He doesn't see the blow that ends Kris's life, by the time he turns around she's lying on the concrete floor, a pool of deep, shiny red seeping out from the back of her head.

'Kris?' Norman steps forward. Stops. Swallows. 'Oh Jesus. . .'

He looks up at Dr Westfield, then down at the bone-hammer in her hand.

His face goes slack and he wets himself.

Calmly she steps over Kris's body and holds up the stainless steel mallet. Clumps of hair glisten on the striking surface and she pauses for a moment to sniff the delicious coppery smell of fresh blood.

'Oh Jesus, no. . .' Tears sparkle in his big, blue eyes. 'Please don't kill me! Please!' He turns to run, but his feet don't seem to be working. He stumbles into the stack of disinfectant and goes sprawling across the blood-slicked floor.

'No, no, Jesus no. . .' Norman scrabbles away on his hands and knees, making for the door. She follows him, staying just far enough back to make him think he has a chance. She lets him get as far as the keypad before raising the hammer in her hand.

'Three, six . . . three, six. . .' He sobs. 'Oh Jesus, what comes after six?'

He can't remember the code. He knows this is his only chance of getting out of here alive and he can't remember the code.

Something warm tingles up and down her body as she watches him struggle. She hasn't felt this aroused in six long, dark years.

She bounces the bone-hammer off the back of his head,

143

not hard enough to kill him, just hard enough to stun him for a while. Then she drags his flabby body into the depths of the supply room.

The man in the toilets doesn't count – she wasn't in her right mind when she butchered him. The Roadhugger crew were deaths of convenience and the halfheads in the back weren't alive in the first place, so *they* don't count. Kris had to die, because two people were too many to control with just a bone hammer, so she doesn't count either. But there will be plenty of time to enjoy this one. This one counts.

'It's going to take a while for the machinery to analyse the data.' George made horrible noises into his hanky. 'You want a cup of coffee?'

'Thought you'd never ask.' Will sat on the edge of the post-mortem table, shivering. It was *freezing* in here. George was wrapped up nice and snugly, but Will was as naked as the stiff on the next slab.

He hopped down to the floor. 'Got a terminal I could use for a minute? Want to check my email.'

George pointed him at the main console, then handed him a cup of coffee and a clean-ish looking labcoat. It wasn't much, but it was better than getting back into those gaudy tatters with blood all down the front.

Will rattled out a quick burst on the keyboard, then nodded at the little pathologist. 'Think your connection's down.'

'What? It was working fine a minute ago—'

Will slapped a hand over George's mouth and pointed at the screen.

`'I think I've been bugged.'`

George read it, curled his top lip, then stared at Will. 'What?'

Will poked at the keyboard with his free hand.

`'They're probably listening right now — I`
`want them to think the test results didn't`
`show anything suspicious. Understand?'`

George pulled Will's hand away and sniffed.

'You have *got* to be kidding me!'

Will made a grab for the fat little man's mouth again, but George ducked under his arm. 'Bloody Internal Services. They've probably cut through the cable again.' His podgy fingers rattled across the keyboard.

`'Might just be temporary paranoia caused`
`by neurological trauma, but if that's the`
`way you want to play it. . .?'`

Will nodded. That was *exactly* the way he wanted to play it.

Three cups of coffee later George returned with the test results, clutching a palmtop to his chest as if it was a hot water bottle. 'Other than a couple of torn ligaments and a bit of dehydration you're going to be fine.' He handed over the palmtop and Will read the message on the screen:

`'You were right. Two subdermal homing`
`beacons and three listening implants. What`
`do you want me to do?'`

Bloody Ken Peitai – rotten little bastard needed taking out and shot. Will tried to force a smile into his voice. 'Dehydration? Sounds like a good excuse for a pint after work.' He unfolded the little keyboard.

`'Kill the listening bugs, but leave the`
`homers in place for now. I don't want them`
`getting suspicious.'`

George emptied his nose into his handkerchief. 'A pint after work?' He took the pad back. 'Any chance of it being your round for a change?'

`'The listeners look like standard 397s.`
`Take them ten degrees above body tempera-`
`ture and they short out. A quick injection`
`and a sauna should do it. The homers are`
`more difficult, they're not like coffin`
`dodgers: they don't wait for an instruc-`

tion to transmit. They're broadcasting your location all the time. There's one just beneath the subcutaneous fat here.' He poked Will in the stomach. 'The other is under your left arm on the wall of the chest. The only way to get rid of them is surgery.'

Not just shot then – Ken Peitai needed castrating.

George blanked the palmtop's short-term memory. 'If you're still sore I can give you a quick injection of muscle relaxants. Then what you want is a sauna and a massage.'

'Good idea.'

Afterwards Will even bought the first round.

The mop slips and slides across the filthy floor – so much blood for one little man. She dunks the head into the bucket, turning the water a delicate shade of rosy pink. Mop, mop, mop. For some strange reason she enjoys the work. It relaxes her. Mopping, rinsing, mopping, rinsing. Empty the bucket, fill the bucket, add more detergent and then back to mopping and rinsing again.

The dark-red stains gradually lighten and then disappear, leaving shiny, wet concrete that smells of pine.

He was good. Wonderfully soft and yielding. And he screamed so beautifully. She already has her souvenirs floating in a plastic of formaldehyde. Such lovely eyes. . .

She'll have to make a little trip to the incinerator later – get rid of Kris and what's left of Norman – but first she pops the top off an ampoule and snaps her medicine into her neck. It's good to be back in control again.

And now that the urges are satisfied, she can prepare: she has people to visit. Labs to break into. Tissue samples to culture.

Revenge to take.

14

Darkness fills the lift shaft like a tumour, pressing against him on all sides, throbbing in time with the drums. Relentless, impenetrable, deafening. Will locks his arms around the rusty maintenance ladder and lets his forehead rest against one of the cool rungs.

What sort of fucking idiot thought this would be a good idea. . .

He tries to laugh, but it comes out as a strangled, painful noise.

Will grits his teeth, screws his eyes shut, and bounces his forehead off the ladder. Stupid. Thump. Fucking. Thump. Idiot.

How could he let them take Private Alexander?

He opens his eyes – even though there's no point: he can't see anything – and stares up into the darkness. Had to be somewhere near the ground floor by now, *surely*. All he has to do is lever open the lift doors on the next level he comes to, find the nearest window, tear off the boarding, smash the glass, jump out and run like Hell.

Freedom.

Get the fuck away from this hellhole asylum.

But he doesn't. Instead he takes a couple of deep breaths

and continues down the ladder. Feeling his way rung-by-rung deeper into the darkness. Towards the drums.

The going's a lot easier without Private Alexander's weight dragging at him. Now the only thing Will has to carry is the Whomper with the dead battery. It might be little more than a high-tech paperweight, but it'll still scare the shit out of anyone he points it at. Maybe that would be enough?

Sergeant William Hunter – second-class – can't just run for it, no matter how much he wants to. Not without Private Alexander. He's come through too much to leave him behind.

Besides, maybe the cannibals have eaten some of the fat bastard by now? At least that'd mean a little less weight for Will to carry.

'That's right,' he tells himself, the words swallowed by the never-ending pounding rhythm. 'Look on the bright side.'

The clock in the kitchen slowly ticked its way to half past nine. Will sat at the little table, nursing a cup of coffee and a foul mood. His head ached, his back hurt, and his eyes felt as if someone had rubbed broken glass into them. That's what he got for mixing nightmares with whisky.

He shuddered, then went back to staring out of the window.

He'd already called the office twice that morning and been told politely, but firmly, that he was on compassionate leave and Director Smith-Hamilton had ordered them not to bother him at home. Not even if he begged.

So he watched the rain hammer Glasgow into submission instead. A thick lid of bruise-coloured cloud lay over the city, hiding the sun, trapping everything in glooming twilight.

The view of Kelvingrove Park he and Janet had paid so much for was a miserable mix of grey and green, fifty-seven floors below, the paths marked by flickering sodiums – ribbons of weak, jaundiced light that bobbed and swayed in the downpour. The other tower blocks that lined the park like a thirty-storey picket fence of glass and foamcrete marked the end of the world, everything beyond that was lost in the storm.

A Hopper sizzled across the sky, engines whipping the rain into spirals and whorls. And then it was gone.

Will got up from the table and rested his forehead against the window. From up here it was easy to believe he was the only person in the whole world.

When the phone rang he jumped, and lukewarm coffee splashed down his front and onto the carpet. 'Buggering hell. . .' He thumped the cup down on the table and stabbed the 'pickup' button.

'What?'

'Will, is that you?' The Network pathologist's face filled the screen on the kitchen wall, then wrinkled into a pinched frown. The image jiggled about as he belted the screen at his end. *'Bloody thing's not working.'*

'It's OK, George.' Will settled back against the work surface. 'Camera at my end's broken.' Which was true: he'd fried the imaging circuits with a soldering iron. 'I can see you fine. What can I do for you?'

'You remember those stiffs I said had VR syndrome?'

Will nodded, before realizing the fat man couldn't see him. 'What about them?'

'I was wrong, that's what.' The pathologist scooted closer, until his round, pink face filled the space between the working surface and the spice rack. *'It's not VR, it just looks like it.'*

'It's not. . .? Then what the hell *is* it?'

'That's the scary bit. I found traces of a chemical in both brains. At first I thought it was just crap on the slides, but it's not.' He ran a handkerchief under his nose and sniffled. *'Whatever it is, I'm pretty sure it's what changed their brain chemistry to look like they had VR.'* He paused, then started hitting the screen again. *'Will? Will, you still there?'*

'I'm thinking. . .'

There was good old Ken Peitai looking after a building

149

full of people with VR syndrome: keeping them safe. Only they didn't *really* have VR, did they? Someone had pumped them full of chemicals to make them look and act as if they had. And Will's prime suspect for that was Ken Bloody Peitai.

And if Mr Peitai was quite happy infecting the occupants of Sherman House with fake VR, planting listening bugs and tracking beacons under the skin of a Network ASD, would he have any ethical problem with tapping that same ASD's phone?

'Damn it.' Should have thought of that earlier. 'Brian, I'm feeling a bit cooped up here, can you meet me in half an hour for coffee or something?'

The pathologist's face wrinkled. *'If. . . em. . . I suppose so. Where?'*

'Remember where we had that birthday bash for Emily last year?'

'Oh, the—'

'That's the place. See you there.' Will hit the 'disconnect' button before George could give anything away.

He grabbed his coat and took the elevator down to the ground floor. Normally he'd just keep going to the sub-basement, hop on the next shuttle, which is exactly why he didn't do it this time: avoiding the predictable. Anyway, he had half an hour. More than enough time to nip across Kelvingrove Park, cut down Sauchiehall Street and meet George.

Turning his collar up, Will stepped out into the deluge. He was wet through before he'd gone more than half a dozen paces.

Maybe this wasn't such a good idea after all. . .

The park was even gloomier than it looked from the kitchen window. Only half of the sodiums seemed to be working, the floating globes hissing and steaming in the pounding rain, like little dying suns. Their light a pale golden glow that shimmered back from the wet path.

No one in their right mind went walking through Kelvingrove Park when the weather was like this. They huddled indoors, plugged into whatever computer-generated rubbish Comlab were pumping through the public channels these days. Or they hopped onboard the shuttlenet, or the nearest bus. What they *didn't* do was squelch along in the rain, going from one patch of yellowed light to the next.

Will kept on walking.

The city sounds were swallowed up by the downpour. Only the flickering holoverts broke the silence – pseudo celebrities pimping unnecessary products whenever he came within range of the sensors. Some public-spirited individual had vandalized a lot of the emitters, leaving blissful stretches of commercial-free peace.

A half-naked woman crackled into existence as Will passed, asking him if it wasn't about time he treated himself to a new head of hair. *'. . .years younger! You. . .'* Fzzzzzzzzzz, pop, *'. . .fin time for that big date!'*

The holo followed him to the edge of the emitter's range, then she blew him a kiss and vanished back into nothingness.

He followed the winding pathways, not taking the most direct route, just drifting in the general direction of Sauchiehall Street. Plenty of time to spare, and it wasn't as if he could actually get any wetter. He heard Mrs New Hair fizz back into life as someone else daft enough to be out in this weather passed too close to the sensor.

Three days enforced compassionate leave – what did Director Smith-Hamilton think he was going to do with all that free time? Take up knitting? Put his feet up and let that nasty little bastard Ken. . .

There was a sound on the path behind him – footsteps, then the unmistakable *click* of a safety catch being disengaged.

. . .Peitai.

Shit.

He'd been set up. SHIT. How could he be so bloody stupid?

He'd thought he was being unpredictable, taking a walk across the park, instead he'd made a target of himself.

Will kept going, pretending he hadn't noticed anything, ears straining for some hint of how many were coming for him. But the rain did too good a job of drowning things out.

Trying to look casual, he checked his watch, using the motion to cover a quick glance back the way he'd come.

There were two of them. One was wearing a long, black cloat with the hood up, hiding his features, the other a thick maroon scarf and wetjacket.

There would be others – lurking in the dark somewhere up ahead. Waiting for him to get far enough into the park to make sure no one saw what was about to happen. Following the signal from the transmitters they'd buried under his skin.

Yeah, way to be unpredictable.

Four against one – if he was lucky – and the bastards would all be Black-Ops trained. Professional killers.

Will forced himself to slow down to a stroll. He still had Brian's Palm Thrummer, at least that was something. And it was fully charged, so the first one to try anything would get their face thrummed off. . . Then it'd be three to one, and they'd kill him.

Will faked a cough and triggered his throat-mike.

'Control this is Hunter,' – keeping his voice low – 'I need you to get a pickup team to Kelvingrove Park, *now*.'

'I'm sorry, sir, but the Director has asked us to make sure you're not bothered by Network business today.'

'I don't care what she says: get me a bloody pickup team!'

'No can do, sir. I have been specifically ordered not to patch through any more calls to or from you while you're on compassionate leave.'

'It's Lucy isn't it?' He paused under one of the sodiums, his eyes flicking across the trees and bushes. 'Listen up, Lucy, I'll be on terminal leave if you don't get someone here right now. I'm getting set up for a hit.'

'Bloody. . . Right: sorry, sir. All active Dragonflies are out on jobs. . .' There was a burst of staccato keystrokes. 'Looks like Delta Three Sixer is nearest. Connecting you now.'

He picked up the pace, trying to put a little distance between himself and the people behind him. It wouldn't be long now. They were already halfway across the park; Kelvin Way was getting closer with every stride and beyond that Sauchiehall Street. They couldn't make their move then; it would be too public.

Lieutenant Emily Brand's voice crackled in his ear, curt and businesslike. 'Talk to me.'

'Halfway across Kelvingrove Park, heading southwest towards Kelvin Way. Two on my tail, probably another two up ahead.'

'Is it a hit?'

'I'm kind of hoping it's a miss.' In his earpiece he could hear the Dragonfly's turbines changing pitch, followed by the roar of a chaingun. 'Where are you?'

'Firefight, corner of Scotland and Carnoustie.'

'Damn.' There was no way they could abandon a combat situation – not even for him. He was on his own.

'We'll get there as soon as we can. I'll—'

'Don't worry about it. Been nice working with you, Emily.'

'Will, don't you dare—'

He killed the link before she could say anything more. He needed to concentrate on what was happening *now*.

Something moved in the bushes up ahead and Will felt for the Palm Thrummer in his pocket, struggling to twist it open one-handed. The tines extending up his sleeve as he flicked the switch to warm the weapon up.

A voice cut through the rain: 'Oi, Grandad. Any last requests, like?'

This was it.

Will didn't turn around. The taunt *sounded* amateurish, but he knew what would happen if he took his eyes off the shadows on either side of the path: he'd never see the other pair sneaking up on him. Clever.

'Who the hell are you calling "Grandad"?' He set the Thrummer to full bore, maximum dispersion. 'Thought you were supposed to be professionals?'

The man laughed. 'Aye? Well how's this for fuckin' professional?' There was the metallic snickt of a power switch. Something big and clunky: modern weapons didn't make noises like that anymore. Maybe it was the same antique P-750 that punched a hole in Private Floyd's shoulder? Didn't matter how old it was, it would still be deadly.

'So what you going to do?' Will slowed to a halt, moving his weight forwards onto the balls of his feet. 'Talk me to death?'

'Am gonnae blow a great big hole in yer arse an bugger aff wi a' yer cards and yer housecode. Then me an some mates are gonnae nick everythin' ye've got. An if yer girl or boyfriend's aboot we'll shag the shit ootae them an fuck'em in the heid wi an ice-pick.'

Will frowned. He knew they were the bastards from the Sherman House 'project', and they knew he knew – otherwise they wouldn't be here. So why the play-acting? Maybe they were filming it? Maybe this was one of the few bits of the park where the CCTV actually worked? No one would go looking for a conspiracy, not when they had it all on tape. A mugging gone wrong. His own fault really, should have known better than to cut across the park. A tragic indictment of today's society. Small state funeral. No questions asked.

Ken Peitai gets away with murder.

Will spun around, bringing the Palm Thrummer up. The one in the cloat was there, but there was no sign of his friend.

'Cloat' wasn't holding a P-750, what he had was even older than that: about as long as the man's arm, all rust patches and visible wiring. It looked more likely to blow up in Cloat's face than do Will any damage . . . Probably a decoy: something to distract him.

A nuclear family strobed into life at the side of the path, the rain rippling through their holographic bodies as they launched into a song and dance about having pizza for tea. Someone must have set off the advertipod's sensor.

Jacket-and-Scarf came out of nowhere, swinging a thick metal rod. Will didn't have time to duck – it slammed into his forehead. Ringing in his ears, bright lights flashing inside his skull. He stumbled and fell, face thudding into the wet tarmac path.

Get up. GET – UP!

An animated dinosaur joined the musical number, telling everyone that on Monday nights kids ate for free.

Will forced himself to his knees, the world roaring in his ears as it span. Jacket-and-Scarf took a run up and kicked him in the ribs, hard enough to send him sprawling across the rain-sodden grass, through the blue triceratops and into the middle of the advert – mushrooms and peppers and chunks of cloned meat swirling all around him, making his skin flicker and glow.

Will coughed up blood. Something inside him was broken. Every breath was a sharp, stabbing pain.

This didn't make any sense. Why were they playing with him? Didn't they know how dangerous it was? Didn't they understand?

'Ha, lookit him: now he's a pizza topping! Whit a fukin' jessie!'

How could they not understand? Will tightened his grip on the Thrummer. It was time to explain it to them.

Jacket-and-Scarf dropped the metal rod and pulled a knife. It was huge, a proper kitchen job: six inches long and three inches wide, tapering to a point. Not the sort of blade he'd been expecting. It glittered as Jacket-and-Scarf stepped through the dancing children and grabbed Will by the throat. 'Time tae play "ah've nae face"!'

Up close Jacket-and-Scarf looked like someone's niece, hardly old enough to be out of school. She drew the knife back, held it there for a fraction of a second then lashed forward.

The Thrummer burred in Will's hand.

Jacket-and-Scarf didn't scream, she just sat back on her haunches, staring at the stump of her left arm – severed just below the elbow – pumping out bright-red, arterial mist into the rain.

A happy dinosaur skipped past.

'Fukin hell!' Cloat aimed his antique weapon at Will's head and pulled the trigger. It clunked.

'No' *again*!' He smacked his hand against the power unit, trying to get something more deadly than a dull whine out of it. 'Work, ye fuckin' piece o'shit!' Cloat backed off, slapping and swearing as Will struggled to his feet. His ribs ached, blood trickled down his face, gumming up his eyes. He rubbed a hand across them. Blinked. Staggered through a small holographic child.

Sparks leapt from the exposed wiring on Cloat's gun when they came into contact with the rain, and the whine changed to a throaty growl.

Suddenly it roared, digging a chunk out of the ground by his feet. Cloat screamed, scrabbled back a couple of steps. Then grinned at Will, eyes wide and bloodshot.

'Yer fuckin' dead! Ye hear me? Yer dead!' He yanked the barrel up and the whole thing went off like Hogmanay. One moment he was standing there and the next he was lumpy rain. Will covered his eyes and waited for the bigger bits to stop falling from the sky.

Jacket-and-Scarf was shivering, clutching her left arm, staring at where it came to an abrupt end.

The pizza song and dance routine reached its big finale, and then it was gone – leaving them in darkness and silence.

'You've got two choices,' said Will, spitting out a mouthful of blood. 'Either you tell me who sent you and what your orders were, or I kill you.'

She looked up at him, face waxy, lips going purple. 'I. . . I. . . My arm! A've nae arm!'

Will planted his foot on her chest and shoved till she was flat on her back. 'Let's try it again!' He was shouting now, the adrenaline burn making his voice tremble. 'You and your friend the smear, were sent here to kill me. Who was it? Who sent you? It was Peitai, wasn't it?'

'Ma arm!'

Will dropped to his knees, straddling her chest, and pressed the Thrummer against her pale cheek.

'It'll be your head next, understand?' He slapped her hard across the face. 'Understand?' Another slap. 'WHO'S HE WORKING FOR?'

'We only wanted some cash! A couple o' cards, some credits! Just enough to get oan wi! We wouldnae've touched yer girl-friend! We wouldnae!' She sobbed. 'Please. . . Ah that stuff Malk wis sayin wis just tae scare ye. We wouldnae've done it. We just wanted a bitta dosh fer H! Ye didnae haf tae take ma arm!'

'I'll take your whole head you snivelling piece of—'

There was a roar above him and a sudden downdraft of hot air. All around them the park jumped into eye-searing focus as landing lights flooded the area, the downpour whipped into a hurricane by the Dragonfly's engines.

A voice buzzed in Will's earpiece, crackling with static.

This is Echo Two Seven, we show landing zone secure.

The cavalry had arrived.

Will looked down at Jacket-and-Scarf. Two more minutes and he'd have got the truth out of her, even if he'd had to take every single one of her bloody limbs off. She wouldn't admit anything now there were witnesses. Even if she made it as far as the Tin, Peitai would find a way to get her out. That or silence her for good.

Will placed the Thrummer against her temple. Maybe he'd save them the trouble.

The holographic advert flickered back to the start: Mum, Dad, and two-point-four children launching into their song and dance again. *'If you're hungry as can be – need to feed your family. . .'*

Someone tapped Will on the shoulder. 'It's OK, sir, we've got her now.'

He didn't have to look to know it was one of the Dragonfly's pickup team. They wouldn't like him blowing Jacket-and-Scarf's head off like this, but they wouldn't say anything about it. They'd close ranks. Delete the footage from the gunship and their helmet-cams. He'd been one of them, riding the wire for almost three and a half years before making the grade as a Network Agent and they knew it. The team protected its own.

A new voice: 'Mr Hunter? Sir?' Will caught a flash of neon-pink trouser leg.

Fuck.

'Sir, are you OK?'

Too late.

He couldn't execute the one-armed bandit while DS Cameron was watching. She wouldn't understand. She still believed in the rules.

'You can let go of her now, sir.'

He closed his eyes and powered down the Thrummer.

'You're bleeding. . .' She helped him to his feet, holding him upright while he hissed breath through his clenched teeth. Definitely a broken rib. Probably two.

'I've had better days.' Will watched someone spray Jacket-and-Scarf's stump with skinpaint. She'd go to hospital overnight for observation; Ken Peitai would make all the charges disappear; it only took a week to grow a new arm; couple of hours in surgery; and she'd be back on the streets.

Will should have killed her when he had the chance.

'Looks like you put up quite a struggle.' Jo pointed at the chunks of Cloat littering the sodden grass.

The dinosaur reappeared, singing, *'On Monday bring your famil-eee, cos kids under twelve eat for free!'* Will pointed his Thrummer at the advertipod and reduced the emitters to dust.

Jo stared at him. 'Not a big fan of pizza then?'

'The dead one had an old S-Nine-Eighty. Looked like it fell off the back of a museum. Blew up in his hands.'

'Long black cloat?'

Will nodded.

'That'll've been Malcolm Albany. He and Samantha here used to work the Green, till Nicholson and Richmond offered to pop their heads in a cruncher.'

'You *know* these people?'

She sighed. 'Know them? I've arrested Samantha McLean more times than I can count. Prostitution, assault, burglary . . . you name it. Been in and out of the Tin since she was six. She's screwed this time – attempted murder. Poor cow's in for a halfheading.'

Muggers. Not Peitai after all.

Will ran a hand over his face. It came away sticky, covered in red. He snorted. Smiled. Started to laugh.

'How hard did they hit you?' Jo stepped in close, peering into his eyes. 'How many fingers am I holding up?'

He grabbed her cheeks with his bloody hands and kissed her full on the lips. 'You,' he said, 'have restored my faith in human nature.'

'I . . . em. . .' She stepped back, mouth working up and down in time with her eyebrows, a blush rushing up her neck. 'I don't understand, sir.'

Will limped towards the waiting Dragonfly. 'Sometimes there *is* no conspiracy. Sometimes people are just basically evil.'

'But why did you—'

The rain-swept sky exploded as a second Dragonfly swung

in over the scene with all weapons pods opened. Deep, dark scars wound their way back along the gunship, smoke trailing from the port engine.

'Hunter, this is Brand, do you copy, over?' Emily. She wouldn't know if he was alive or the filling in a body-bag buttie.

'Panic's over, Lieutenant.' He turned and beamed at Jo and her ridiculously colourful suit. 'DS Cameron saved the day. They were just muggers. Can you believe it? Muggers.' He started to laugh again and didn't stop until they'd snapped a blocker into his neck.

The hospital's busy in the run-up to lunch: lots of things going on, people trying to clear their desks before noon. Buzzzzzzzzzzzzzzzzzzzzing about the hospital like busy, busy bees. No one paying attention to anyone else. Always the best time to get things done.

She takes a good look around before hauling the trolley out of the storeroom and into the corridor. Body-bags would be too suspicious – they don't let halfheads push dead people around – but general-purpose refuse sacks are another matter entirely. You just have to cut the dearly departed into smaller bits.

She pulls the door shut behind her and trundles along the corridor to the incinerator. It's been six years since she last needed it: Gordon Waugh. She'd kept the furnace door open that time, turning the heat down so it wouldn't instantly reduce his mangled corpse to ash . . . smiling as Gordon hissed and crackled in the flames. That night she'd gone out and had a huge plate of roast pork.

But she doesn't have time for fun now. So she just throws the eight heavy refuse sacks into the furnace and cranks the heat up full. Soon there is nothing left. Bye-bye Kris, bye-bye Norman.

Dr Westfield waves, then abandons the trolley in favour of a mop and wheely-bucket, pushing it in front of her like a bag lady pushing a shopping cart full of empty plastics. Focusing on the soapy water as if it's the only thing in the world.

The service elevator is crowded – just as she expected it to be. Four doctors, three interns, and a nurse. They move over, just enough to let her in without actually acknowledging her existence. Even though two of them used to work with her every day. . . Back when she was a human being.

Dr Stephen Bexley – the one with the salt and pepper beard, reading a patient's chart on his datapad – even went to the trial. He wept as she took the court through the list of names, telling them exactly what she'd done to their bodies, both before and *after* death. It was the post-mortem activities that seemed to upset Stephen most of all. Once upon a time he'd claimed to be her friend. Now he doesn't even recognize her.

Poor Stephen.

His face is much the same as it's always been: leathery, hook-nosed and bearded. He's got a lot more hair than he had at the trial – cloneplants, the saviour of balding men. Did he get one of his minions to perform the procedure, or do it himself? Always the perfectionist. Always the huge ego.

The floors pass and one by one the others leave until she is alone in the lift with Stephen. Oblivious to her presence he works one of his delicate surgeon's fingers up that huge, hooked nose. Round and round and round he digs, before dragging something out and peering at it.

She closes her eyes and does not watch him eating what he has found.

The lift shudders to a halt and she waits for him to leave the car first – just like a good halfhead should – then follows him out into a cluttered reception area. The walls are peppered with inspirational posters, pictures of happy, smiling children, thank you letters, news clips and awards. The cloneplant ward of Glasgow Royal is one of the best in the world. And Dr Stephen Bexley is it's grand vizier.

The security guard checks Stephen's ID, running it through the scanner as if he were a potential terrorist instead of the head of the department. Only when the reader plinks 'ALL CLEAR' does the guard smile and ask him how his wife and children are.

He has a family now. A new head of hair, a pregnant wife, and children. How sweet. That makes things a lot easier.

Stephen shares a few pleasantries with the guard, then walks through the doors. No one bothers to check the ID of the halfhead with the mop and the bucket, she just shuffles past into the depths of the cloneplant lab.

It's bigger than she remembers it. The equipment in here is all new to her, but she's a fast learner. She mops the floor, up and down between the rows of work benches, nice and slow, watching what the technicians are doing. The first stage seems easy enough: place patient samples in a sequencer to fabricate stem cells. The next bit is harder: working out how to direct the growth. There will probably be stored procedures in the system to get the results she wants, but she needs enough time to find the proper commands. So she keeps on mopping until the lunch bell goes and they all bustle off to sample the canteen's deep-fried delights.

They'll be back in forty minutes: she has to work fast.

Getting the sample for the sequencer isn't easy. She needs good, healthy tissue. There's no way she can scrape cells out of her cheek, or her oesophagus; so she peels a strip, five millimetres wide and ten millimetres long, from her abdomen with a fresh blade. It's not a deep wound, but it stings and bleeds more than she expects. She presses a handful of sterile wadding over the wound, stopping the worst of it. A small sacrifice to get her real face back. To be *herself* again.

Should have taken a tin of skinpaint from the storeroom,

but she never expected to get this far so soon. Ah well: *carpe diem*.

With her free hand she slips the rectangle of flesh into a fresh crucible – a circle of complicated plastics and electrics sealing off a bag of growth medium. She snaps the top back on, slides the whole thing into the sequencer and sets it in motion. From here on everything is automated; all she has to do is tell the system what she wants the cells to grow into.

Which is more complicated than it looked.

She's still searching for the right commands when people start returning from lunch: she can hear them chatting in the reception area, dragging their heels, not wanting to get back to work too quickly.

The sequence has to be in here somewhere. . .

Her left leg starts to tremble.

Where the hell is the damn sequence?

Bees and broken glass.

The door clicks open and the staff drift in, heading for their work areas.

Time to give up. Come back later. Don't take any risks.

She tabs through the command list as quickly as she can, speed reading from one file to the next.

Someone sits down at the next bench along, talking into his finger: 'Yeah, no, a pint sounds great. . .'

A sequence flickers up on her monitor, every last cell division worked out in perfect detail. It's a lot more tissue than she needs, but she doesn't have time to search for something else.

'Hey, what's that damn halfheid doin' tae ma desk?' The voice is rough, coming from the other end of the room.

The man sitting at the next bench looks up at the noise and then glances at her.

It's just enough time to peel the wadding off her bleeding stomach and pretend to polish the desktop with it.

'Cleaning,' says the man. 'What'd you think it was doing, Rob, reading your pornmail?'

They laugh, and Rob blushes. 'Shut up.'

She stabs the button, downloading the instruction sequence into the crucible.

'What's all the hilarity about?' Dr Stephen Bexley stands at the front of the room, running a hand through his new hair.

'Rob thinks the halfhead's reading his dirty emails.' More laughter.

'No ah don't!'

'Children, children.' Stephen smiles at them, always the self-appointed father figure. 'Play nice.'

The workbench is covered with thin streaks of blood where she's been rubbing it with the wadding. She dips the cloth into the bucket at her feet and wipes it clean before anyone can see.

The crucible drops down the feeder rack and slips off to the incubation room. The first cell division will already be under way, expanding and growing at an accelerated rate.

Now all she has to do is wait.

15

'Feelin' any better?' Special Agent Brian Alexander plonked himself down on the end of Will's hospital bed. The little private room was comfortable enough, if you liked machines that pinged and gurgled at random intervals. 'You look like a mouldy jobbie, by the way.'

'What took you so long?' Will swung his legs out of bed, then stood, his hospital-issue smock flapping open at the back. The left side of his face felt as if it had been stretched over a head three times too big for it. And every breath was like being stabbed in the chest.

'Last time I do you a favour.' Brian sniffed. 'We knew they took all your clothes in as evidence, so me an' Jo went *shoppin'*!'

Will stared at him. 'Oh, no. Tell me you didn't let. . .' He ground to a halt – DS Cameron was standing in the doorway. She was still wearing the same florescent pink, triple breasted suit she'd had on in the park that morning. Given her taste in work clothes, and the dirty big grin on Brian's face, Will got the nasty feeling they'd bought something that would make him look like a complete idiot. He forced a smile. 'I mean. . . Thanks.'

It was the thought that counted. And besides, whatever

fashion-disaster they'd bought, he'd only have to wear it from here back to the apartment. Twenty minutes, half an hour tops.

Will reached round and clasped the gown closed at the back, making sure DS Cameron didn't get subjected to an eyeful of buttock. 'Honestly, you shouldn't have gone to all that trouble.' They *really* shouldn't have: they could have just gone past the flat and picked him up a change of clothes – and Brian knew it – but that wouldn't have been as much fun as buying something hideous.

'Oh no,' Brian's smile grew wider. 'It was a pleasure! Wasn't it, Jo?'

DS Cameron handed Will a bulky bag in luminous yellow with something trendy written on the side. 'Hope they fit.' Was she blushing?

Suddenly Will felt very uncomfortable. 'Em . . . thank you.'

Brian let the silence drag on for a bit, before taking DS Cameron by the arm and leading her out into the corridor so Will could 'get some privacy'. Wink, wink. The bastard was loving every minute of this.

Will dumped the bag down on the bed and opened it gingerly. There was no sudden flash of electric green, or yellow and blue stripes, or any of the other fashion eye-burners that were all the rage on Sauchiehall Street. Not believing his luck he tipped the contents out onto the scratchy sheets and began to dress.

Outside the room, Jo shifted from foot to foot. Brian nudged her. 'You needin' a pee?'

'Don't be daft.' She scowled and stopped fidgeting. Then started again. 'Think he'll like them?'

'Ooh, I get it,' Brian's eyes sparkled as he started to sing: 'Jo and Wi-ill, up a tree, H.U.M.P—'

Smart arse.

She smacked him one.

'Ow! Better watch that DS Cameron – don't think Will likes rough girls.'

Jo turned and leant against the wall. 'Tell me about him.'

'OK. . .' Brian held up his hands, pulling back the cuffs of his jacket. A ragged line ran all the way around the left wrist. The arm looked normal enough, but the hand didn't – it was smaller than the right, and the skin was a strange pink colour: as if he'd borrowed it from someone shorter who didn't get a lot of sun. Up till now she hadn't even noticed there was anything wrong with it. So much for impressing everyone with her Bluecoat powers of observation.

He held both hands side by side. It just emphasized the difference. 'Eleven years ago we were workin' in one of them Rapid Response Teams, doin' our best to stop them riotin' bamheids from killin' each other. Thirteen Service personnel got grabbed at Dexter Heights: poor sods were only there to pick up the dead. So we go in after them.' He leant against the wall next to her. 'There's me: out on a wire with the rest of the pickup team, shootin' back at a bunch of wee radges with Shrikes and Whompers; no way in hell we're gonnae rescue the hostages, the buggers have got way too much fire-power. So we do a runner: hard D, me and the guys all danglin' about underneath the Dragonfly when it jumps into the air. Only we don't make it.'

The smile slid from his face. 'Somethin' big hits the ship and we do a nosedive right into Sherman Heights. Bang!' He slammed his hand with the funny borrowed fingers against the plasticboard.

Jo tried not to flinch.

'Everyone on a wire gets flattened against the wall, an' this is like thirty-nine storeys off the deck, mind. Will's the only one still movin'. Pilot and Copilot's dead, so's the rest of the pickup team: squashed like fuckin' bugs on the side of a dirty big buildin'.'

He pursed his lips for a moment. Frowned. 'I'm no' a

167

hunnerd percent sure what happens next cos I'm all busted up and out ma face on blockers, but somehow Will hauls me back into the drop bay. Then he carries me on his back for about two days, climbin' down the stairs an' lift shafts: tryin' to stay away from the locals. You know, proper hero stuff.' Brian dropped his voice to a whisper. 'They wis goin' tae make a big film out of it, but the Ministry called copyright on everything involving government personnel. Thievin' bastards. Anyway. . .'

Brian straightened up and showed her his hand again. 'At some point in the proceedin's Will gets jumped by the natives, and while he's fightin' them off, some noseless wee turd carries my poor, unconscious body away intae the depths of the buildin'. I come round for like about five minutes, an' it's real hazy: I'm in this parkin' lot on one of the sublevels, and some bugger's chewin' on a severed hand. . . Takes me a while to realize it's mine.'

He stared at that strange, pink-skinned palm. 'So I scream. Will appears, chaos ensues, an' next thing I know we're out – him runnin' hell for leather, me slung over his shoulder like a sack of tatties. He'd never set eyes on me before the crash, could'a left me to die on the wire, or in the basement, or half a million other times, but he didn't. Came back for me, even though I wis a total fuckin' stranger. You want to know what he's like? *That's* what he's like.'

Jo looked at the hand again. 'Not a very good cloneplant, is it?'

Brian shrugged. 'Had it done eleven years ago; they've got a wee bitty better at it since then. James keeps tellin' me to get a new one grown, get this one replaced. But I'm buggered if I'm gonnae sit back and let anyone cut ma hand off again.'

Jo had to admit he had a point.

Will examined himself in the mirror above the sink in the tiny en-suite shower room. Brian had been right – he looked bloody awful. The left side of his face was swollen and tender, covered in dark-purple bruises. An off-colour patch sat on his temple – just above the eyebrow – where Jacket-and-Scarf had tried to cave his head in with that metal rod. The surgical team had filled the wound with skinpaint, but it would take a while to blend in.

The rest of him looked . . . almost stylish. Black trousers, grey T-shirt, and a collarless thing in stone-blue. The unders weren't covered in little hearts or bunny rabbits. They'd even thrown in a jacket that must have cost someone a small fortune.

Will limped out into the corridor with a small, 'Tada.'

'You still look like shite,' said Brian, head on one side, 'but at least now you look like well-dressed shite.'

'This lot can't have been cheap.'

'Aye, well remember that when you're signin' my expenses this month.'

DS Cameron still hadn't said anything. Maybe he'd offended her by being an ungrateful bastard when she'd turned up with the clothes. Will cleared his throat. 'Thank you . . . both of you. These are really great.'

She smiled, obviously pleased. 'It's OK.'

Brian tugged at the jacket's lapels, lining them up. 'I wanted to get you somethin' a bit more *vivid*, but she wasn't having any of it.'

Jo shrugged. 'Just thought these would suit you better.'

She looked at the floor, twiddling with her hair while Will tried to think of something to say.

'So. . .' Brian grinned. 'Are we goin' or no'?'

They'd almost made it as far as the escalator when a reedy voice piped up behind them, 'And where do you think *you're* going, Mr Hunter?'

'Home?'

A short woman with greying hair and glasses marched in front of them, blocking the lifts. Dr Euphemia Morrison – if you worked for the Network, and you went into combat, sooner or later you ended up in her care. 'You *are* kidding, right? You nearly died this morning, remember?'

'Er. . . Pressing business. Can't be helped.'

'You just had major surgery.'

'*Really* pressing business.'

'Apart from anything else, you've got a concussion, you need constant supervision.' Dr Morrison pointed back towards the private room. 'Get your arse back in that bed.'

No one moved.

She stared at him, but Will didn't flinch.

'Fine. . .' She said at last. 'But if you drop dead in the middle of the night, don't come crying to me.' She turned on Brian. 'Keep an eye on him this time, for God's sake. If I have to glue his ribs back together again there'll be no bloody bone left.'

Dr Morrison poked Will gently in the stomach. 'Your insides are one big gristly ball of scar tissue. Next time I'm cutting all that gubbins out and replacing it, whether you like it or not.' She handed Will a packet of blockers, the finger-length plastic tubes fluorescing slightly under the UV lights. 'No more than one an hour. And I want to see you back here at four thirty on Sunday for a follow-up.' She poked him again. 'Don't make me come and get you. And try to stay off your bum for a while, keep those bruises moving or you'll seize up.'

'Yes, Mum.' He planted a small kiss on her cheek.

'Don't you "yes mum" me, you cheeky wee bugger. Go on: out. I have sick people to attend to.'

Will hobbled after Jo and Brian to the lifts, riding down in silence, till Jo finally asked, 'So your mother's a doctor?'

'What?'

The doors pinged open and they stepped out into the hospital's busy lobby.

'The doctor: I didn't know she was your mum.'

'She's not. Doc Morrison is like that with pretty much everyone. Even more of an old mother hen than Brian is.'

Brian didn't rise to it, just kept barging a path to the front doors.

Will limped along behind him. 'So what's the plan?'

'We're givin' you a lift home, then me and Jo gotta crash a birthday party full of dead folk.'

'Why don't I just tag along with you?'

'No chance. The Tiny Terror would have my balls: you're on compassionate leave till Monday.'

'Look, you heard what the Doc said – I've got a concussion. Someone needs to keep an eye on me just in case something—'

'Nice try. You're goin' home.' The automatic doors swished open.

Outside, it was still chucking it down.

People dashed in from the deluge, collars up, plastics down, looking miserable. The only ones not rushing about trying to get into the dry were the halfheads – they just went about their daily business, emptying the bins, polishing the plaques, mopping up the dirty water tramped in from the streets – as if today were a day no different from any other.

They didn't mind the wet, because they couldn't feel it. Some would get flu, some would get pneumonia, some would probably even die and no one would care. Not even them.

Brian hurried out into the rain, sploshing through the puddles towards the car park, while Jo and Will huddled under the hospital's portico – watching the people go by.

Neither of them saw the halfhead shivering its way through the deluge towards them, pushing a wheely-bucket piled high with refuse sacks. They didn't see it, but it saw them.

* * *

She recognizes Him, even with all the bruising and casual clothes. He's lost some hair and gained some pounds, but it's Him all right: The Man In The Dark-Blue Suit. The man who did this to her.

The BASTARD who did this.

He's dead. He's still walking about but he's dead. Right now. Dead.

There's a scalpel in her pocket – not as delicate as a surgeon's wand, but it'll open him up just as well. Spill his guts all over the concrete floor. Blood like a fountain. Screams. Begging to be put out of his misery as she jams her hand into his hollow stomach cavity and reaches for his heart. . .

Everything is bees and broken glass.

She steps forward, the scalpel's handle cold against her palm.

And then stops. Too quick. It'll be over too quick. The Man In The Dark-Blue Suit deserves to suffer.

We begin by splitting the lower jaw.

Deep breaths. Calm. Deep fucking breaths.

A battered people carrier pulls up outside the hospital entrance – The Man In The Dark-Blue Suit limps over and opens the back door, clambering inside, followed by some woman dressed in garish pink.

They drive off, sending up a wall of spray.

She stands there, watching as the car disappears into the waterlogged traffic.

It takes a lot of effort to calm her breathing. Slowly the buzzing in her head subsides and she can think clearly again. Focus. Not focusing leads to mistakes. Mistakes lead to getting caught.

It has taken her four hours to traverse the city, depositing her bargaining chip in a safe place. Safe for her, but not so safe for her old friend Dr Stephen Bexley.

She has dozens of apartments dotted all over the city, all neat and clean, safe and tidy. The people who used to live

172

in them are all dead. Have been for years. She didn't list their names in court, kept them secret.

During the trial, the NewsNet channels had gloried in the size of her body count, gleeful indignation as the roll of the dead grew and grew. But to her it was little different from reciting a shopping list. No one cries when the fleshworks harvest their great vats of cloned meat do they? No, they eat their CheatMeat burgers and go on with their happy, dead, little lives.

It's not her fault she has more refined tastes.

She stalks the corridors beneath the hospital buildings. Pushing her wheely-bucket and its special cargo.

All that fuss about a few hundred dead bodies. Ridiculous. Imagine the outcry if they'd discovered the *real* number of victims was even higher. But they didn't. And best of all, they never found out about 'Harbinger'. If they had they'd have rounded up all her special children before they had a chance to blossom and grow. And that would have been a *terrible* waste.

Back in the storeroom she finds a box of datapads and spends a happy fifteen minutes programming one. Then, when everything is perfect, she goes visiting.

Dr Stephen Bexley's office is on twenty-nine, one level down from the incubators where her cells are multiplying and dividing. It takes all the control she has not to skip out into the corridor when the lift doors open on the right floor.

The people she passes up here don't give her a second glance. They don't notice that her wheely-bucket doesn't contain the usual load of foamy water, just a bin-bag and a brand new datapad. They don't wonder why, as the floors are all carpeted on this floor, a halfhead would need a mop in the first place. Because they don't see her at all.

She pushes into Stephen's office, pulling the bucket and mop behind her.

He's alone. Good.

Stephen looks up as the door clunks shut. His eyes slide across her, then return to the papers on his desk. Just another halfhead. Nothing to worry about.

Mistake.

'So what's the story then?' Will climbed out of the people carrier's warm interior and into the cold rain.

'The story,' said Brian, locking the car, 'is that you're no' here. Old Frosty Knickers has it in for me as it is. She finds out I let you muscle in on my investigation when you're supposed to be on compassionate leave, I'll be up to my ears in shite. So if anyone asks, you're a figment of their imagination. Understand?'

Will popped a quick salute. He was feeling a lot better than he had when they'd left the hospital, mostly due to the blocker he'd snapped into his neck on the way over. Blockers *always* made the world a happier place. And given that he'd almost executed a mugger this morning, it'd probably do him good to get out of the house for a while. Stop obsessing about Ken Bloody Peitai and what was going on at Sherman House. Get a bit of perspective.

He looked up at the building Brian had parked in front of.

Montieth Row was an expensive address, commanding views of Glasgow Green that cost more money than Will would ever see in his life. The old red sandstone buildings were long gone, replaced by a gothic complex of terraced granite and pewtered glass. Buttresses leaped over the pavement into the road, creating parking bays big enough to hold a dozen private Hoppers.

'The Kilgours lived at number forty-seven,' said DS Cameron as they climbed the front stairs. 'Six victims: two males, four females. Houseman found them sixty-seven minutes ago. Preliminary team ID'd the bodies and called for SOC support.'

Which explained the rumbling vibration Will could feel

174

through the soles of his shoes as he pushed through the double doors.

'Victims: John Kilgour and his wife Jocelyn. Agness Kilgour, her partner Ian Preston, and their daughter Trent – she was four. Mrs Helen Kilgour, John and Agness's mother.'

'What happened to Mr Kilgour senior?'

The lift doors opened on a little wonderland of polished wood and leather upholstery. Brian pushed the button for the eleventh floor. 'Hopper crash nine years ago. Died before they could get him into surgery. The mother sues the arse off the ambulance firm and the other driver, takes the compensation and makes a killin' on the stock market. That's how come they live here. Nuevo riche.'

'Any other relatives?'

'Only the one.' Brian pulled out a datapad and fiddled with it. 'Jillian Kilgour, John and Jocelyn's daughter. This wis meant to be her eighteenth birthday party. I've got a team out lookin' for her, but. . .' He shrugged.

They flashed their ID badges at a trooper Will didn't recognize, ducked under the crime scene tape, and into the huge apartment. The sonics were in full swing through in the lounge, making conversation impossible, so they picked their way through the other rooms, not touching anything.

The Kilgour home was palatial – just what you'd expect in this part of town. The walls were a warm shade of cream, punctuated with tasteful abstract art in minimalist frames. Expensive furniture in deep red velvet and burnished wood. The carpet was speckled with tiny clots of blood, hard and shiny against the cream pile.

A flicker of hot green light spilled out into the hall, and the gurgling roar of the subsonics shuddered and died. Then came the swearing, followed by a couple of cloinging kicks of boot on metal. It sounded like Private Beaton.

The lounge was huge, broken up into three different areas:

eating, relaxing, and entertainment. The sonic booms and readers were arranged around a large dining table, and so were the Kilgours. They all sat bolt-upright, brightly coloured party hats perched on their heads, faces pulled into freakish smiles. The carpet beneath their chairs was stained, and there was the distinct aroma of old urine and faeces. Will didn't blame them.

A roasted joint of CheatMeat took pride of place in the middle of the table – one of the expensive ones, cloned around ceramic bones, not just a slab of flesh from the vats – the surface dried out and beginning to go mouldy. Wrinkly green peas and leathery-looking potatoes slumped in blue serving dishes. The gravy looked like burnt shoe polish.

Brian sagged. 'What a waste of good food!'

Private Beaton looked up from fiddling with one of the scanners. 'Afternoon, Brian. Wondered when you'd drag your. . .' She shot to attention when she saw Will and snapped off a salute. 'Sir! I didn't know you were there. Aren't you supposed to be—'

'Apparently I'm a figment of your imagination.' Will took a look around. This one room was bigger than his whole flat. 'Having fun?'

'Bloody SOC duty again. The Lieutenant says I have a talent for the kicking and the swearing, sir. Says it would be a sin to let that go to waste.'

Beaton seemed to have got over her ordeal at Sherman House. It was strange to think that Private Stein had died only four days ago. A lot could happen in four days.

'Have a look at this,' said Brian, peering at Mrs Kilgour senior's head, 'be right up your street.'

The back of the old woman's skull was missing, the edges of the wound soft and rounded, no signs of cracking or impact. Impressive.

Will snapped on a pair of gloves and ran a finger around the opening. 'See how all the arteries are sealed off? This guy's

176

a whiz with a Thrummer.' He picked a butter knife off the table and inserted it into the hole. 'Must have taken it real slow and gentle, there's not even any brain matter on the back of the seat.' Will tilted the knife until it clanked on the roof of the skull. 'Whole head's completely empty. All the guests the same?'

Brian wrinkled his nose. 'Far as I can tell. No' a brain cell between the lot of them.'

Beaton gave the scanner's casing one last kick and it roared back into life, rattling the cut-crystal on the table.

'Hallelujah!' She turned and shouted over the noise, 'Anyone still in here in five seconds will forever remain part of the crime scene.'

'Shite!' Brian grabbed Will by the arm and dragged him out into the corridor. 'You're no' supposed to be here!'

Private Beaton squeezed out into the hall with them. Standing in the middle of a dark brown bloodstain she stuffed both hands in her pockets and leaned back against the door.

'Funny thing is,' she yelled, 'you kinda get used to the noise after a bit. Did you meet the newbie?' she pointed out through the hallway towards the front door.

'Have you done the other rooms yet?'

'Did them first. You can touch anything you like. . .' She looked down at the butter knife in Will's hand, closed her eyes, and gritted her teeth. 'Where did you get the cutlery from, sir?'

'Oops.' Will handed it over.

Private Beaton swore, stomped back into the dining room, switched off the scanner, reset all the booms and put the knife back where it'd been before he'd interfered with the crime scene.

Brian shook his head as the array started up again. 'You're a disaster, Will. A total disaster.'

He had a point. Will sloped off before Beaton got back and

scowled at him some more. He found DS Cameron on her hands and knees in one of the flat's three bathrooms, backside stuck in the air as she peered round the back of the sink. It was far from being an unpleasant view. Will opened his mouth to say so, then shut it again. That was the trouble with blockers, they did a great job of killing pain *and* common sense.

He cleared his throat and tried not to stare at her bum. 'Found something?'

She glanced up at him. 'Tiny specks of blood. Looks like our killer was a clean freak. Outside of the sink's been given a going over with some sort of detergent. Probably washed his hands and then cleaned the place up to remove any prints.'

Will dropped to his knees to take a look. Jo was right, no bloody hand prints, just minute flecks of scarlet on the skirting board. There wasn't so much as a streak on the sink itself. And it smelled lemony fresh too.

He sat back on his haunches, and when Jo did the same, their faces were only a breath apart. . . They stayed like that for a moment, neither one of them saying a word.

It was Brian who finally broke the silence, peering in from the bathroom doorway. 'All clear. Beaton says the scannin's done.'

Will hadn't even noticed the noise had stopped.

'Says if youse want tae poke about in the lounge you'd better do it now, before it gets bagged and tagged.'

'Yes.' Will clambered to his feet, awkward and formal.

'Right.' Jo jumped up beside him.

Brian raised an eyebrow, a smile blossoming on his podgy face. 'I can come back later if you like.'

'No. No need.' DS Cameron brushed some invisible lint from the front of her bright-pink trousers.

'OK. . .' Brian stepped back, leaving the doorway clear. Then winked. 'I'll be givin' Beaton a hand if you need me.'

'No, we'll just . . . em. . .' She pointed.

Will said, 'Good idea.'

Private Beaton and Agent Alexander stuffed the scanning booms back into their canister, while Will picked his way around the dining table, staring into the backs of the Kilgours' heads. Every single one of them had been hollowed out – not so much as a scrap of cranial matter left. Very, *very* impressive work.

Not surprisingly, the family's freakish smiles were artificial. Someone had looped translucent wire through the corners of their mouths, hauling the lips back and stitching them to the gums at the back, near the molars. Happy families.

Were they alive while their guest evacuated their skulls, one by one? Sitting there, waiting for their turn? Will looked at Trent – the little four-year-old girl – dressed up in her party frock, grinning away like the rest of them. Christ, he hoped not.

He stood back and took in as much of the room as he could. Only one of the chairs was empty, the place setting surrounded by birthday cards with 'EIGHTEEN TODAY!' on them. The messages flickering as the batteries died. Jillian Kilgour – the birthday girl.

A pile of presents sat in the middle of the floor. Only half of them were unwrapped, the rest probably being saved for after dinner. The wilted corpses of a dozen gold and silver balloons. A streamer with her name on it, stretching across the wall.

Slowly, Will swivelled left to right and back again, eyes slightly unfocused, just letting the scene sink in: waiting for something to nag at him, something that was out of place. He found it over by the bay window.

The view was spectacular, even through the rain. The monsoon had turned Glasgow Green into a lake – same as it did every year – the water dotted with islands and fancy little

179

restaurants, raised up on stilts. A meal there would set you back a week's wages, if you weren't feeling too hungry. They'd strung golden lights between the trees, turning the scene into a glittering water world. . .

But that wasn't what had drawn his attention. The VR unit was on, a plain grey cable snaking out from it across the carpet – the gold jack glinting against the oatmeal weave. Will picked it up, then squatted in front of the unit, searching for a headset. There had to be one: Trent was only four, too young for a cranial implant.

He found the headset. 'Oh, that's just brilliant. . .' It was tiny, pink, and covered with little white daisies. He plugged the gold jack into the socket and loosened the head strap as far as it would go. It still wouldn't fit over his bruised and battered head, but he was able to peer in at the pair of tiny screens.

It was tuned into one of the children's channels, all bright colours, unicorns, and talking toadstools, waiting for him to play with them. Squeaky voices coming from the earpieces, *'Hey, I know, why don't we go on an adventure, Jillian? Wouldn't that be cool?'*

Jillian: still configured for the last person plugged into the system.

Will dropped the headset.

There was something wrong with the carpet in front of the VR unit: a circular patch, about the size of large pizza, was a slightly different colour. Cleaner than the rest of the floor. He reached out and stroked the surface with his fingertips. They came away dry, but with that same lemony smell as the bathroom sink.

Clean freak.

The birthday girl would be lying right here, plugged into a cheery kiddie's VR game, hands and feet tied, sobbing behind a gag, wetting herself in terror while the mystery visitor Thrummed the back off granny's head.

Dirty girl. Leaving a mess. Couldn't have that.

'When you bag and tag this lot,' said Will, making for the door, 'grab any cleaning materials you can find. Watch for prints.'

Brian looked up from forcing one of the scanning booms back into its casing. 'Why, where you off to?'

The muffled screams. The fake smiles. Everyone waiting for their turn to die.

'Anywhere I can get a bloody stiff drink.'

An electronic voice breaks the silence. 'HELLO STEPHEN. DO YOU REMEMBER ME?'

Stephen's head snaps up as if someone's just rammed an electric prod into his rectum . . . which isn't a bad idea.

He frowns, making little creases between his eyebrows. 'Is there somebody there?' he asks, completely ignoring her standing in the corner of the room. Holding the datapad.

She hits the next button, and that same disembodied voice says, 'WE WORKED TOGETHER OVER SIX YEARS AGO.'

'Is this some sort of joke?' Stephen sits forward in his chair. 'Show yourself or I'm calling security!' He reaches for the phone and she slams the datapad down on his hand – hard enough to sting, but not hard enough to damage those delicate, skilful fingers.

His eyes go wide as she pushes him back in his chair.

'Hey! What. . .' Look left, look right, look very, *very* scared. 'Who's doing this?'

She types in two words into the pad: 'I AM.'

His face falls open like a gash. Then his lips start to tremble. The poor wee soul must think he's having a nightmare.

'Who are you?' he whispers.

As predictable as ever. She only has to punch a button to bring up the preprogrammed reply. 'STEPHEN I'M INSULTED. SURELY YOU REMEMBER ME? YOU WEPT WHEN THEY SENT ME AWAY FOR SURGERY.'

'Oh God. . .'

Ah: *now* he remembers.

'How did you. . . I saw you. . . But. . . Oh God, you can't be—'

She slaps him. Blood wells up from the new split in his lip.

'I REQUIRE A NEW FACE, STEPHEN. A JAW, A LARYNX, VOCAL CHORDS, CHEEK MUSCLES, EVERYTHING THEY TOOK AWAY FROM ME.'

'I can't—'

She hits him again.

'A CLONEGRAFT HEAD IS GROWING IN THE VATS. YOU WILL PERFORM THE SURGERY.'

'This isn't happening. . .'

This time she doesn't slap him; she balls her hand into a fist and smashes it into the bridge of his nose. Stephen's head snaps back, blood spraying from his nostrils. He grunts. Groans. Clutches both hands over his broken face. Probably in a lot of pain.

Good.

'YOU WILL PERFORM THE SURGERY AND YOU WILL TELL NO ONE.'

He glares up at her, blood seeping out between his fingers. 'I'll see you rot in Hell first!'

At last, the mouse is showing some balls.

Time to castrate him.

'YOU WILL COOPERATE. I HAVE TAKEN OUT INSURANCE.' There's a framed holo sitting on his desk. A happy family group, grinning at the camera somewhere exotic. She picks it up. 'YOU HAVE TWO CHILDREN,' says the electronic voice. 'MARTIN IS FOUR. HE LIKES DINOSAURS AND WILL NOT EAT HIS VEGETABLES. JASMINE IS THREE. HER FAVOURITE THING IN THE WHOLE WORLD IS TEDDY ORANGE. YOUR WIFE IS BLONDE.'

Stephen's hand falls away from his face as she pulls a clump of long golden hair from her bucket and throws it onto his

182

desk. There's a palm-sized chunk of bloody scalp attached to it.

He's making that whimpering sound again.

'I . . . I don't believe you!'

She punches his home phone number into the unit on his desk.

'What are you doing?'

It rings for a moment, then an unfamiliar face fills the screen, a Bluecoat uniform just visible beneath the double chins. The man frowns. *'Who's this?'*

Stephen grabs the desktop. 'Dr Bexley. Where's my wife? Where's Marilyn?'

'You know your nose is bleedin'?'

'I want to talk to Marilyn!'

The officer looks down, out of shot, as if consulting something. *'You Dr Stephen Bexley? Two, two, three, seven, Niven Towers, Cowcaddens?'*

'I. . . Yes.' He goes pale. Swallows. 'What's happened?'

'We got an anonymous nine, nine, nine call. Said two wee kids were here unsupervised.'

'My children?'

The officer's frown turns into a scowl. *'You do know it's an offence to leave minors on their own?'*

'Oh God.' That's all he says, over and over. 'Oh God.'

The man on the other end of the phone sighs. *'Look, sometimes it just gets a bit too much for the mums every now and then, you know? Your wains are fine, but I need you to organize someone to look after them, OK? Then talk to yer wife. Give her a bit of support, but.'*

Stephen snivels. 'Oh God, Marilyn. . .'

'Dinna worry, she's probably just out takin' a breather. Doin' some shoppin'. Blowin' off steam.' The officer pauses, staring out of the screen at Stephen. *'I'd get that nose looked at if I wis you.'* And with that the Bluecoat kills the connection.

Stephen picks the chunk of scalp off the desktop with trembling fingers, sniffs the blonde hair, and starts to cry. It's sweet the way people become attached to things. A wife's fragrance. A clump of skin. A limb. Their lives.

Dr Westfield lets him have his little moment before holding up the datapad again. It says: 'I HAVE HIDDEN HER SOMEWHERE SAFE. IF I DO NOT RETURN TO FREE HER, SHE WILL DIE. SLOWLY. IF YOU DO NOT PERFORM THE SURGERY, SHE DIES. IF YOU TRY TO CONTACT THE AUTHORITIES, SHE DIES. IF YOU DO NOT DO EXACTLY WHAT YOU ARE TOLD, SHE DIES. DO YOU UNDERSTAND?'

His face moves as if there are snakes buried under the skin. 'But you can't . . . she's pregnant! You. . . I'm calling security!' Stephen goes for the phone.

She grabs him by the lapels and drags him across the desk. Throwing him to the floor. Papers go flying, the heart-warming family holo hits the floor and she stands on it. Stephen's family goes crunch beneath her feet.

'LOOK AT ME.' She hammers one-handed at the datapad's keyboard, as he scurries backward into the bookcase, nose streaming blood down his pale face. 'WHAT CAN THEY DO TO ME TO MAKE ME TALK? WHAT? WHAT HAVE I GOT TO LOSE?' All spoken in that same, flat, artificial voice.

'You can't do this!'

'I ALREADY HAVE.'

'Please. . .' He struggles to his knees, hands clasped in front of him, tears streaming down his face. 'Please, I'm *begging* you! Let her go, for the sake of the baby. It's not too late—'

She would laugh if she could. 'DO YOU REALLY THINK ONE MORE TINY DEAD BODY MAKES ANY DIFFERENCE TO ME?'

He slumps back against the bookcase and sobs. 'Please . . . give me back my wife!'

She tilts her head to one side and watches him bawl like a small child covered in cigarette burns, then gathers up her bucket and mop and makes for the door.

'CELL DIVISION WILL BE COMPLETE IN THIRTY-TWO HOURS. MAKE SURE THERE'S A PRIVATE OPERATING THEATRE READY FOR THE TRANSPLANT.'

'What. . .' He wipes a hand across his eyes, leaving a bloody smear. 'What if I can't get a theatre ready in time?'

She stops at the threshold.

'THEN YOUR WIFE DIES AND WE MOVE ON TO YOUR CHILDREN.'

16

The Dog and Diode squatted beneath the Western Flyover, between two of the heavy support pillars. It wasn't the best pub in the world, but it was within easy walking distance of Network Headquarters, and some days that was all that mattered. Inside, the bar was decorated in mockwood and leatherette. Booths lined the walls, loose tables filling the remaining space. A handful of off-duty agents were celebrating someone's promotion by getting them blootered on happy hour drinks. So Will sat on his own in the corner – away from the speakers pumping out a mixture of frosty music and old rock classics – nursing a pint of Black Douglas and a large Macallan.

Trying not to think about the Birthday Party of the Damned. And failing.

The Kilgours were still alive as their unexpected guest worked his way around the table. Cutting a hole in the back of their heads, carefully evaporating their brains in a cloud of pink-grey mist, then stitching that obscene rictus grin in place. Before moving on to the next one in line. They watched their family die, unable to do anything about it, but wait for their turn.

Will shuddered and downed the last of his whisky.

Whoever the Thrummer man was, he'd done it before: there was no way anyone became that skilled at cranial evacuation without a *lot* of practice. What happened to the earlier bodies – the ones before the Kilgours – was anyone's guess. Certainly the Network had never found them.

A shadow fell across Will's table.

'Penny for your thoughts?' It was Brian, dripping from the downpour outside.

'You don't want them. Trust me.'

Brian shoogled himself into the booth and popped the console out of the tabletop. 'Drink?'

Will clinked his empty whisky tumbler against his empty beer glass. 'Where's Jo?'

'Reportin' to Central. She's got her Bluecoat mates runnin' tests on the stuff we bagged and tagged at the Kilgours'.'

'What about building security?'

Brian pulled a face. 'Place that fancy, you'd think they wouldnae skimp on the cameras and scanners and that, but they got a cheap-arsed system. Bargain basement time. Whole bloody lot was hacked: sod all on the hard drives going back a week and a half.' He ran his fingers over the drinks console, then struggled out of his coat while they waited for their order to arrive.

'The missing girl: Jillian, wasn't it?'

Brian nodded.

'If our friend with the Thrummer wanted her dead, she'd be sitting at that bloody table with the rest of her family. He's got something special in mind for her, something that's going to take time and solitude.'

'Jesus. Poor cow. . .'

An old man hobbled up to the table, plonked their drinks down, collected Will's empties, and hobbled away again without saying a word.

'Come on, put it away for the night.' Brian helped himself to a Guinness. 'Let the Bluecoats handle the legwork; you an' me'll get blootered, grab a curry or something.'

'What about James?'

'We've got an understanding. I don't moan when he's out with his horsey friends, and he doesn't moan when I'm out with mine. Anyway, he knows fine you'll keep me out of temptation.'

Which was true.

Half an hour later, George appeared, sniffing and snorting, all wrapped up in winter woollies. He had to peel himself like an onion before he could even fit into the little booth.

'Sodding bucketing down out there.' He blew his nose, then stared at Will. 'What happened to you this morning? Twenty minutes I was waiting there. Felt like a right prat.'

'Yeah, sorry about that.' Will pointed at his bruised face. 'Had a near-death experience in Kelvingrove Park with a couple of muggers. You'll probably get one of them in the mortuary tomorrow. . . if they can scrape enough of him up.'

'Oh thanks, *just* what I need: more work.' The little pathologist ran a hand across his forehead. 'Any chance of something medicinal? I'm dying here.'

They ordered another round, and when the old man had hobbled off with the latest set of empties, Will got George to tell Brian what he'd discovered in the brains of the bodies they'd dragged back from Sherman House.

'You're kiddin' me,' said Brian when he'd finished. 'They're givin' people VR syndrome on *purpose*?'

George gulped at his double brandy and blue. 'Yup. I went back to the mortuary and had another look at the bodies when Will didn't show up; they've both got old injection marks at the base of their necks. At least two dozen each. Whoever it is, they're going around manually infecting people.'

Brian said, 'Dirty bastards. . .' and Will had to agree with him.

George held up a podgy hand. 'No, no: this is good news.'

'What? How the hell is *any* of this good news?'

'They're still injecting people.' He paused, obviously expecting some sort of reaction. Then sighed when he didn't get one. 'Look, VR syndrome is at its worst when loads of people get it at the same time, right? But this lot are still having to infect their test subjects by hand. You'd need to do a big chunk of the block simultaneously to really kick things off, and you can't do that going round with a needle; you need to get it airborne, or in the water supply.'

Will sat back in his chair. That was all they needed: Glasgow exploding into violence all over again. People killing their friends, neighbours, family and anyone else they could get their hands on. Little cabals of madness getting bigger and bigger until there were only two kinds of people: the cannibals and the dead. 'If they can weaponize this stuff—'

'The whole bloody city turns into bamheid central.' Brian scowled at his beer. 'Aye, and no' just the connurb blocks like last time, everyone: you, me, Emily, Jo, James. . .'

The fat pathologist slurped at his vivid blue drink. 'You don't come up with something like this overnight. Whoever made this stuff spent a lot of time and money developing and testing it. Probably years.'

'How the hell do you get away with pulling shite like this for years?'

Will closed his eyes and sighed. 'You get away with it,' he said, 'by having someone very big and very powerful standing behind you.'

'Corporate? One of them bio-research outfits?'

'Whoever it is, they're well connected – Governor Clark was on the phone to Director Smith-Hamilton shouting the odds about Emily and me being there half an hour after we left Sherman House.' Will drummed his fingers on the tabletop. 'Peitai said he was with the Ministry for Change, kept going on about finding a cure for VR—'

'Bollocks,' said George. 'This is weapons research, or I'm a ballerina.'

Will rolled the last of his whisky round his mouth and placed the empty tumbler in the centre of the table. 'Question is, what do we do about it?'

'We stop them!' Brian thumped his fist down, making the glasses rattle. 'Even termites've got a right to live without some murderin' bastard usin' them as guinea pigs. We go in wi' all guns blazin' and take the bastards down!'

'Don't be daft.' George emptied his glass and placed it next to Will's. 'You can't just march in there and start shooting. Could be hundreds, *thousands* of people already infected. Go in there and spark something off, you'll be looking at a lot of dead bodies.'

Will held up his hands. 'OK, we can't storm the place, so we do what we always do: build a case. Find out who that little git Ken Peitai's really working for, what else they're up to. Then shut the whole place down.'

Brian snorted. 'Aye, right – like the Poison Dwarf's goin' tae authorize an investigation with Governor Clark breathing down her cleavage. She's after a seat on the board and there's no way in hell—'

'By the time we're finished with him, Governor Clark's going to be pushing a mop about with half his face missing. Just because you don't like her, doesn't mean the Director isn't good at her job. We go to her with this, she'll take it all the way.'

'Still say you're mental.' Brian swallowed the last of his Guinness and plonked the empty down alongside the others. 'I'll get an incident room and team organized—'

'No! No team.' Will shoogled forward in his seat. 'This has to be low key. Just the three of us.'

Brian rolled his eyes. 'Fine. I'll get Emily to—'

'Emily can't hear a word about this. I don't want Peitai to know we're after him.'

'What? You've known her for years! She's saved your arse more times than I can count, how can you no' trust her?'

'It's not her he doesn't trust.' George pulled the console over and ordered another round. 'If they put listeners and trackers in Will they put them in Emily. You speak to her you're speaking to them.'

'Fuck. . .' He frowned. 'Jo, then?'

'Fewer people know about it the better. Besides, this thing's a potential career-killer. I'm not putting her in that position.'

'Aye.' Brian winked at George. 'It's OK to kill ours, but.'

Will grinned. 'Brian, your career couldn't get any more diseased if it tried. It'd be a mercy killing.'

'What would?' Emily's voice made all three of them jump. She was standing at the end of their table, her concrete-coloured jumpsuit replaced with a snazzy two-piece in dark burgundy, a blue overcoat leaving puddles of water on the pub floor. She hung it up, then squeezed in next to Will and stabbed her thumb down on the drinks console, ordering the same again.

'Er. . .' Will looked across the table, but no one came to the rescue. 'We were . . . talking about how we can't go back to Sherman House.'

'Yup, it's not safe.' Sniff, snort.

'Aye, place's a fuckin' powder keg.'

'Bunch of old wifies.' She shook the water from her close-cropped hair. 'There's something going on over there and that little MFC weasel Peitai is a lying tosser. "Finding a cure for VR syndrome" my mum's hairy backside.'

'You don't know that, Emily.' Will shifted in his seat. 'If there's any chance they *can* find a cure, we can't risk jeopardizing it.'

'Did those muggers knock something loose between your ears this morning?' Her voice was rising. 'Peitai's bastards zapped us and tied us to a bloody chair! I am *not* turning a blind eye just because some jumped up little social-working shitebag—'

'I'm serious, Emily. And it doesn't matter anyway: Director

Smith-Hamilton has ordered the place off limits till things have calmed down.'

'Since when did you give a toss about what Smith-Hamilton says? Look, if we can get back into that underground lab I think I can—'

'No! As far as the Network, you, I, and everyone else is concerned, Sherman House does not exist.'

'Don't be so bloody—'

Will slammed his hand down on the tabletop, making the glasses jump. 'End of discussion Lieutenant! You are not to go near Sherman House, and that's an order!'

Emily stared at him, eyes narrowed, top lip curling. 'Yes, *sir*.' She stood, grabbed her overcoat off the hook, then threw him a curt salute.

'Emily don't—'

'If you'll excuse me, *sir*, I have to get some fresh air. It suddenly stinks of shit in here.'

Emily turned and marched out of the pub, back straight, chin up.

As the door slammed shut, the old man reappeared, his tray loaded down with two of everything, and a single glass of Methven Bay chardonnay. Emily's drink.

When he'd shambled off again, Brian reached forward and picked a large Jack Daniels from the collection. Took a sip.

'That went well,' he said into the silence. 'I *particularly* liked the bit where you pulled rank on her. Good move. Smooooooth.'

'Oh bugger off.' Will sank back in his seat. 'Didn't see either of you two leaping in to help.'

'You know,' said George, helping himself to another brandy and blue, 'looking on the bright side: anyone listening in is going to think they're safe.'

Will shrugged. 'Suppose you're right.'

But it didn't make him feel any better.

* * *

She snuggles deeper into her little nest of toilet paper, feeding tube in her arm, warm, comfortable, and content. Two kiddiewinks and a pregnant wife. Dr Stephen Bexley, you virile stud you.

Pregnant, pregnant, pregnant. . . She loves pregnant women – they add such a sparkle to proceedings. Especially when it comes to the vivisection.

She makes a sound that could be mistaken for a sigh. On Sunday she'll lie back on an operating table and have her face restored. Her very own face. . . Of course, the *sensible* thing to do is take someone else's face. But she doesn't want to be sensible. She wants to look in the mirror and recognize the person looking back. She wants to be whole again. Then, when she's all healed and beautiful, she'll have to leave the country.

A shame. This city has been good to her – let her hunt its inhabitants for years – but if she remains in Glasgow someone's going to recognize her. At first they'll see nothing more than a striking resemblance to the notorious Dr Fiona Westfield, but then they'll begin to talk. And eventually someone will listen.

They'll start asking difficult questions. Then someone takes a fingerprint, or a DNA sample and they'll know she's not dead. Then they'll strap her to another operating table . . . only this time she won't come back.

She shakes her head and tries to think happy thoughts. But Stephen Bexley and his screaming wife no longer light her candle. All she can see is a long dark tunnel with an operating slab at the end. The sound of bees and broken glass.

Deep breaths.

It's just paranoia. Nothing to worry about. Don't let it take control.

Deep breaths.

Kill something.

That'll make her feel better. Kill something *slowly* and bathe in the screams.

No.

Deep breaths.

Kill something.

Not yet.

Please.

Focus!

She snaps another ampoule of medicine into her neck and waits for the chemicals' soothing touch.

Focus.

She can't risk staying here. Soon as her new face has healed, she'll leave. Bye-bye Glasgow. Bye-bye Scotland. Well. . . First she'll see how her children are getting on and *then* she'll leave.

Yes. Somewhere far, far away.

But not before she pays an old friend a visit.

His face doesn't have the long, winding scar she'd given him anymore, which is a shame. It suited him: raw and painful. He was limping as he ran for the people carrier, bruised and battered, probably fresh from surgery. . .

Perfect. If he's had medical treatment he'll be in the hospital records – she can just waltz up to any terminal and find out what was wrong with him and where he lives.

She stretches in her toilet-paper boudoir like a cat in the sun.

It's been a long time since she has visited friends.

The birthday girl sobs and moans as he drags her off the bed and over to the chair. The older woman – the one he found in a bar a week ago – lies on the table next to the window. She was a lawyer, but now she's all peaceful and still. Content and happy. Ready to become one with the angels.

He hauls the new girl into the chair. She struggles, but a punch in the face quietens her long enough to shackle her arms and legs. After all, it wouldn't do to have the birthday girl falling off and hurting herself. Not when she's so close to finding salvation.

Then, when she's all nice and secure, he turns to the older woman, stroking her cold white cheek. It's got that lovely, waxy pallor of the soul departed. Lucky lady.

He pulls an old, battered, but well-loved Palm Thrummer out of his pocket, twists it open, and powers it up. Then opens the living room window, high above the streets. The rain hisses and roars outside, tearing from the sky in its rush to know the ground. Silly rain. The sky is where it should be. The sky is its home.

The Thrummer buzzes in his fingers as he strips the woman's face away, leaving nothing but a bare, empty skull behind. The skin and fat and fibre of her sinful life is whipped into a dark purple mist that drifts out the open window into the night, pulled away by the rain. The body will take a while to dissolve, but it's worth the effort to give her salvation.

He purses his lips, whistling the DinoPizza jingle while he works.

In her seat the birthday girl watches, screaming behind her gag: knowing that she's going to be next.

17

Will dragged himself out of bed and groaned his way to the bathroom in the dark. There was a fuzzy shape in the mirror above the sink. A rough, hungover outline that wouldn't stay in focus.

'Lights.'

The whole apartment exploded with brightness, driving red-hot knitting needles into his eyes and out through the back of his head.

'Aaaaaaarrrrrrrrrgh! Down! Down!'

They dimmed to something less head-splitting and Will stood there, blinking and swearing till he could see again. God. . . he looked as bad as he felt. His face was grey-green on one side and purple-green on the other.

He grabbed the edges of the sink and retched. But nothing came, and gradually the swell of nausea passed. How much did he *drink* last night? The last thing he could remember was singing rude songs with Brian in the curry house. After that it all became a bit of a blur.

There was an open packet of blockers in the medicine cabinet, courtesy of his hospital visit yesterday. He fumbled one out and popped it into his neck, then let his head thunk against the cool mirror, waiting for the chemicals to work their magic.

By the time he walked into the lounge all traces of pounding headache and churning stomach were gone.

Will told the room's controller to open the curtains: they slid back, revealing yet another wet, dark morning. The lounge reeked of stale beer, garlic and greasy meat. Seven or eight empty plastics of Greenmantle were lined up on the coffee table beside a half-eaten, ill-advised kebab.

Abandoned dataclips made an abstract mosaic on the carpet between the couch and the controller. They were all Janet's: her favourite cookery books, films, the birthday message she'd recorded one year as a surprise, wearing nothing but his old suit jacket. Carefully, he placed them back on the shelves. It'd been a while since he'd been drunk enough to go looking for her.

He said, 'Music,' and the controller bleeped softly – the opening bars of *Alba Blue* sparkling into the air. Janet's favourite opera, the one they'd played at her funeral. He left it running and went to make breakfast.

An hour later he closed the door on a tidy apartment; he'd even thrown his new clothes through the cleanbox. Seemed a shame not to give them a second outing.

Director Smith-Hamilton had told him to take a couple of days off, but hadn't said he couldn't spend it doing a little 'unauthorized data access'. Whoever Ken Peitai worked for they had to keep records of some kind. The only problem was finding them. The easiest way would be to hack into the files from Ken's underground laboratory, but there was no way of getting in there without arousing a lot of suspicion.

Unless he took Ken up on his offer of lunch. . .?

Will grimaced. The idea of having to eat with the slimy little turd was bad enough, but if Smith-Hamilton found out he'd gone back to Sherman House – and she would – the repercussions would be a *lot* more severe than a couple of days' enforced leave.

So he made his way downtown instead.

Central Records was an imposing mock-Victorian pile of red brick and sandstone, straddling Cadogan Street. For some reason known only to the planning department, it didn't have its own shuttle station, so Will had to slog through the rain from Wellington Street, stopping off to pick up a plastic of wine for the evening; this morning's hangover totally forgotten. He squelched in through the front door, submitted to a geometric scan, and found himself a quiet corner with a private study booth.

The monitor buzzed and crackled into life. He spent a couple of minutes entering convoluted search criteria, before sending the system off looking for old ministerial directives. It didn't matter if they found anything or not, he just wanted to make sure there was a record of him doing something legitimate.

Rule Number One: always establish your alibi *before* you do anything wrong.

While the machine plodded away, searching and cross-referencing, Will slipped the cracker out of his pocket and popped open the service panel under the table. He checked to make sure no one was watching, then teased a pair of wires out of the main data trunk and slapped the cracker over them. Then hacked his way into the main system and started doing a little searching of his own.

Three hours later he switched the cracker off and stifled a yawn. Ken Peitai didn't work for any of the biotech companies, none of the big conglomerates, or any government department. His National Insurance Number didn't connect to anything – no driver's licence, passport, or pension. The man was a ghost.

The only record Will could find was a bonus payment made half a dozen years ago in the PayFund database. It was a considerable sum of money, which was the only reason he'd found it: large payments had to be approved by the PayFund Manager, and that meant there were records. It also meant

Peitai really did work for the government . . . or at least he had six years ago.

The payment record was staggeringly short of detail. Will had been hoping for a home address, bank account, phone number, but no joy: whoever Ken worked for back then, they kept their information well away from the main channels.

Will stretched the knots out of his back and checked the time: twelve fifteen. Lunch. Brian wasn't answering his phone and neither was George, and unless hell had frozen over in the last twelve hours, there was no point calling Emily. It'd be weeks before they were on speaking terms again.

He raised his eyes to the large stained glass window at the end of the records hall. He could hear the rain hurling itself against the multicoloured panes. Still chucking it down . . . but he wasn't that far from the West George Street Bluecoat Stationhouse – where Jo worked when she wasn't at Network HQ. Maybe she'd be in?

That'd be nice. More than nice, actually.

Will ran a hand through his hair and checked his reflection in the study booth's monitor. He still looked like crap.

Ah well, too late to worry about that now, wasn't as if he could do anything about it.

OK. . .

He rubbed his palms on his trousers. No problem. Not like he was asking her on a date was it? Just two work colleagues having lunch together.

He closed his eyes and murmured, 'Just try not to make an arse of yourself. . .' Then he pulled out his mobile, called the Bluecoat switchboard, and asked to be put through to DS Cameron. Three minutes and twenty-seven seconds later Jo's face appeared on the tiny screen, one eye an opaque, milky grey.

'DS Cameron, can I help. . .' A small crease appeared between her eyebrows. *'Who is this?'*

With a small start Will realized he was sitting there with

his thumb over the phone's camera. She'd be looking at a blank screen. 'Ah, sorry,' he moved his hand so she could see his face in all it's bruised glory, 'force of habit. It's Will, Will Hunter.'

The frown disappeared, but didn't quite turn into a smile. *'Afternoon, sir. Why the anonymous act?'*

'I'm over at Central Records and I was wondering if you'd like to have lunch.' He shrugged. 'Thought you might be hungry.' He paused. 'As it's . . . er . . . lunchtime.' He cleared his throat. So much for not making an arse of himself.

She stared at him for a moment, then said, *'Where?'*

'Downtown?'

'When?'

Will did his best to look nonchalant. 'Look, if it's a bad time it's not a problem, I can—'

'Chiswick's: fifteen minutes.' A smile flickered across her face and then it was gone, disappearing into a little grey dot as she cut the connection.

Will put the phone back in his pocket, then caught sight of his reflection, grinning away in the monitor screen like a hormonal teenager. The smile slipped. He'd spent the wee small hours looking for his dead wife's memory, and now look at him.

Lunch, with a side order of guilt.

Fourteen minutes later he was sitting at a corner table, examining the menu. Chiswick's was small, cheap, and just close enough to the West George Street nick to attract a handful of blue uniforms.

'This seat taken?' There was a bright flash of colour and Detective Sergeant Jo Cameron slid into the chair opposite. Electric Lime and Volcanic Orange: gathered in tight at the waist. The jacket was surprisingly flattering, hugging her chest like a . . . Will tore his eyes away from the area in question. He'd not been on many dates in the last six years, but he was pretty sure that staring at a woman's breasts wasn't the way to make a good impression.

And then she took off her jacket, exposing a fashionably clingy emerald top.

'Nice bruises,' she said.

'Thanks. Picked them out specially.'

She laughed. 'So what have you been up to today then?'

'Not much.' He nudged the plastic of wine in its bag under the table. 'Just getting a few things in for tonight. You?'

'Loads. We took your advice and grabbed all the cleaning stuff we could find at the Kilgours.'

'Lemon-scented bathroom cleaner?'

'Yup: three partials and one perfect thumb print. They don't belong to any of the family or the cleaners. We're ninety-five percent certain it's our boy.'

'Any luck on a match?'

'Not yet.' She grabbed a menu. 'We've got the system churning through every record for the last twenty-five years. If he's been tagged we'll get him. Just a matter of time.'

'Good.' He watched her reading the menu, the little pink tip of her tongue poking out between her lips from time to time. That clingy emerald top stretching every time she breathed. Will tried really hard not to stare.

'See anything you fancy?'

'I . . . em. . .' He could feel his cheeks flush. 'Er . . . whatever you're having.'

Jo smiled, and Will couldn't help smiling back. Even if he did feel like an idiot.

She punched their order into the tabletop. 'What did you do to Brian last night? He's done nothing but eat pickled onion crisps and swig coffee all day.'

'Ah, the Agent Alexander patented hangover remedy. We got a bit hammered last night; kind of drowning our frustrations.' He fiddled with the tomato sauce. 'Director Smith-

Hamilton's banned all return visits to Sherman House until things calm down over there.'

'So we can't go anywhere with the Allan Brown investigation.' She scrunched her face up. 'Arse. . .'

'Sorry, Jo.'

'Damn it. I thought this time we'd actually be in with a decent chance of proving something.' She sat back in her seat and sighed. 'Like I said, it's pretty clear one of the Road-hugger crew did it, but still. . . Be nice to get closure for a change. How long's it off-limits for?'

'No idea. The whole square's under quarantine till further notice.'

The starters arrived – two bowls of Cullen Skink – and they ate their soup in silence. Slowly the mood began to lighten. They talked about old cases, movies, made fun of the sour-faced passers-by scuttling between the puddles. The main course was barely on the table before Jo sat bolt upright in her seat, her left eye going from golden brown to milky grey. 'Sod it. . .' She dug a bright-red fingerphone from her jacket pocket and slipped it on. Pointed it at herself.

'DS Cameron, go ahead.'

Will paused, fork halfway between a bowl of ruby-coloured goulash and his mouth.

'Negative.' She pushed her plate away. 'I'll be at the station-house in about thirty seconds. Fire up a Hopper, we'll meet them there.'

Jo stuck the fingerphone back in her pocket and stood. Will followed her. 'What's up?'

'Got a match on the Kilgour prints.' She dragged her green and orange jacket back on. 'Pickup team are waiting for me.'

'I'll come with you.'

'Oh no you don't: you're confined to barracks, remember?'

'But—'

'No buts.' She pushed him gently back into his seat. 'Stay. Eat your dessert. I'll let you know how we get on.'

Then she was gone, running out of the door and into the pounding rain. Will watched until her brightly coloured suit was swallowed up by the drenched crowd. A minute later the café's windows rattled and the roar of a Hopper's engines cut through the lunchtime rush.

Slowly he sank back into his seat and looked down at the plate of clotting, dark-red lumps. He just wasn't hungry any more.

The hospital's hum has become as familiar to her as her own breathing, warm and reassuring. She sits in her cosy nest of toilet paper, with a datapad on her lap, doing a little light reading. Her personal research notes have always been part of the PsychTech files, hidden away amongst the endless records of bed-wetting, insomnia, shoplifting, father-hatred, mother-love, sibling-rivalry, and all the other mental debris of the people she and her team interviewed.

But her files aren't like the other PsychTech files: her files are secret, hidden away in an obscure subdirectory. Password protected, and encrypted.

PsychTech. She headed up the project for five happy years, monitoring a cross-section of Glasgow's most vulnerable citizens, making sure they didn't become a danger to themselves or others. Of course it was all *her* idea. She campaigned for it, pushed it through committee, dazzled them with her dedication and brilliance. Made them see that if you knew what the criminal mind looked like, you could start going through the population, picking out people who fitted the profile. People who might not have done anything wrong *yet*, but had all the right screws loose to do so in the future.

And who knew more about the criminal mind than her?

So she rose up through the ranks, her budget and remit snowballing as she climbed. It was a Ministry for Change flagship project – a vast psychological experiment designed to make Glasgow a better, safer place.

She wriggles deeper into her nest.

They didn't have a clue about her own special project: Harbinger.

Her fingers stroke the datapad, opening the secret research notes. . . Opening. . . She stops. Frowns at the screen. There's something not right, something that tugs at the holes in her memory.

Something. . .

Never mind, it'll come to her in time.

Dr Westfield works her way through the case notes, following her children's progress from the first time she saw their parents. There's a lot to read through; some of them weren't even born when she started to mould their psychological development. When the Ministry shut down the PsychTech programme they cut off her children. No therapy, no analysis, no one listening to their problems and twisted little fantasies. Six years without her guidance and advice.

Such a waste.

There are twenty-seven of them: boys, girls, and some not quite certain what they are. The girls are the most challenging to work with: they don't mould as well as the boys do, female killers being more suited to the spree than the serial. The uncertain ones were the easiest; sexual dysfunction is a wonderfully fertile playground for the seasoned psychologist.

Gently she taps the datapad against her exposed teeth. Six year is a long time. Who knows what mischief they've been getting up to.

Twenty-seven opportunities for beautiful carnage. Twenty-six of them still out there, primed and ready to explode.

At the trial they'd thought Alastair Middleton was the only killer she'd created. Poor Alastair: her first real success. Just a shame he hadn't been a bit more careful in his choice of prey. If he had she wouldn't be sitting here with half her face missing.

This is *his* fault: if it wasn't for him she'd have a seat on the Ministry board by now. All because that stupid shit couldn't keep his fucking dick in his trousers. Filling her world with broken glass, turning her into a mutilated freak. ALL HIS BLOODY FAULT.

She pulls another ampoule of medicine from the pack and snaps it into her neck with trembling fingers. Calm. Calm. Deep breaths.

It's no one's fault. It's no one's fault.

The chemicals rush through her bloodstream. Alastair was only doing what she'd taught him to do.

Calm.

It was bad luck, nothing more.

Calm.

Her eyes drift back to the datapad in her hands.

Six years. Most of her children would be in their late teens or early twenties by now. Perhaps Alastair Middleton wasn't the only one who'd achieved his potential. Perhaps his wouldn't be the only halfheading she'd find in the Glasgow Royal Infirmary database. Dr Westfield punches her children's names into the hospital search engine and settles back to wait.

The results, when they come back, are encouraging.

Three have suffered minor breaks – nothing serious, just arms and legs. Four are getting treatment for psychotic disorders and she spends a happy hour or two reading through the psychiatrists' notes. Of course the questioning isn't anywhere near as insightful as her own would have been, but then she has a unique perspective.

Five of her children are already dead: two stabbings, one shot during a 'Police Action', one suicide, and one cut up so badly in a public toilet that they needed a DNA match to identify him. Details on the two stabbings are slim, little more than post mortems, but the shooting victim is a lot more interesting. Duncan Clark, multiple Thrummer wounds to the face and head. His post-mortem holos are a 3D treat in vivid red and purple; his head looks as if it's been skinned then sandblasted. She calls up the NewsNet, runs a search for 'Duncan Clark'.

An entire documentary pops up. Duncan Clark is a success story.

The presenter speaks to Duncan's neighbours and mother – who looks every bit as deranged as she did when Dr Westfield got her hooked on Tezzers. Addicts are so very malleable.

There's even footage of the hostage drama that marked the start and end of Duncan's campaign to silence the voices in his head. He's wearing black-and-grey urban camouflage, with an assault weapon over his shoulder. And then there's the naked woman. He's got a handful of her hair, holding her up while she screams and sobs and struggles, blood trickling down between her legs. Duncan presses a serrated knife to her throat, shouting at the Network pickup team, his pale, blotchy face speckled with targeting beams.

And then he slashes her open from ear to ear. Blood sprays out in glorious slow motion. The woman's eyes bulge, her knees buckle, then Duncan's face explodes in a cloud of pink mist. There's just enough of a breeze to let the camera record every last beautiful detail as his features are boiled away. It only takes a second.

He falls on top of his victim – probably the closest he's ever been to a naked woman – twitching. Muffled screams come from the ragged, bloody hole where his mouth used to be. There are no eyes, no cheeks and most of his jaw is gone.

The documentary goes into maudlin detail about the seventeen other people in the fast food joint: fathers, wives, sons, daughters. Not one of them survives the trip to the operating theatre.

Well done, Duncan. You've made mummy very proud.

Dr Westfield rewinds to the point where he cuts the woman's throat, then pauses, her fingers caressing his evaporating face.

So pretty.

If only she could have spoken to him in the run up to that spree, could have found out what finally pushed the buttons she spent so many years setting in place.

There's no NewsNet coverage for Allan Brown – the one they had to ID from his DNA – but his post mortem reads like the inventory of a butcher's shop. There are a lot of holos in the file: close-ups of his hands, face, genitals, and belly, all torn and shredded. It's beautiful workmanship. Strangely familiar. . .

Still, none of that matters. The important thing is that the remainder of her study group, all twenty-one of them, are still out there. Shrouded in the brittle comfort of bees and broken glass. Ready for that little push to send them right off the edge.

She has a lot of catching up to do.

Four hours later and the rain was still hammering down. Will stood on the edge of Blythswood Square, dripping quietly as he watched the halfhead.

It was dragging a buggy along behind it, picking up sodden litter from the drenched streets. It speared a discarded crisp packet and transferred it into the buggy's bin. Strange to think that the thing cleaning the square had been human once. A creature of violence and destruction.

Now look at it.

Will stepped out from beneath the tree he'd been sheltering under, wincing as he crossed the square towards the figure in orange and black. Doc Morrison had told him to keep moving or he'd seize up, and now he knew what she meant. It was as if he'd come down with a bad case of rigor mortis. That's what he got for spending all day sat in front of a monitor looking for Ken 'The Invisible Man' Peitai.

In the end he'd had to admit defeat: if there was any information on Peitai out there, Will couldn't find it. Instead he'd just ended up thinking about Jo and whether or not Janet would have liked her, wondering if his dead wife would approve of his seeing another woman.

Then he went looking for Alastair Middleton. It didn't take long when you knew which databases to hack into.

The halfhead didn't even look up as Will walked up to him and stood watching yet another bit of sodden rubbish disappear into the bin. There was something almost peaceful about halfheads. Something timeless and serene. There was never any rush. They had nothing left to worry about.

'Afternoon, Alastair,' said Will, shifting his grip on the carrier bag with his shopping in it. 'Long time no see.'

If Alastair Middleton heard him, he didn't give any sign, just went on picking up the trash and depositing it in his little buggy.

'Been thinking about you a lot over the last couple of days. Your old mentor's dead. Did you know?'

Alastair didn't say anything, but then again he couldn't: his mind and lower jaw had been taken away long ago.

'Got burned to death in a Roadhugger that crashed. Just like that. No more Dr Fiona Westfield.' He stuck his hands in his pockets and shrugged. 'Don't suppose that means an awful lot to you though, does it? She just used you the same way she used everyone else: wound you up and let you go.'

Water ran down the truncated features and dripped off the exposed upper teeth, making the thing that had once been Alastair Middleton glisten.

'You know, I sometimes wonder if it wouldn't have been kinder to kill you when I had the chance: boil your chest away just like you did to Janet. What do you think? You happy as you are? No longer a menace to society?'

A group of about a dozen schoolgirls – all of them clearly stoned out of their heads – staggered across the square, giggling and tittering in their long red cloaks. Will watched them jump from puddle to puddle, shrieking with the joy of being young and off their faces.

'Yeah, well,' he said when they'd gone. 'Just wanted you to know she was dead.'

Will didn't wait for a reply – there wasn't any point – he turned his back and squelched his way to the nearest shuttle station.

Brian and Jo would be in the pub by now, having the traditional booze-up to celebrate catching their bad guy. And God knew Will could do with celebrating something.

There was no sign of the pickup team in the Dog and Diode, so Will dragged out his mobile and called Brian's. No response, so he tried him at home.

The little screen crackled and fizzed for a bit before Brian's face swam into focus. Will was on his best behaviour. Didn't even obscure the camera.

'Brian, how. . . God you look terrible!'

Agent Alexander's face was pale and baggy, his eyes bloodshot, his nose red. He sighed. *'Will.'* That was it, no niceties, no hello, no merry banter.

'Are you all right?'

'No.'

'Jesus, Brian, what happened?'

He rubbed at his eyes. *'You don't want to know. And I really don't want to talk about it.'* He took a couple of deep breaths. *'I'm sorry Will. I'll . . . I'll talk to you later. I can't do this right now.'*

Someone appeared at his shoulder and Will recognized James's voice as he wrapped Brian up in a hug. *'Shhhh. . . Come on. Let it go. It's all right.'*

Then the connection went dead.

Will frowned at the flashing 'CALL TERMINATED' icon. It wasn't like Brian to let things get to him. Not like that.

Will called the West George Street Bluecoat station. A

harassed-sounding sergeant told him he could go screw himself if he thought they were going to hand out a DS's private number to some wanker in a pub, before slamming the cut-off switch. Will was left with the 'CALL TERMINATED' icon again.

He could always dig Jo's number out of the Bluecoats records when he got home. And anyway, he had a plastic of wine and a pizza delivery menu waiting for him. Who could ask for more?

She pushes the datapad away and stretches. It's taken her most of the day, but she now has addresses for all her remaining children. Surprisingly, most of them live in the same place. Three stay out in the lower suburbs, but the other eighteen are all bundled up, nice and snug, in Monstrosity Square. Strange that fate made them gravitate together like that. Strange, but convenient – visiting them will be nice and easy.

She'll have to get herself a little insurance first. Pick up a few choice items from one of her weapons caches. Wouldn't do to fall prey to her own children. That would be too ironic.

Dr Westfield rolls out of her nest and drops to the supply room floor. Sadly, no one's come to visit since Kris and her friend. No one to see the excellent job she's done cleaning away the evidence. But that's probably just as well: they might wonder about the two jars, resting against the back wall, full of preserving fluid and body parts. She likes to take them down from their shelf and dance around the room with them. Hold them up to the light and watch as it flickers and dances between the strings of flesh. Pop open the lids and. . .

She stops, one hand on the lid, one on the cool plastic container. She just had to open them. Her case files should have been locked tight. Passwords. Encryption.

The jar drops from her hands. It hits the concrete floor and bounces, spilling eyes and testicles and ovaries in an explosion of bitter-smelling liquid. Bouncing back up from the floor, it spins, spraying out the last of the preserving fluid, before sinking back to dance and skitter to a halt at her feet.

She shouldn't have been able to just open up the Harbinger files. She'd erased all open versions when that Network bastard came snooping. Everything else was hidden. Stored. Compressed. Booby-trapped. The only way those files would be accessible was if someone had unlocked and disarmed them. And she sure as hell didn't do it.

Someone has been tampering with her work. Someone has been meddling.

Someone is going to *pay*.

The front door bleeped at him, and Will put down his keyboard and stretched. The twinges were back, but he only had a couple of blockers left and wasn't going to waste them. Instead he took another sip of wine and slouched through to the hall to pay the DinoPizza delivery girl for his twelve-inch Cheat-Meat feast.

He stuffed a slice into his mouth, settled back on the couch and pulled the terminal closer. Hacking into the government network didn't take long – their security was a joke. If he weren't in the habit of using it to sneak into other, more suspicious, systems he would have said something. The main Bluecoat computers weren't any better, and he spent a couple of minutes skimming their arrest records to see if any names would leap out at him. They didn't. So he pushed on – through the firewall surrounding their personnel files – and called up Detective Sergeant Josephine Cameron's record.

Most of it he'd seen before, but he read through it again: commendations, verbal warnings, an impressive enough arrest list. Three applications for transfer to the Network. He'd not seen those in her public file. No wonder she'd jumped at the chance to act as liaison officer, it was a back door into the service for her. Three or four knock-backs weren't unusual;

the Network liked to make sure new agents really wanted to be there.

Her disciplinary record wasn't too bad – the most recent entry was over two years old, so it looked as if she'd learned to play the game. Politics: the bane of law enforcement agencies everywhere. It wasn't enough to be good at your job, you also had to be sensitive to the machinations of your superiors.

Will took another bite of pizza. It was getting cold, the cloned pepperoni greasy, the cheese beginning to congeal.

He moved on to her personal details: address, mother's maiden name, height, weight and home number. He punched it into the phone and settled back on the couch, only remembering at the last minute she wouldn't be able to see anything because he'd killed the camera.

'Damn.' Never mind, it was too late to do anything about it now.

It rang and rang and rang and rang. In the end the answerphone clicked on and he was confronted with a pre-recorded DS Cameron telling him that she wasn't able to come to the phone right now, but if he felt like it, and didn't expect an answer anytime soon, he could leave a message after the beep. Will hung up.

He washed a chunk of pizza crust down with a mouthful of wine. Just because no one wanted to talk to him, it didn't mean he couldn't find out what happened today. If Jo had submitted any paperwork it would be filed on the Bluecoat mainframe. He dragged the case reference out of her day log and went hunting.

He was almost there when the doorbell went. Twice in one evening, something of a record.

Cursing, he shut the screen down, slipped the keyboard back under the coffee table, then answered the door.

He barely recognized the woman on his doorstep. There was no sign of the trademark eye-melters she normally wore, instead DS Cameron was clad in sombre blues and greys. Freed from its usual asymmetric bun, her hair hung round her face like a mourning veil, hiding her eyes, curling in round her cheeks in tight, black curls. There was a lot more of it than he'd suspected.

He smiled at her. 'Hi.'

She didn't say anything.

Will tried again. 'You OK?'

'Can I come in?' Jo's voice was thick and a little slurred. Not much, not falling-down-pissed-as-a-fart, just enough to let Will know that she'd been drinking.

'Em. . . Yeah, of course.'

She followed him through to the lounge. 'Got your address out the files.'

Will frowned. 'My address is in the public files?'

She shook her head and a small smile flickered across her lips. 'Nope.'

So she'd been up to the same thing he had.

'You want something to drink? Got some cold pizza I could reheat.'

'Drink's good.'

He popped a couple of tumblers out of the cleaner and onto the countertop; somehow Will got the feeling this wasn't an occasion for wine. A generous glug of whisky was accompanied by the briefest splash of water.

Jo took a deep sip and rolled it around her mouth. Her eyes were pink and swollen, just like Brian's had been.

They sat side by side on the settee making stilted small talk. The weather, Will's bruises, the view from his apartment. . . When the change of subject came, Jo's voice faltered.

'We found Jillian Kilgour,' she said into her glass.

Will settled back and waited for her to tell it, but she didn't. Instead she bit down on her bottom lip and her shoulders started to tremble. There was no noise at first, just a gentle rocking back and forth and then the tears started. They balled up in the corners of her eyes like tiny fists and rolled down her coffee-coloured cheeks. Then she dragged in a ragged breath and bit down again. Will placed his glass on the coffee table and put his arms round her shoulders.

'It's OK,' he said as she buried her face in the crook of his neck. 'It's OK.'

He held her until she had no tears left.

The mess is all cleaned away, mopped and polished until there is no sign of spilled preserving fluid or body parts.

Broken glass and bees. Filling the storeroom with their incessant, sharp-edged buzzing.

Someone has been in her files.

Some bastard has been interfering with her work.

For a moment she comes close to exploding; it would feel very good to start smashing things. But she can't do that. The storeroom's internal sensors will notice that much destruction, someone will be sent down to investigate. She can do nothing to draw attention to herself. Nothing.

So she sits on the edge of a pile of surgical gowns and seethes. Someone has hacked into her Harbinger files. Someone has been rifling though her research. Someone. . .

She stops and looks at the monster reflected in the polished steel of the central unit. Only one person has ever managed to get into her files. A long purple scar winds its way across the left-hand side of his face. He wears a dark-blue suit.

Dr Westfield scowls at the datapad in her hand – the open Harbinger files. He should have known better. She won't let him get away with it a second time.

Her fingers dance over the datapad, accessing the Network admissions sheet for the last three days and there he is. Three broken ribs, cranial trauma – nothing too serious – and a follow-up appointment made for four thirty tomorrow. The bastard will be right here in this very building. . .

She closes her eyes. If she goes after him *now* she risks

214

everything. With trembling fingers she snaps an ampoule of her medicine into the soft skin at the nape of her neck.

Calm washes through her on a chemical tide.

Soon her cloneplant will be ready and Stephen will make her whole again.

She'll be whole again and Assistant Section Director William Scott Hunter will begin his new, painful life.

She calls up his personal information and copies down his home address.

They'll spend some quality time together. Just the two of them and a scalpel, a bone hammer, needles, blades, screams, blood. His lovely face. . . Death is fast and permanent. But with the right treatment, The Man In The Dark-Blue Suit can suffer for years.

She picks a dissection blade from a pack of twelve. It feels nice in her hand, comfortable, heavy, shiny. Mutilating him will be therapeutic. And she has always known the benefits of good therapy.

18

Jo was sleeping with her mouth open, lips pouted, showing off a glimpse of teeth and the soft pink tip of her tongue. Will picked his head up off the pillow and watched her breathing. Slow and gentle. The first time had been wild and furious, the second a lot gentler.

She hadn't told him what had happened that afternoon.

He pulled his arm out from under her head and Jo shifted, making herself comfortable. Will pulled the duvet up, tucking her in so that only her face showed, framed by an explosion of curly black hair. Then he leant forward and planted a soft kiss on the end of her nose. She wrinkled it and brushed the back of her hand across her face as he slipped out of the bed and into the lounge.

Outside, the rain continued to pound the city into submission. It drummed against the glass, danced on the balcony, wrapped itself around the world for as far as he could see. Low black clouds, laced with reflected sodium-yellow, blanketed his world. Ten thirty on a Saturday night – even with the heating turned up full blast he was overwhelmed by the urge to shiver.

Will picked a tumbler from the coffee table and poured himself another small whisky. Wasn't as if he had anywhere to go tomorrow. The liquid went down smooth and warm, worked its magic, soothed away the chill.

The terminal was still on – he'd only switched off the screen – so, pushing the discarded socks, pants, and trousers to one side, he pulled the keyboard onto the coffee table and went back to reading Jo's notes. She didn't want to talk about it and he wasn't going to force her. But he wasn't prepared to let it go.

Jo's files were impressively tidy, she even had live footage – captured from Sergeant Nairn's headset as they went in – all cross-referenced and annotated.

Will spilt the screen and let the footage play on one side as he sifted through the background notes.

Colin Mitchell: twenty-seven, single, no family. He'd had three lots of psychiatric treatment, two for arson and one for assault, even did a short stretch in the Tin.

On the right hand side of the screen the picture crackled with static. That would be the Dragonfly landing. And suddenly the ship's drop bay was full of green light as weapons came online.

It was too dark for Will to make out anyone's face as they leapt out into the rain, but he recognized the voices. Sergeant Nairn's hands popped into view, holding a powered-up Thrummer.

Three years ago Colin Mitchell invites a young woman back to his small flat on the lower south side and gets her stoned on Mouse. When she's unconscious Colin removes her clothes and ties her to a chair. Then he masturbates over the back of her head. That's it. No other sexual contact.

When the woman wakes up she kicks up hell and calls the Bluecoats. Colin gets seven months in the Tin for indecent assault and illegal imprisonment, and another round of therapy.

Will watched two figures jog down the corridor, one holding a Bull Thrummer – that would be Dickson, she was the only one cleared to operate siege weaponry – and another with a Whomper. They counted off the doors as they went, until Dickson flattened herself against the wall and made a fist. The one with the Whomper took the other side of the door and gave the same gesture. Nairn nodded and Will got a good view of the hall carpet before the apartment door was kicked in.

The psychological notes on Colin Mitchell were a lot more comprehensive than Will had expected, and he skimmed through them as Nairn and his troops slunk from room to room, weapons at the ready. Their lightsights cast a ghostly green glow across the walls.

Social dysfunction, brief flirtation with VR syndrome during the riots – nothing unusual in that, half the city went down with the damn thing – but mostly Colin's problems seemed to stem from a general sense of dislocation. The people around him had nothing to do with his life, they were just shadows, they weren't real.

There was a spare bedroom, towards the rear of the property, the window boarded up, leaving the room in darkness. A dozen cleaned skulls sat on a shelf against the back wall, the bone covered with engraved squiggles. They'd been hollowed out, just like the Kilgours'. You could tell by the way the lightsights shone through the empty sockets and onto the wall behind.

Mitchell's mother and father had been in therapy, getting treatment for alcoholism and anger management. Referred on by social workers. . . Will's breath caught in his throat. Their therapist was Dr Fiona Westfield.

He gulped down the whisky and poured himself another.

No big deal. It was a surprise, that's all. Hadn't been expecting to see her name like that.

Bloody woman was like the bogeyman, even dead she still had the power to make his skin crawl.

Will settled back in front of the computer.

Colin Mitchell's parents never wanted kids, resented the little brat, blamed him for ruining their lives, used that as an excuse to repeatedly beat the hell out of him. During one therapy session the mother claimed her husband was sexually abusing the boy, but there was no evidence. She retracted the statement later, said it was just the drink talking.

A small camp bed sat against one wall, two pairs of chains snaking out onto the plastic-coated mattress.

Colin's father died from an overdose of H when the boy was eight, and after that his mother caught a bad dose of God. It just meant Colin got beaten more often.

There was a chair in the centre of the bedroom, surrounded by plastic sheeting. Shackles were attached to the arms and legs: big ones, with locking pins down the sides.

Colin's mother died three and a half years later. Back on the booze, she'd slipped and fallen down the apartment block stairs. Four floors. By the time she reached the bottom she had two shattered legs, a fractured wrist and a broken neck. Colin wasn't charged, but he went straight from the inquest to a care home.

The troopers on the right-hand side of his screen froze and Will turned the sound up.

Nairn said, *'Can you hear something?'*

The camera made a slow sweep of the room. There was nowhere to hide. No cupboards, nothing under the bed.

A hand swam into view and the picture crackled as Nairn flipped the viewing monocle into place. The screen went black, and when it faded up again the troopers were bright yellow and red balls of heat in the cold room. Another slow sweep, left to right, and then the camera stopped: there was a patch of pale orange on the wall, beneath the shelf with the skulls.

Nairn moved forward and the image on the screen grew. There were two figures, one wrapped round the other. Will couldn't see the hidden entrance, but Nairn obviously could – he dug his knife into a join in the wall and twisted.

Sudden motion. Swearing. A jumble of limbs. Someone making a run for it. Shouting. The hard crackle of a Field Zapper at full charge. More shouting, the words all running together, then, *'Jillian? Can you hear me, Jillian?'*

Jillian Kilgour, eighteen years old, was curled in a ball on the floor of the hidden alcove.

Someone knelt down next to her and felt for a pulse. The trooper hauled her upright, cradling the young woman in his arms as he checked for wounds: making sure there was nothing life threatening. There was something wrong with the back of Jillian's head. Will leaned forward in his chair to get a better look, but the picture was too fuzzy. He could see the trooper's hand come away from the bulge at the base of Jillian's skull:

'What the fuck?' The voice was low and shocked. The trooper stared at the back of the young woman's head: *'Oh Jesus Christ. . .'*

And then Jillian's body was on the floor again, dropped so the person holding her could be sick. The eighteen-year-old just lay there, shivering quietly until someone covered her up.

The other troopers gathered round . . . and then the signal died, leaving Will with nothing but angry, grey static. He didn't need to read the duty doctor's report on Colin Mitchell to guess what happened next. He was given a kicking. Not enough to kill him, or do any *serious* damage. Just enough to really hurt. The report would say he'd fallen badly when they zapped him. That he'd caught his head on the door handle. That he'd broken a rib on the occasional table. That someone had accidentally stood on his hand hard enough to dislocate all of his fingers.

Will turned down the sound on the film window, waiting for the picture to come back while he called up the hospital report on Jillian Kilgour.

'What you doing?' Jo's voice made him jump. He looked

around and she was standing just behind the couch, looking rumpled and sleepy. She hadn't bothered to dress.

'Reading your notes on the Kilgour case.' He pointed at the screen, there was no point in lying.

'It was horrible.' She picked the other tumbler off the tabletop. The motion was casual, but it was enough to get Will's heart, and other parts, throbbing.

'Want to talk about it?'

Jo shook her head. 'No.' She pulled the top off the whisky and filled the glass half-way up.

'OK.' He switched off the screen and pushed the keyboard away. He didn't power down the machine or close the connection, though.

She wandered over to the patio doors and stood there, sipping her drink and staring out into the rain. Will watched transfixed. She was so unselfconscious. There was no way he could have paraded about in the nip like that. Not with the blinds open.

'He fell down a bit when we arrested him.'

Will nodded, but didn't say anything.

'Nairn was all for taking him out on the roof and seeing if the fucker could fly.' She wrapped an arm round herself, her skin golden caramel in the reflected city light. 'Had my vote.'

He picked himself up out of the settee and joined her in front of the glass, slipping a hand round her waist. Jo leaned against him, her skin hot to the touch.

'Jillian Kilgour was dead before we got her back to the Dragonfly. Duty doctor said she was lucky: if she'd lived she'd've spent the rest of her life in a tank. Neurological trauma.' Jo sniffed and Will could see her teeth clamping down on her bottom lip again.

She dragged in a couple of deep breaths and wiped her eyes on the back of her hand. 'Mitchell thrummed a hole in the back of her head, just about here.' She tapped Will's skull at the very back, just above the line of his left ear. 'Doctor said the hole went straight through to the prefrontal lobe. All the way through.' She let her hand drop back to her side. 'He used a hot-glue-gun: fixed a condom to the back of that poor girl's head.'

Will had a nasty feeling he knew what was coming next.

'He was fucking her. In the head.' The tears were flowing freely now. 'He was sticking his dick in the back of that girl's head and fucking her. It. . . It. . . He. . .'

Will folded her in his arms and sank to the floor with her, rocking her back and forth until she cried herself dry.

19

Dawn broke, but it made little difference to the day outside. The dense clouds and pounding rain wouldn't let the daylight through. Everything was grey and miserable.

Will sat on his own at the dining-room table, wrapped up in his dressing gown, huddling around a hot mug of tea. He yawned. Rubbed at his gritty eyes. Sighed. It had been a long, difficult night. Jo had tossed and turned in her sleep, when she could sleep at all, and he hadn't been much better: the nightmares were back in stomach-churning Technicolor.

Will's enforced compassionate leave was officially over tomorrow. He'd been looking forward to going back to work, but now that Jo was here, he found didn't really want to. There was more to life than paperwork and crime statistics.

At least they'd have the day together. A lazy Sunday breakfast, maybe a walk in the rain – anywhere other than Kelvingrove Park – late lunch, go do something fun. OK, so they'd have to detour past the hospital for his follow-up appointment with Doc Morrison, but other than that he had nothing on. . . Which was another good idea: spend the day in bed.

He gave Jo another hour before making a pot of tea and

carrying it through to the bedroom. She was already awake and half dressed. As he walked in she jumped and clutched her shirt to her chest, hiding her bra.

'Will, sir, I think I—'

He didn't let her finish.

'Before you say anything,' he said, settling the teapot down on the bedside table, 'I want you to know that I don't consider last night to be a mistake. I've liked you since the first day we met.' He paused and shrugged. 'Well . . . except for that bit with the dismembered body in the toilet of course.'

She kept her mouth shut, so he soldiered on.

'It's Sunday and I'd like you to spend the day with me. We could go out to Comlab Six, save the world from Martian invaders, or rampaging dinosaurs, maybe go somewhere fancy for dinner. Whatever you like.'

She looked at him, then down at the carpet. 'I've . . . em . . . got a lot of paperwork to catch up on.'

'I see.' He picked the tea up and carried it back into the living room, leaving her to finish dressing in peace.

When Jo emerged from the bedroom five minutes later she looked ready to leave. 'Did you mean what you said back there?' she asked.

Will nodded.

'I really *do* have a lot of paperwork to get through,' she said, slinging her bag over her shoulder, 'but if you like we could meet up after lunch and go save the world?'

Will got himself another cup of tea and sank down on the couch. Smiled. She wanted to see him again. OK, so it wasn't quite the day of indulgence and nakedness he'd been hoping for, but it was a better than nothing.

Much better.

So why did he still feel guilty?

His love life had been sparse since Janet died. Three and

a half years of celibacy, followed by a one-night stand with an executive from Dis-Com-Lein over on a junket from the small South African country her company owned. Her cloned, faintly oriental features had been a feature of his life for almost four whole hours. She'd phoned him a couple of times, but he never called her back. The memory of Janet was still too raw. The next two had suffered the same fate. He'd start out well enough, but in the end he just couldn't let them in.

Maybe six years was long enough to mourn.

Sighing, he pulled the keyboard out from under the coffee table and powered the screen up again. He'd not had any joy finding Ken Peitai yesterday, so it was time for a different approach. Will opened up the old bonus payment he'd found.

The digital signatures were all stored with the docket. Received by Ken Peitai. Approved by Julius Grond – PayFund Manager. Requested by Tokumu Kikan. That would make him Ken's boss, and he obviously thought highly of him, given the number of zeroes on the deposit.

Will leaned forward in his seat. Tokumu Kikan. He'd never heard of him, but any friend of Ken's was a friend of his.

He sent a cluster of stealth engines off to look for anything relating to Ken's boss.

Ten minutes later he was still no further forward: there was no sign of Ken or his boss in any of the government systems, other than that one bonus payment. PayFund was one of the few services every ministry shared, so that was Will's next target.

He called up the Network's payment system and slipped in though a back door he wasn't supposed to know about. From there it was a struggle to work his way back to the main PayFund servers without leaving a footprint. PayFund was a high-security system for a reason: it handled every single penny the government collected and spent. Screw around in here and you could bankrupt the whole country. They had every type of guardian software known to man in operation, all of it monitored around the clock for intruders. Which was why Will had to take it slow and careful, covering his tracks as he went.

He slipped into the budget allocations and went looking for any mention of Ken Peitai, Tokumu Kikan or Sherman House.

Half an hour passed and all he had to show for it was a blinding headache. He was having to work harder and harder to keep the software from finding him in its daughter's bedroom with his pants round his ankles. If he stayed in here much longer someone was going to notice.

Ken Peitai: one – William Hunter: nil.

He worked his way back out of the system, making sure he'd left nothing incriminating behind, then slumped back on the sofa, massaging his eyes.

OK. Time to try something else.

He couldn't find anything on the people *running* the Sherman House project, but what about the people they were experimenting on. The two bodies they'd dragged back from the place: Allan Brown and Kevin McEwen. Two men living two doors away from each other. One a serial killer, the other a family man who decided one morning to murder his wife and kids.

They'd only managed to ID Allan Brown because his DNA was on file with PsychTech, but maybe there'd be something in there about Kevin McEwen as well.

There wasn't.

Will swore. Then tried a couple of the other systems. As far as he could tell Kevin McEwan had been a perfectly normal citizen. Until Ken Peitai infected him with VR syndrome. So Will went back to PsychTech and called up Allan Brown's case notes.

There were a lot of them, just like Colin Mitchell's,

describing his development, step by step, into the monster they'd finally caught. But there were other chunks of data in the PsychTech files. Data that wasn't meant for public consumption. Data he'd never have found without root access to the archived records. Data logged against Dr Fiona Westfield's username.

Damn. Every time her name came up, Will felt that familiar tightening in his stomach. And the more he read, the worse the feeling got.

'Jesus. . .'

Her notes detailed every session with Allan Brown's parents: how she encouraged beatings, sexual fantasies, feelings of resentment, drug and alcohol dependence . . . Allan Brown was doomed from the start. Parents hate him, abuse him, leave him. Boy drifts into a violent fantasy world. Boy starts burning things. Boy starts hurting things. Boy starts killing things.

'Boy ends up torn to pieces in a public toilet.'

Will called up Colin Mitchell's records. He found a similar set of notes, all logged by Dr Fiona Westfield as she methodically ruined Mitchell's life.

Everyone thought Alastair Middleton was the only monster she'd made, but now it looked as if she'd been a *lot* more productive. Taking vulnerable children and twisting them into carbon copies of herself.

First thing Monday morning he'd get a team to slog through everything – see if they could spot anyone else Westfield had manipulated.

'How many more of you are there? How many more of you did she make?'

She stands outside the incubation room, pretending to clean the window, but really staring at what's growing inside.

It's beautiful. Most of her new head is covered with skin: soft and pale and lovely. It hangs, suspended in its pouch of growth medium, surrounded by a nimbus of thick, golden hair. The face looks like she did when she was eighteen. Back when she was just beginning to experiment with dismemberment. Ah, to be young and innocent again. . .

The nose is slightly too big, the chin slightly too wide – the way it was before Daddy paid for that little round of cosmetic surgery. Helping nature on the way to perfection.

Her heart tingles as she watches her new face floating there. Tonight Dr Stephen Bexley will make sure she can speak, and eat, and look just like a real person.

Tonight she gets her human mask back.

She finishes wiping the glass and drops the rag back into the wheely's cleanbox.

Time to make sure everything is arranged.

She pushes into the good doctor's office, pulling her mop and bucket behind her. When he sees her he flinches. He's lost weight over the last two days; dark circles shroud his bloodshot, grey eyes. He has always had beautiful eyes. It seems to take him a minute to figure out whether this is really her or just some brain-dead, menial slave. She sees the sweat prickling on his face. He knows who she is.

Dr Westfield pulls the datapad from her pocket and presses a button. 'WELL?' it says in its flat, artificial voice.

'Theatre Six: half past eleven.' Stephen fumbles with the pens on his desk. 'It's the earliest I could get without anyone seeing.'

'ACCEPTABLE.'

He rubs a hand across his face. 'I . . . I'm not sure that I can do the whole procedure on my own.'

He wants someone to hold his hand. Share the honour.

'I mean . . . I mean who's going to assist? Who's going to handle the anaesthetics? I can't do everything! What if something goes wrong?' There are tears dribbling down his cheeks and she wonders if she's pushing him too hard. Perhaps she should have sprung the operation on him at the last minute, instead of giving him time to worry. He's obviously terrified for his family, not been sleeping. Panicking. Imagining his pregnant wife being skinned alive.

Hmm. . . Dr Westfield frowns. A miscalculation on her part: she needs him at his best, not exhausted. But it's too late to worry about that now.

Her fingers dance over the keypad.

'IF ANYTHING GOES WRONG YOUR WIFE DIES.'

'But I—'

She punches the 'speak' button again:

'IF ANYTHING GOES WRONG YOUR WIFE DIES.'

He buries his head in his hands and cries.

'MAKE SURE EVERYTHING IS READY. WE START AT ELEVEN THIRTY PROMPT.'

She steps back from the desk and stares at him. Snivelling like a frightened child. Disgusting. Weak.

When she kills him – after he's fixed her face – she'll be doing him a favour. A long, slow, painful favour.

'DO NOT DISAPPOINT ME, STEPHEN,' says the datapad in her hands. 'YOU WILL NOT LIVE TO REGRET IT IF YOU DO.'

He won't live anyway, but sometimes a little hope can go a long way.

They stood beneath the awning of a burger van, sheltering from the pounding rain, eating cloned-meat patties and over-cooked onions. George was tucking into his with relish. Brian ate his with tomato sauce. Will peered at his suspiciously, as if a cat had just crapped in it.

'So what's the verdict then?' said Brian between chews.

'I found out who Ken's boss was six and a bit years ago. Other than that: nothing. It's like they don't even exist.'

'How can there be nothin'? No one's invisible these days, no' even ministry spooks.'

'They've got no Social records, nothing in the Services data-base and, other than one hefty bonus, bugger all in PayFund either. I couldn't even find a budget allocation for Peitai's project at Sherman House.'

'And you're sure they're no' corporate?'

Will nodded. 'No private company's got enough clout to keep something this big a secret.'

Brian growled and bit into his bun. 'If they're no' on the official budgets, they're dark funds. That makes 'em Special Ops, or SIS, or some covert department shite.'

George raised an eyebrow, grease glossing his chin. 'Is that bad?'

'Aye, them bastards don't play by the rules. I used to go out with a guy worked Special Ops – this was years ago mind, just after they'd won the World War Cup: everyone wanted tae shag a soldier – he used to brag about what they did tae people what got in their way. Thought it wis sexy. We're gonnae have to go real careful here: even if we get proof. . . They'll bury us, literally.'

Will swore, risked a bite of his burger, and swore again.

'We're in way over our heads,' said Brian, as Will looked around for somewhere to spit. 'We'll have to be a right sneaky bunch of bastards to get away with this.'

George took a mouthful of Irn-Bru, belched. 'I've sent those brain samples off to the labs. Get them back tomorrow. At least then we'll know what Peitai's injecting the poor buggers with.'

Will stuffed the rest of his burger in the bin. It wasn't much, but it was a start. 'What about you, Brian?'

'No one's talkin'. I've twisted every arm I can think of; whatever they're up to, they're keepin' it real quiet.'

'Then all we've got is one mysteriously fake-shabby apartment, two corpses, and George's chemical residue.' Will scowled out at the rain, watching it hammer into the pavement hard enough to jump back to knee level. 'There's something else: Dr Westfield.'

Brian raised an eyebrow, 'Oh aye?' George just went on eating.

'Turns out Alastair Middleton wasn't the only one Westfield was grooming. Colin Mitchell and Allan Brown: she was their therapist too. I found case notes detailing how she screwed up their parents, then did the same to them. Twisted them till they went out and started killing.'

'Shite. . .' Brian shivered. 'If she did three, who's to say she didn't do more?'

'That's what I was thinking. Bit of a coincidence isn't it? Westfield was manufacturing killers, and now good old Ken Peitai's doing the same thing. Only a bit more high-tech and—'

The alarm on Will's mobile bleeped. He checked his watch: one thirty. Time to go spend the afternoon with Jo.

'Got to run. Keep me up to date, OK?' He dashed out into the downpour, heading for the nearest shuttle station.

'Afraid we've had a couple of problems, sir.'

The room was dark, lit only by the screens that lined the central table. Ken's boss didn't say anything, just twisted the test tube round and round in his fingers, keeping the liquid inside from settling.

Ken Peitai kept his eyes dead ahead. 'Mr Moncur and Mr Stevenson had a . . . lapse of judgement. They've been kinda negligent in their monitoring of our brood mother.'

Ken's boss stopped fiddling with the tube and placed it down on the table with a delicate clink. 'Go on.'

Ken nodded. 'I passed on your instructions to get Dr W brain-fried for good, but Stevenson came down with the flu and Moncur's been up to his eyeballs with other projects. I checked their logs: she's not been in for over three weeks. That means she's not had her medication. And that means—'

'I'm quite aware what that means. Find her. Find her and bring her in *now*.'

'That ain't going to be necessary, sir. She's in the morgue. Roadhugger she was in went for a flying lesson off the ring

231

road and smacked bang into a bus. Boom!' He mimed a small explosion. 'No survivors. Hospital morgue ran a DNA check on Westfield's remains – idiots got the sample wrong, but Moncur says he gave them a false positive anyway, just in case they decided to dig any further. ID chip matched, so it's OK: all taken care of.'

The old man pursed his lips. It made his face look even more aerodynamic than usual. 'Moncur and Stevenson?'

'This is the first time either of them has screwed up, Mr Kikan. I gave them a first and final warning. One more breach and they're testin' the next batch of mixture.'

'Three weeks.' Kikan frowned. 'When I give an order to have someone lobotomized, Ken, I expect it to be carried out immediately. If Dr Westfield had gotten "out of hand" without her medication it would have raised some very awkward questions.'

'Yes, sir. But she didn't and now she's dead.' He watched his boss pick the test tube up and set it dancing again.

'And the other thing?'

'Ah . . . yeah . . . the other thing. You remember that Network guy we had in the other day: William Hunter? Assistant Director?'

'The one you were supposed to be keeping an eye on?'

Ken cleared his throat. 'Yeah . . . that's the one. Publicly he's been making all the right noises about steering clear of the test zone, but we're monitoring his home line and he's been poking around in the PsychTech files.'

'So?' There was a hint of boredom in the man's voice, but Ken knew better than to believe it.

'He's also been runnin' searches on you and me. Hasn't found anything yet, but the guys in statistics say there's a six point three percent chance he's going to find something we'd rather he didn't.'

'How did he get my name, Ken?' The old man's eyes were like ice.

Ken stuttered. 'I . . . I don't know how—'

'This is supposed to be a discreet operation, Ken. First the Westfield woman is allowed to outlive her usefulness and now this. I am not pleased. Not pleased at all.'

'No, sir. I understand, sir.'

'Then you know what to do, don't you?' He slipped the test tube back in his pocket and stood.

'Actually. . .' Ken shifted from foot to foot. 'You think I should maybe have a friendly chat with him first?'

The old man stopped on his way to the exit, his cloat slung over one shoulder. 'What *is* this strange aversion you have to killing the man, Ken?'

'He's a hero, sir. I've read through his file and William Hunter's one of the good guys. I'd kinda prefer not to go rubbing him out unless I absolutely have to.'

Kikan shook his head and smiled one of his rare smiles. 'Just make sure he doesn't cause any more trouble than he already has. The first sign of anything inopportune I want him removed. Understand?'

'Yes, sir!' Ken snapped off a smart salute. 'Don't you worry about Mr Hunter, I'm gonna make sure he stays nice and friendly. And if he don't I'm gonna make sure he stays nice and dead.'

20

Will looked back over his shoulder and watched the city burn. The air was misty with evaporated flesh: soft pink clouds drifting gently to the ground, leaving a faint slick of human cells on anything they touched. He turned his attention away from the funeral pyres and palls of thick, greasy smoke and examined the Whomper in his hands. It was less than half full; whatever Jo was going to do she'd have to do it soon.

The barricade he was hiding behind rocked under another onslaught. Chips of smoking concrete rained down all around him. The noise was deafening. Over in the distance, through the fog of skin and bone, he could just make out Jo's outline, hiding behind the wreckage of a school bus. The vehicle looked as if it had been put through a mangle, and Jo didn't look much better. Her jumpsuit was stained and scorched, the middle section slashed almost in half, exposing swollen, burnt flesh.

She looked back at him, their eyes meeting over the barrel of her Crackling Gun. For a moment Will just crouched there, not moving, then the man standing next to him exploded.

The gun in Jo's hands howled.

They were running out of time.

He vaulted the barricade, and sprinted across the war-torn street, trying not to get his head blown off. The pavement buckled beneath his feet as he ran towards the dark-red troop carrier, chunks of concrete shattering all around as the gunners tried to kill him.

Jo's Crackling Gun howled again, her siege weapon carving bite-sized chunks of metal out of the carrier's hull. Will slithered to a halt, skidding on a patch of someone as he drew level with the craft. He snatched up his Whomper and turned the driver's head into a green-grey stain on the vehicle's roof.

The passenger snatched up something shiny and pointed, like an electric squid, lights twinkling along its length. Will didn't wait to see what it did, just turned the Whomper on him and thumbed the trigger, spreading him all over the inside of the cab. He didn't even have time to scream.

Comlab's computer-generated fantasies always made Will feel vaguely uncomfortable. Here it was OK to kill anything you liked and, as he jumped about the game ring like a lunatic, he couldn't escape the feeling that it was all just a little bit too real. As if the boundaries between what was, and what wasn't, didn't apply here. But that didn't stop him playing.

Will leaned back against the dispenser, totally knackered. Sweat ran down his back and pooled in his unders; he never wore the right thing to play in the game rings. Jo was a lot more sensible: she'd ditched her day clothes and slipped into an all-in-one that clung like a second skin. Her hair was plastered to her forehead, a thick red line marking where the headset had sat. But she was smiling.

He ran a hand over his face, then wiped his damp hands on his trousers. 'How did we do?'

Jo gulped her plastic of fizzy down. 'Not bad,' she said,

suppressing a belch. 'Not the highest score ever, but we kicked some serious Martian arse.'

'Glad you came?'

She rubbed at her forehead. 'Been years since I had to wear a headset. Forgot how much it throws you off. Full immersion is a hell of a lot easier. Less sweaty too.' Jo looked at him for a moment. 'You *really* don't have a jack point? On an Assistant Director's salary?'

'Yeah. . . Sorry about that.'

'Nah, it was fun. Kinda nostalgic.' She reached up and touched his cheek, then grimaced. 'Urgh. . . You're sopping!' She backed off towards the female locker rooms. 'I'm going to shower and change. If you weren't such a mincehead, Mr "Outside Clothes Will Be Fine", you could do the same.'

'Blah, blah, blah. I'll see you in the cafeteria, OK?'

'Try not to stink the place out.' She stepped closer and for a moment Will though she was going to kiss him. Then something happened and she changed the movement into a smile instead, turned, and disappeared through the locker-room door.

They'd been like that all afternoon; as if last night had never happened and they were back to acting like nervous teenagers. It was driving him mad.

Slinging his new jacket over his damp shoulder Will went for a stroll through the gaming hall to cool down a bit. The place was mobbed, as usual: the last shift of gamers milling around, talking over their latest adventure, even though they'd only finished playing it five minutes ago; the next shift plugged in and ready to go. As he walked around he watched them logging on. It was one of the funniest bits for him, over a thousand people, standing in wide, elevated rings eight feet across, doing the hand jive: hitting buttons only they could see. Loading up pre-saved characters and scenarios so they could get on with the violence and the sex.

Slowly the noise level began to rise as the games got

underway; the players staggering around the game rings waving invisible swords/rocket launchers/Whompers/dildos. Each ring had a little viewing screen hooked up next to the command ports and Will paused from time to time, looking in to see what was going on. You could tell when people were playing 'pink disks' because the screens were blank while the people in the middle of the ring got on with whatever filth took their fancy.

'You like to watch?'

The fake mid-Atlantic accent made Will freeze. He took a second to plaster a smile on his face, then turned to see Ken Peitai standing behind him, leaning back against a game ring. He was dressed in one of those lounging robes they wore in the deep-immersion suites, where you didn't need a headset to experience the best in Virtual Reality, you just stuck a wire in the back of your head.

'Ken, good to see you.' That was a lie.

How did the sinister little turd know he was. . . The homing beacons, that's how – buried under Will's skin. Out of sight and out of mind.

Ken smiled, the corners of his eyes crinkling as if he actually meant it. He swept a hand around, indicating the room full of gamers. 'One of my few vices: I like to save the world every now and then. What about you?'

'Just finished: Red Conquest.'

'Great stuff. How did you do?' The smile got bigger. Look at me, I'm so friendly and approachable. . . For a murdering bastard.

'Not bad. We saved Aberdeen, but Dundee's a write-off.'

Ken sighed. 'Too bad, I kinda like all the casinos. All that razzmatazz, yeah?'

There was an awkward silence.

'You know, Will. . . I can call you Will can't I?' He didn't wait for an answer, just took Will by the arm and began to walk. 'Great. I know you were interested in what we were doing at Sherman House—'

237

'Excellent project.' Will laid it on thick. 'I can't think of anything more important than preventing another round of Virtual Riots.'

'Thanks. We've gotta keep it all so hush-hush, no one ever gets any good feedback. I'll tell the team you said that, though.' He flashed the same smile again. 'They're gonna be thrilled. Anyway, Will, I told you all about the project, but you never told us anything about yourself.'

'No. I was a bit tied up at the time.'

Ken laughed a lot harder than was strictly necessary. '"Tied up at the time." I like it! "Tied up." Ha! . . . But seriously, what are you guys in the Network up to these days?'

The greasy little bastard was actually trying to weasel information out of him. 'Well, you know what it's like at Network HQ: there's always so much going on.'

'Yeah, all those guys and gals, running round, keeping us all safe. What about you, though? You working on anything juicy?'

'Just having a couple of days off.'

'Right, right. I heard on the grapevine that you'd caught someone for that hole in the head thing. Good work. Fast. You gotta be proud of your people for getting the guy that quick.'

'Yes.' Will was finding it more and more difficult to smile back. Colin Mitchell had been caught less than twenty-four hours ago, and Ken Peitai already knew about it.

'Can I be frank, Will? Can I? Good.' Ken stopped. They were by the west exit. Outside the double glass doors the rain hammered against the concrete forecourt, sparkling in the spotlights as it leapt back into the air.

'You know, Will. . .' Ken sounded as if he were picking his words very carefully. 'The funny thing about national security is how some of the weirdest things turn out to be sensitive information.' He paused as if waiting to see if Will got it. 'Sometimes it's the silliest little things, things that don't seem

238

at all connected, that can cause real big problems further down the road. But you know that, right? You deal with sensitive stuff all the time.'

He punched Will on the arm and winked: all mates together.

Jumped-up little shite.

'So what I'm saying is *I* know, and *you* know there's nothing wrong with you pokin' about in the PsychTech files or searching for a bit of info on me and my boss. Don't blame you at all: after what happened you're bound to be interested, right? But there's a couple of guys upstairs who know a lot more about the big picture than I ever will and they're worried something's gonna get out that'll jeopardize what we're trying to do over at Sherman House.' He shrugged. 'Seems daft to me, but what do I know?'

He obviously knew Will had been going through the PsychTech database. Just like he knew they'd caught Mitchell. . . Will wondered if he went back to Network HQ right now and played the SOC recording of Mitchell's flat, would he see little grey blobs of no data in the corners?

'If you work for the Ministry for Change, Ken, why are you worried about national security?'

Ken's smile faltered a little, but he rode it out like a pro: 'Hey, ain't we all concerned about the security of our nation in these troubled times?'

Will stared at him and said nothing.

'Look, Will, I know you got your suspicions. Hell, be surprised if you didn't. But we're on the same side here. We. . .' Ken's eyes did a quick sweep of the gaming hall. 'Your mate the pathologist, he found chemical residue in Allan Brown and Kevin McEwan's brains, right?'

So he'd been right – they were monitoring his phone. No point lying about it then. 'He thinks they've been injected with something that gives them VR syndrome.'

Ken sagged back against the double doors. 'I know how it looks, but. . .' He stopped and took a deep breath. 'Will, what

I'm gonna tell you can't go any further. I mean it, man: this stuff is like code-black, OK?'

'Tell me.'

'OK.' Ken lowered his voice. 'Look, you're right, we *are* infecting controlled groups with something that makes them act like they've got VR syndrome.' He held up his hands. 'I know, I know, it's a crappy thing to have to do, but we got no choice. We don't know what started the last set of Virtual Riots. We can't study it in the wild. And we can't afford to sit about with our thumbs up our asses waiting for the next outbreak to come along.'

He looked away. 'I gotta tell you, I hate this. I hate pumpin' our own guys full of shit and watchin' them go off their heads, but it's the only way we're gonna find a cure before it comes back again. You know how many people died last time?'

Will did, but he kept his mouth shut.

'Three million. Three million Scottish citizens *died*. World-wide the total was like, what: fifty, sixty million?'

'So you're giving our own people VR.'

'Will, we infect controlled groups and keep them under real close observation. We work on what's goin' to keep them alive and sane. We work on ways to diffuse the triggers before they occur. We tried using simulations and computer models but it wasn't working, there's something about the way the diseased population interacts, a kinda feedback loop you can only see in the wild. Makes the condition a hell of a lot worse.' He shook his head. 'All that stuff I told you when I showed you around was the God's honest truth: we're doin' our best and we're gettin' there. Next time it happens we're gonna be ready. We're not gonna sit back and watch another three million poor bastards die.'

Will had to admit Ken sounded as if he meant it. As if he believed every word he was saying. But Will had dealt with lying wee shites before. 'What about Allan Brown? He was killing for years: how come you never stopped him? You're up there monitoring the whole place and he's out butchering halfheads.'

Ken's smile slipped a bit. 'We're not perfect OK? Like I said: we don't got cameras in all the flats yet.'

'He's been at it for over five years, Ken. You telling me you didn't notice anything?'

The smile disappeared all together. 'Listen, all I know is the VRs turned America from a superpower into a third world fuckin' country. I ain't gonna sit back and let that happen here. Not again. Will, I'm tellin' you: this gets out we're all in for a whole world of hurt.' Ken stared at him. 'You gotta understand, man: we're doin' what we gotta do. I'm asking you to be one of the Good Guys and just leave it alone. Let it drop. We'll go on lookin' for a cure and you and your team can go on doin' what you do. No one needs to get hurt, OK?'

No one needs to get hurt? The little shite had just threatened him. Will had a sudden urge to kick Ken's backside up and down the gaming hall. But instead he stuck out his hand and said, 'One of the Good Guys.'

Ken beamed 'OK!' They shook hands. 'Well, gotta go. There's this kingdom needs saving from a fire-breathing Dragon and a buncha Goblins. You have a nice day.'

Will said, 'Thanks,' but he was thinking about twisting Ken's head round until his neck went pop.

She's so excited she can barely stand still. The operating theatre will be ready in just over eight hours. Eight hours. How can she possibly wait that long without bursting?

The automated storeroom gleams like a brand-new pin. She's polished and mopped and dusted and scrubbed – anything to make the day go faster. Kill the time. . .

Deep inside her, a need is growing. A need to kill more than time.

She's taken her medicine today, twice the normal dosage,

but the need won't go away. It's the excitement; it makes her body tremble.

Eight hours to go.

Eight hours. . .

She walks round and round the store, straightening the piles of surgirags and skinglue and sharps and sheets and disposals and everything else a large modern hospital needs. She has counted each and every sheet in the pile, every box of nutrient and she still can't rest.

There has to be a release. There has to be a release *soon*, or she won't be able to think straight. And if she can't think straight she'll start making mistakes. And if she makes mistakes she'll be caught.

Justification.

She stops pacing and closes her eyes, pleased with herself.

If she doesn't kill something, she'll be caught.

She grabs a fresh blade from a pack and slips it into her orange and black jumpsuit. This is the last day she will ever wear this nasty polyester uniform. After tonight she'll be back to her elegant best. Perhaps, once the swelling goes down, she'll stroll down Sauchiehall Street and burn a hole in someone's bank account. That will be nice. A manicure and a facial and a lovely lunch down at the Green. What could be better?

Then afterwards she'll pay Assistant Section Director William Hunter a visit and congratulate him on his promotion.

Dr Westfield pops some supplies in the bottom of her wheely-bucket and saunters off towards the exit. There are a lot of people in Glasgow Royal Infirmary, many of whom will live to a ripe old age. And one who isn't going to live to see tomorrow.

As the storeroom door slides closed behind her she wonders who it will be.

* * *

'What's up with you?' Jo appeared in the Comlab Six canteen where Will was busy nursing a half litre of imported lager and a foul mood. She stood in front of his table, hands on hips, hair hanging slightly damp round her face. On her it looked good.

'Nothing.' Will forced a smile. 'Nothing's wrong.'

DS Cameron raised an eyebrow. 'Bollocks, nothing's wrong. I've interviewed thieves and murderers remember? I know a lie when I hear one.' She dumped her kitbag on the table and sank down into the seat opposite. 'Spill the beans.'

'Honestly, there's nothing—'

'William Hunter, if you expect dinner, dancing or anything else this evening you'll come clean. Understand?'

'"Anything else"?' This time the smile was genuine. 'And just *what* did you have in mind?'

'Talk.'

After a moment's silence he nodded and said, 'I bumped into an old friend when you were getting changed. Told me to keep my nose out of the PsychTech files, told me to stop digging for information on him and his boss. Said if I played nice, "no one would have to get hurt".'

'He *threatened* you?'

'Yup.'

'But you're a Network Assistant Director!'

Will just shrugged.

Jo frowned. 'Why the hell would someone care if you went rooting about in a defunct, debunked, psychology programme that died years ago?'

'No idea.' Will stood. 'I've got to go see Doc Morrison at Glasgow Royal Infirmary in forty minutes. Would be a shame if I *accidentally* hacked into the PsychTech files while I was there. Want to tag along?'

'Just how dangerous is this "old friend" of yours?'

'That's what I'm trying to find out.'

Jo hauled on her jacket. 'What we waiting for then?'

* * *

She walks through the wards like a diner examining the menu. There are so many to choose from: some that no one will miss, others that will leave a family in mourning. Some are young, some are old and none of them look as if they're going to put up much of a struggle. She likes that best of all. This is no time to take any unnecessary risks. A quick, clean kill and then a little bit of post-mortem fun. She's not due in surgery till half eleven: she can take her time with the remains.

But first she has to get them downstairs.

The dumb-waiters are no good, they're only designed to transport things *up* from the automated storeroom, not down. Being inside one when it collapses into the wall and starts its rapid descent back to the basement would be . . . messy. Nothing left to play with. Nothing but mush and a few broken bones. Where's the fun in that?

She pulls her mop from its bucket and spreads some disinfectant over the floor. It's a mundane task, but it helps her think. When she has her real life back, whether it's in the New Republic or Asia Major or even the Colonies, she's going to have the cleanest home in town.

In the next bed a small child cries. It can't be much more than four or five years old: too small to be any real sport, though it would just about fit in her bucket if she snapped its arms and legs. But its head would stick out of the top, someone would see. . .

She drifts through to a more grown-up ward.

There are a few other halfheads working the room. One manoeuvres a floor-polisher back and forth across the scuffed terrazzo; another pushes a disposal buggy from one bed to the next, picking up the patients' wastepaper baskets and emptying them into the big box on wheels. She stops for a moment to watch him – or her – work. Pick up the bin, tip it into the buggy, put the bin back. A nice undemanding job, just the thing for a surgically edited mass murderer. Or rapist. Or hedge-fund manager. Or whatever it was the thing in the orange jumpsuit had done to deserve half its face being cut off.

A nice big buggy, just the right size to take a fully grown adult. Perfect.

She crosses to the end bed. The man lying beneath the crumpled white blanket is wearing stripy pyjamas and a VR headset. His hands are above the covers, so whatever fantasies he's living out can't be too rude.

Dr Westfield takes a look up and down the ward: no one is watching. So she goes up to the curtain, grabs it and walks it round until the bed is hidden from view. The man doesn't even look up.

His name is Liam Holdstock and – according to the case notes that flicker across her datapad – he has an infected liver. Better not eat it. . . And then she remembers she hasn't got a mouth to eat it with. Not yet anyway.

Seven and a half hours and counting.

She balls her right hand into a fist, then taps Liam on the shoulder.

'Whatta hell d'you want?' he grumbles, still buried in his little computer game. 'Can you no' see I'm busy. Jesus, hiv youse lot nithin better tae dae wi' yer time than bug me?'

She taps him again, enjoying herself as the moment stretches out.

'*What?* Jesus-effin-Christ. Can ye no'—' He pulls up the side of his headset and peers out. He frowns, slack mouth hanging open. There's no one there, just some stupid halfhead. 'Aw, fer fucksake,' he says at last. For a brief second he glances up at her and his flabby face breaks into a smile. 'Aye, an' you can fuck aff as weil, y'bucktoothed wee bast—'

She hits him across the bridge of the nose, breaking it. Blood pours down his face. His hands come up, palms open and facing out. Classic defence posture. But she's not playing that game today. She grabs the clock from his bedside cabinet and smashes it over his head. He goes limp.

For a minute she just looks at him lying there, not moving, and then she reaches forward and feels for a pulse. And there it is. She hasn't hit him too hard; he'll survive the trip downstairs. But not what waits for him there.

Right on cue, the halfhead with the disposal buggy pushes through the curtain, looking for Liam Holdstock's bin. She takes the buggy and steers the lobotomized slave to the other side of the bed, where she presses her mop handle into its hands, then pushes it back out into the ward.

Liam's heavier than he looks and getting him into the buggy isn't easy, but she manages it, forcing him down into the basket. She doesn't want him making any sound on their little trip down to the storeroom so she pulls a tube of skinglue from her pocket and with quick, economical movements draws a line of surgical adhesive on both his lips, then presses them together. He looks funny like that, as if he's forgotten to put his teeth in. Just to be safe she runs a spiral of the same glue onto both of his palms and slaps them over his ears. Hear no evil, speak no evil, but he'll be able to see and feel everything.

Emptying Liam's waste-paper basket over his head she pushes her way through the curtain. The halfhead is still standing there, frowning at the mop in its hands. She has confused its little brain. It was emptying bins, but now it's mopping floors. Sooner or later its training will kick in. She doesn't have to worry about it.

Which is just as well, because she's got an appointment in the basement with a man who isn't going to enjoy the next few hours even half as much as she is.

Will and Jo squelched their way through Glasgow Royal Infirmary's lobby, en route to the private Network wards, a good half hour early for Will's follow-up appointment with Doc Morrison.

On the thirteenth floor he led the way through security,

then down the corridor to the doctors' consulting rooms. Doc Morrison wasn't in, so Will slipped in behind her desk, powered up her computer, and asked Jo to keep an eye on the door.

'Right,' he said, hacking his way into the hospital network. 'Let's see what the little gimp was so keen to hide. . .' He entered 'KEN PEITAI' and 'TOMUKU KIKAN' into a stealth engine and sent it off to look at every single record on the hospital servers. They weren't listed in PsychTech – he'd checked before leaving the house this morning – but they were bound to be somewhere, and the hospital's systems were the only ones Will hadn't broken into yesterday. Ninety percent of them weren't accessible from outside the building.

Only the rattle of the air conditioning and the hum of the doctor's terminal broke the silence.

Jo stood with her back against the wall, arms crossed, face working its way round a frown. 'Will,' she said at last, 'when we were in your house this morning I noticed all these pictures of a woman. . .'

So that was it.

Not exactly a conversation he'd been looking forward to.

'It's. . .' He cleared his throat. 'Her name's Janet. We were married.' He closed his eyes; this was even harder than he'd thought. 'She . . . she died six years ago.'

'You still miss her.'

'I. . .' He couldn't look her in the eye. Sigh. 'Yes, I still miss her.' Six years. Six whole fucking years and he still couldn't let go.

'I see.'

Silence settled back over the room like a shroud.

Fucking useless blubbery BASTARD!

Liam is spread out on the concrete floor with hardly a mark on him, dead. He barely lasted ten minutes.

Useless fuck.

She stops pacing up and down the storeroom to kick him in the face. Hard.

He bounces: flopping like a great, flaccid rag doll. It didn't say on his chart that he had a heart condition.

She kicks him again, smearing his nose over his waxy features.

If they don't put things like that on the chart, how is she supposed to operate?

This time she stamps on his face with her heel, again and again and again – useless – bastarding – fuck – until the whole front of his skull caves in.

There are still seven hours on the clock and she's got nothing to keep her busy but getting rid of fat Liam's disgusting corpse. This is so *unfair*. All she wanted was a little distraction to while away the time, was that so much to ask? Was it?

Something to make the fucking bees shut up.

Stamp, stamp, stamp.

She stops when she realizes that all she's doing is making a bigger mess for herself to clean up. Liam's head looks like an old cushion, and all the stuffing is leaking out over the storeroom floor. She steps away from the body and breathes deeply, in and out through her nose, not the little vent glued into her throat.

Calm.

This is all just temporary. Just make-work. Killing time till the operation, nothing more.

Calm down. Deep breaths. Deep breaths and calm, cool thoughts.

Useless *bastard*.

Grabbing a drip stand from a nearby rack she beats at his chest until one of the wheels breaks off and the sharp edge punctures his flesh.

Seven hours to go. Just seven hours. She can make it, she can. All she needs to do is clear her mind.

248

The drip stand rattles and clanks as she drops it to the floor. Calm, cool thoughts. Calm, cool thoughts.

She snaps yet another shot of medicine into her neck and sinks down against a stack of internal thermometers.

Calm, cool thoughts.

She'll need to wrap the body in something, then she'll have to clean the floor. Get rid of the evidence. Something deep inside her likes that. Mopping and scrubbing will be therapeutic, calming. Then she can throw the body back into the disposal buggy and wheel it down to the incinerator.

Calm, cool thoughts.

But inside she *burns*. She wanted a release – deserved one – and Liam didn't hold up his end of the bargain. She needs to let off steam. She needs it. Even with three shots of medicine in her she can't sit still.

Bees and broken glass.

Dr Westfield looks from the battered corpse of worthless Liam to the clock on the wall. It's just after four: nearly seven and a half hours to go. She can't last that long. She just can't.

A shudder runs down her spine. The Man In The Dark-Blue Suit has to come back to the hospital at half past four: she read about the appointment in his medical records. She has half an hour to clean stupid Liam away before the man responsible for all this shit arrives in the building.

She was going to save William Hunter for later, for when she's all fixed up and can taste his fear and his blood, but she needs something now. And William Hunter will do nicely. Escort him back down to her storeroom-operating theatre and give him the worst seven hours of his life.

21

The Network has its own private floor of Glasgow Royal Infirmary. Different from the rest of the building, its walls are thicker, its floors are reinforced, its ceiling covered with shielding. Troopers stand guard at the main bank of elevators; anyone without a pass is escorted off the thirteenth floor at the point of a Whomper. But she walks right past them as if they weren't even there.

She wanders slowly around the private reception area, picking up the wastepaper baskets and emptying them into her buggy. Fat, useless Liam is just another layer of ash in the hospital furnace, the storeroom is nice and clean, and she still has ten minutes before The Man In The Dark-Blue Suit arrives for his appointment. Ten minutes to find out where he'll be going. Ten minutes to get into position. Ten minutes to decide what she's going to do to him.

So many beautiful options. . .

Her medicine makes little stars twinkle at the edge of her vision, the world fizzing on chemical ripples. The base of her neck is sore from repeated injections. She's had far more than the recommended daily dose.

The buggy creaks as she pushes it through the double doors, following the orange line. The place is quiet, but then four twenty on a Sunday afternoon is hardly peak time. She passes wards, scanners, and operating theatres. The consultation rooms are at the end of a short corridor.

There's a waiting area in the middle of the room – comfy chairs, pot plants, a coffee machine – and treatment rooms down either side. Each one with a display screen next to it, listing the doctor's name and upcoming appointments.

There's no one around to see her checking the screens for William Hunter's name. She finds it down at the end of the row.

Seven minutes. His appointment is in seven minutes.

Perfect. All she has to do is wait in the little room. She's not worried about the doctor already being there – doctors die just as easily as everyone else. And when William Hunter turns up she'll wait till he's not looking, then use the injector in her pocket to pump him full of sedatives. Heave him into the buggy, just like useless Liam. Only when she gets him down to the storeroom he'll last a lot, lot longer.

Mmm. . .

Her hand freezes on the doorknob; there are voices inside the consulting room. She frowns at the display, checking. No one should be in there – it's reserved for The Man In The Dark-Blue Suit. How dare they! How *dare* they get in the way! And then the voices say something that makes her flinch.

'Peitai. . .'

The word makes her skin burst out in pins and needles.

A cold room, keys beneath her fingers and tubes in her arms.

She lurches back from the door, heart thumping in her chest.

Peitai.

Pictures of her children, flickering lights, questions, electricity, pain. She staggers into the buggy and it sends one of the pretty pot plants crashing to the ground.

Peitai. . .

*   *   *

251

'What was that?' Jo jerked upright.

'I said that Ken Peitai—'

'Shush!' she crossed to the door and put her ear against it. 'There's someone out there!'

Will nodded. 'Yeah, it's a *hospital*. There are thousands of people out there.' It was a stupid thing to say, but it was out before he could stop himself. Ever since she'd asked about the photos in his living room there had been a layer of glass between them. Something that couldn't be seen, but kept them apart. He was acting like a tit and he knew it.

Jo scowled at him. 'You know what I mean. We're hacking into the hospital records, you think your doctor's going to be happy about that?'

'Good point.' He started hammering commands into the keyboard. 'You see who it is, I'll copy the files and shut this thing down.'

Lights: too bright for her to bear, shining straight in her eyes. A short man in green, an older one dressed like a crow. Questions. More questions. She stumbles to the seats in the middle of the waiting area and collapses into one.

Hot noise races through her head; the interrogation chair; stabbing bursts of pain; questions. Peitai and his keeper – the man in the long black cloat with the delicate fingers that make her writhe in pain.

Someone says something, but she ignores it. Her head is burning from the inside out.

A hand touches her shoulder and she explodes out of the chair. No. No more. She won't answer any more questions!

Something goes 'crack' and suddenly all the noise and light and pain vanish.

She's in the waiting area, standing over the body of a woman. The woman isn't moving, she's just lying there on the floor, a Palm Zapper nestling in a shoulder holster, just visible through her open jacket.

Dr Westfield grabs it.

It's all gone wrong. Unravelling. . .

She stares at the consulting room door with his name next to it.

This is too dangerous. Too big a risk. She has to get away from here. Now.

She grabs her trolley and makes for the exit. Walk, don't run. If she runs they'll know something's wrong. If she runs they'll catch her.

Will shut down the doctor's computer with a satisfied click. There were only a couple of references to Peitai and his boss, Mr Kikan, but it was still a lot more than he'd had this morning. And now the files were all downloaded to his cracker where he could read through them at his leisure.

He put everything back the way he'd found it and stood, waiting for Jo to return. When she didn't he crossed to the treatment room door and stuck his ear against it: silence.

'Jo?'

He pulled the door open and saw her body lying sprawled across the floor. A bloody graze on her forehead.

'Jo!' Will dropped to one knee and felt for a pulse. She was still alive, but it looked as if she was in for one hell of a lump. 'Jo, can you hear me? Who was it?'

No reply.

'Damn!' He stabbed his throat-mike. 'Control, this is Hunter: Network treatment rooms, Glasgow Royal. I have an officer down.'

'Roger that, Security is on its way. . . Wait a minute, "officer"? Don't you mean Agent?'

'No I don't.' He dragged his Palm Thrummer out of its holster and snapped the thing on. 'Get a med team here on the double! You'll find DS Cameron outside Doc Morrison's room.'

'Where will you—'

He killed the link.

There was no sign of which way the bastard had gone.

Left or right? Left. He sprinted back along the corridor, making for the exit and the lifts, barged through the first set of swing doors and almost fell over a halfhead. The damn thing was right in the middle of the passageway, but Will dodged it just in time and kept on running.

He was breathing hard when he battered through the next set of doors and into a ring of heavy weapons.

'Hud it right there! Hauns far I can see 'em!'

Will was looking down the business end of a Whomper on full power – telltales blinking away on the assault rifle. He did exactly what he was told.

'Drop the weapon, pal, or I'm gonnae drop you!'

He let the Palm Thrummer fall to the floor. 'ADS Hunter. I've got a Bluecoat DS in need of medical assistance back there and whoever did it is still running loose! Has anyone passed you?'

'What?' The assault rifle drifted away from his face as the spokesman frowned. 'There's been naebody down this end.'

'Then they're still on this level!'

Will pointed at the trooper with the Whomper and the sergeant's stripes. 'You come with me.' He turned towards two others: 'I want you and you to do a sweep of the floor, search the bloody bedpans if you have to.' Then he grabbed the remaining trooper. 'Get back there and guard the lift, no one in or out. Understand?'

'Hud oan.' The Whomper drifted back towards Will's head. 'Afore we go runnin' about like good wee doggies, let's see some ID.'

She can feel the sweat beading on her forehead. The corridor is full of armed guards, but they're not interested in her; they're interested in the man trying to order them about. The man she came here to kill. Their guns point at *his* head, not hers and she wants to keep it that way.

254

Her heart thumps faster and faster as she wheels the creaking buggy past.

Calm. Stay calm. They don't even bother to look as she slouches by, even though she knows she must be shaking like a schoolboy in a brothel. And then the doors swing shut behind her and she is in the reception area, praying with every step.

God must love her, because no one says a thing as she walks into the lift.

The doors slide shut and a shudder runs through her body.

She's going to get away with it.

Will ran back towards the consultation rooms, trailing his armed escort behind him. Jo's body was still lying where he'd left it and he skidded to a halt. Thank God, she was still breathing.

'Search the rooms!'

He knelt beside her, stroking her cheek as the sergeant with the Whomper started kicking in doors. Jo's eyelids fluttered, then she murmured something. He had to lean in close to hear what it was.

'Well,' he said, sitting back on his haunches, 'there's obviously nothing wrong with your swearing gland.'

Jo grunted, opened her eyes, then closed them again, clutching her bleeding forehead. 'Bastard. . .'

'Are you OK?'

'No.' She struggled to sit up. 'Did you get him?'

'No sign of anyone. Did you see which way they went?'

She nodded her head, winced, then pointed off towards the main reception, where Will had just come from. 'Heard the door slam.'

'What? But there wasn't anyone. . .' He stood, watching the sergeant kicking in another consultation-room door. They'd said no one had passed them, and Will hadn't seen anyone on the way back.

He clicked his throat-mike. 'Has anyone tried to leave this floor?'

Jo almost fell over in the rush to pull her earpiece free. 'Not so loud!'

He shrugged an apology as the voice of the trooper guarding the elevator crackled in his ear.

'Negative. Just a halfhead with a refuse buggy.'

'Stop the lift!'

'What?'

'Stop the damn lift!'

'OK, OK! I'm stopping it!'

Jo sagged back against the row of seats, cradling her head in her hands and groaning.

'Will you be OK?'

'Go. Catch him.'

Will didn't need telling twice; he charged back up the corridor and into the reception area. The trooper stood at the lift's control panel, the open casing exposing neat braids of multicoloured wire and a small terminal.

'I thought I told you no one in or out!' Will said, storming across the floor.

'It was just a halfhead! How could it have been the half-head? It's got nae brain!'

'Not the halfhead, you idiot: the buggy. You said it was pushing a refuse buggy.'

'Aye.'

'Big enough to hide a man?'

'Shite.' The trooper's face fell.

'Shite is right. Override the safeties on the lift. We don't want him cranking the doors open and jumping out.'

'Yes, sir!' The private punched something into the elevator's console. 'Safeties are killed. He's going nowhere.'

'Where is he?'

'Lift's stopped between the lobby and the ground floor.'

'Right.' Will checked the charge on his Palm Thrummer.

'Stay here and make sure no one else gets out this way. And this time when I say no one I *mean* no one! Got it?'

'Yes, sir!'

Idiot.

Will called the sergeant and told him to round up more bodies and meet him in the hospital lobby.

Tears roll down her cheeks when the lift shudders to a halt between floors. She was so close. So very, very close. Twenty seconds longer and she'd have been free.

Stupid, stupid, stupid.

She could have sat on her backside, down in the storeroom, and waited for her surgical appointment, but no. She has to have *revenge*! She has to risk everything for a little venal pleasure.

She deserves to be caught.

Deserves it.

But she'd been so close. . .

Dr Westfield reaches into her jumpsuit pocket and fingers her new Palm Zapper. She won't make it easy for them. The little pebbled disk is powered up, its dial twisted past 'HEAVY STUN' all the way to 'FULL POWER'.

She looks at what's left of her face, reflected in the lift's mirrored doors. If they catch her they'll burn her brain away again. And this time they'll do it properly. This time there will be no coming back.

The Zapper is warm in her hands.

They won't take her alive.

They clustered round the lift entrance, all weapons pointed at the doors. A small crowd was beginning to form behind the Network team, but just like the residents of Sherman House, everyone observed the mythical six-foot barrier.

Will clicked his throat-mike, 'I'm going to give the word and I want you to bring the elevator down nice and slow.'

He checked the cordon of heavy weapons surrounding him. They had enough firepower to take on a small army. 'Do it.'

With a delicate *ping*, the double doors slid open and the sound of electronic firearms gearing up filled the air like wasps in a blender. There, standing behind a disposal buggy, was a solitary halfhead.

'Shite.' The sergeant took a step forward and swept the lift from top to bottom. 'There's no one here.'

Will could have sworn the truncated face relaxed as the sergeant spoke . . . but that was ridiculous.

'Hold on.' Will motioned one of the troopers forward, pointing at the disposal buggy. He'd been right: it was easily big enough to take a fully grown man. The trooper nodded and held his Whomper vertically, the butt-end brushing the ceiling tiles inside the lift. The barrel was pointing straight down into the open buggy.

'Sorry, sir,' he said at last. 'Nothin' in there, but crap.'

'You sure?'

'Yup.' The trooper stabbed the assault rifle down into the basket, sweeping it through the rubbish, letting it clang off the buggy's walls. When he pulled it out again there were unpleasant things sticking to the barrel.

Will stepped into the lift. It was beginning to get a bit crowded: three Network personnel, a halfhead, and a disposal buggy. He peered inside the open top, but the trooper was right, there was no one hiding in there. This had all been one big waste of time.

They stood back and let the halfhead get on with its business, moving between the foyer's rubbish bins, picking them up and tipping them into the disposal buggy as if there was nothing more important in the world.

'Damn it!' They were back to square one.

The trooper with the dirty Whomper wiped the barrel clean and said, 'Y'know the wee bugger may still be up there, sir?'

The sergeant nodded. 'Aye, and there's always the stairs.'

'You're right.' Will powered down his Palm Thrummer and slipped it back in its holster. 'Sergeant, take enough men to search the whole Network level. The rest of you, watch the exits.'

'Aye, sir.'

'Jo, you picking this up? DS Cameron, can you hear me?'

'Not so loud! I hear you. God my head hurts. . .'

'Glad to hear you're feeling better.' Will stepped back into the lift, his finger pushing the button for the thirteenth floor. 'Can you describe the man who attacked you?'

'I'm kinda fuzzy. I came out of the doors and . . . and I think there was a halfhead sitting on the seats. . . And I . . . I remember going to see if it was OK. . . Next thing I know: you're standing over me and my head feels like it's splitting open.'

'You didn't see anyone else?'

'Just the halfhead.'

He froze as the lift doors slid shut. It couldn't be . . . could it? He stabbed the 'hold' button and dragged his Thrummer back out. It was a stupid idea, but he could have sworn he'd seen the expression on its face change: as if it'd been expecting trouble that didn't happen. He squeezed through the doors and ran out into the lobby. There were people milling about everywhere, but no sign of the halfhead with the disposal buggy.

'Where are you?' Will pushed his way through the crowd to the middle of the floor and hopped up onto one of the seats.

'Hey, get down from there!'

'Shut up, Peter, can you no' see he's got a gun?'

Will ignored them, searching the throng for the familiar truncated features and orange and black jumpsuit. There: over by the drinks machine! He jumped down from the chair and saw another halfhead before he'd even hit the floor. And another and another. Suddenly the foyer was full of them, all slouching their way towards the exit.

'What the hell?' He barged his way to the front doors.

There were even more of them outside, all shuffling off the back of a bright-yellow Services Roadhugger. It had pulled in, right under the hospital's portico, keeping out of the rain, and a fat man in dirty grey and blue overalls was manhandling more halfheads down from the tailgate. Will grabbed him, spinning him round.

'Hey, get yer hands aff me, ya bampot!' The man puffed and flustered, smoothing away imaginary creases in his uniform.

'I want you to keep your halfheads away from the hospital ones!'

'Aye, that'll be shinin'. It's changeover time, James, this lot have tae go in an' sweep the floors an' pick up the jobbies.'

'Just hold them here!' Will stuck his ID under the man's nose and watched the assembling halfheads.

'Well, well.' He took Will's ID card and squinted at it. 'Hey Dougie, look at this: it's a bigwig fae the Netwurk!' The fat man turned and showed it to his colleague, the one dishing out the mops and buckets. 'Are we no' honoured?'

'Oh, aye, I'm honoured all right.' Dougie laughed, showing off a random collection of lopsided teeth.

Will snatched his ID back. 'Fancy a three-week holiday in the Tin? Because that's what you'll get if I do you for obstruction!'

'Aye, aye, keep yer wig on, James. There's nae need tae get a' huffy.' The fat man waved a hand at his partner. 'Douglas,' he said in a mock Morningside accent, 'be so good as to line all oor guests up against the truck so that they does not mix wi' those ruffians ower there.'

'Aye, aye Mon Capitan. I'll just shoogle 'em over here oot o' harms way.' He gave an elaborate salute and shoved his charges back against the Roadhugger's side. 'Come on ma wee darlins, let's be havin' ye.'

'There ye go, James, all present and correct.' The fat man

added, 'Sah!' then clicked his heels and grinned. Will came within an inch of punching him on his squint, sarcastic nose.

The halfheads from the previous shift were beginning to get restless. Every evening they would drift out of the hospital and onto the Roadhugger, go home to the depot to be fed and washed. They lived by their routine and the change was making them nervous. One by one they abandoned their wheelies and their buggies; milling about, looking distressed. Will tried pushing them into some sort of order, but it was like juggling cats: they wanted to get onboard the Roadhugger and there was going to be no standing still until they did.

'Oh, for God's sake! Put the bloody things on the truck.'

'Keep them aff, pit them oan, dae the hokey-cokie. . .' The fat man executed a courtly bow to his friend with the awful teeth. 'Douglas, would you be a dear an' help oor passengers aboard th' good ship Lollypop?'

'My pleasure, Captain!' He turned and made a megaphone out of his dirty hands and irregular mouth. 'All aboard the Mudlark!' To Will's surprise the halfheads started shuffling forwards. 'Come on ladies an' gentlemin, lets be avin' yeeeew!'

They brought their mops and their buckets, their buggies and their brooms with them. Dougie relieved them of their burdens, then Captain Fat and Sarcastic helped them up the back step and into the Roadhugger. Will stood at the tailgate, looking into their faces as they were pulled onboard. Searching for some sign of life. There was no way to tell if any of them were the halfhead in the lift; they all looked alike to him. Every single one of them seemed to be brain-dead.

'Ye happy now?' asked the Captain, when they were all on board and strapped into their bays.

'How many did you bring with you?'

'The same number they gave us at the depot. Whit *is* it wi' you?'

'How many?'

He hooked a thumb over his shoulder at the ones lined up along the side of the truck. 'That many.'

'You must keep some sort of records—'

'Look, Mister, we ain't their keepers. We just picks them up and drops them off. OK? Gie's a break!'

Will dropped off the tailgate and stared at the line of new halfheads, all clutching their cleaning materials and waiting for instructions. This was madness: they were halfheads. Between them they wouldn't have enough brains left to break wind, never mind assault a Bluecoat officer and evade a Network security team. It wasn't just unlikely, it was impossible. He was just making a fool of himself.

'We all done here, James? Entertaining as this is, Dougie an' me gottae go dae some actual work, but.'

Will gritted his teeth, forcing out the words, 'Thank you for your cooperation.' Then he turned on his heel and stomped back into the hospital, doing his best to ignore the derisive laughter that erupted behind his back.

She watches him leave: face all crumpled, shoulders all slouchy. Poor thing. What he needs is a woman's touch. She gets a warm feeling inside at that. A woman's touch, with a very sharp blade.

It was easy to change lines, to become one of the incoming domestic slaves, rather than the outgoing.

When the line snakes away from the Roadhugger and in through the hospital doors she goes with it. They all line up like good little soldiers, then a bored-looking orderly assigns them their tasks.

She tries to look completely bereft of intelligence as the bored man tells her to go and mop the floors in the mortuary. As she slouches off towards the lifts she sees the orderly get to the end of the line and examine his clipboard.

'We got one too many. . .' He frowns, then shrugs. 'Ah well, waste not want not.'

Dr Westfield catches sight of the big glass and bronze clock hanging over the reception desk. It's not even five o'clock yet. She still has six hours to go.

Six hours and a head full of bees and broken glass.

Peitai. . .

She will find herself a nice private room and have a shower. A long, hot shower to cleanse away all the dirt and filth and menial labour of the last six years.

Then she'll be nice and clean for Dr Stephen Bexley. He'll give her back her face and her life, and she'll take his. Then she'll pay that nice man from the Network a home visit.

He almost had her tonight – almost ended everything before it had really begun.

One good turn deserves another.

Will sat on the edge of the treatment bench and tried not to wince as Doc Morrison poked and prodded his bruised ribs.

'You know,' she said, standing back, watching him sitting there in his pants and socks, 'you're becoming a bit of a fixture round here. How about you stay out of trouble for a month or two? Let absence make the heart grow fonder.'

'I'd like to,' Will smiled, 'but you're just too much woman for me to resist.'

'Very funny. Get your clothes on.' She slapped a couple more blockers into his hand and invited him, politely, to get the hell out of her office.

Jo was waiting for him outside, a patch of bright pink sitting on her forehead where the graze used to be.

'That looks nice,' he said as they walked towards the lifts.

'So much for natural flesh tones.' There was still a touch of frost in her voice. She punched the button for the rooftop landing pad and they stood side by side, waiting for the lift to show. 'How's your ribs?'

Will shrugged. 'Doc says they're healing. What about you?'

'Slight concussion and a patchwork head.'

He smiled and wrapped an arm round her waist. 'All in all a lovely day then?'

'Yeah. Great. Remind me to go out with you next time I'm feeling suicidal.'

'Oh. Sorry.' He let go of her and tried not to sound hurt. They stood in silence.

Will bit his lip and took a deep breath. He wanted to apologize, tell her she was important to him, that he didn't mean to push her away. . . But looking at her standing there, her face all clenched tight, he couldn't find the words.

He looked away.

He'd screwed it up again.

22

Doctor Stephen Bexley stands in the middle of the operating theatre. He's on his own – good boy. She watches him though the observation window as he twitches and fidgets. Her new head sits on the operating slab beside him, beautiful and radiant in its bath of nutrients.

She should be happy, but all she feels is sick and twisted. The episodes are getting worse: flashes of pain, bright lights, and the old man. The past won't leave her alone.

She pulls out her datapad and picks her way quietly down the stairs and into the operating theatre. Stephen doesn't hear her enter, he's too busy biting his fingernails. He shrieks when the cold, artificial voice says: 'ARE YOU PREPARED?'

'I . . . I was beginning to think you weren't coming.' He looks around the room as if seeing the large banks of machinery for the first time. 'I've disabled the cameras and set up an artificial anaesthetist and. . .' He runs out of words and just stands there, slack and silent. The dark circles under his eyes have grown and his salt and pepper hair is uncombed.

He doesn't look fit to operate on a cat.

Her hands dance over the datapad's keyboard as she gives him some words of encouragement. 'STEPHEN, YOU ARE THE FINEST CLONEPLANT SURGEON IN THE COUNTRY. YOU WILL DO A

WONDERFUL JOB AND MAKE ME BEAUTIFUL AGAIN. NO ONE ELSE CAN DO THIS AS WELL AS YOU.'

He doesn't look as if he believes her.

'REMEMBER THE JENKINS'S CHILD? YOU MADE HIS LIFE WHOLE AGAIN. YOU ARE A GENIUS.'

Something like pride sparks in Stephen's eyes and he nods, then straightens up. Stands a little taller. He must be desperate if this kind of banal flattery makes him feel better about his miserable little life. Or the short portion that's left of it.

'Yes, well,' his voice has become a lot firmer, almost masterful, 'if you could hop up on the operating table we'll get you plugged in.' His hands shake as he prepares the IV drips. Then he takes a deep breath and slides the needles into her skin like the expert he is. She barely even feels it.

Numbness creeps out from the centre of her chest. She can smell her own fear. The last time she lay back on an operating slab they took everything away from her. Everything. She fights to keep the panic in check, but it's acid, eating at her belly. She can see Stephen busying himself with the preparations, but it's the other surgeon she hears: the one that stole her life.

We begin by splitting the lower jaw.

Her breathing becomes erratic, rapid, and somewhere behind her a machine starts to bleep – upping the sedative.

From the corner of her eye she can see Stephen wheeling the surgeon's wand into position. There's a test block mounted beside the wand, a chunk of polished granite, nicked and scarred from previous operations. She wants to scream, to make it all stop, but the drugs hold her solid.

Stephen pulls the operating hood over his face. 'We'll begin by marking the edge of the peel area,' he says, talking to an audience of junior surgeons, students and nurses that isn't even there.

Doctor Westfield can barely feel the tug of the marker on her skin as he runs it around her neck. She's slipping away into chemical darkness, still terrified by the surgeon from six years ago, his long thin fingers and the pain they bring. Her mind caught in a loop of panic and horror. She doesn't even hear the low buzz of the wand or feel her old face being whipped away into a thin, red mist. But an image flashes before her – his name, written on her medical records.

She knows who the old man is.

The apartment was as cold as it was empty, but that suited Will's mood just fine. He sat in the dark, *Alba Blue* belting out through the speakers, an open plastic of whisky on the coffee table, and the keyboard in his lap. The only light in the room came from the screen in front of him, the notes he'd 'liberated' from the hospital's computers casting a ghostly white glow.

He hadn't managed to speak more than a dozen words to Jo as the Dragonfly took them away from the hospital. Instead he'd just stood there like an idiot, trying to get something to come out of his mouth. Trying to say something that would make her understand that he didn't mean to be distant. That he liked her a lot. That he wasn't really an arsehole.

'Remind me to go out with you next time I'm feeling suicidal.'

Great. Just what he'd wanted to hear: Fucking perfect.

Forget about it. It didn't matter. So Jo didn't want him any more. Big deal. He was happy here anyway. On his own. In the dark. Going slowly mad.

No wonder he was seeing things.

Chasing halfheads through Glasgow Royal Infirmary like a lunatic.

Still, at least he'd managed to salvage something from today's fiasco – the files he'd downloaded from the hospital servers.

He poured another measure into his glass.

Ken and his boss had been busy half a dozen years ago.

Mr Tokumu Kikan, Ken's employer, had been a registered

267

surgeon at Glasgow Royal Infirmary for almost six months. From the look of things he'd managed to perform nearly every halfheading the hospital did at that time. His list of 'clients' read like a *Who's Who* of Glasgow's criminal over-belly. Serial killers, kidnappers, rapists, politicians: you name it he'd. . . Will froze, his heart pounding, as he read the name 'Doctor Fiona Westfield'.

Maybe he had something to thank Ken and his boss for after all: they'd mutilated that evil bitch.

According to the records, Kikan only performed the pro-cedure on a handful of others after her. As if no one else was really worth the bother.

Ken Peitai started working for the hospital not long after Doctor Westfield's crimes became public knowledge. He'd been employed to work on the PsychTech database, tidying things up before the project was unceremoniously dumped.

Will checked the dates against the bonus payment he'd found. They matched. When Peitai finished working on the PsychTech database, Kikan made sure he got a massive golden handshake.

Why would a surgeon care about a glorified datamonkey?

Will scowled at the screen. 'What were you really doing, you nasty little squit?'

What was in the PsychTech files that Peitai didn't want him to see?

He took another swig of whisky.

Of course, the *real* question was: why were Peitai and Kikan playing doctors and nurses in the first place?

The world doesn't hurt as much as she'd expected. It's cold and clammy and her throat feels as if she's swallowed razor wire, but it's bearable. She reaches up with a trembling hand, almost afraid of what she's going to find.

'You'll feel groggy for an hour or two.' Stephen's voice has lost its nervousness; the surgical arrogance is back. 'The operation was a complete success. I'm particularly happy with the nerve regeneration.' He makes a theatrical gesture that oozes self-satisfaction. 'Some of my finest work.'

Her shaking fingers brush against something that feels tight and swollen: her chin. It worked! The hand carries on up her face; there are lips, taut cheeks, a smooth forehead and hair. Long, matted, sticky hair, still full of nutrients.

'Try not to move about too much,' he says as she peels her eyes open.

The light stings: makes her head swim, makes her stomach lurch. Stephen stands beside the operating slab, close enough for her to reach out and squeeze the life out of him.

She wants to ask for a mirror, but all that comes out is a hissing grunt.

'Don't try to speak. Your new vocal chords need time to settle in.'

It takes an almost Herculean effort to pull herself upright. Something's not right. Burning pins and needles race up and down her body. She shouldn't be feeling like this.

'Having problems?' He's gloating . . . the bastard has *done* something to her!

She tries to grab him by the throat, but he dodges easily. Grinning. Her arm flails out, throwing her off balance. She tips off the edge of the operating table and crashes to the floor – pain rips through her entire head. New nerve endings screaming and burning.

'Not so fucking big now, are you?' He spits at her: a thick globule of white, frothy sputum that splashes on her face like jism.

Stephen takes two steps back – getting a bit of a run up – and then his boot smashes into her stomach. More pain. 'WHERE'S MY WIFE?'

She drags herself onto her hands and knees, but Stephen kicks her again and sends her sprawling.

'Feeling a bit under the weather? That's what happens when you mix your narcotics.'

A tiny moan escapes her brand-new lips.

'How about it, *Doctor*? Want me to hurt you some more?' He aims a kick at her ribs and she can only bounce with it. 'Where is she? GIVE ME BACK MY WIFE, YOU BITCH!'

Oh God. . . everything hurts.

She lies there, on the floor, gazing up at the theatre lights, trying not to cry. This wasn't meant to happen: he was beaten, he *belonged* to her.

Stephen grabs her shoulders and drags her across the polished marblette, back towards the operating table. All she can do is wave a feeble hand in his direction. With a grunt he hefts her off the ground and throws her down on the stainless steel surface. She didn't know he could be so strong. So masterful.

'You have a lovely face you know,' he says as he drags her all the way up the table. 'You were right: I *am* a genius. Oh, it's a little swollen just now, but that'll all settle down in a day or two.' He wheels the surgeon's wand back into place, then grabs a mirror and shows her just how beautiful she is. 'Such a pretty face. Be a shame to ruin all my hard work, don't you think?' The wand screeches as he fingers the hair-trigger, slicing a corner off the test block, sending it clattering to the floor.

'You told me you had nothing to lose. Well now you do.' He holds the wand's cold tip up against the swollen end of her chin. 'How would you like to go back to the way you were?'

'Drrrrrnt. . .' It is barely a word, but she forces it out through her aching throat.

'Was that a plea for help? Was it?'

She nods her head, hot tears running down her cheeks.

'Pllllssssssssssssss drrrrrnt. . .'

He drops the wand to the tabletop, where it skitters and

clanks on the cold metal surface. 'Tell me where my wife is!'

'Cnnnnnnnnnt tlllllllk.'

He grabs her datapad and presses it hard against her face. Nerves creak and burn.

'You can't talk, but you can type, you fucking bitch! Tell me where she is, or so help me I'll peel your head apart!'

Her hands fumble with the smooth ceramic rectangle and it slips, bounces off the edge of the operating table and falls to the floor.

'Stupid, clumsy *bitch*!' He slaps her. It's like a knife's being driven through her face. Skinpaint and skinglue shift beneath the surface of her cheek, threatening to tear the muscle loose. It's not been attached long enough for the fibres to bind themselves to the bone.

She curls up agony as he stoops to pick up the dropped datapad. She has worked so hard! This isn't how it's meant to happen!

Something cold and hard rolls against her forehead and she reaches up, snatching it with both hands.

'Right, you cow.' He grabs her by the shoulder, wrenching her over onto her back. 'Type!'

The wand screeches in her hands and Doctor Stephen Bexley screams. 'Jesushhh, oh fucking Jesushhh!' He's on the floor on his hands and knees, clutching at his left cheek – there's a big hole in his face that goes all the way through to his tongue.

Carefully she swings her legs out over the edge of the slab and lurches to her feet. Her head pounds and her ribs ache and for a moment she comes close to fainting . . . but she doesn't. Instead she yanks the test block out of the wand's holder and batters Doctor Bexley over the back of the head.

She feels a lot better now. The operating theatre's bio-scrubber is plugged into her arm, pulling the blood out and purifying it, before pumping it back in again. Naughty old Stephen's chemicals are being flushed clean away.

He lies on the operating table, strapped in nice and tight, his eyes as wide as dinner plates. He's scared and so he should be.

She pats him on the cheek – the one without the golf-ball-sized hole in it – and pulls her new face into a smile. It's hard work. She hasn't done it before.

'Yvvvvvv bnnnnnn nnnnnte. . .' She has to admit: she doesn't sound good.

But she's still doing better than Stephen. The only sound he can make is a strangled sob from the smooth-edged hole in his cheek. If she peers into it she can see his tongue, ringed in a circle of cut-through teeth.

Poor lamb. And his day's about to get even worse.

She pulls out the datapad and types the words for him.

'YOU HAVE BEEN NAUGHTY,' says the cold, artificial voice.

He doesn't reply, but then he can't: his lips are stuck together with skinglue.

'WE HAD A DEAL, STEPHEN. AND YOU TRIED TO TAKE MY FACE AWAY.'

Tears roll down the sides of his face like tiny waterfalls. The wound in his cheek must be causing him some discomfort. She could give him a couple of blockers, make it easier for him, but she doesn't want to.

'I TOLD YOU WHAT WOULD HAPPEN TO YOUR WIFE IF YOU DISOBEYED ME.'

He bucks and writhes against his restraints. It doesn't help. She checks the clock on the theatre wall: nearly half past six in the morning. People will be here soon, cleaning and polishing and preparing for the first operation of the day. But she really wants to make Stephen's last few minutes special.

'I WAS GOING TO LET HER DIE. BUT NOW I HAVE TO MAKE AN EXAMPLE OF HER.'

He screws his eyes shut. Bangs his head off the stainless steel tabletop. Cries.

'SHE WILL TAKE DAYS TO DIE BECAUSE OF YOU. LONG, PAINFUL DAYS. PERHAPS I WILL SEND HER HEAD TO YOUR CHILDREN AS A KEEPSAKE.'

She pauses and makes a noise that could almost be mistaken for laughter. It is rough and it hurts, but it feels so good! She leans in so close that her eyelashes sparkle with his tears.

'WOULD YOU LIKE THAT, STEPHEN?'

The sobbing is louder than ever, his grimace opening up the smooth edges of the wound, making it bleed.

'MUMMY'S HEAD IN A BOX.'

But he's stopped listening; he's lost in his world of despair. He's just sentenced his wife and her unborn child to death, and that's something he'll have to live with for the rest of his life. Dr Westfield glances back to the clock again. Which will last exactly eighteen minutes, give or take thirty seconds. She wants to be out of here in plenty of time to avoid the rush and prying eyes.

Speaking of eyes. . .

She climbs up onto the operating table, straddling Stephen's groin. With gentle, rhythmic motions she rocks back and forth, trying to get an erection out of him, but he isn't playing. Shame. But never mind: she's got something that'll take his mind off his poor dead wife.

She twists the top off a tube of skinglue and runs a thin line along the top and bottom lids of both his eyes. With gentle fingers she pulls them open and sticks them down. He looks like a startled cartoon character.

She leans forward and tries to lick his right eyeball, but her tongue is too unruly, too swollen to comply, and all that comes out is a stream of spittle. It spirals down onto his cornea and pools in the deep red folds underneath. Her left hand reaches out and plucks the surgeon's wand from its holder. With a hot buzz it comes online and she eases the hair trigger back and forth, feeling for the right level. She wants this to be nice and gentle.

'Yyyyy hvvvvvv awwwwwways hddddddd boooooffffflllll eyyyyyyysssssssss.'

The wand's nozzle comes to rest over the pupil of Stephen's left eye and she opens her mouth slightly, trying not to pull the muscles too hard. She takes a breath: it tastes of anti-septic and recycled air and Stephen's sweat.

Her finger caresses the trigger.

Now the air tastes of eye.

23

'Sometimes, William, I think you're hell-bent on destroying your career.' Director Smith-Hamilton made a big show of massaging her temples. Her office was nice and warm, in contrast to the day outside, rain hammering against her panoramic window. 'Do you really think I've got nothing better to do than run around cleaning up after you?'

Will kept his mouth shut.

'Why must you always be so *difficult*, William? Why must you always cause trouble?'

'At no point did I contradict any of your standing orders. You said to steer clear of Sherman House and that's exactly what I'm doing.'

'Then why did I have Ken Peitai on the phone this morning telling me how much he enjoyed your little *chat* yesterday? Oh he was full of lovely words about you William, "what a solid agent he is", "fine head on his shoulders", "credit to the Network".'

That didn't make any sense – why would the slimy little bastard call the Director with a glowing character reference? 'I'm sorry, ma'am, but I'm confused: did Mr Peitai complain about any aspect of my behaviour?'

She scowled at him from under the razor-sharp edge of

275

her fringe. 'No, but Governor Clark did. *Again*!' Director Smith-Hamilton sank back into her executive chair and went into the head massaging routine again. 'Why were you speaking to him at all? I told you to stay away from Sherman House!'

'I did!' Getting irate wasn't going to help, so Will took a deep breath and tried to sound reasonable. 'I was at Comlab Six on a teambuilding exercise with DS Cameron when Mr Peitai approached me. He told me to stop digging for information on him, his boss and the PsychTech programme. Said it was a matter of national security.'

'National security?' Her mouth stretched into a thin line, turned down at the edges.

'I managed to get into Glasgow Royal Infirmary's main computers and—'

'William! What have I told you about unauthorized data access!'

'Peitai and his boss both worked at the hospital six years ago: Kikan was a halfheader, Peitai was a PsychTech data-monkey. Whatever they're up to, it's got something to do with the PsychTech programme. I've got profilers and analysts going over the files and—'

'I've told you time and time again not to go traipsing around in other people's computers without my *express* permission! Do you have any idea how much trouble you've got us into?'

'Turns out Alastair Middleton wasn't the only killer Doctor Westfield built. I've got proof that—'

'Ah, I see.' She settled back in her chair, arms tightly crossed across her chest. 'Now we get to it.'

Will pulled a datablock from his pocket and slapped it down on Director Smith-Hamilton's desk.

'These are the files I got out of the PsychTech programme. They prove Colin Mitchell was another one of her 'little projects', and so was Allan Brown. All three of them turned into killers by that murdering bitch. She—'

'This is all about you getting revenge isn't it?'

'What? No. Peitai and Kikan are—'

'Don't think I can't see the connection. Doctor Westfield scrubs toilets at Sherman House, so you can't stay away. One of your own people gets killed because of your obsession – don't interrupt – and even though you're told not to go back again, you do. *Then* you go gallivanting off looking for files from the project she was in charge of and Detective Sergeant Cameron suffers severe head injuries!'

She slammed a hand down on the desktop, making the holo of Mars jiggle. 'And now Services tell me you were running around yesterday trying to arrest halfheads. Halfheads! And you sit there trying to justify your bizarre behaviour with a spurious tale about some big conspiracy!'

'That's not true! Peitai and Kikan—'

'Work for some very important people, and I won't have you interfering with their project!'

Will played his last card: 'They're giving people VR syndrome.'

Her eyes widened. She hadn't been suspecting that. No matter how much political pressure she was under, Director Smith-Hamilton still knew right from wrong. Hopefully.

She sat there with her mouth hanging open for a moment, staring at him. 'You have proof?'

Will nodded. 'We've got two corpses in the mortuary, both with traces of a chemical residue in their brains. It mimics the effects of the syndrome perfectly. George has sent samples off for analysis.'

She leaned across her desk and picked up the datablock with the PsychTech files in it, turning it over in her hands. 'I don't like this, William. I don't like this one little bit. You should have informed me right from the very start. How dare you go behind my back and set up a major investigation without my knowledge!'

'I—'

'Your behaviour has gone rapidly downhill ever since Doctor

Westfield died. I checked with our counsellors, you haven't made an appointment with any of them!'

'I didn't think it would be—'

'You will go back to your office and make an appointment for a week of extended therapy sessions.'

'But—'

'Or you can go downstairs and clear out your desk. Your choice.'

Silence.

Then Will said, 'Yes, ma'am.'

'You will then make yourself useful and go supervise your team! Agent Alexander has one of the poorest clear-up rates I've ever seen. It's supposed to be *your* job to make him produce results.'

'Yes, ma'am.'

'Shape up, Mr Hunter. Shape up or you'll find yourself looking for something else to fill your day. Do I make myself clear?'

'Yes, ma'am.'

'Now get out of my sight.'

She sits in her toilet-paper nest, examining her lovely new face in a stolen mirror. The skin's swollen and puffy, black and blue, but to her it's beautiful. Dr Stephen Bexley – God rest his tortured soul – really was a genius. Before his unexpected, messy, *painful* death.

The bruises will disappear within twenty-four hours, as long as she keeps taking the post-operative drugs. The swelling will take a little longer. It makes her face lumpy and bumpy, as if she's stuffed her skin with half-chewed fruit gums.

Her long blonde hair is still sticky and matted, clinging to her head like strangled string. She can't wash it till this evening when the skinpaint has fully cured; the last thing she wants is for her new face to start melting.

The handful of blockers she snapped into her neck after getting rid of Stephen's body have left her blissfully relaxed, but she longs to get away from this dungeon, with its racks of bedpans and piles of plastic sheets. She wants to feel sunlight on her new face.

She slides out onto the storeroom floor and peels off Stephen's old surgical gown. He doesn't need it anymore: he's all burned away.

The clothes Kris wasn't wearing when she and her boyfriend were caught *in flagrante delicto* are clean and disinfected: washed by hand in the little sink. The lacy confectionary pretending to be Kris's undergarments is a bit cheap and tarty for Dr Westfield's tastes, but she slips into them anyway. The bra hangs on her, its cups empty and sad. She hasn't got breasts any more, just a pair of U-shaped scars where the surgeon hacked them off – de-sexing her so no one would be tempted to live out their filthy fantasies by screwing a serial killer. She cheers the bra up with a few handfuls of toilet paper. The panties are slightly more disturbing: her catheter makes a tiny tent in the front, like a little erection. As soon as she's taken care of business here she'll go somewhere new and book herself some more surgery. She will be a woman again.

Dr Westfield pulls on Kris's green trousers, T-shirt and white trainers. They make her look like an intern, but there's nothing she can do about that. So she throws the white labcoat over her shoulders and examines her reflection again.

Her new face makes her look . . . odd, unfamiliar. It's not just the swelling, or her old nose – it's the bottom jaw. She hasn't had one for six miserable, brain-dead years. Carefully she pulls back her top lip and exposes her teeth. *That's* what she's used to, that hideous parody of a human face.

She slips her new credit cards into her pocket – Kris, her dead boyfriend, and Stephen won't be needing them any longer – along with one or two medical supplies that'll come in handy later. Then Doctor Fiona Westfield says goodbye to the storeroom that's been her home for the last five days.

She doesn't look back.

Will stood in the rain with his collar turned up and his mouth turned down. On the other side of the 'CRIME SCENE' tape half a dozen of Glasgow's finest were slowly picking their way through a mountain of rubbish skulking beneath the Kinning Park flyover.

Agent Brian Alexander was knee-deep in filth, directing the search with all the joy of someone who's just found a jobbie in his bathtub. Will ducked under the yellow-and-black tape, trying not to think about what he'd just stood in. It was brown and it squelched, and that was more than he really wanted to know.

'Why is it,' he asked, dragging his shoe along the side of a pile of sodden paper, 'that you always end up with cases like this, Brian?'

Brian grunted. 'Because the Bitch Queen hates my guts, that's why. I mean look at this!' He waved a fat arm at the vast pile of rain-soaked garbage. 'Why does this need real people? I could've grabbed a bunch of halfheads to grub about in the shite, but no! That would be too easy. What we want is some poor Network bastards up to their knees in pish!'

Will stood with his back to the wind, watching a Behemoth from Dis-Com-Lein drift across the leaden skies towards Glasgow Central, and wondering what the cloned publishing executive he'd slept with all those years ago was doing now. Probably *not* wading through stinking mounds of garbage.

At least here, under the expressway, they got a little shelter from the rain. All they really had to worry about was the dirt, the germs, and the disease-carrying vermin.

Will pointed at the team going through the unofficial landfill site. 'What's the story?'

'Two Bluecoats, missing since Friday.' Brian dug his hands

into his pockets. 'Station commander didn't do anythin' about it till Saturday afternoon. Says he's no' got enough manpower to do a proper search. Tosser. He finally gets round to tellin' us about it and we have to fight him all bloody weekend to get their coffin dodgers turned on. He says they're only used as a last resort. Like PC Douglas and MacDonald're out there eatin' chip butties and skoofin' Irn-Bru!' Brian sniffed back a drop hanging on the end of his nose and spat it out into the rubbish heap. 'Anyway, we broadcast their ident codes first thing this morning and bingo. Both signals are comin' from this pile of shite under the expressway. So now here we are, diggin' through it by hand, lookin' for them.'

Will nodded, looking out over the mound of mouldering debris. 'How come there aren't any Bluecoats helping?'

Brian grunted again. 'Station commander couldn't spare any. Can you believe it? No' even to look for his own people! Unbe-fuckin'-lievable.'

Will had to agree.

They walked the perimeter of the rubbish heap, Brian bemoaning his fate and Will making distracted soothing noises, not really listening. He was going over the chewing out he'd got from Director Smith-Hamilton instead. She'd taken what was pretty damning evidence and dismissed it out of hand. It wasn't like her at all.

And she had the cheek to say *he* was the one acting irrationally.

'You know,' he said, watching a Network trooper in a filthy grey jumpsuit digging through a multicoloured pile of trash. 'Director Smith-Hamilton thinks I should go get some therapy. Thinks I've got "issues".'

'There's a fuckin' shock. You've no' really been the same since that cow Westfield turned up burnt tae a crisp. I mean I'm no' surprised: what with her deid and all the shite goin' on at Sherman House. . .'

'Don't you start.'

281

'Look, you're only babysittin' me today cos Her Majesty tore a strip off your arse.' He turned and poked Will in the shoulder. 'She used to think the sun shone out that very hole. People are beginnin' to think you're a born-again bamheid.'

Will laughed. 'You know something? They might be right.'

Something crackled and sniffed in his ear followed by George's voice: *'Will, Brian, is that you? Hello? Hello?'*

'You don't have to shout George, we can hear you.'

Brian's response was a bit more to the point: 'Quiet down ya snotty wee bastard!'

'Oops, sorry. I've got some bad news . . . and some worse news. The labs have lost the samples I sent them.'

'Soddin' hell, that's just bloody typical.'

'Never mind,' said Will, 'we've still got the original bodies right? We can just take more samples and—'

'That's the worse news.' A loud sniff rattled their eardrums. *'Services came by while I was out at a meeting and picked up the wrong bodies – they were meant to take the two jumpers we scraped up last week – but they took the Sherman House ones instead. They've gone to the great barbecue in the sky. I only found out when I went to get another slice of brain to send off.'*

'Tell me we still have the SOC recordings!'

'Oh . . . I didn't check. You want me to?'

'Please.'

The pathologist's voice clicked off and Brian shook his head. 'They'll be gone too, you know that don't you?' He spat another glob of phlegm onto the garbage at his feet. 'We're fucked: we've got no evidence left.'

'We've got one last bit, but I don't know how it fits in yet.'

Brian raised an eyebrow. 'Oh aye?'

'Peitai wanted me to keep my nose out of the PsychTech files, so I went digging. I've got a team going through everything I downloaded, looking for something that implicates the weasely little shite. Something we can use.' He gave that same bitter laugh again. 'Not that Her Royal Highness will do anything about it – Governor Clark's been on the phone again. They're putting serious pressure on her to bury the whole thing.'

'Shite. . . So what we goin' to do?'

Will looked up at the mountain of rubbish. 'Keep digging.'

The apartment used to belong to an unmarried man. He said he liked nursery rhymes, so she cut off his tail with a carving knife; other than that she can't remember much about him. The rooms are tidy and ordered – unlike some of her other places – and a small layer of dust covers the surfaces, but a quick once round with a damp cloth will put that right.

She drops her shopping bags on the couch and lowers herself into an armchair. What a lovely day. She's managed to max out all three credit cards in the space of an hour and a half. The lovely Kris, her boyfriend Norman, and good old Doctor Bexley have bought her more comfort than she's known in six years. Kris's cheap, lacy underwear is gone, replaced by the finest silk, the toilet paper padding replaced with soft pink cashmere. It's vain and silly, but it makes her feel good to have breasts again, even if they're only make-believe.

And she has bought herself a little *treat*. She pulls a small glass jar from one of the bags. It was expensive – even by her standards – but definitely worth it. She twists open the top and breathes in the rich, earthy scent. Savours it. Then dips a finger into the sticky liquid, coating her skin like amber. Real honey from real bees. Like the ones in her head. Rare and exquisite. Decadent. It tastes of summer: sweet, warm, and wide, the flavour almost overpowering after all this time without a mouth.

She allows herself two more dips, then screws the jar shut again and unlaces her brand-new, slender-heeled boots. God . . . that's better. For years she's worn nothing but utility footwear; she deserves to be pampered. Even if it does result in blisters and sore feet. A good soak in the tub will help, but before she can run a bath she has a little matter to attend to.

Stephen's wife is in the bathroom, surgi-taped into a black plastic body-bag with just her face showing. Dr Westfield leans into the tub and looks at her. She's almost angelic, up to her prefrontal lobes in sedatives, but the effect is somewhat spoiled by the large chunk of scalp missing from the top of her head – the wound covered in a layer of skinpaint to stop it oozing red everywhere. The nutrient pouches plugged into her arms are almost empty; this evening she'll start to dehydrate and after that death won't be far away. After all, she's pregnant. She'll be dying for two.

Unless she accidentally gets gutted first.

Dr Westfield unhooks the IV pouches from the shower pod and lets them fall to the bathroom floor. She hauls the body-bag out of the bath, smiling as she hears something nasty sliding about in there. The woman's bowels have obviously been productive. It's only to be expected. The poor thing must be terrified. And that turns Dr Westfield's smile into a grin.

She drags the bag through to the dining area and wrestles it into place on one of the chairs, securing it tightly with more surgi-tape. Mrs Stephen Bexley won't be going anywhere. Not alive at any rate.

Dr Westfield pulls the intravenous sedative from the woman's neck and throws the bag in the bin. It will take three or four hours for the drugs to wear off, enough time to have a nice hot bath. Then, when Mrs Bexley is all awake and terrified, they can have a little chat about how Stephen was naughty and how much pain that's going to mean before his wife finally gets to die.

With a happy smile Dr Westfield pats the woman on the cheek. It's not *her* fault she married a weak man, but it's too late to worry about that now.

* * *

'Sir! Over here, we've found one of them!'

Will struggled up the pile of trash to join the knot of jump-suited figures. They stood around a shallow hole in the rubbish, looking down at what used to be a man. The body was tied up in a bundle with orange packing tape: knees against chest, arms against knees, hands curled into stiff claws. The Bluecoat's head was tilted back onto his left shoulder, sightless eyes staring up at the expressway, mouth hanging open, the skin waxy and yellow like rancid butter.

Brian hunkered down at the edge of the makeshift grave and ran a reader over one of the constable's fingertips. He waited for the print to come back from Central Records, then read out the results. 'Stephen Mackay: twenty-five, male. Bluecoat. Rank—'

'Police Constable.' It was Jo, standing on the edge of the group, dressed in a yellow suit and scarlet cropped cloat: the kind the horsy set always wore. The hood was up, hiding her eyes and she sounded as if she hadn't slept in a month. 'Married. Wife: Louise Mackay. One child: Cheryl, three years old.'

She pulled a palm-sized transmitter out of her pocket, punched the dead PC's code into it and handed it to Agent Alexander. With a gentleness that would have surprised anyone who didn't know him, Brian cleared some rubbish away from the back of Constable Mackay's head, pressed the transmitter against the base of his skull and pressed the 'send' button.

'Better?' He asked one of the troopers.

'I don't. . . There! Got a positive lock on the other one.'

The team headed down the other side of the rubbish heap, leaving Brian, Will and DS Cameron alone with the dead body.

'Jo,' said Will.

'Sir,' said Jo.

Not exactly friendly.

'Oh fer God's sake. . .' Brian picked himself up, slipped the transmitter into his pocket and tried to brush some of the muck off his coat. It didn't help, just smeared it further. 'You're like a pair of wee kiddies.' He watched them standing there in silence, then sighed. 'Fine, we'll keep it professional: the two coffin dodgers was interferin' with each other. We couldn't get a good signal lock on either of them.'

Will stared down at the packaged-up body. 'Any idea why they were killed?'

'Who knows these days?' said Jo. 'Wrong place at the wrong time? Asked the right people the wrong questions? Looked at someone funny?' She straightened her shoulders. 'Anyway, if you'll excuse me, sir, I'll go supervise excavating the other body.'

'Of course.' He watched her picking her way carefully down the slippery mound to where the team were already digging.

'All right,' said Brian when she was out of earshot. 'Let's hear it: what did you do?'

Will closed his eyes. Might have known this was coming. 'Nothing. I didn't do anything.'

'Bollocks. I wondered why she was so quiet this mornin'. Yev done somethin' stupid haven't you?'

'Brian—'

'Don't Brian me! If you think I'm gonnae stand around while you piss away the best thing that's happened to you in years you've got another think comin'.'

'It's not—'

'You listen to me, William Hunter. For years I've watched you buggerin' about, never gettin' close to anyone cos you're still hung up on Janet. It's been six fuckin' years! You think she'd want you to be a miserable, lonely old bastard? Do you? Cos that's what you're turnin' into!'

Will took a step back. 'Where the hell did that come from?'

'That woman down there cares about you! Or at least she did before you fucked it up.'

'I know! OK, I know.' Will sighed, looking down at the dead constable at his feet. 'She asked about Janet and I freaked. I . . . I still miss her, Brian.'

Brian's voice was softer, his big hand falling on Will's shoulder. 'I know you do, but you're no' the one who died.'

Jo was standing back from the excavations, watching as the Network troopers dug the second corpse out of the rubbish. With her bright yellow suit and short red cloak she looked like a fruit cocktail.

'She has the most appalling dress sense I think I've ever seen,' said Will with a small smile. 'I like her a lot, but I don't think she's too keen anymore.'

'Aye well,' Brian gave him a wink. 'You just leave that to me – they don't call us the Clydeside Cupid for nothin'.'

'Talk to me.'

'Yes, sir.' Ken's voice was calm, even though it felt as if a weasel was playing the bongos on his heart with a pair of ice axes. 'After speaking to Mr Hunter yesterday I got the guys to put a monitor on any data searches using your name or mine. Yesterday evening they got one: Glasgow Royal Infirmary.'

'And?'

Ken shifted from one neatly polished Cuban heel to the other, trying to make the gesture look casual. 'The search turned up some files from the hospital database.'

'You told me you had deleted all reference to our involvement there, Ken.'

'We. . . We didn't know the files were being held in a backup, sir. We didn't have access to them. When the hospital records crashed five years ago they must have been restored with historical data. The files we got rid of sort of . . . reappeared.'

Quiet settled in as the old man steepled his delicate, long-boned fingers, tapping the tips against his narrow lips, face closed and eyes on the middle distance. 'Who was doing the searching?' he said at last.

This was the part that Ken had been dreading.

'Access was hacked so we have no positive ID, but Assistant Section Director William Hunter and Detective Sergeant Jo Cameron were involved in an incident at that location two minutes after the last file was copied.'

'I see.' The old man sat back in his chair and pulled the test tube from his pocket, twisting it in and out of his fingers as if it was alive.

'I got the guys monitoring Mr Hunter's DataLink to take a real close look at what he's been accessing. He downloaded the whole PsychTech database yesterday morning.'

Ken watched the test tube dance between his employer's knuckles, feeling himself drawn into the old man's silence. Unable to stop himself.

'The . . . em . . . Harbinger files weren't encrypted.'

The older man's eyebrows shot up, and small beads of sweat began to dampen the nape of Ken's neck.

'I pulled Moncur and Stephenson in; seems the guys were using their 'initiative' and trolling though Westfield's original notes looking for more data. Unfortunately they neglected to re-encrypt the files afterwards. Hunter's got access to everything Doctor Westfield did before she was caught.'

'I see. . .' The old man's gaze was a solid object, sharp and cold, like the pin in a lepidopterist's display case. The younger man swallowed and tried not to fidget with his tie as those cold, grey eyes bored into him.

'Kenneth, when the Network discovered Doctor Westfield's unsavoury activities you asked me to let you go through her notes, to see if there was anything we could use. I agreed. When you discovered her programme to breed serial killers and suggested we take it over, I let you run with it. When you asked me to make sure she wasn't properly halfheaded so we could tap into her knowledge, I even went so far as to perform the operation myself.' He sat forward in his seat, teeth clenched. 'We've spent six years questioning her and monitoring her damn children. Six years! And what do we have to show for it?'

'Sir, I. . .' Ken swallowed. He'd never heard the old man this angry before.

'Nothing! That's what. *You*, however, got a big bonus cheque!'

'Sir, if we hadn't been working with her we wouldn't have come up with the idea for the formula. We—'

A long, thin hand slammed down on the tabletop, making Ken jump.

'Enough!'

Ken stood up straight and stuck his chin out. 'Sir, if you want my resignation—'

'Oh, you're not getting out of it that easily, Ken.' The old man settled back in his chair and placed the test tube on the table in front of him. 'What do you intend to do about Mr Hunter?'

'Find out how much he knows and who he's told.'

'And then?'

'Kill him.'

24

The last sliver of daylight disappeared into the low clouds, leaving the city to the night and the rain. Standing on opposite sides of a mortuary slab, Assistant Section Director William Hunter and Detective Sergeant Jo Cameron tried to make small talk. Brian had been as good as his word, talking Jo into taking the trip back to the mortuary with the bodies, and then buggering off out of it.

'Look,' said Will when they finally ran out of things to say about the crappy weather, 'I'm sorry about what happened yesterday.'

'Yeah, well, my getting bashed over the head wasn't your fault.'

'I didn't meant that – I'm sorry about behaving like an arse.'

Jo didn't say anything and neither did the trussed-up corpse of PC Sandy Douglas.

'When you asked about Janet I . . . I didn't know what . . . I reacted badly: got defensive. I'm sorry.'

She nodded.

'Janet. . .' He took a deep breath. 'Janet died six and a half years ago. We'd been married four years. I was looking for a guy who'd already killed seven people. He liked to use a

Thrummer – not like Mitchell – Alistair Middleton's speciality was the human heart. He used to boil the. . .' Will closed his eyes and tried again, 'He used to boil his way into their chests and hold onto their hearts till they stopped beating.'

'He . . . he phoned my office, pretended to be a witness in another case. I used to have this big picture of Janet and me on the wall, and he saw it. I didn't know who he was. I just talked to him like he was a normal person and all the time he's staring over my shoulder at Janet's picture.'

Will grabbed the edge of the post-mortem table. 'Three hours later I got another call: it was Janet. She wanted to know if I could bring a plastic of wine home with me, something fizzy. Said she had something special to tell me. She . . .' He cleared his throat, gripping the table so tightly his knuckles were turning white. 'The doorbell goes and she says, "Hold on, I'll just be a minute." And that's when I saw him again. Alastair Middleton, the man I'd spoken to on the phone. He was in my house with a big bunch of flowers for my wife. And she's smiling as she invites him in. I can see them talking and then he just punches her in the face.'

'Oh God, Will.' Jo reached over the dead Bluecoat and took Will's hand.

'I shouted at him, tried to get him to stop, but he kept on hitting her and hitting her.' Will shuddered. 'I told Control to get a pickup team over there, but there wasn't time. . . He. . . She was wearing this Fair Isle sweater I'd bought her for her birthday and I watched him boil it away. And all the time he's singing, "Hush little baby don't say a word. . ."'

'Will, I'm so sorry.'

'So am I.' He took a deep, ragged breath and straightened himself up. 'I miss her . . . but I've been alone for six and a half years. I really like you; you're bright, sexy, colourful.' He managed a smile. 'And I'm not just talking about the suits.'

Her hand left his, travelling up to rest on his cheek. 'Listen, buster, I only wear them for work, OK?'

She leant forward slightly – reaching over PC Sandy Douglas's corpse, still done up in its parcel-tape bundle – and pulled Will's face towards her.

'Why?' he asked.

'Maybe I'll tell you later,' she said, as their lips met above the mortuary slab. 'But only if you're very, very good.'

She sits alone in the bedroom, trying to ignore Stephen's wife's whimpering. Honestly, just because she's about to be tortured to death, there's no need to make all this racket!

The gag isn't working – too much noise leaks out. Perhaps it would be best to just kill the woman and get it over with?

Dr Westfield smiles at the thought and runs the brush through her hair again, making it shine like molten gold. The skinpaint holding her new face together has cured perfectly, you can barely see the joins. And even those pale pink lines will fade over time. Soon she'll be perfect again. The bruises are fading and so is the swelling. The skin is soft and smooth, free from the mark of age. No more crow's feet, or laughter lines. She looks eighteen again.

One last brush and she admires her long blonde hair in the mirror. She's beautiful. When she was younger she always hated her nose. But now it gives her face character. It's not big, it's proud. Her chin isn't wide, it's strong. Appropriate for who she's become. Stephen really was a brilliant surgeon.

She comes to a decision: as a tribute to his skill she won't slit his wife open and strangle her with her own intestines. Mrs Bexley will get to die of dehydration instead. Yes, it's slow and painful, but a lot more dignified. Never let it be said that Dr Fiona Westfield couldn't be merciful.

Even if the bitch does make one hell of a racket.

Dr Westfield closes the bedroom door, shutting out the muffled sobs. She needs silence to plan her next move.

All this time she's been obsessing about the man who caught her, but William Hunter is only part of the picture. He discovered her crimes by accident. If Alastair Middleton had called someone else that afternoon – if he hadn't killed the Network man's wife – he might never have been arrested and 'interrogated'. He wouldn't have told them all about his special therapy sessions, and William Hunter wouldn't have come after her.

It was an accident. A twist of fate. Nothing more.

But Peitai and Kikan are a different matter entirely. There was nothing random about what they did to her. If she concentrates hard she can still smell the interrogation room: old leather and bitter-almond aftershave.

Yes, William Hunter was the one who caught her, who built the case against her, who made sure she went into mutilated slavery, but he's not solely to blame. He'll still have to suffer, but he'll have company on the way.

Peitai and Kikan. Peitai and Kikan. They stole her children, tortured her for information: interfered with her research. They didn't see the *skill* involved, the artistry needed to take a perfectly normal person and turn him into something that wouldn't think twice about killing a total stranger, cutting a hole in their stomach, and fucking the corpse.

She was creating masterpieces; all Peitai and Kikan wanted was mass-produced killers.

Philistines.

She'll pay Mr Hunter a visit tonight and then, while he's still got a mouth to scream with, she'll ask him where to find the old man and his weasely sidekick.

She'll show them what it feels like to have six years of their lives ripped away. One painful slice at a time.

*   *   *

293

He didn't think the rain could get any heavier, but it did, obliterating the city beyond, hiding it in the angry roar of suicidal water drops.

Will took a sip of whisky, looking out through the patio doors at the downpour, but not really seeing it.

'Thought you were coming to bed?' Jo stood in the middle of the lounge, hands on hips, buck-naked.

'Hmm? Sorry: miles away.'

'Are you always this damn moody, Will? Only I'd like to know before I get too deep into this thing.'

He managed to crack a smile. 'Normally I'm a lot worse.' He planted a soft kiss on the nape of her neck. 'You ask Brian.'

'I did. He told me some cock and bull story about you being this big, all-conquering, sensitive hero type. Whatever you pay him to talk you up, you're getting value for money.' She plonked herself down on the edge of the settee. 'So why all the brooding?'

'I've just had a lot on my mind lately.'

She blew a raspberry. 'Strike one! Try again.'

'We . . . I mean Brian, George and I, have been investigating that bloke I told you about yesterday.'

'What Petty?'

'Peitai, yes. He's running some sort of experiment up at Sherman House; they've got a drug that gives people VR syndrome. He's been testing it on the inhabitants.'

'Holy shit! You're kidding!'

Will shook his head. 'We had evidence. The bodies you saw in the mortuary, tissue samples from their brains, SOC recordings of the flats at Sherman House. But it's all gone.' He took another sip of whisky. 'Lab lost the samples, Services destroyed the wrong bodies, and George called back to say maintenance had a little 'accident' this afternoon: they erased all the recordings we had.'

'Cover-up?'

'I told Director Smith-Hamilton about the evidence we had against Ken Peitai and his boss, and six hours later it disappeared. She even stopped the team I had going through the PsychTech files: confiscated the data. Governor Clark's been on her case all week, so as far as she's concerned none of this ever happened.'

Jo stood and wrapped her arms round his neck 'You want to bring him down?'

'It's not just him. Clark's an arsehole, a mouth for hire. Someone's pulling his strings. Someone who doesn't worry about threatening a Network Director.' Will closed his eyes and rested his forehead against hers. 'And I don't have any evidence. They destroyed it all.'

'You listen to me, Will Hunter.' Jo stepped back and held his head in her hands, forcing him to look her in the eyes. 'There is no bastard in this world well-connected enough to get away from us! If Ken Petty wants a fight I will kick his scaly arse from here to Inverness. You want to bring them down? We'll bring them down. Those sons of bitches don't stand a fucking chance.'

He smiled. She had a lot of guts. And her nipples went all pointy when she was angry. 'Such language from a young lady.'

'Ah, you love it when I talk dirty.' She pulled him down towards her and for the next two hours he forgot all about Ken Peitai and Sherman House.

She stands at the apartment window, watching Glasgow sparkle in the night rain. She loves this city more than any other. It held her to it's bosom, allowed her to feed off its inhabitants for nearly a dozen years and never once complained.

Peitai and Kikan. . . Definitely a challenge. Hunter will be easy enough – she got his home address from the hospital files. All she has to do is turn up at his home tonight, and introduce him to a little home surgery. Peitai and Kikan will be a lot harder to track down. Even if William Hunter knows where they are, it's going to be a lot more difficult to get at them.

Still, that's a problem for tomorrow; tonight is a night for fun! And knives.

There's a row of blades laid out on the kitchen work surface, all nice and sharp and shiny. She spends a happy five minutes picking the ones for tonight. In the end a paring knife, three scalpels, and a small portable triage wand go into her pack, along with halfheading sedatives, four tubes of skinglue, and a plastic of good wine. It would be rude to visit and not bring something.

Mrs Bexley is quiet for once, sitting there strapped to the chair.

'Now, I want you to behave yourself when I'm out, OK?' Dr Westfield's voice is still a little gruff, but it's getting better all the time.

She ruffles Mrs Bexley's hair – the woman screws her eyes shut and flinches, breath hissing in and out of her nose. Terrified.

Westfield smiles. 'Are you hungry? Thirsty?'

The woman nods, tears spilling down her cheeks.

'Good.' Westfield pulls on the brand-new cloat she bought from a very expensive boutique this afternoon. Armani. Very stylish. She's almost out the front door when she remembers the Palm Zapper she picked up at the hospital. Tonight is a night for fun and knives, but a Zapper set on low can do some interesting things when applied to the right parts of the human anatomy. Interesting and very painful.

Out on the streets there are still signs of life, even thought it's half past one in the morning and there's a monsoon in progress. Clubbers run between sheltered spots, or just plod on through the downpour, eating chips and cloned kebab meat. Some drunk, some high, some looking for a fight, some looking for love. She could take a dozen home with her and bathe in their blood, and no one would even notice.

Crossing Glebe Street, she descends a slippery flight of stairs to the local shuttle station and takes the next car going west. It'll be a shame to leave this beautiful city, but when the bodies start showing up again people will talk. So she'll just have to start again somewhere new – somewhere they don't know her *modus operandi* – but she will miss Glasgow so much.

As the shuttle car arrives at the platform, she sees her face reflected in the curved plexiglass window. It's the face of someone who has earned a little fun. A little revenge.

In the dark bedroom, Will tried to identify the noise that had jerked him awake. The flat's heating popped and pinged away gently to itself; the ever-present hum of the control panel; Jo, breathing deeply beside him, the duvet wound round her like a boa constrictor. . . He lay still, holding his breath, straining to hear it again.

Silence.

Probably just the rain, or the fridge, or the idiot downstairs.

But now he was awake Will knew he wouldn't get back to sleep until he'd looked in each and every room to make sure there weren't any bogymen hiding in the closet. Quietly, he slid out from under the covers and into his bathrobe. His Palm Thrummer was hanging in its holster, draped over the end of the bed, and he pulled the metal tube free, twisting it open. It came alive beneath his fingers, the batteries ready to turn whatever it was pointed at into a cloud of ionized dust.

Will hesitated at the bedroom door. Someone was out there, he was certain of it. Heart pounding, he twisted the door-knob and inched out into the lounge. The large patio windows were partially covered, the blinds three-quarters drawn, letting the city's sodium glow trickle into the room. The dead yellow light only seemed to make things darker, turning the shadows into solid things.

Padding through the lounge he made straight for the kitchen. It was empty, the study too. The guest bedroom hadn't been used for eight years, not since Janet's father had come to visit them the year he died. Will opened all the closets, but didn't find any skeletons he didn't already know about. And yet he was certain there was someone. . .

It wasn't loud, little more than a dull scrape, plastic on plastic.

Creeping out of the spare room Will stood staring back towards the front door. Light seeped in through the gap between the door and the floor. There were shadows moving out there in the corridor, outside his flat.

The soft scraping sound came again and he heard a small bleep. Tiny and discreet. The sound of his front door lock disconnecting.

Quietly he backed into the bedroom, pulling the door almost shut behind him. Someone was breaking into his apartment in the dead of night and he was pretty damn sure it wasn't the Jehovah's Witnesses. Peitai. The little git had used Governor Clark to lean on Director Smith-Hamilton, but it looked as if Will was about to get something a lot more permanent.

He settled back against the wall, cursing under his breath. An assault team was the last thing he wanted in his home at quarter to two on a Tuesday morning. They'd have light-sights, they'd have infrared, they'd have Zappers, Screamers, Whompers, and God knew what else. All he had was a Palm Thrummer . . . and Detective Sergeant Cameron.

With one hand he grabbed the duvet and dragged it off the bed. Before Jo could start swearing he slapped the same hand over her mouth and pointed at the bedroom door with his Thrummer. She scowled up at him in the gloom, and then another clunk came from somewhere inside the flat. Her eyebrows shot up.

Will let go of her, put a finger to his lips, and went, 'Shh. . .'

She mouthed the word, 'Fuck,' then scrabbled through her discarded clothes.

Will clicked his throat-mike and activated the emergency channel. 'Control, this is Hunter: do you copy?' he whispered, stuffing the earpiece into place.

'Sir?'

'I need a pickup team here and I need it *now*.'

'Sir?'

'Just do it!'

'Sir, all our teams are out on—'

'I don't care if you have to call in your sick granny! Reserves, anything! Just get them—' Will's earpiece exploded into a barrage of static and he dragged it out.

Jo whispered, 'How we doing?' She was stark naked, holding a brand-new Field Zapper. The thing was three times the size of her original sidearm, the telltales casting a soft blue glow over her caramel skin. She caught him looking and shrugged. 'What? Thought if I was going to hang around with you I'd better pack a bit more firepower.'

'They're jamming the coms channels. We're on our own: nothing in, nothing out.'

She swore quietly. 'How many?'

'Couldn't tell.' Will cranked his Palm Thrummer up to full. 'At least four.'

'So what's taking them so long?'

'How the hell should I. . .' He cleared his throat. 'Sorry. Get a little tense when people are trying to kill me.'

They sat side by side in the dark, both weapons pointing at the partially open door.

'Maybe they're doing a room to room search?'

Will shook his head. 'If they've got infrared goggles they can see our heat signatures. They don't need to search.'

'What if they're on low-light?'

Will opened his mouth to say: 'Don't be daft', but it *would* explain why they hadn't just charged straight into the bedroom. A smile tugged at his face. If they were using light-amplification goggles, they were in for a nasty surprise.

He crept towards the bedroom door, keeping close to the wall. 'Cover your eyes and get ready to run.'

Outside, in the lounge, he could hear soft, careful foot-steps. They were getting closer.

Will risked a glance through the slit between the door and the frame, into the living room beyond. A strange-looking creature with goggles over its eyes looked straight back at him. In the split second it took them to recognize each other Will took in the troop boots, the vid-helmet, the heavy gloves and the full-sized Thrummer.

He closed his eyes and shouted, 'Lights!'

Suddenly the entire apartment exploded into brilliant daylight – he could see pink through his eyelids – and then the flat was full of swearing.

'Lights off!' He grabbed Jo's hand and charged out through the bedroom door.

Will's night vision was still good as he barged into the trooper with the Thrummer and sent him flying. The man smashed through the coffee table, hands clasped to his goggled eyes, blinded by the sudden brilliance. The room was full of them, staggering around clutching their heads. Will ran for the front door, Jo hot on his heels.

She snapped her Field Zapper up and sent a blue arc of lighting into the chest of the nearest invader. He screamed and flew backwards as every muscle in his body contracted, sparking like a Catherine wheel into the control panel. The Whomper in his hands barked and something red and wet sprayed across Will's cheek. He turned, just in time to see a man in combat gear, with a shark-sized bite out of his torso, twitch and judder to the floor.

Will didn't stop at the front door, just ran straight through, shouting, 'Lights!' again as he crossed the threshold. He could hear swearing erupt for a second time as he and Jo sprinted for the lifts.

She was spray-painted raspberry red all down one side. Naked or not, it wasn't an erotic sight.

They skidded to a halt at the end of the corridor. Will punched the button for the lifts. It bleeped back at him and the doors slid open, revealing a startled-looking woman in combat fatigues, her Thrummer unhitched and resting against her foot.

'Shite!' Jo shot her in the face with the Field Zapper.

The trooper's head crackled with hot blue sparks and a deafening roar filled the lift as the Thrummer went off, taking the woman's left foot and a chunk of flooring with it.

'Will you stop doing that!' Will leapt into the lift. It was full of pink mist that smelled of raw meat and roasting ozone. Hot red blood pumped from the woman's truncated leg, spreading out in a slippery puddle, dripping through the hole in the floor. Fifty-seven stories straight down.

'Stop complaining and get us out of here!' Jo dropped to her knees and wrenched the Thrummer from the unconscious trooper's hand.

Will pressed the button for the building's shuttle bay and sank back against the cool mirrored wall as the doors slid shut and the car started to accelerate downwards.

Jo wrestled the crash webbing off the twitching body in the middle of the floor. 'You see how many?'

'Seven that I counted, plus this one. Standard pickup team is ten, not including the pilot. My guess is there's another two covering the exits.'

'Catch.' She threw the webbing at him and he fastened

it over his dressing gown, twisting it round the right way so the spare power cells for the Thrummer were easy to get at. When he was all buckled up she passed across the assault rifle and then laughed at him. 'What *do* you look like?'

'At least I'm wearing something!'

'True.' Jo unsnipped the catches on the front of the woman's jumpsuit and sat her up, pulling the limp arms out of the sleeves. 'How much longer?' she asked, trying to drag the jumpsuit's one remaining leg over the trooper's heavy boots.

'Thirteen floors.' They were already decelerating.

'Damn!'

'Ten, nine, eight, seven—'

'I can't get the bastard thing over her bloody boot!'

'Two, one.'

The lift went 'ping' and Will braced himself against the back wall, Thrummer pointing at the twin doors. As they gently slid apart Will looked out through the opening gap into the shuttle bay. Two men were standing on the platform – one carrying a Whomper, the other a Screamer, both weapons pointed in his direction.

Will didn't wait for introductions, just jammed his thumb down on his Thrummer's trigger, tearing a hole in the lift doors at chest height. The two men dived for cover as he held the button down, filling the air with vaporized metal and the sound of tortured bees. He slapped the control panel with his other hand and sent the elevator back up to the ground floor, the lift shaft clearly visible through the new four-foot hole in the doors.

'Got it!' Jo stood, a blood-soaked, tattered jumpsuit in her hands. She managed to get one leg into it before the elevator juddered to a halt and Will shoved her out into the building foyer.

'What the hell was that for?' She staggered against the

302

wall as, behind them, the floor of the lift exploded upward. The unconscious body of the one-legged trooper jerked as round after round tore into it. 'Ah, got you.'

Mr Duncan, the building's night porter, came scuttling round from behind his brass and marblette fortress.

'Fit'i hell's ga'in oan?'

'Get back behind your desk and keep your head down!' Will ran for the front entrance, pulling Jo along behind him. 'And call for help!'

They burst out into the street and the rain.

Jo struggled her arms into the jumpsuit. 'Which way?'

'There.' He pointed across the street to the path that led away into the darkest depths of Kelvingrove Park. 'We go anywhere else and people are going to get hurt.'

'Trust me,' she said, running after him through the park gates, 'those bastards come anywhere near me, people are going to get hurt.'

Will was already soaked to the skin, his bathrobe flapping out behind him like a towelling cape. The Thrummer in his hands still had a good two-thirds charge left and he had another pair of power cells strapped to the webbing. If they could find some decent cover they might actually get out of this alive.

They hammered, barefoot, down the path, between hissing yellow orbs of light, setting off holo adverts as they passed. Will tried his throat-mike again.

'Control, do you read me?'

The response was garbled – small spurts of words interspersed with waves of hard, white noise.

'Anything?' Jo was breathing hard now and so was he.

'Jammer's breaking up the signal. Backup might be on the way, but I don't know how long it's going to take.'

He looked back over his shoulder, just in time to see seven heavily armed troopers explode out of the front door of the building and screech to a stop on the pavement. For a moment it looked as though they might have got away with it . . . but one of the figures must have seen the chain of glowing adverts Will and Jo had left in their wake, because he pointed straight at them.

'Bastard! We've got to hide.' Jo grabbed a handful of Will's soaking dressing gown and ran off at ninety degrees to the path, dragging him into the darkness.

Cold, slippery grass whipped at their shins, the rain and the night swiftly gobbling up the sodiums' feeble glow. There wasn't enough light to see his hand in front of his face, let alone where he was going. Will went down hard, twisting his ankle and slithering to a halt in the mud beneath a sharp-edged bush.

From his skewed vantage point he could see the assault team charging along the path like polished beetles, the sodium light glinting off their wet body armour.

'Will?'

'Shhh!' he hissed through clenched teeth. 'Get out of here. I'll hold them back.'

'Bollocks you will.' She dropped down next to him in the mud.

'We stand a much better chance if we split up.'

She shook her head, but Will reached out and held her face in his hands. 'You need to go. You need to get as far away from here as possible.'

'I'm not leaving—'

'No you're not. We're just splitting up, that's all. Making it more difficult for them to find us.' His ankle was killing him: he was going nowhere fast and he knew it. 'Once you're out of the park, get on the nearest shuttle and go anywhere. Soon as you're out of jammer range, call control and get a pickup team out here.'

'I—'

Will pulled her down to him and placed a soft kiss on her lips.

'Over there!' The shout was followed by the high-pitched whine of a Whomper on full. It barked, blasting a chunk of waterlogged turf into muddy rain right in front of them.

'Go!'

Jo didn't need another telling; she picked herself up and charged off into the bushes.

Will pulled the Thrummer up and flicked on the light-sight. Its hard green line streaked out from under the bush, into the middle of the shouting trooper's chest. Will pressed the trigger and the man's torso evaporated. Four troopers watched, mesmerized, as the man's shoulders slumped into his hips, before the whole grisly mess slapped into the path in a mist of red. When the green targeting beam leapt to the next one in line they hit the deck hard. But not before Will got off a second shot. The Thrummer growled and someone lost everything between their left elbow and their spine. The survivors scrabbled to their feet and ran for it, doing their best to get the hell out of there before Will fired again.

He picked one at random and stripped the skin off their back before the weapon chimed empty in his hands.

'Three out of seven. Not bad for a half-naked man in a bathrobe.' Will racked the Thrummer upright and shot the battery pack out into the mud. He could hear them crashing through the bushes on either side, trying to outflank him while he reloaded. With a grim smile he slapped the next power cell into the slot and cranked it up to speed. The tell-tales danced along the body of the weapon as the tines began vibrating inside.

The night lit up with a blue flash. Over to his left a bush was torn apart into its component molecules, the fragments of chlorophyll swept away in the torrential downpour. He took a guess at the source and swept the area with his Thrummer. Undergrowth leapt into the air, crackling with static electricity. The weapon's roar filled his ears, shaking the teeth in his head as he swung it back and forth, decimating anything in its path. It was deafening.

He didn't hear them coming up behind him until they were almost on top of him.

Will span round, the Thrummer coming with him, tearing its way through shrubs and earth, his finger still hard on the trigger. The first one into the clearing caught the weapon's wake full in the face. His body ran on another step before it realized there was nothing giving the orders anymore and went down, fountaining arterial crimson into the rain-battered grass. The second trooper dived in beneath the Thrummer's arc and slammed into Will's chest, sending him sprawling into the bloody mud.

Something hard crashed into the side of his head, snapping it around. Hot yellow blobs filled his vision. The world span. And then someone clambered on top of him, straddling him, locking his arms against his sides, pushing him down into the quagmire. Pain burst across his scalp as the woman grabbed a handful of hair and forced his head back. Her fist hammered into Will's nose, sending warm salty blood pouring down his throat. The next blow closed his left eye, smashing his head further into the mud.

He tried to heave the bastard off, but her weight was solid, pinning him, immobile.

The fist caught Will's left cheek and he heard, with surprising clarity, a muffled 'pop' as the bone broke.

Will's hands scrabbled in the mud, looking for something, *anything* to fight back with. His fingers brushed against a boot – the other trooper, the one with no head.

The fist hammered down again. Pain cracked through Will's mouth as teeth snapped. He retched, blood exploding from his split lips.

A voice above him shouted, 'Gah! You filthy fucker!'
Another punch.
Will grabbed the boot, working his hand around. Boot knife:

306

please God let there be a. . . Bingo. He fumbled with the strap holding the knife inside its sheath. The handle was cool beneath his fingers as he slid the blade free. Head swimming.

Difficult to think.

Dizzy.

Darkness. . .

Someone was yelling at him, bellowing into his battered face, dragging him back to consciousness. He saw, through his one good eye, the woman on top of him curl her fist back again. Will rammed the boot knife into the back of her ankle and twisted till he could feel the hamstring snap.

A scream. The weight fell away. She rolled in the mud, clutching at the knife sticking out of the back of her leg.

'You bastard! My fucking leg! You bastard! Agghh Jesus!'

Will rolled onto his side and vomited blood, bitter and salty. The roaring in his head came in waves, fading the world in and out, in and out.

'You fucking bastard!'

He tried to move, but nothing worked. All he could do was lie there as the trooper struggled to her knees and dragged his fallen Thrummer out of the mud. Her face was pale, teeth gritted, eyes angry, dark slits, but there was no mistaking her. The first time they'd met she'd been wearing tribal scars and eclectic rags. The second time she'd been wearing casual clothing and talking to a man in a long black cloat. Big-boned rather than fat. Her ginger hair hidden beneath a combat helmet.

'Fuck orders, you're fucking dead!'

The telltales danced along the sides of the assault rifle, and a hard blue crackle filled the air. The lightning caught her square in the chest and Will felt the harsh roar of the Thrummer as all her muscles contracted involuntarily. Blue sparks fizzled out across her rigid body and then, with a wet splatch, she keeled over into the mud.

Will wanted to laugh, but all that came out was a rasping

gurgle and one of his back teeth. Still alive. He lay there, bleeding into the rain-soaked earth. Then quietly slipped into unconsciousness.

25

'What do you mean, you lost him?' Ken Peitai stood in the darkness of the Hopper's cargo hold, watching the monitor in front of him and not liking what he saw one little bit. He'd arrived with ten heavily armed troopers, to pick up *one* guy, and the useless bastards got their asses kicked. One dead in Hunter's apartment, another unconscious. One in little pieces at the bottom of a lift shaft. Three dead on the path in Kelvingrove Park. One with no head in the bushes and another one out for the count. Only two left and they'd lost the God-damned target.

'Sorry, sir. There's no sign of him. We're widening our search pattern—'

'I don't care if you're sticking a pineapple up your ass: find him! And find that Bluecoat bitch he's got with him. If either of them get out into the real world I will *personally* make sure you spend the rest of your miserable life helping research test the next batch! Do I make myself clear?'

'Sir, yes, sir!'

Ken stabbed the 'off' button. The old man was in a bad enough mood already – he'd hit the roof when he found out they'd cocked this up.

Should have been a piss-easy assignment: get in, pick up

Hunter and get out; take him somewhere safe; torture, question and kill his ass.

So how come Ken had six dead troopers and two zapped into unconsciousness?

The guy was a Network Assistant Director, not bloody superman.

'Captain,' Ken activated the intercom next to the monitor. 'Get this hunk-a-junk in the air. We're doing a sweep of that damn park.'

'Sir? Our orders are to keep a low profile—'

'You want me to come up there and *make* you do it? That what you want?'

'No, sir.'

The engines came online, filling the drop bay with a low pulsing throb. Ken felt the floor surge under his feet and then the Hopper dropped over the edge of the building and accelerated towards the centre of the park.

Hunter wasn't going to get away from him a second time.

Detective Sergeant Jo Cameron hit the ground like a sack of gravel. Someone scrambled onto her back, forcing her face-down into the wet earth. She lashed out with an elbow and felt it slam into something solid. Her attacker grunted, slipped – Jo dug her knee into the sodden grass and heaved, keeping the momentum going, throwing the bastard all the way off.

With a twist she came round on top of the guy, and rammed her Field Zapper in his face, hard enough to break four of his front teeth.

'Bad move, Cuddles.' She thumbed the power up to maximum. 'You've got exactly thirty seconds to tell me who the hell you are and where you're from, before I electrify your head. You get me?'

The man just stared at her. Blood trickled from his broken mouth into his beard, before being washed away by the torrential downpour.

'Twenty-five, twenty-four, twenty-three. . .'

He didn't move a muscle.

'Twenty, nineteen, eighteen. . .' She rammed the Zappper forward again, the sight gouging a slice out of his cheek. 'I'm not fucking kidding around here!'

'Twelve, eleven, ten, nine, eight. . .' She smashed the hilt against the side of his face.

He just grunted.

'Fuck it.' Jo looked down into the bleeding man's eyes and spat. 'You're not bright enough to know when you're screwed.'

She sat back and stuck the weapon's barrel underneath his hairy chin. 'Bye, bye.'

She didn't see the other trooper behind her, but she felt the butt of his Screamer as it smashed down on the back of her head. Hot orange sparks exploded in front of her eyes.

The Zapper dropped from her fingers and she slowly keeled over into the mud.

The Hopper twisted sideways in the rain, dodging the glowing sodiums that hovered over the path. With a deafening roar the engines turned and battered the grass flat before the whole thing settled into the soft earth on three articulated landing legs. It looked like a large metal flea, devoid of any visible weaponry, the logo of a nonexistent engineering firm stencilled on the side in flaking orange paint.

Ken Peitai walked down the rear ramp, a vid-helmet on his head and a fully-charged Whomper in his hand. As he stepped out into the monsoon he flicked his headset onto low-light, the goggles pulling hot green outlines and soft green shapes from the darkness. Three bodies lay nearby: one with nothing between its hips and shoulders; another sporting a large hole where its heart, left lung and arm should be; the third slightly further away, her spine little more than a foggy memory, the tips of white ribs poking through the smooth mess of her back.

311

Ken flicked on his throat-mike. 'Get your scaly ass out of that cockpit and get these stiffs onboard.'

'Sir, I don't think that's a good—'

'So help me if I have to tell you again. . . Get out here and pick them up, now! *I* will go see what the hell is taking the rest of your halfwit buddies so long.'

This was ridiculous. Someone in his position shouldn't have to go stomping about in the mud looking for morons who were supposed to know how to do their friggin' jobs! 'Right you hairy-assed bastards, sound off like you gotta pair!'

'Sir, it's Armstrong. We got one, sir!'

'About time!' Ken smiled into the falling rain. 'Which one you got?'

'Female: Five nine, wearing one of our jumpsuits. How'd she get one of our—'

'Never mind that. Is she dead?'

'No, sir. Just unconscious.'

'Good, get her back here.' He swept the park with his goggles, looking for the other trooper. 'Buncha monkeys.' It wasn't even as if they paid peanuts. 'Where the hell's Carter?'

The same voice sounded in his ear: *'I got Carter with me, sir.'*

'What, he can't talk for himself?'

'No, sir: broken jaw. The young lady kicked his arse for him.'

'Just what I need, a bearded fuckin' mute.'

The pilot grunted past, dragging one of the corpses into the Hopper, leaving a trail of smeared blood behind him. Like a haemorrhaging snail. From the way the bodies had fallen it was a safe bet that whoever shot the shit out of them had been hiding in the bushes.

'Can the hairy asshole carry the woman?'

'Yes, sir.'

'Then get your ass out there and find Hunter.'

'Em . . . how?'

'What d'ya mean, "How"? Use the trackers for God's sake!'

'*The jammer's blocking the signal – all I'm getting is static.*'

'Jesus. . .' Unbelievable. What was the point of burying transmitters under people's skin if you couldn't use them? Ken grabbed the pilot as he stomped out to get the next body. 'You: get back in there and switch off that damned jammer.'

The pilot looked at him. Opened his mouth. Shut it again. Closed his eyes for a moment. 'Sir, if we turn off the jammer, every CCTV camera in the place will be able to see us. Any Network ship in the area will get us on sensors. We'll be screwed.'

He was right.

Ken stared out into the darkness. It was all falling apart. 'Get those corpses onboard.'

'Yes, sir.' The pilot did what he was told. For once.

'Armstrong,' Ken clicked his throat-mike, 'the jammer stays on.'

'*But how am I—*'

'Just get your arse out there and find that Network bastard.'

'*The park's massive, I can't—*'

'Do you want to test out the next batch? Do you? That what you fuckin' want?'

'*Sir, no, sir!*'

Assholes, he was surrounded by assholes.

Ken set off towards the bushes, the Whomper up and ready to rock. Just past the outer layer of greenery the place looked as if it had been sheered off at ground level. Some poor bastard was lying in the grass with nothing to put his hat on any more. A second trooper had a dirty big knife sticking out the back of her leg like a handle.

It looked as if someone had been dragged off into the undergrowth – away from the scene. Ken took three steps along the trail before coming to a halt: the woman was in custody, Hunter was at large, and the retrieval team were all accounted for. So who dragged a body out of here?

'Armstrong,' he said into his mike, 'where are you?'

'*Looking for Network Future Boy. Like you said, sir.*'

'You don't have him with you?'

There was a pause. '*No, sir, I don't. If I had him I would have told you. Sir.*'

'Then who the hell else is out here?'

'*Winos? Zippers, Bean-Heads, Tezzers, H-monkeys, perverts, muggers—*'

'Alright! Enough already, I get the picture.' Ken looked around the devastated clearing, searching for inspiration, but all he could see were the two bodies. 'Shit.'

'*Sir?*'

'Get your ass over here on the double, Mister.' He scowled into the green-tinted night. 'Where the hell are you, Hunter?'

She drops to her knees and peers at his battered face. One eye is already swelling up. His nose is broken and caked with blood, and the left side of his face doesn't sit right. She reaches out and pokes it, feeling bone move beneath the tips of her fingers.

At least he's still breathing: she can see his chest rise and fall, see the blood washing away in the rain. . .

Disappointing. This isn't how it's supposed to be. It was supposed to be perfect. She's been looking forward to this moment for so long, but now that she's here – with him all battered and helpless – it just doesn't feel right. He should be awake and terrified. He needs to know that she's taken *everything* from him: his wife, his future, and his life.

He's meant to suffer.

She sits back and watches the rain falling on his pale skin.

She could reach out, right now, and end it all. Smash her fist into his throat – crush his windpipe and let him choke to death. Or take one of the blades from her pack and slit his throat. Or just take the skinglue, seal up his nose and mouth, and let him suffocate. . . But what's the point if he doesn't know it's her?

She strokes his cheek, feeling the rasp of stubble beneath her fingers. The people in combat gear have spoiled her revenge. Ruined everything.

She looks off into the park, back along the drag marks, towards the place where she found him about to be Thrummed apart by a fat woman with a knife in her leg.

She recognized the uniform: Special Ops combat gear. The kind of thing the guards wore in Peitai and Kikan's torture chamber.

'Peitai. . .'

There's no point killing William Hunter, not when he's like this, and Peitai and Kikan still need to be punished.

She leans forward and kisses Hunter on his bruised and bleeding forehead. There will be plenty of time to torture him when he's feeling better.

And that's when the cavalry arrives.

'Hud it right there!'

She freezes. A Bluecoat sidles around the edge of a big rhododendron bush. Female, carrying a heavy Field Zapper. The weapon's powered up, rain sizzling against the hot barrel.

Dr Westfield stands. 'You've got to help me!' Her voice is nearly perfect, just a slight rasp to show she's not had vocal chords for six years.

The Bluecoat's Zapper doesn't waver. 'I told you tae stand still.'

'This man's been attacked!'

'Aye,' the officer inches closer, 'an' who's to say you're no' the one attacked him?'

Hunter twitches and moans, a small, painful sound, but it's just enough to take the Bluecoat's eyes off hers. Westfield leaps at the woman, knocks her to the ground, and runs away into the dark.

Sir, we have serious problems!

'Jesus, what now?' Ken turned on the spot, sweeping his

Whomper across the undergrowth. The bushes all around him had grown thicker and darker, and the drag marks had run out. He was soaked to the bone, he didn't have Hunter, and the last thing he needed was more whinging from that slack-assed pilot.

'We have incoming, sir. Network gunship. Two minutes twenty.'

Ken spat into the rain – tonight just kept on getting better. 'Options?'

The pilot didn't even pause. *'Run for it.'*

'Unacceptable.'

'We can't make a stand: this piece of shit isn't designed to go up against that kind of firepower, sir.'

Ken clenched his teeth; the whole operation was one big cluster-fuck. Even if they did have the Bluecoat, going back without Hunter was as bad as going back empty handed. The old man would kill him.

'ETA: One minute fifty. We need to go now, sir, or they'll be right up our arses!'

'FUCK!' Ken backed towards the waiting Hopper. 'We've got your bitch, Hunter! You hear me?' He squeezed off a couple of shots at random, sending up plumes of mud and vegetation. 'We've got her, and if you open your fuckin' mouth so much as an inch I'll slice her fuckin' face off!'

The Hopper's engines were bellowing full blast as he stepped onto the ramp.

'One minute thirty seconds.'

'YOU HEAR ME HUNTER? I'LL SLICE HER FACE RIGHT OFF!'

The ramp wasn't even fully closed before the ship leapt into the sky. Ken staggered through the Hopper's hold, lurching as the thing accelerated away, hugging the streets. Getting as far away as its two massive turbines could carry it before all hell broke loose.

The bays lining both sides of the hold were full of dead people. Some had no heads, some had no backs, some had

316

no inside bits. Useless bastards. The two unconscious troopers lolled against their harnesses, swinging back and forth with the ship's motion. And there, at the far end, was the consolation prize for this evening's fiasco: Detective Sergeant Josephine Cameron.

A thin trickle of blood ran down the nape of her neck from where Armstrong had cracked her on the back of the head. Ken grabbed a handful of hair and pulled her head up. She was pretty. Not stunning, but not bad either.

Six dead, two unconscious and one broken jaw.

'You better be worth it.'

26

The Dragonfly banked hard to the right and dropped like a roller coaster for suicidal maniacs. More than half the bays were empty, their regular inhabitants being un-contactable at two o'clock on a Tuesday morning. The ones who had shown up lurched with the ship's motion, clutching their assault weapons, rubbing the sleep from their eyes, and grumbling. Up front, Lieutenant Emily Brand scowled at the monitor, watching a blurry echo disappear from her screen. Probably just interference from the engines, but she could have sworn she'd seen something hiding in the fuzz. She reached for her throat-mike.

'Oliver, I've got—'

'Targets acquired!'

The screen flickered and an infrared view of the park sixty feet below appeared. Two human-shaped heat signatures filled the centre of the frame, yellow and orange: one lying flat out, the other standing waving.

'Hit the lights!'

A soft 'crack' rang through the hull and a patch of Kelvingrove Park lit up like a very wet summer's day. Emily toggled the display and got a view from the external cameras: in the foreground rhododendron bushes writhed – buffeted by the downdraught – and just behind them a Bluecoat stood over a body. The body was wearing a filthy dressing gown and looked as if it had taken one hell of a beating. The body was William Hunter.

'Damn! Control, we have an agent down!' She stuck her head through into the cockpit. 'Get this thing on the deck NOW!'

The Dragonfly's legs hadn't even touched the ground before Emily cracked open the side hatch and leapt out into the rain. She hit the ground and rolled, coming to her feet with her Whomper ready and armed, sweeping the park like a conductor's baton, looking to orchestrate a little death and destruction.

'What are you waiting for, ladies?' she said. 'Defensive perimeter, *now*!'

Behind her, the rear hatch hissed open and four knackered troopers slogged out into the downpour.

'You!' Emily's Whomper was pointing right at the sodden Bluecoat's face. 'Hit the deck!'

'Yes, ma'am!' The constable dropped her weapon, jumped for the ground and hugged it like a long-lost friend.

'What happened here?'

'He's been attacked and beaten up.'

'I can see that.' Will looked as if someone had run over his face with a steamroller. Emily slid in closer and kicked the police-issue Field Zapper just out of reach, keeping her Whomper trained on the Bluecoat. 'Who did this?'

'Didn't get a good look at her – it was dark – but it was definitely a woman. She was standing over him when I got here. I challenged her and she ran for it. Bitch knocked me flying.'

'You let her get away?'

There was a pause. 'Not by choice. The victim was still alive. I tried to call it in, but they—'

'I know: jamming field.'

'I started to chase her, but the victim looked like he needed assistance so. . .'

'You did good.' Emily stooped down and helped the muddy Bluecoat up. Then started shouting orders: 'Nairn, Dickson secure the perimeter. Nothing in or out. Floyd, Patterson you've got stretcher duty. Move it people, we're not getting paid by the hour!'

The Bluecoat stared at Will's battered head. 'Is he going to be OK?'

Good question. 'Where's that damn stretcher?'

Patterson and Floyd squelched to a halt, dumped the stretcher on the wet ground and carefully lifted Will into place. They strapped him in and switched the thing on. It rose into the air, the sensors beeping and humming. Floyd pulled out a couple of blockers and a stim, snapping them into Will's neck as they hurried him back towards the waiting gunship.

'Grnnnnnkin insn nnnsnsssnnn. . .'

'Easy, Tiger,' Patterson pushed Will's head back against the platform. 'Someone's kicked seven shades of shite out of you.'

Emily followed them up the rear ramp and into the Dragonfly's warm, dry interior. 'Nairn, Dickson, report!'

'Nothing out here, ma'am, just a sodding huge bloodstain, two hundred yards from the pickup point. Other than that, nada.'

Emily looked out at the torrential downpour. 'You found bloodstains in this?'

'No' as hard as it sounds, ma'am, there's a hoorin' lot of it.'

She stared down at Will's battered face. 'What the hell did you do. . .?' There'd be time to worry about that later. 'Nairn, you and Dickson get back here. Next stop Glasgow Royal Infirmary—'

A hand grabbed her wrist. 'Nnnnrrr Dccccccccctrsssss.' The stims were starting to take effect.

'Don't be daft. Your head looks like an inflatable turnip.'

'Nnnnrrr Dccccctrsssss. Nnnnrrr timmme!' He struggled to sit up, but the platform's restraints held him fast. 'Whrrrrrssss Jo?'

'Jo?'

'Jo! Dtttttttectiffffff Srrrrrgnntttt Camerrrrrrnn.'

The Bluecoat grabbed Emily's sleeve. 'Just before you turned up, someone was shouting, "We've got her." They were going on about cutting her face off if anyone opened their mouth.'

Will thrashed against the medistraps. 'Gtttt me out offfff thizz.'

'You're going nowhere till you've seen a doctor.' Emily keyed her throat-mike. 'Nairn, Dickson, you going the bloody scenic route? Get your arses back here now!'

Two soaked and muddy troopers squished their way up the rear ramp.

'What kept you?' Emily slammed her hand on the button, and the rear doors squealed closed. 'Get us out of here,' she told the pilot. 'Glasgow Royal and step on it.'

Will grimaced at his reflection in the hospital mirror. Having his cheekbone welded back together wasn't something he ever wanted to experience again. A triangular patch of skinglue and bracing pulled his face into a constant, lopsided smile, whether he felt like it or not. His nose had been reset for the umpteenth time and new toothbuds stitched into his gum.

The black eye was already beginning to fade – as were all his other bruises, thanks to a hefty dose of anti-ecchymosis medication – but the sight still wasn't pretty.

Someone had been dispatched to his flat to fetch a change of clothes and discovered the place in ruins. All the corpses were missing: no dead bodies in the apartment, no dead bodies in the lift, no dead bodies in the park. All that remained were two huge bloodstains on the lounge carpet and some sticky bits of skin on the lift walls. Short of a DNA match they weren't going to get any names.

'We need to get back to base,' he told Emily as she stood watching him dress.

'You need to get back to bed. You look as bad as you smell.'

He glared at her. 'We haven't got time for this! If they've got Jo. . .' And then he remembered the listening devices sitting beneath Emily's skin. Everything he told her went straight into the ears of that stumpy wee bastard Ken Peitai. Deep breath. 'Sorry.' He pulled on his trousers. 'It's the blockers. I'm not thinking all that clearly. You're right. I need to go to bed.'

Her eyes narrowed. 'Oh no you bloody don't. Come on: "if they've got Jo," what?'

'Nothing. It's been a rough—'

'What is *wrong* with you Will? Why won't you talk to me any more? What the hell did I do to you?'

'I. . .' He shut his mouth and forced his arms into the sleeves of his shirt. The blockers cut the pain, but he was still stiff. 'You've not done anything. It's me. You heard the doctor, too many bangs on the head. Concussion. It's not. . . I'm not. . .'

'Don't give me that shite Will. The people who attacked you got DS Cameron. We're going after her!'

Will smiled; it twisted his face even further out of shape. 'Thought you didn't like her.'

The pause was only a heartbeat long, but it was there. 'She's on the team. We don't hang our own out to dry.'

Carefully he pulled on an old jacket and stood, looking at his bruised and battered reflection in the mirror, but seeing Jo: running for her life, dressed in a jumpsuit scavenged from a dead body.

Emily paced up and down the little hospital room. 'We get them to set off her coffin dodger. We pull in the reserves. We push every button we can until someone squeals. We lean

322

on people. We oil the wheels. We do whatever it takes to get her back.'

A good suggestion, but utterly hopeless. Whoever it was Ken Peitai worked for, they weren't going to be hanging around in bars, ready to spill their guts for a pint of special. But it would give Emily something to do, and everything she did would be relayed back to good old Ken. Let him know they were getting nowhere.

'You're right. Get it started.' He laid a hand on her shoulder and even though he felt like a complete bastard for lying to her again said, 'I'm going home.'

Out in the corridor, the constable they'd picked up in the park was waiting. The mud had dried on her bright-blue tunic, turning it the colour of old lentil soup. She'd made some attempt to brush it off, but the thing was still a long way from clean.

'Has there been any news?' she asked as they drew level.

Will shook his head, winced, and decided not to do that again for a while. 'Lieutenant Brand's setting up a search. I'm going back to bed. Doctor's orders.'

The Bluecoat looked surprised. 'Is it going to be safe there, sir?'

Emily nodded and consulted her watch. 'We've got two of the nightshift over there watching the place: Bull Thrummer and a Screamer. No one's going to get anywhere near.'

'Even so, sir.' The constable stood to attention. 'I'd like to escort you back. I know it's probably not necessary, but—'

'Good idea.' Emily placed a hand in the small of Will's back and propelled the pair of them in the direction of the lifts. 'Gives me one less thing to worry about.'

'You know,' said Will as they climbed into the shuttle, 'you saved my life, and I don't even know your name.'

The constable looked down and picked a lump of mud from

the ID tag on the front of her filthy tunic. 'Catherine McDonald.' She pulled the tag, showing it to him. 'But you can call me "Cat" if you like, sir. My DS does.'

A frown crossed Will's battered face. 'Have we met?'

'Oh, not again.' She sighed. 'Listen, I don't make a habit of getting drunk at official functions, OK? And it was bloody years ago. Can we just drop it?'

'Consider it dropped.' He reached forward and punched 'NETWORK HEADQUARTERS' into the destinator, then settled back in his seat as the shuttle slid forward and clacked onto the hospital exit ramp. The brightly lit tunnel walls disappeared behind them as the car picked up speed, leaving them with the internal light. It turned the wraparound windshield into a dusty mirror, reflecting back one battered Network Assistant Director and one filthy Bluecoat. The first of the stanchion lights vwipped past, wiping their images off the glass and back on again, like the flickering lines on an old display screen.

'You're not going back to your apartment?' said Constable 'Cat' McDonald as the shuttle bumped onto the main shuttlenet.

'No, I'm not.' Will dragged out his mobile. 'I'm going to Network HQ, I'm going to get my hands on some very big guns, and then I'm going to blow some very big holes in the people that grabbed DS Cameron.' He dialled Brian's home number, waiting for it to connect.

The constable shook her head and placed a hand on her sidearm. 'Oh no you're not.'

'Trust me, there's no way—'

'*Grmmmmmmf?*' A bleary face – squeezed too close to the camera – peered out from the little screen. '*Will?*' it said prising its eyes open, '*Fuck's sake, do you no' know what time it is?*'

'Brian, I need your help.'

The face pulled back a bit and frowned. *'What the hell have you done to your head? Looks like a fat bird's jumped on it.'*

'Shut up and listen. They broke into my flat. They got Jo.'

'Jesus!' Brian suddenly looked a lot more awake. *'When? How?'*

Will told him everything, watching the Bluecoat out of the corner of his eye. She fidgeted with the Field Zapper on her hip, a frown on her face as he got to the part where she saved his life. Will held the phone out to her. 'Tell him what you heard.'

'I didn't see anyone, but I heard some American bloke shouting that if anyone did or said anything he was going to cut the DS's face off.'

'American?'

Will took the phone back. 'That'll be Ken Peitai. Speaks like he's just jumped off the tunnel. Newnited States? I'll bet he's never been west of Govan in his life.'

Constable McDonald pursed her lips and frowned. 'And you're going after him?'

'And his bastard boss. Anyway,' said Will going back to the phone, 'I'm stopping by the office to get tooled up. I can't ask you to come with me Brian, but—'

'Away and shite. You know fine well I'm no lettin' you go off after the buggers without me.' He turned to look at something off camera and smiled. *'James here can make his own breakfast for once.'*

The Bluecoat was still staring off into the middle distance when the destinator finally chimed their arrival at Network HQ. Will reached out and gently touched her shoulder – her hand flashed up and wrapped round his wrist like a vice.

'Are you OK, Constable?'

She blushed and let him go. 'Sorry, sir, I was miles away.'

'Don't worry about it. I've got to go arrange things here. Thanks for the escort. You can take the shuttle back to your station—'

'Oh no you don't, sir.' She followed him out onto the platform. 'If you're going after the DS I'm going with you, whether you like it or not. She'd do the same for me.'

'Fair enough.' Will turned and swiped them both in through the staff entrance. 'You know where the armoury is?'

She shook her head.

'Ask at Reception. Tell them you've got orders to draw some Whompers, a tracker and anything else that takes your fancy. They can confirm by calling me.'

'Where are you going to be?'

Will straightened his shoulders and headed for the lifts.

'There's something I have to take care of first.'

Most of the lights were off in the mortuary, filling the antiseptic room with thick chunks of darkness. Will sat on the edge of a post-mortem slab with a surgical blade in his hands and blood running down his left side. An Anglepoise lamp cast a hot-white spotlight on his left armpit, making the scarlet blood sparkle and shine. With gritted teeth he cut deeper, pulling the edges of the wound apart. It didn't hurt – the last of his hospital-issue blockers had seen to that – but the sights and sounds were making him nauseous.

George had said one of the trackers was beneath his left arm, on the wall of his chest, but Will was beginning to realize that finding the transmitter wasn't going to be as easy as he'd hoped. The blood was making everything slippery and difficult to see.

The blade slid from his fingers for the third time in as many minutes, clattering against the stainless steel tabletop.

Fucking thing.

How was he supposed to hold onto it when it was slick with blood? How hard did this have to fucking be?

He grabbed the handle and hurled the knife away into the darkness. It clanged off something metal hidden in the shadows.

He put his bloody hands over his eyes and slumped back on the cold post-mortem table.

This was impossible. He couldn't go anywhere near Sherman House with a pair of locator beacons buried under his skin. They'd all be dead before they even set foot in the place.

An angry voice burst into the cold room. 'Who's in here?'.

'George?'

The short, fat pathologist stood framed in the doorway, slippers on his feet and a bone hammer in his hand. The lights flickered on, killing the shadows.

'Will? What the hell are you doing down here? It's half three in the morning!'

'Could ask you the same thing.'

George shrugged and waddled across the squeaky floor. 'Explosion in the Queens Cross shuttle station. Forty-one dead. I was getting a couple hours kip before going back to. . .' He sniffed, then stopped, staring at the blood oozing out of Will's side. 'What the hell are you doing?'

'I'm trying to get rid of the—'

'You're bleeding all over my lovely clean mortuary!'

He pushed Will flat on the slab and peered at the open wound in his side.

'What did you use, a cheese grater? This is a mess!'

'You try operating on yourself! See how easy—'

'You're not even cutting in the right place!'

'Well you do it then, if you're so damn clever.'

George stepped back and bit his bottom lip. 'I only operate on dead people.'

Will placed a hand on the little pathologist's shoulder,

leaving a dark red stain. 'They've taken Jo. I can't get her back if they know I'm coming.'

'Lie back, I'll go get the wand.'

Will pushed through the double doors into the Network shuttle station. His chest and stomach ached a little, like a background noise not quite loud enough to identify. George might be happier working on the dead, but he was no slouch with the living either. Even if he did narrate everything as if he was doing a post mortem.

Constable Cat McDonald was waiting for him, a brand-new Bull Thrummer slung over her shoulder. It dwarfed the Field Zapper strapped to her hip, reaching down to her shins and up past the top of her head. There was a small buggy at her feet, heaped with weapons from the armoury.

She'd changed out of her mud-encrusted Bluecoat into Network-issue concrete-grey camouflage combat gear. 'Got a set for you too, sir,' she said, handing over another jump-suit.

Two minutes later a shuttle pulled up at the platform and Brian clambered out. He looked as if he'd fallen out of bed and into his fatigues.

'Somebody call for a taxi?'

'Here,' said Will, giving him one of the Whompers and a shoulder pack of assorted crowd-control devices, 'make yourself useful.'

When they were all ensconced in the shuttle – the massive Bull Thrummer jammed in at an angle to make it fit – Brian stuck his hand out to the new girl. 'Special Agent Brian Alexander. Who're you when you're no' tooled up to go shoot some toley beanbag?'

The constable smiled and shook Brian's hand. 'Cat McDonald: Bluecoats.'

'Do I no' know you?'

She stopped smiling. 'I was drunk, OK?'

Brian threw a wink in Will's direction. 'A woman after me own heart.'

With a small clunk the shuttle left the Network's private station and slipped into the main tunnels. As the car hummed up to cruising speed, Brian asked the big question: 'So how're we goin' tae find her then?'

Will dug the tracker out of Cat's shoulder pack and tossed it across the shuttle to his friend.

'Coffin dodger.'

Brian flipped the thing open and scowled at the empty fizzing display. 'Aw come aff it! It'll take days to get that bugger Station Commander to switch the damn thing on!'

'Who says we're going to ask him?' The shuttle's console flickered under Will's fingers as he hammered his way out through Network security and straight into the Bluecoat's dispatch system. Within minutes there was a small click and then the tracker in Brian's hand lit up like a carnival ride.

'We have lift off!' Brian squidged his face close to the screen, lips moving slightly as he read.

Will sat forward. 'Well? Where is she?'

'Hud yer horses, it's comin' up. . .' He frowned as the map appeared on the tracker's screen. Jo's coffin dodger was a big red circle that constricted to a point as the city's network of receivers triangulated the signal. 'Southeast: other side of the river, past the firestacks. . . Shite.' Brian looked up. 'It's—'

'Sherman House.' Will finished for him.

'Aye, Sherman House.' Brian sighed. 'Arseholes.'

'Look on the bright side,' said Will as he powered up his Whomper, checking the charge, 'you'll get to meet the lovely Mr Peitai.'

Brian shrugged and slapped a new battery into his assault rifle. 'Her Majesty's goin' tae go mental when she finds out. She'll have our goolies for earrings.'

'Only if we get out of this alive.'

Brian beamed and slapped their new friend Cat on the back. 'Aye, he's right. Always look on the bright side.'

27

Outside the shuttle's windows the stanchion lights vwipped past, their cold-white glow making the carriage flicker as Brian dug his way through the pack of crowd-control devices Constable Cat MacDonald had liberated from the Network armoury – lining them up on the floor. She'd been pretty thorough: Crispies, Jammers, Sticky Willies, and NightFog. All the toys.

Brian stuck them back in the bag while Will filled Cat in on Ken Peitai's 'social research' project, the sub-dermal tracking and listening devices, Peitai and Kikan's spell at Glasgow Royal Infirmary and what he'd found hidden away in the PsychTech files.

When Will was finished, Brian dumped the full pack on the seat next to him and said, 'You find out why the wee dick and his boss were messing about with PsychTech?'

'Not yet.' Will stared out of the window, watching the bars of light streak past. 'Westfield was building killers, Peitai is too. Maybe it was a kindred spirit kind of thing?'

Cat MacDonald raised her hand, as if asking permission to go to the toilet. 'She was trying to see if the textbook model of serial killer development was valid, yes?' Cat picked at the Field Zapper in its holster. 'Perhaps they thought they could hijack her research?'

Will nodded. 'That's what I thought.'

There was a small lurch as the shuttle left the main net and clacked onto the Monstrosity Square branch line.

Will checked the destinator. Almost there.

'Lock and load, people.'

He pulled his Whomper upright and popped the power cartridge out into his hand, checking the contacts were clean and the charge was full, before racking the battery back into place. Watched as Brian and Cat did the same.

They coasted the last fifteen feet into the shuttle station beneath Sherman House in absolute silence. Their car bumped to a halt against the station buffers and, with a soft hiss, the doors slid open, letting in the bitter reek of stale urine. Faded sodiums flickered incontinence-yellow against the grubby concrete as Will stepped out onto the deserted platform.

'Which way?'

Brian wrinkled his nose. 'Jesus. . . It *honks* in here!' He peered at the tracker's screen, then did a slow, lumbering pirouette, holding the device in front of him as he turned. At last he lifted a grey-clad arm and pointed off the end of the platform and into the dark of the shuttle tunnel: back the way they'd come.

'Goin' to have to walk.'

Constable MacDonald almost choked. 'You're kidding, right?' She looked at the shuttle and then the black hole. 'Do you have any idea what speed these things go at?'

Will pulled his Whomper round into firing position and started towards the platform's far edge.

'Sir, if we're in the tunnels when a shuttle comes we'll be spread all over the walls like pâté!'

Brian shrugged and slung his rifle over his shoulder. Holding the tracker in front of him, he followed Will down the ladder at the end and onto the trackway, leaving Cat alone on the station platform, clutching her massive Bull Thrummer and spluttering.

'Am I the only one who sees how stupid this is?'

'Aye,' said Brian, 'Looks like it.'

Will marched into the darkness, the hot green circle of his lightsight sweeping the track in front of him.

The room sparkled like a surgical blade. Harsh light bounced back off the wraparound mirror, illuminating the figure strapped to an interrogation chair. Sneaky bitch was slumped sideways, trying to pretend she was still unconscious, but the monitoring equipment told a different story. She was awake and they knew it.

The old man rested a hand against the observation suite window, staring through the glass at William Hunter's girl-friend.

'Have you managed to glean any information from our guest?' His voice was soft, but Ken could hear the menace in it: like a teddy bear full of razorblades.

'Well, sir, we had a friendly little chat and it seems Hunter knows a damn sight less than we thought he did. That or he's not told Pocahontas here the whole story. Either way. . .' Ken flexed his hand, feeling the tight pull of fresh skinpaint on his scraped knuckles. 'She's been very cooperative.'

'You persuaded her?'

Ken nodded, pointing at the monitors. 'Chemical, electrical and kinetic. She's got nothin' more to hide.'

The old man turned his back on the observation window and pulled the test tube from his pocket, sending it dancing between his fingers, keeping the thick, liquid contents moving. 'You still haven't found Mr Hunter.' It wasn't a question.

'We're lookin' for him, sir. I got three teams sweepin' the city as we speak.'

'And are they going to be using the tracking beacons we implanted under his skin to find him this time? Or have you got them charging around like headless chickens again, wearing low-light goggles instead of infrared?'

Ken could feel his cheeks flushing in the darkness. 'We couldn't use the trackers in the park, sir, the jammer blocked the—'

'I don't like excuses, Ken, you know that.'

Tokumu Kikan smiled and placed a hand on the back of Ken's neck. The old man was easily a foot taller than him – even with the Cuban heels – and Ken had to try really hard not to flinch as the long, cool fingers wrapped around.

'I would so hate for this to come between us, Ken.' Pause. 'Don't let it come to that.'

'Yes, sir. Definitely, sir. I'll get onto the teams and make sure they know—'

'Find Hunter for me. Maybe we'll forget all about your errors of judgement.'

'Yes, sir. Thank you, sir.'

The test tube stopped its dance and Ken watched the liquid inside slide back down the sides of the glass into a thick green pool.

'And if you can't. . .' Kikan shrugged. 'If you can't, well, we always need people to help us test the formula.' He slipped the test tube into Ken's top pocket and patted it gently.

'It's not goin' to come to that, sir, I swear it.'

'Good lad.' The old man smiled again and turned back to look through the window at Detective Sergeant Jo Cameron pretending to be unconscious.

Interview terminated.

Ken got the hell out of there as fast as his cowboy boots would go. If the old man was pissed at him it might be better to keep on running. Make himself disappear before an assault team broke *his* door down in the middle of the night and did it for him. Maybe hop a Trans-Atlantic shuttle, set up shop in one of those half-assed redneck republics. Get a new name and a new face and keep his head *way* down. Not even the old man could live forever. . . But Ken knew it wouldn't

334

work, the Newnited States wasn't far enough: they'd still find him.

No choice then. Have to see this out to the end.

The control room was quiet, the bank of monitors covering one wall flickering from apartment to apartment in the building above. A mousy blonde in a headset sat behind the large, crescent-shaped desk. Ken parked himself on the edge of it and demanded a progress report.

'Not much, sir.' The controller hit a button and the monitors flickered, all the pictures merging into one. An aerial shot of Finneston slid past, the distinctive pug nose of a Hopper just visible on the left of the frame. 'Team two is doing a segment sweep, but they're not getting anything on the tracker.'

She hit another button and a Network Dragonfly shot across the wall, its navigation lights winking red and green in the rain-drenched night.

'Team three picked up this blip fifteen minutes ago: the codes don't match, but.'

'That'll be Lieutenant Brand: the one that crippled Arkwright. Forget about her, she's. . .' Ken stopped, remembering the old man's fingers wrapping around his neck. 'Second thoughts, stay on her: she's wired for sound. If Hunter tries to get in touch I want to know.'

'Yes, sir.'

'What about team one?'

'Spiral search pattern out from Network Headquarters. He was in Glasgow Royal Infirmary for a couple of hours getting his head stitched back together, but we couldn't touch him: too much security. He took a shuttle to Network HQ an hour ago. Twenty minutes later we lost the tracking signal.'

'God damn it.' Forty minutes – bastard could be anywhere by now. 'You pull in every extra man we've got. I want to know where this sonuvabitch is.'

*　　*　　*

'There we go.' Brian's voice was little more than a whisper, but it still echoed uncomfortably loud in the dark, empty hollow of the shuttlenet tunnel. Up ahead, just visible as a faint semicircle, was an unmarked branch off the main line.

Will swept the green beam of his lightsight up the near-side wall and then snapped it off, leaving them in absolute darkness.

'Anyone see any cameras?' he asked.

'No, sir.'

'How're we supposed to see cameras? You've switched the bloody light off!'

'Stop moaning.' Will reached out, searching for the person nearest to him and finding Constable MacDonald. 'You grab the back of my harness, Brian'll grab yours. Single file.' He inched forward, feeling his way in the dark towards the private branch line.

'Sir?' Cat whispered. 'Sir? What are we going to do when we get there?'

'Grab the first person we find, ask them where Jo is. Then we rescue her and do a runner before they send in the Marines.'

'Great.' She sighed. 'A well thought out plan. Nothing left to chance. How could it possibly go wrong?'

'You want a list?' asked Brian from the back of the line.

'Would you two shut up!'

They crept on in silence, off the main line into the private tunnel – using the maglev track in the middle as a guide. The tunnel swept away from the Sherman House station and, after what seemed like hours sneaking along in the dark, Will shuffled to a halt. He felt his way back along Cat's arm to where Brian was holding onto her battledress.

'How much further?'

There was a click and a faint grey glow lit Brian's face from beneath. The light was turned down so low it was almost off, but after the pitch black of the tunnel it was like a search-light.

'Two hunnerd and fifty feet . . . Jesus.' He snapped the screen shut, plunging them back into darkness. 'We're right on top of the damn thing.'

'Right, here's what we. . .' Will ground to a halt, staring back down the tunnel. It wasn't much; just a faint flicker of light, but it was getting brighter. He stuck his arms out to encompass Brian and Cat and leapt for the tunnel wall. They slammed into the concrete as the light bars on either side of them burst into life, stinging their eyes. A pressure shock-wave made his ears pop and he hung on for dear life as the shuttle screamed past. It decelerated rapidly, settled into a stately glide and coasted to a halt at the research facility's private station.

On either side of them the stanchion lights flickered out, plunging them back into darkness again. Globes on the station walls blossomed into life and Will had to squint to make out anything more than a harsh, painful blur. Three figures stepped out of the car and onto the platform. The sound of a punchline wafted down the tunnel – just audible over the ringing in his ears – and the newcomers laughed, slapped each other on the back, and disappeared through the station doors.

'Shite that was close!' said Brian when they'd gone. 'My whole life flashed before my eyes. . . Mind, the dirty bits were good, but.'

Will turned his head and found his face less than an inch away from Constable MacDonald's. Her hips hard against his, her breath hot on his neck where they were all squashed together against the tunnel wall. The adrenaline of almost getting killed was making this feel a lot more erotic than it should. She smiled at him, licked her lips, and said: 'My hero!'

'Yes, well. . .' He backed away into the middle of the tunnel. 'We'd, erm, better get moving.'

Will led the way across to the vacated shuttle and up onto the platform. He pulled his Whomper round, hit the 'on' button, and the assault rifle came online with a soft electric whine. Brian powered his up. Then they waited for Cat to get the Bull Thrummer going.

Nothing.

She poked at the buttons and flicked the switches. 'It's a different model to the one I'm used to, OK?'

Brian turned it on for her and the siege weapon growled, drowning everything else out.

'Right,' said Will, 'here's what we're going to do: single file from here on. I'll take point; Cat in the middle; Brian, you're tail-end Charley.'

'Shite. No' again.'

'Yes again. The place will be wired so. . .' He dug into Brian's pack and pulled out a portable jammer. 'It's got a range of about two hundred meters.' He flipped the switch and stuffed it back where he got it. 'They'll be able to guess our position as the cameras go out ahead of us, but there's nothing we can do about that.'

'Aye there is.' Brian winked at Cat. 'Will's supposed tae be the brains of the organization, but I'm no' just a pretty face maself.' He pointed at a big grey box marked 'DANGER OF ELECTROCUTION!' welded onto the concrete wall with about a ton of foamsteel. 'See that? That's the main power line goin' in tae the place. Cat, you want to do the honours?'

'What?'

Brian sighed. 'Thrum the damn thing.'

'Oh. My pleasure.' She swung the massive siege weapon round and thumbed the trigger. Nothing happened.

Brian rolled his eyes and sighed again.

'It works better when you've no' got the safety on,' he said, reaching over and clicking it off for her.

'Thanks.' This time the tines began to tremble, sticking out behind her like an angry metal porcupine. And then the Bull

Thrummer bellowed. Cat rocked back on her feet as a hard blue pulse surged forward, ripping through the foamsteel as if it was made of jelly. Tiny ionized particles of metal and concrete exploded under the Bull Thrummer's touch, whirling round in a cyclone of powder-grey dust, crackling with static electricity.

Cat McDonald was grinning like a maniac as the siege weapon thundered its way through the power line.

The noise was deafening, amplified by the tunnel walls. Sparks showered out of the ravaged foamcrete and all the lights in the station cracked off. The roar of the Bull Thrummer died away, leaving nothing but the sizzle and fizz of the dust storm, glowing with its own discharging electricity. And then they were back in darkness once again. Tinnitus ringing in their ears.

'THERE YOU GO,' Brian yelled. 'NO POWER. NOW ALL THE CAMERAS ARE ON THE BLINK.'

Will just smiled, shook his head, and pushed through the doors into the darkened facility.

He switched the Whomper's lightsight on, painting the place in soft green monotone. It wouldn't be long before they brought the backup generators online and Will was determined to get as far as he could before that happened. He charged up the main corridor, trying to remember as much of the layout as he could from Ken Peitai's tour. Cat was hot on his heels, sweeping the Bull Thrummer back and forth while Brian brought up the rear, tracker in one hand Whomper in the other.

'Talk to me, Brian.'

'Up to the end then left . . . no right. Shite, the thing's all over the shop, must be the jammer!'

Will kicked his way though the doors at the end of the corridor and swept the area with green light.

There was a large woman standing beside a vending machine, a plastic of something hot and dark in her hand. 'What the hell's goin' on?'

Will pointed the Whomper straight at her and she had to squint in the lightsight's glare, her orange hair bleached green in the targeting beam.

'Buchan, is that you?' She hobbled forward a step. One leg was encased in plaster to the knee, but she still stood like a rugby player.

'On the floor now!'

'I don't understand—'

'Get your arse on the ground before I blow it off!' Will thumbed the trigger, not with enough pressure to fire, just enough to make the weapon snarl in his hands. The woman dropped to the floor fast, coffee splashing across the dark terrazzo.

Will jabbed the Whomper into the back of her neck. 'Where is she?'

'I don't know what you—'

'Will?' That was Brian, sounding worried. 'What you doin'?'

'This was one of the pickup team that got her.' Will said. 'This is the one that put me in the hospital.' He turned his attention back to the redhead and made the Whomper growl again. 'I SAID WHERE IS SHE?'

'I don't know what you're talking about – I don't even work here!' She covered her head with her hands, face pressed against the floor. 'Please don't hurt me. . .'

Brian placed a hand on Will's shoulder. 'Hud oan. You don't want to do this. You're no' that kind of person.' Brian gently pushed the Whomper's barrel away from the big woman. 'But I am.' He kicked her in the ribs. Hard. Something dark splashed out of her mouth and Brian kicked her again.

'Right, sunshine,' he said balling his fist and grabbing the coughing, gasping woman by the throat. 'We know who you are.' He slammed the fist into her face, spreading her nose like meat paste. 'You know who we are.' He loosened a couple of teeth for her. 'And you know where our friend is. Okey doke?'

'Jesus, Brian!'

'No' now Will, I'm workin'.' He grabbed her arm and twisted it round through ninety degrees, locking the elbow. 'How about a nice wee game of *This Little Piggy*?' Brian took a firm hold of her index finger. 'Where is she?'

'I don't know what—'

'This little piggy went to market.' He jerked it back. A soft 'crack' sounded and she squealed.

'Where is she?'

'Bastard! I don't—'

'This little piggy stayed at home.' *Crack*.

'Ah Jesus! I don't—'

'This little piggy had roast beef.' *Crack*.

'Aaaagghh!'

'And this little piggy—'

'She's in the main interrogation suite! Down the corridor, first left, second right!'

Will jumped past them, leaving them in darkness.

'There you go,' said Brian, as if he was about to give the ginger-haired wifie a lollypop, 'that wasnae so hard now was it?' He let go of her hand and she pulled it against her chest, sobbing. Poor wee soul.

'Come on, Cat.' He struck a heroic pose. 'Will's only gonnae get himself in all kinds of shite if we're no' there to bail him out.'

'First things first.' Constable MacDonald placed the barrel of the Bull Thrummer against the woman's battered head. 'You have beautiful eyes.' One second the big-boned woman was there, the next there was nothing left but a dark, sticky mist that tasted of iron.

Brian stood, mouth hanging open, eyes wide. 'But. . . You. . .'

'What?' Cat hoisted the weapon. 'Like we're going to leave her alive to raise the alarm and shoot us in the back? I don't think so.'

Brian watched her disappear up the corridor after Will. Jesus: they were a lot tougher in the Bluecoats than they'd been when he was a sergeant.

The lights flickered on above Will's head. They'd got the backup generators online already. So much for all the cameras being out.

He pulled up outside the double doors marked 'HOSPITALITY SUITE'. The roar of a Bull Thrummer sounded behind him, swiftly answered by the bark of a Whomper. More gunfire echoed down the corridor. The lights were on and someone was home.

Will stabbed his throat-mike: static crackled in his earpiece – the jammer was still going.

Cat sprinted around the corner, screeched to a halt and yelled, 'Down!' The hallway sizzled with blue light as her Bull Thrummer bellowed again. Brian came scrabbling after her; the hair on the back of his head a lot shorter than it had been fifty-seven seconds ago. He slammed into the wall at Cat's feet, turned, and fired his Whomper back the way he'd come.

'BRIAN!' Will yelled over the noise, 'KILL THE JAMMER, I NEED TO CALL FOR BACKUP!'

Agent Alexander fumbled in his pack and the static filling Will's ear died.

'Control, this is Hunter, put me through to Lieutenant Brand!'

'Sir? Half the city is looking for you, Director—'

'Put me through to Lieutenant Brand, now!'

'Yes, sir!'

Brian dug a Sticky Willy out of the pack, pulled the pin and hurled it down the corridor. Someone shouted 'Fire in the—' and a wet whoomping noise rattled the ceiling tiles as everything in the blast radius was coated in a thick layer of polymer adhesive.

Cat's Bull Thrummer roared again.

Will's earpiece popped and a tired, irritated voice came through loud and clear: *'This better be bloody important!'*

'Emily, shut up and listen. We're in a secret research facility under Sherman House. You know the one, you've been here.'

'What the hell are you doing there? You told me you were going home!'

'We've found DS Cameron, but we're under heavy fire.' He ducked as a section of wall exploded into hot plastic shrapnel.

Cat MacDonald heaved the Bull Thrummer back and forth, teeth bared.

Someone screamed.

Will fired a couple of shots into the thick cloud of Thrummer dust. 'Lock onto my signal and get your team down here ASAP!'

'Damn it, Will, You lied to me!'

'I didn't have any choice. When they caught us they stuck listening bugs under our skin. Trackers too. If I'd told you anything they would have known.'

'They put listeners under my skin and you didn't tell me? You should have told me!'

'Just get yourself down here pronto, OK?'

There was a pause and in the background Will thought he heard the Dragonfly's engines changing pitch, though it was difficult to tell over the roar of Cat's Bull Thrummer.

'ETA two minutes thirty.'

'Thanks Emily, I owe you one.'

'You should have told me.' She killed the link.

Will sighed and turned to face the hospitality suite doors. Brian and Cat were keeping the facility's guards busy; Emily and her team were on their way; all he had to do now was rescue Jo.

How hard could it be?

The Whomper sang in his hands as he drew back his foot and kicked the door off its hinges.

28

Light, so bright it was painful. Will skidded to a halt, blinking, one hand up in front of his eyes. Nothing was visible past the broken door – the rest of the room hidden behind the lights shining straight into his eyes.

'Mr Hunter,' said a familiar, mid-Atlantic accent, 'hey, nice to see you again. Drop the gun.'

Will snapped the Whomper round, pointing it straight at the voice.

'Whoa there! You shoot, you blow a hole in the lovely DS Cameron! Want to see her head explode when you whomp it? You want that? Cos if you do, go right ahead.'

Will squinted into the glare. 'Jo, are you OK?'

Silence.

Then Ken said, 'Don't be rude, Sweetheart, the nice man asked you a question.'

'Kaaaaaaaarl thhhfugin basstdd Will, shoothfuger. . .' Her voice was weak, slurred and swollen, but it was Jo alright.

'I want to see her!'

'OK, but remember: you use that cannon of yours, she's not gonna need a party hat for Christmas.' The light flickered and dimmed.

The shapes were fuzzy at first, just blobs, reflected again

and again in the wraparound mirror, but as Will watched they resolved themselves into three figures: a gorilla in fatigues standing against the back wall, carrying a Thrummer; Ken Peitai standing beside one of the interrogation chairs; Jo strapped into it.

Her face was swollen and bruised, her left eye little more than a puffy, prune-coloured slit. Blood caked the side of her mouth, her lip split like the skin on an over-ripe tomato. Half a dozen wires were taped to her head and two intravenous lines ran from her arm to a small, cat-sized box festooned with little blinking lights.

Will twisted the focus on the Whomper's lightsight until the green point sat dead between Ken's shifty eyes. 'Bye, Ken.'

Peitai flinched. 'Henderson!'

The gorilla in the suit hauled his Thrummer round and Will shot him in the face. The Whomper's bark echoed around the circular room as Henderson's body twitched its way to the floor, fountaining bright red up the mirrored wall.

'Nice shootin' Tex.'

Will swung the Whomper back, but Ken wasn't in the same place – he now stood directly behind Jo, one hand wrapped up in her hair, the other holding a Palm Screamer.

'Now you got that out of your system, what say we have us a little chat like civilized human beings? OK?'

'Let her go.'

'You put that thing down or I do us up a batch of sizzlin' long pig. You catch my drift?'

'I said—'

Ken placed the Screamer against Jo's right arm and thumbed the trigger. Hot noise burst from the weapon and her skin swelled and cracked, letting out puffs of steam and the smell of roasting meat. She turned to look at the cooking joint, her face slack, eyes not quite focused. . . And then the screaming started. It began as a low moan, barely audible over the pop and crackle of her flesh as it baked, then it got louder and more piercing, as painful to hear as it was to watch.

'You like your meat rare or well done?'

Will tore his eyes away from the sight and the Whomper growled in his hands.

'Now, now,' said Peitai. 'You put that thing down or it's brains next on the menu.' The Screamer rested lightly against Jo's temple.

'Do it and I'll kill you.'

A grin split Ken's face. 'Yeah, but then she'll be dead and I'll be dead and the man standin' behind you's gonna turn your insides to mush.' Will felt something hard jab into the small of his back. With all the light bouncing back and forth from the mirrors he hadn't seen anyone else enter the room.

Ken winked. 'So you'll be dead too. Now where's the point in that? Much better you put down the Whomper and we see if we can't figure out a solution to our little misunderstanding. DS Cameron here can always get herself a new arm when we're done.' He shrugged. 'Can't get herself a new head.'

The box hooked up to Jo's arm bleeped and her screams faded to a dull whimper.

Will lowered the Whomper to the floor.

'There we go – all one big happy family.' Ken pointed the Screamer at Will's discarded weapon and melted the casing into plastic slag. 'Lincoln, help Mr Hunter to his seat.'

Hot blue sparks exploded behind Will's eyes as all the muscles in his back contracted at once. He fell to the floor, twitching. The Zapper must have been on light stun, or he'd be unconscious by now. Rough hands grabbed his shoulders, dragging him into an interrogation chair.

Will gritted his teeth and tried to punch Lincoln in the throat, but his arms weren't working. Pins and needles pulsed through his arms and legs as Lincoln strapped him down and wired him up to a bank of monitors. 'There's a pickup team on its way, Ken. It's finished. You're through.'

Peitai shrugged. 'I'm gonna give you a chance to think things through, Will.' He clicked a panel open on the box attached to Jo's arm and started flicking switches. 'We're not like them other shlubs in Special Ops, we're Unit 731. You're just Network. Trust me, if we need you to disappear, you go bye-byes. My boss: he wants to see you filling a little jar on his shelf. Me: I think, even though you've been a right royal pain in the ass, you're one of the Good Guys, like me.'

He finished fiddling with the box and put a hand on Jo's shoulder. A thick line of drool silvered her chin. 'I think you and me could do a lot of good here, Will.

'You know what, Ken?' The sensation was starting to come back – Will tried to work one of his hands loose. 'You're not "one of the Good Guys". You're scum.'

'I'm deeply hurt to hear that.' Ken sighed. 'I know it looks bad, but it's the only way we're gonna win the war.'

'We're not *at* war!'

'Will, Will, Will. We're *always* at war. You just don't get to hear about it any more. Sure we let the armed forces wave the flag when they're off on them international peacekeeping missions, and all that humanitarian bullshit, but that's not where the real fight is. It's here.'

'Bollocks.'

'You know how people in Oldcastle always look so damn stupid? Know why that is? Cos some bastard put this chemical in the water that retards neural development. An' you wanna know who did it? It was one of our allies. Not our enemies, our *friends* did that to us.' Ken shook his head. 'Unbelievable.'

'You see,' he said, settling back against Jo's chair, 'it ain't about land or religion or any of that crap anymore. It's about money. They make enough of us stupid – we can't compete with them. They make enough of us infertile and we got no workforce in twenty years. They make us riot and kill each other. . .' He shrugged again. 'We can't prove the VRs weren't caused by a manmade pathogen, released into the wild on purpose. We need to have an antidote in case they decide to do it again.'

'Don't speak shite. You're not looking for a cure; this is a weapons programme!'

The smile disappeared from Ken's face.

'OK: you got me. We're buildin' a weapon, so what? "*They*" do it all the time: look what happened to Oldcastle.'

'Chemical warfare is illegal!'

'Jesus, Will, grow up. This ain't the God-damn World War Cup, this is real life. All's fair in love and war, remember?' He slapped another smile on his face, straightened his tie and gently slipped the IV lines out of Jo's uncooked arm.

'You're using human beings as lab rats!'

'Eggs and omelettes, Will, eggs and omelettes. How we supposed to fight the bad guys if we ain't got any weapons?'

Ken turned and faced a seam in the mirrored wall, popping it open to reveal a hidden door and a small, quiet passageway beyond. 'Down the end of that corridor there's a shuttle bay.' He pulled the electrical pickups off Jo's forehead and dropped them on the floor. 'I can put her in a car and away she goes to A&E. She's got so much crap in her veins she's gonna remember none of this. All you need to do is get with the programme. Help your country.'

Will scowled. 'And if I don't?'

'She dies. You die. The two monkeys you came here with die . . . if they're not already dead. We can't have you out there shootin' your mouth off, Will. When we use this stuff we gotta make sure there's nothin' linkin' it back to the powers that be. Can you imagine the world of shit we'd be in if they found out the Scottish Government infected a foreign country with VR?'

Will watched as a thin stream of gravy leaked out of Jo's roasted skin.

'How the hell can you do this?'

'Cos I have to. We ain't evil monsters and this ain't my idea of fun.' He ran a hand across Jo's bruised and shiny fore-head. 'What d'you say sport? Last chance: you gonna join us?'

Will closed his eyes and hung his head. 'You promise you'll let her go.'

'Give you my word. You join the team and she goes free. We'll pay for any care she needs. The two of you live happily ever after.'

'And the others?'

'Well, they'll have to make up their own minds, but at least they'll get the option.'

Play the hero and get everyone killed, or join the bad guys. Become responsible for atrocities. Save Jo's life. . .

Will hung his head. 'I'll do it.'

Ken nodded and looked at his own green-suited reflection in the mirrored wall. 'You get that, sir?'

A cold, disembodied voice floated out from hidden speakers. *'He's lying.'*

'Are you sure he isn't—'

'Positive. You know what to do.'

Ken sagged. 'Yes, sir.' He looked Will in the eye. 'Jeez I hate this bit.' He took the Screamer and pointed it at Will's head. 'I'm real sorry about this. I thought we could make it turn out different.' Ken pressed the trigger.

A faint heat washed over Will's face and then the Screamer went 'plink'.

'Sonovabitch.' Ken turned the device over in his hand and peered at the power reading. 'Empty. Lincoln, you want to do the honours?'

'Aye, sir.'

Will felt the cold barrel of a Whomper pressed against the

side of his head. He glowered at Peitai. 'I *will* kill you. This world or the next: I'll find you and I'll kill you.'

Ken smiled sadly. 'Guess it's gonna have to be the next, buddy, cos your time in this one is up. Do him.'

The man on the end of the Whomper said 'Aye, s—' and then exploded.

29

Lumps of red meat spattered against the floor, an arm thudding off the side of the interrogation chair, then twitching where it fell. Blood dripped from the low ceiling tiles. The front of Lincoln's Whomper hit the deck in pieces, like a bag of spanners, clattering and clanging against the tiles. Ken backed away, dropped his empty Screamer and dived through the mirrored door, slamming it shut behind him.

Will craned his head round to see Brian, cheeks freckled with dark red dots, teeth bared, snarling. The Whomper in his hands jumped and the mirrored door exploded in a whirl-wind of shattered glass.

'GET ME OUT OF THIS!' Will had to shout over the deaf-ening noise.

Brian looked through the gaping hole to the passageway beyond, then back to Will.

'Cut me free! The bastard's getting away!'

'Arse.' Brian yanked his boot knife out and sliced through the straps.

Will staggered to his feet as Constable Cat MacDonald burst into the room, her eyes sparkling like cold, feral diamonds.

'Through there!' Will pointed at the section of wall Ken had asked for instructions – where the observation suite had to be. 'Kikan's in there: Peitai's boss. Bring the bastard down!'

'Yes, sir!' She grinned and the Bull Thrummer roared, turning the mirror into a fog of ionized particles. With a whoop she dived into the cloud.

Will knelt next to Jo. Her eyes were glazed, sweat dripped off her battered face. She was unconscious and Ken was getting away.

'Look after her, Brian.'

He grabbed the Thrummer from Henderson's headless corpse, and dived through the shattered doorway, sprinting after Ken Peitai. The weapon buzzing in his hands.

Left alone in the interrogation room, Brian crossed to where Jo was slumped in her seat and brushed the hair from her face with a gentle hand. Poor cow looked like shite, all battered and broken. The sweet, meaty smell of roast pork rising from her blistered arm.

Brian's stomach rumbled . . . then lurched.

The whole thing was cooked from fingertips to elbow. No *way* that was healthy.

He whipped off his belt and wrapped it around her bicep, hauling it as tight as he could. It might not help, but it couldn't hurt.

'Don't you worry, hen,' he told her. 'We'll kill the fuckin' lot of them.'

The passageway ran straight for about a hundred yards and so did Will, the Thrummer held out in front of him like a battering ram. He smashed through a security door at the end of the corridor and burst back out into the shuttle station, twenty yards down from the main doors.

The platform was still shrouded in heavy clouds of ionized dust from when Cat had decimated the power lines. The dirty white outline of a parked shuttle was just visible in the gloom, it's tail lights blurry red balls in the fog.

'Ken!' Will made sure his new Thrummer was powered up and ready. 'Where are you, you little bastard?'

Something moved in the murk and Will pushed the Thrummer's trigger, whipping the dust into a frenzy. It blasted a hole straight through the cloud to the main entrance, tearing the double doors apart, making the fog there even thicker.

'It's OK, Ken, you can come out now. I'm not going to hurt you!'

The shuttle doors hissed open. The lights inside the car flickered on, and Will could just make out the a blurry shape frantically punching something into the destinator. As the car began to lurch forward Will pulled the Thrummer into his shoulder and stepped to the edge of the platform.

'Oh no you bloody don't!'

The assault rifle shivered in his hands, then let out a deafening howl – ripping into the shuttle's rear end, turning a big chunk of machinery into crackling powder. But the shuttle was already on its way, building up speed as it powered away from the platform. It listed hard to one side and slipped off the maglev track, still accelerating. The nose dug a groove out of the tunnel wall and ricocheted back, twisting as it bounced over the guide rail and ploughed into the concrete on the other side. It scraped along in a shower of hot-metal sparks, shrieking against the wall.

The tunnel turned right, but the dying shuttle didn't; momentum spent, it ground to a halt. The safeties finally kicked in and shut the whole thing down, leaving the car's lights clicking on and off in emergency-warning orange. Darkness. Orange. Darkness. Orange.

Will walked to the edge of the platform and dropped down to the tracks, the Thrummer's lightsight a solid bar of green in the dust.

Behind him he could hear Brian staggering through onto the platform. 'Holy mother of shite. . . Will?' He had Jo slung over his shoulder, her face covered with a thin film of dust and sweat.

'He's mine, Brian, understand?'

'You don't have to do this.' Brian climbed carefully down to the tunnel floor. 'I'll slit the wee bastard like an envelope if you want me to. No one'll ever know.'

'I will.'

They marched towards the crashed shuttle, bathed in the on-again, off-again light of the warning beacons. Ken was inside, struggling with the door catch. A long gash snaked down one side of his face, spilling dark red onto his collar, saturating his shirt. With a final heave he hauled the doors open and fell out onto the tunnel floor.

They watched him struggle to his knees and then his feet.

Will powered down the Thrummer and handed it to Brian.

Brian frowned. 'You *sure* this is a good idea?'

'You don't shoot him, you got that? You don't shoot him unless he kills me and tries to get away. Then you blow his fucking head off.'

They could hear Ken talking to himself as he lurched away from the wrecked shuttle car. 'No, no, no. . .' One hand was clutched to his chest, the other held out against the wall, trying to hold himself upright. 'Aw Jesus no.' He slipped and fell sideways, bouncing off the wall as he slithered to the tunnel floor. 'Why'd the old bastard have to do that? Aw Jesus!'

'PEITAI!' Will picked his way through the wreckage. 'Told you I'd track you down.'

'Why?' Ken looked up as Will closed the gap. 'Why'd he have to do it?'

'Stand up, you piece of shit. Stand up or I swear I'll kick you to death where you sit.'

Ken held his hand out for Will to see. Shards of glass glittered in his palm and through the breast pocket of his torn jacket.

He let out a weird, high-pitched laugh. 'I'm already dead. . .'

It's darker in the observation room: the light that bleeds in from the interrogation suite does little to banish the gloom, nor do the flickering monitors. There are no heartbeats or brainwaves for them to register; instead they twitch away to themselves, displaying nothing but static.

Pretty.

She steps into the centre of the room and sniffs: old leather, and bitter-almond aftershave, she can smell it even over the stink of ionized glass. The old man has been here.

She lets the Bull Thrummer drift around the room, looking for a target.

The place is empty, but it hasn't been that way for long: the door at the end is still drifting shut. She sidles over and nudges it open with her foot.

Outside a corridor runs left to right with a pair of lab-coated women crouching at the furthest end, looking nervous and flustered, picking up printouts strewn across the floor – as if someone has run past and knocked them flying.

She's so glad she decided not to kill Hunter when she saw him outside the hospital. If she had, she wouldn't be here right now. And this is much, *much* more fun. William Hunter will kill Ken Peitai for her and then, after she's caught up with her old friend Tokumu Kikan and given him his present, she'll pay Mr Hunter a house call and say thank you in person.

She laughs and sprints down the corridor, past the scrabbling scientists, and on to the end of the passageway, following the trail of destruction and bitter-almond.

The old man is running for his life. She is so looking forward to seeing him again.

* * *

Ken shuddered and twitched. Red spittle frothed at the corners of his mouth, his hands flapped and skittered, the little shards of glass sparkling in the palm of his right hand.

'What's the wee bugger shooglin' about like that for?'

Will frowned. 'No idea.'

Ken's head snapped back, smacking off the tunnel wall with a resounding thunk. Slowly the trembling eased and he slumped into himself. Not moving.

'He snuffed it?'

Will took a step back and said, 'Lets find out.' He kicked the sagging figure in the chest as hard as he could. Ken bounced back against the wall and then slid gracelessly to the floor.

Brian spat a long, phlegmy, gob onto the back of Ken's motionless head. 'And there was me lookin' forward to seein' you beat seven shades of shite out of him.'

'Damn it.' Will kicked him again for luck.

Nothing.

Dead or unconscious. Either way, he wasn't fighting back.

Will reached up and keyed his throat-mike. 'Lieutenant Brand, this is Hunter. Where's your team?'

'Sherman House. Where the hell are you? We've searched the whole lower floor and we can't find an entrance to that damn lab.'

'We were on the forty-seventh floor when they zapped us, and we woke up in the lab. Easiest way to get us down here would be the lifts.'

'Floyd, get that lift console jimmied open.' Emily's voice was curt and businesslike. 'We'll be there as soon as we can.'

'Thanks I—' But the connection was dead. She'd cut him off. 'Great.'

Brian gently lowered Jo to the tunnel floor, then fumbled about in his pack for a med-kit. 'We need tae get her to the hospital. Her arm's fucked, and Christ knows what they've pumped her full of.'

Will nodded, and sank down beside Jo, stroking her swollen

cheek. When he'd told her to leave him in Kelvingrove Park, he'd thought *she'd* be the one to escape. . . And now look at her. It was all his fault, he'd got her involved in this. With that bastard Peitai.

'Will?'

He looked up to see Brian staring at him. 'Yes. . . Right. Emily's upstairs, we'll take the Dragonfly.'

'Good. I've had about enough of this shitehole for one day.'

'Call Cat and tell her to get back here. I don't want her wandering about on her own when Emily's lot come charging in, all guns blazing.'

Brian stood and clicked his mike. 'Cat?' He paused and tried again. 'Cat? Can you hear me?' He shook his head, pulled his earpiece out, peered at it, then stuck it back in. 'Everythin's buggered. . . Constable MacDonald, do you read?'

He scowled at Ken's twisted body. 'If any of your bastards have hurt her, I'll kill them!' He threw a kick into Ken's ribs, hard enough flip him over onto his back. The body groaned.

'Did you hear that?' Brian knelt and felt for a pulse. 'The wee shite's still alive. Happy days!' He grabbed Ken by the lapels and backhanded him. Ken's head snapped to the side, another groan. His eyelids fluttered, then opened.

Brian dragged him to his feet, singing, 'Oh Kenny boy, the pipes, the pipes are callin',' as he slammed him back into the wall.

'Brian, don't.' Will sighed and looked away. The initial burn had gone, leaving a bitter taste behind. The Network didn't make people disappear, it hauled them into court. All above board and legal. 'Read him his rights, he's got an appointment with an operating table.'

'After what this wee shite did to Jo? Halfheadin's too good for him.' He stuck his face inches from Ken's blood-caked features and shouted, 'Wakey wakey, Kenny, it's time to get the shite kicked out of you!'

Ken still hadn't said anything, but his eyes were wide,

dancing back and forth, his cheeks twitching, teeth gritted. Brian slapped him again.

'Your lucky day Kenny: two beatin's for the price of—'

It was if someone had run a thousand volts through Ken's battered body. He exploded off the wall, hands wrapping round Brian's head, teeth snapping like a rabid dog. Sinking them into Brian's cheek, ripping, tearing. . .

'Aaah!' Brian shoved him away. 'Ya wee bastard!'

Ken spat out a chunk of Brian's flesh, then lunged, going for the throat.

Brian whipped his head back and then forward again, smashing his forehead into Peitai's nose. *Crack*. They both staggered off: Brian into the middle of the tunnel, blood pulsing out from the hole in his cheek, Petai groping along the wall. The maglev rail caught Brian in the back of the knees and he went down like a sack of tatties, banging his head off the floor.

Will grabbed Ken on the rebound and smashed his elbow into the little bastard's face. Ken's nose burst like an egg, but it didn't even slow him down. He bared his teeth again and jumped, knocking Will off his feet. They crashed to the floor in a tangle of limbs.

Will scrabbled backwards, trying to get away from those blood-stained teeth.

Ken's hands groped for Will's cheeks and for a heartbeat the flashing emergency lights sparkled off the glass embedded in his right palm. The blood that dripped from the sharp, curved edges wasn't clean and red: it was tainted with some-thing green and viscous. Something that had turned Ken Peitai rabid.

Will stopped trying to fight off the teeth and grabbed the back of Ken's injured hand, forcing it over on itself – trying to snap the wrist. Peitai kept coming.

'BRIAN!'

Blood poured out of Ken's shattered nose and the gash

across his face. Lunging forward he sank his teeth into Will's eyebrow. Sharp, stabbing pain.

'Argh! Get off me!' Will rammed his right thumb into Ken's eye socket all the way up to the first knuckle. *That* got his attention. He let go of Will's face with a gargled scream, and struggled to his feet, one hand pressed against his ruined eye, trying to hold the contents in.

Then he lurched back into the middle of the tunnel and staggered away into the dark.

Will picked himself off the floor and grabbed his stolen Thrummer. His torn eyebrow throbbed and stung, blood dribbling into his eye. He wiped it clean on his sleeve – grimacing as the fabric pulled at the wound – but it just filled up again.

Brian was still lying flat on his back, groaning and swearing.

'Look after Jo.' Will flicked on the Thrummer's lightsight and headed off down the tunnel, following the sound of Ken's footsteps.

Everything smelt of damp and mildew and hot copper and oil and death.

'You won't get away, you know that don't you, Peitai?'

No reply.

Dark splashes of blood sparkled in the lightsight's green glow, like slicks of oil. The little bastard was moving fast and Will had to jog to keep up. Whatever Ken had in his top pocket it had done more than turn him bug-crazy, it had given him a whole new lease of life.

The tunnel twisted off to the left and Will stopped for a moment, straining his ears, trying to tell where Peitai was. It wasn't easy, but he could just make out the *scuff-click, scuff-click* of cowboy boots in the darkness.

The air was changing: he could feel it on his face as he moved. It was warmer here than it had been back at the platform, less musty – that meant the main line was close. He stopped again and listened. . .

Nothing but silence.

Either Ken had stopped running or that handful of glass and chemicals had finally killed him.

Will stepped into the middle of the tunnel, one leg brushing the cold metal of the maglev rail. He swept his Thrummer back and forth like a spotlight, looking for a target, but all he could see were shadows, haunting the empty alcoves between the stanchions and the end of the tunnel, where it joined the shuttlenet.

'Where are you, you wee—'

Something snatched at his ankle and pulled.

The floor disappeared beneath Will's feet and he tumbled backwards, hitting the concrete hard. The Thrummer roared in his hands, filling the dark tunnel with blue light that danced in an expanding ball of dust as a chunk of ceiling evaporated. His head cracked against the tunnel wall and the weapon jumped out of his hands, skittering away down the passageway. It clattered to a halt, the lightsight pointing back up the tunnel, casting grotesque shadow puppets across the concrete as Peitai leapt on him. Teeth flashing in the green glow.

A hand grabbed Will's face and he sank his teeth into it – not caring if there was glass in the palm or not.

Ken screamed, a bellow of animal pain with nothing human in it.

Will scrabbled away from the reaching hands. Not fast enough. Something slashed across his cheek and he felt the hot sting of flesh parting beneath multiple tiny blades of glass.

Bastard! He drove his knee into Ken's groin, hard enough to jack-knife him three feet into the air. Peitai collapsed, vomiting, clutching his groin.

Will scrubbed at the cuts on his face with the sleeve of his jump suit. The little bastard had infected him!

'Damn it! Damn it! Damn it!'

There had to be something in the jumpsuit's med-kit he

could use. He fell to his knees and fought the pouch free from its clips, spilling the contents across the floor.

'Blockers, skinpaint, dressing,' His hands fumbled through the pieces, spreading them far and wide. 'Skinglue. . . Where the fuck's the Biolene?' His fingers wrapped around a tube of sterilizing paste. It wasn't perfect, but it was all that he had. He ripped the top off with his teeth and mashed the sticky gloop into the cuts on his cheek. Then did the same with his torn eyebrow, just in case whatever it was could be transmitted through Ken's infected saliva.

He looked up, suddenly aware that he'd taken his eyes off the evil little bastard for far too long. Peitai wasn't rolling around on the concrete holding his ruptured testicles any more – he was on his feet, limping, knock-kneed down the tunnel towards the fallen Thrummer. Will scrabbled after him, but it was too late. Ken had made it out of the branchline and into the main tunnel, snatching the assault weapon up off the deck.

Peitai screamed at him, the words making no sense, jumbling into one another like meat in a grinder as the Thrummer's lightsight caught Will in its green gaze.

A soft whisper of air stirred the dust cloud of evaporated ceiling. Will looked about for somewhere to hide, but all he could see was empty tunnel. His eyes darted back to Ken – the little man seemed to be lit up from within, a soft nimbus of white light sparkling around him, getting brighter with every heartbeat. . .

The shuttle hit him hard enough to spread him all over the inside of the tunnel like pâté.

30

She follows the old man as he hurries through the facility, making for the hidden exit to Monstrosity Square – the one they used to sneak her through for their little Twenty Questions torture sessions. He knows the value of discretion when the Network comes a-rampaging armed to the teeth. She lets him get all the way to the doorlock before she stops him.

'Hold it right there!' She bathes him in the Bull Thrummer's targeting beam.

He doesn't flinch, she admires that. Instead he pulls himself up to his full height and turns on her. 'I don't know what you're trying to do here,' he says, all clipped and educated, not moving a muscle. 'But I can assure you I am *not* someone you want to interfere with.'

She swings the Bull Thrummer up and evaporates a chunk of roof above his head. Concrete particles drift down over his tall, black-cloaked shoulders like microscopic dandruff.

He coughs and splutters as the dust settles. 'You have no idea who you're dealing with. Your Network friends aren't going to save you. I can make you disappear, just like that!' He snaps his long, surgeon's fingers and she laughs.

'I've already disappeared.' She pulls a pebbled disk from her jumpsuit pocket, then twists the Palm Zapper's power dial down to 'LIGHT STUN', keeping the Thrummer on him at the same time. 'Now it's your turn.'

He sticks his chest out like a fighting cock. 'Do you have any idea who I am?'

'You,' she says, pointing the Palm Zapper at his face, 'are Tomuku Kikan. You stole my research, you stole my face, you stole my life.' She smiles: a cold, sharp, hard-edged thing. Broken glass. 'Did you really think you'd get away with it Tomuku? Did you?' Her finger caresses the trigger gently and little sparks dance around the disk's rim. 'You should have known better than that.'

'Who. . .' There's uncertainty in his eyes now. 'Who are you?'

She just smiles and shoots him.

The shuttle didn't even slow down. It sped away down the main line, the stanchion lights fading out behind it. Will stood in the growing darkness with chunks of Ken Peitai congealing on his jumpsuit.

The sound of small arms fire filtered down the tunnel behind him, punctuated by the unmistakable clatter of Whompers and Thrummers. Will turned and staggered back towards the shuttle platform and the orange flashing emergency lighting.

When he'd got as far as the crashed shuttle he slumped back against the twisted metal. The wreckage groaned in sympathy.

'Where's the wee shite?' Brian swung his Whomper across the tunnel behind Will.

Will looked down at his splattered and stained jumpsuit. 'I think that's his ear.'

'Don't be a bamheid.' Brian peered at him. 'That's a kidney.'

Will peeled it off the front of his chest and dropped it to the floor. 'Yeah, you're probably right.'

A soft 'thump' sounded from further up the tunnel and what was left of the platform doors exploded in a whirlwind of glass and plastic. Two figures, just visible through the thick pall of dust, picked themselves out of the debris. They tried to return fire, but something large roared, turning them both into a fine red mist.

'Jesus!' said Brian. 'Emily's no' takin' any prisoners.'

Someone stalked out of the ruined doorway onto the platform, a Bull Thrummer growling in their hands.

'Cat!' Will clambered to his feet and jogged back up the tunnel towards the murky figure.

'Hold it right there!' It wasn't Cat; it didn't even sound human.

'Dickson? That you?' Will had to squint, the siege weapon's targeting beam had turned the foamcrete and human dust into solid green soup.

'On your knees, hands where I can see them!'

Will sank to the floor and did as he was told. Something alien emerged from the mist, all lumpy and misshapen. The figure flipped up its visor and pulled the breather off its face.

'Lieutenant,' Dickson said into her throat-mike, 'I've found him.' She gave Will a small smile and clipped the mask back over her mouth. 'You can get up now, sir.'

'Agent Alexander and DS Cameron are back there, near the shuttle wreck. We need to get Jo to a hospital ASAP.' He pointed at the Bull Thrummer in her hands. 'There's another member of my team, a Bluecoat, carrying one of those. She's still in the facility.'

'I've not seen anyone, but I can ask.' Dickson put out the call and another strange, alien figure emerged out of the mist. Two gold pips painted on the chitin's shoulder plates, a glowing digital readout with 'Brand' on the chest. Emily.

The three of them walked back towards the flickering orange hazard lights in uncomfortable silence.

'The cavalry's here,' he told Brian, trying to break the permafrost.

Lieutenant Brand snapped her visor up and nodded. 'Brian.'

'Took yer bloody time.' He winked. 'No' got any chips on you, have you? I'm starved.' The sound of gunfire was less frequent now; only the occasional roar and pop breaking the silence.

'Greedy bastard. . .' Emily looked down at Jo's battered face and broiled arm, then keyed her throat-mike. 'Floyd, Patterson, get your arses and a stretcher down to the shuttle bay. I've got an injured DS for you.' She turned and addressed Dickson. 'You're on escort duty. See them back to the ship and make sure they go straight to the Royal. I hear they stopped off for a couple of pints and your arse is in a sling.'

'Yes, ma'am!'

'Emily. . .' Will paused as she turned and stared at him, eyes cold and hard. 'We've got an officer missing, the Blue-coat—'

'I heard. If she shows up we'll let you know.'

Dickson and Patterson jogged out of the mist carrying an evac platform. Gently they lifted Jo into place, strapped her in and set off back to the surface, taking Private Dickson and her Bull Thrummer with them.

Emily turned to follow them, but Will held her back.

'Look, I'm sorry I—'

She ripped the breather from her face. 'YOU SHOULD HAVE TOLD ME!'

'I didn't want—'

'They put crap under my skin! You knew!' Her hand struck him like a cannon-shot, snapping his face to one side. 'Bastard!'

'What was I supposed to do?' He spat a long stream of blood at the tunnel floor. 'If I'd told you they'd have heard. They killed Stein and they damn near killed Jo. They would have come after you too. . .'

'You should have told me.' She pulled the mask back over her face and walked back into the mist. Will watched her disappear.

A large hand settled on his shoulder.

'Fancy a curry?'

Will sighed. 'She's going to hate me for ages, isn't she?'

'Come on, let's go see if we can find Cat.'

She breaks an ampoule of halfhead sedative into Kikan's twitching body. His eyes widen as the chemical takes hold and the shuddering subsides. Now he can't move, but he can see, and he can hear, and he can *feel* everything.

Lucky boy.

Hefting Kikan's limp body over her shoulder is no trouble at all. All those years of hard physical labour have paid off.

It's a shame she'll have to leave the Bull Thrummer behind. A lovely toy, but it's just too big. She can't carry that and the old man at the same time.

Pity. . .

Ah well, she'll just have to buy herself one when she gets to her new home.

She pushes through the door. Outside, Sherman House is a dark silhouette against the sodium-tainted clouds. Doctor Westfield closes the door behind her, then slips away into the rainy night with her new best friend.

She has a lot of fun activities planned for Mr Kikan.

The facility was full of dust. Down in the interrogation room a handful of technicians and plainclothes military types were lying face down on the floor, hands snared behind their backs. Someone had thrown a cloat over Henderson's head-less body, but bits of Lincoln were still stuck to the roof, floor, walls. . .

'No sign of her anywhere.' Sergeant Nairn wiped a hand across his chitin's breastplate, leaving a clean patch. 'We found a Bull Thrummer up on the top level, near an exit to the square, but. . .' He shrugged. 'Sorry.'

A familiar voice echoed down the corridor, getting louder

all the time. 'What's going on here? I want an explanation for all this and I want it now!'

'Shite, it's Her Royal Bitchiness!' Brian spat onto one of the prone figures. 'Where's the nearest terminal?'

Nairn pointed through the hole Cat had blasted in the mirrored wall to the observation suite.

'You've no' seen us, OK?' Brian grabbed Will by the arm and pulled him into the little darkened room before Director Smith-Hamilton appeared.

The unmistakable sound of power heels on tiles clattered through from the other side of the mirrored wall and they ducked down behind a bank of monitoring equipment, keeping out of sight.

Brian pointed at a terminal and whispered, 'Hack into the Bluecoat system again and set off Cat's coffin dodger.' He dug the tracker out of his pack. 'We find her fast enough, maybe we all live to see breakfast.'

Will hammered commands into the keyboard, not even bothering to cover his tracks. Fifteen seconds later the tracker in Brian's hands burst into life.

'Got her!' He grinned, then frowned. 'In the name of the wee man. . .' He slapped the tracker and peered at the readout again. 'It's no' workin' properly.'

Will held out his hand. 'Let me see it.'

'It's buggered. According to this she's way over the other side of town.'

Will stared at the map flickering on the tracker's screen. 'Maybe whoever grabbed her has a hopper?'

'Aye, that'll be. . . Hud oan, she's no' movin'. Signal's stationary.'

'Right. We need transport.' Will clicked off the terminal and crept through the door at the back of the observation room.

There was a brand-new Wraith parked in the middle of Monstrosity Square. It was sleek and impressive, the engines idling; ready to bounce away at the slightest sign of trouble. Will and Brian marched straight over to it.

Will knocked on the cockpit window, and when the pilot opened it said, 'We're commandeering this vehicle.'

'Aye,' she replied, 'that'll be shining. This is the Director's private flyer, I'm no' goin' anywhere without her say-so.'

'You want to call her?' asked Brian. And when the pilot said she did, he punched her on the nose and dragged her out of the cockpit.

'Brian!'

She rolled into a ball on the rain-soaked concrete, clutching her face and groaning.

Brain shrugged and threw his Whomper in the back. 'We're in a hurry.'

They scrambled aboard and strapped themselves in, then Brian grabbed the controls and the Wraith leapt into the downpour, engines howling as it accelerated away from Sherman House.

'Where we goin'?' He tossed the tracker to Will.

Will squinted at the little screen. 'Kelvingrove Park.' He frowned. That didn't make sense. . . Why would they take Cat back there?

From above, the park was a vast patch of darkness, the only light coming from a thin line of sodiums burning amber in the incessant rain. Brian brought the gleaming ship in low, whipping the bushes with the engines' wash as he landed.

Will grabbed the Whomper and leapt out into the frigid monsoon. The tracker bleeped at him as he squelched through the mud and bushes, and then, at last, he found her.

It was difficult to equate the battered, naked body at his feet with the Bluecoat they'd stormed Ken's underground facility with. Her face was smashed beyond recognition: battered so badly there were no features left, her skin pale and waxy.

'Aw Christ, Cat.' Brian sank to his knees in the mud next to her. 'You poor wee kid.'

Will shifted from foot to foot, powering up the Whomper. Something wasn't right.

'What the hell's she doing out here, Brian?' He swept the weapon across the darkened park. 'Why's she been stripped?'

'Give me the tracker.' Brian's voice was low.

'Brian, something's wrong '

'Enough! Alright? Enough. . .' Brian scowled at him, then looked away. 'Course somethin's fuckin' wrong: she's dead. We're too late.' He took a deep breath and held his hand out. 'Just gimme the tracker.'

Will handed it over.

Gently, Brian reached out and killed the transmitter embedded in Constable Cat McDonald's skull. There was nothing else they could do for her.

The rain was turning icy, lashing against Director Smith-Hamilton's window. Her office was far too warm and Will would have been fighting to keep his eyes open, if she wasn't in the process of giving him a bollocking.

'What the hell were you thinking? You had no authority to raid that research lab. You had no sanction to massacre its staff. You shouldn't have been there at all!'

New skinpaint and skinglue covered one side of Will's face like a patchwork quilt and he did his best to stand up straight and not answer back.

'You can consider yourself damned lucky, Mr Hunter,' she said, picking up a thick folder and shaking it at him, 'that the Ministry are blaming last night's little fiasco on the man who ran the Sherman House project. You have a lot to thank Mr Tokumu Kikan for, if we ever find him. If it wasn't for him you'd be facing a tribunal faster than you can say "Criminal Negligence".' She slammed the folder down on the desk.

'And you can tell Agent Alexander to thank his lucky stars my pilot isn't pressing charges!'

'Yes, ma'am.'

She stood and straightened the creases out of her dress uniform. 'We will discuss your disciplinary hearing once the press conference is out of the way.' Director Smith-Hamilton glowered at him as she crossed the thick pile carpet to the office door. 'The Ministry may want to give you a medal, Mr Hunter, but I *warn* you: one more step out of line and you'll be swelling the ranks of the unemployed. Do I make myself clear?'

'Yes, ma'am.'

31

The flat is clean from top to bottom: not a speck of dust or a spot of blood anywhere. Which is quite remarkable considering what's happened here over the last five days.

Her new guest is nice and quiet, standing in the middle of the lounge where she can fuss over him. There isn't as much of him as there was when she dragged his limp body through the door on Tuesday morning, but what's left feels no pain. Now Tokumu Kikan's face ends at his upper jaw – everything underneath that is gone, hacked away with a boning knife, the spare flaps of skin stuck down with far too much skinglue. But then surgery was never really her forte, not the kind you survived anyway.

And he has told her so many things. So many secret, dirty, dangerous things.

Dr Westfield moistens the edge of a silk handkerchief and wipes away the little flecks of dried blood that sit in the corners of his eyes. The holes are hardly noticeable, she's made a good job of it: a full-frontal lobotomy done the old-fashioned way. She tells him do a little twirl, showing off his new orange and black jumpsuit. Very smart.

'Right,' she says, 'time to go.'

She takes the old man's hand and holds out the other one

for Mrs Bexley. Stephen's wife looks nice in the grey outfit Dr Westfield bought her. It flatters that big, pregnant bulge. With a pretty silk headscarf hiding the patch of bare skinpaint where she was scalped. Her eyes are glassy and vacant as she shuffles into place. Drugged up, docile, and most important of all: *silent*.

Westfield leads her little family out of the flat, her travelling case trundling along behind. They walk, hand in hand, down the corridor and into the lifts.

'Now then,' she says, picking a stray dot of lint from the collar of the old man's jumpsuit as they descend to the ground floor, 'I want you to behave yourself out there. Always do what the nice people at the depot tell you and remember to rinse out your mop.' The lift doors ping open and she smiles. 'This is what happens when you interfere in someone else's research. You should have kept your naughty little fingers to yourself.' She tweaks his prominent nose. 'Yes you should. Yes you should.'

But he doesn't reply. He can't.

She tells Mrs Bexley to go and wait for her by the front door, then guides Tokumu Kikan over to the janitor's locker and pulls out a wheely-bucket and mop. It's heartening to see the old man as he carefully fills the bucket with a mixture of hot water and detergent – just like he's been taught – then he takes the mop and starts to clean the dirty grey tiles beneath their feet. He's as happy now as he'll ever be.

Her research is ruined. Kikan and Peitai contaminated the study with their heavy-handed amateurish methods. It's worthless now, her children's potential squandered: the point was to study serial killers as they developed in the wild, not churn them out like cloned burgers.

Never mind, she's had a lot of time to think since the fun and games in the research lab. Mrs Bexley's unborn child will be the first of a new breed – not manipulated third-hand through their parents, but taken directly under her wing. In a few months' time she'll be able to start all over again. A brand-new child, and a brood mother to breed more from. Exciting times . . .

With a spring in her step she takes Mrs Bexley's hand and skips out into the freezing downpour. Glasgow is cold and wet, but it's nice and sunny where they're going. In just a few hours they'll be sipping margaritas in the Southern Republic of the Newnited States.

Crossing the street she heads down to the nearest shuttle station, pausing only to drop a package in the post on the way. A little parting gift.

'Will? You've got a parcel.' Jo stuck her head around the kitchen door and frowned when she saw he still wasn't dressed. 'We're going to be late for that funeral if you don't hurry up!'

Special Agent William Hunter sighed and poured the last of his tea down the sink. He'd seen enough good men and women planted in the long walk to last him a lifetime. But Cat had fought alongside him, helped him rescue Jo. He owed her, even if she was a terror with a Bull Thrummer.

'Come on.' Jo threw his coat at him. 'Are you wearing your medal?'

'No.' His demotion hadn't hurt *that* much, not compared with getting Constable Cat MacDonald killed, but he'd felt like a fraud when they pinned that shiny bauble on his chest. 'Not this time.'

He had to admire Jo's resilience. She'd got over the events at Sherman House a lot quicker than he had, and he wasn't the one who'd been tortured. She struggled into her jacket – the stump of her right arm waving about in random circles as she fought with the sleeves.

Will pulled on his overcoat and helped Jo with the brass buttons on her dress uniform, trying not to get them covered with fingerprints.

'Come on,' she said as he started to pick at the wrapping on his parcel, 'Take it with you, you can open it later. We have to go.'

The rain was like ice, bouncing off the circular headstones beneath their feet. Mourners huddled together for warmth beneath a drumming curtain of black umbrellas as the priest worked her way through the eulogy.

Standing off to one side Jo, Brian and Will watched as the sealed casket was tipped up on its end and slid slowly into the freshly dug hole. As it sank into the ground the assembled Bluecoats struck up *Abide With Me*, singing as yet another of their number was consigned to the cold, dark earth. At last the casket clicked into place and the priest dug a handful of dirt from the box at her side and intoned the ritual words:

'Ashes to ashes. . .'

'Jo,' said Brian, 'what did Cat do at that official function? Y'know, when she was pished?'

'Hmm? No idea. Only met her a couple of times.'

Will frowned as six Bluecoats stepped forward, forming a circle around the grave. 'She said you were her DS.'

'Nope. I think she worked for DS McLeod.'

The roar of Thrummers filled the air, turning the heavy rain above the grave into freezing fog.

Jo shrugged. 'I can ask if you like?'

The Thrummers sounded again and Will looked down at the order of service in his hands for the first time. There was a holo on the inside cover of a red-haired Bluecoat with freckles and squint teeth. Beneath it were the words: 'CONSTABLE CATHERINE MACDONALD. GONE BUT NOT FORGOTTEN.'

Oh . . . shit.

He shoved the holo into Brian's hands. 'Look.'

'Who the hell's this?' Brian stared at the stranger on the card. 'That's no' Cat!'

Jo took the order of service from him. Checked. 'Yes it is.'

'Will. . .? If *that's* Cat, who the hell was with us?'

Will didn't say anything; he knew now why he'd recognized her.

He pulled the package out into the rain and fumbled it open. It contained two items: a note saying 'SEE YOU SOON!' and a human jawbone.